Albert H. Hall

Star of the Cheechikois
A Canadian Flag Fantasy

Steven Rainmaker is a peacenik boy for whom the goal
of a world fraternal and at peace is synonymous with the
greatest of all wishes. Though impressed by his teacher's
declaration that, to Canada's newlycome, the Maple Leaf is
a flag that grants wishes — especially the wish for freedom
and refuge — he has no kind words for flags that usurp and
divide the land of his ancestors. It comes about that he
takes refuge from a storm in an old shaman's cabin.
Carried away by the shaman's account of a visit by the
spirits to the ancient Cheechikois when the Elder Woman
of Lots (Dame Fortune) left a miraculous balm by way of a
five-lobed leaf of which the identity is hidden in a riddle,
he finds himself a page boy in the Dame's Court. In a
repetition of the legendary visit involving a clash with high
technology, witchcraft, and didactic virtue, he learns how
flags, wishes, and the maple leaf are bound together in the
dispensation of fortune. The key to the riddle issues from a
stormy finale, but awakening to the aftermath of the storm
outside his night's refuge — and its toll of the shaman —
Steven cannot clearly separate reality and dream. He
nevertheless gains proof that the maple leaf is indeed the
legendary miraculous balm, and that the Maple Leaf flag is,
therefore, symbolic of Dame Fortune's preceptual guide to
the healing of political differences and the generation of a
world fraternal and at peace — the greatest of all wishes.

Star of the Cheechikois

A CANADIAN FLAG FANTASY

Albert
H.Hall

GAI-GARET
design &
publication ltd.

Published by
Gai-Garet Design & Publication Ltd.
Box 424
Carp, Ontario, Canada K0A 1L0
(613) 839-2915

ISBN 0-921165-08-0
Printed and bound in Canada
© 1990 by Albert H. Hall

Art direction by Wendelina O'Keefe
Cover illustration by Ray Knowles
Printed by the Runge Press Limited, Ottawa, Ontario

Canadian Cataloguing in Publication Data
Hall, A.H. (Albert Henry), 1914-
    Star of the Cheechikois

ISBN 0-921165-08-0

    I. Title

PS8565.A44S73 1990   C813'.54   C89-090481-2
PR9199.3.H34S73 1990

Dedicated to
Edith Elizabeth Banks
and
Angela Claire Vaugeois

1

In all parts of the world there can be found rivers of peace, which are rivers that came to stand between peoples who were divided and could not otherwise resolve their differences. Those who followed have built structures to bridge the water, and some have found wisdom to bridge their differences, though divisions still remain. It was by the fortunes of geography that from the earliest of times the great river had separated the tribes on either side, but that is not to say they were divided. Division was a measure of the newcomers who conceived a line to partition the ancient waterway, assigning the southern half to the United States of America, and the northern half to the Dominion of Canada.

Among the tribespeople who boated across it, the imaginary line of division had held little meaning until the arching span of a bridge, rising high above the masts of the river traffic, offered them an alternative passage for their daily exchanges. Then it was that the line acquired a certain reality to be found midway between two lofty flagpoles guarding the approaches to the bridge — one bearing the fluttering Maple Leaf, the other the rippling Stars and Stripes.

More than that, two highways arriving from the north and south met at the bridge. There being linked, they discharged into each other's lanes a selfsame cavalcade of vehicles carrying goods and travellers whose consuming interests seemed always to be elsewhere. Yet, despite its dedication to the service of a passing world, the highway came to shed upon the local newcomers the favours of accessibility. Among those favours were the towering domes of atomic power stations that stood in lordly silence at the river's edge where they drew upon the passing water to cool their vitals. So it was that the newcomers, whose towns had risen to prosper in the shadow of their flagpoles, came to enjoy a mounting variety of endeavours very much in contrast with the changeless reservation on the other side of the highway.

Of the opportunities and wealth the highway brought within everyone's reach, Miss Adley was only too aware. A young woman of social conscience and professional commitment, she was a familiar sight in the line of traffic that flowed to and from the bridge, her grey and maroon convertible conspicuously sandwiched between the dwarfing eighteen-wheelers. So the regulars, looking down from the height of their highway behemoths, would toot a lighthearted farewell to their diminutive escort as Miss Adley, each morning without fail, turned her convertible from the highway and into the reservation, there to teach the tribespeople's children.

From the weathering schoolhouse that sat atop a hillside overlooking the highway, there was a clear view of the bridge and its guardian flags, and when turning from the blackboard to face her class, Miss Adley could glimpse the ceaseless flow of life and purpose to and from the bridge. Dropping her eyes to the attentive faces in front of her, she would hesitate before the disparate lot of those whose inheritance was the range of a continent and the blessing of two flags that pledged freedom and equality for all. Then catching herself, she would resume the lesson, silently wishing her enduring students an eventual place in the affairs of the highway, leading away from the reservation and towards the fulfillment of a meaningful and rewarding life.

Miss Adley was not alone in her wishes for the children's welfare. Being only two familiar with the bustling thoroughfare and the exciting world it served, the children themselves knew there was much to be wished for. Especially on a balmy summer's night when the earth fairly rose into the heavens and hovered there among its sparkling neighbours, the youngsters watched breathlessly for a runaway star to break loose and make its fleeting streak across the sky. Seizing upon it as a sign to outdo each other's fancy, they filled the air with wishes of every description, never forgetting the wish for a miraculous vehicle to race up the highway and into the reservation, loaded with extravagant favours.

Among the older students, it was Steven Rainmaker, class leader and one for whom Miss Adley held the greatest of expectations, who harboured the more solemn wishes. Observant and thoughtful, Steven's upturned face was among those who followed the screaming military jets that swept over the somber reactor domes and across the peaceful reservation with unending urgency. Awakened in the night by their troubling sounds which were sometimes far off and lonely, sometimes near and defiant — approaching, passing overhead and dying away in the distance — Steven would be left staring into the darkness long after their going, still and listening. So in his mind the vigilant interceptors gave life and reality to the computer games that were to be found in the back room of the townspeople's video store. Under the compelling force of misgivings and curiosity, he would steal there, when not likely to be missed from the reservation, to watch the intense players who gathered to match their wits and dexterity in games of war. Quietly looking on from a corner, Steven seemed scarcely to be noticed, though if as it happened someone begrudged his place, sympathetic voices would be raised to say, "Leave the kid. He's from the school," and the contest would continue amid shouts of prowess on the destruction of enemy missiles. So, unlike his classmates to whom the commotion of a passing jet was nothing more than a diverting thrill, Steven scanned the intruder for its friendly markings, and wondering over the possibility of some day looking up to see instead the markings of a deadly enemy, dreamed the greatest of all wishes — the living paradise of a world fraternal and at peace.

It was thus that affairs in and about the reservation fostered a variety of wishes, some of them special to the reservation, and some no different than in the world at large. Although few if any wishes seemed ever to be granted — unlike experience in the world at large — the number seeking Dame Fortune's nod continued to go forward in undiminished volume and with undiminished faith. While this might be expected in the nature of a forbearing people, it was in the greater part a measure of Miss Adley's method of encouraging the children to broaden their horizons and stir their ambitions. But if she encouraged wishing on the one hand, seeing in it the germ of ambition, she emphasized on the other hand that faith was its handmaiden. No less reverent than the next, she held firmly to the belief that faith could not only move mountains but must be so employed lest it become a weakness instead of a strength. "Faith," she would assert, "is something to be lived," and throwing back her head before a flagging class, would make the rafters ring with her admonition, "Wish for the moon and strive with faith, for faith is to be embraced as the champion of success, not the consolation of defeat!"

True to her calling, Miss Adley preferred the carrot to the goad, but faced with the reservation's climate she found her own resources sorely tested in her drive to subdue disillusionment and stimulate resolve. But in her trial, providence was offering some assistance, for Steven, while endowed with the customary attributes of a boy, was redeemed with a most promising talent. It was the talent of his pen and a lively imagination to feed it. Whence came Steven's tales of olden days wherein the tribespeople's superstitions were most often flavoured with the ways and foibles of the newcomers, but ancestral tribal wisdom always emerged holding the key to a better world — especially for the weak and oppressed. Although his classmates saw in this the humour only of the olden tribespeople acting like newcomers, Miss Adley was quick to recognize and encourage the greater talent, for whether it sprang from his inheritance or from his covert visits to the video store, it revealed a spirit that sought fulfillment in the cause of brotherhood and equality — the cornerstones of democracy — and democracy being what the highway was all about, Miss Adley saw in Steven a kind of Pied Piper. His success would be an example for the other children to follow — out of the reservation and into the open arms of the highway, there to seek their rightful place in a great society on the move.

There were others besides Miss Adley who watched Steven's progress with interest, and each for a different reason. They were those who made up Steven's only family: his younger sister Stella, grandfather Gorse, and Aunt Becky. It was in Aunt Becky's hands that fate had cast the orphaned children, though it was not that alone that held them close to each other and coloured their outlook in the same hue. No, it was old Gorse who was the greater influence. He found in his grandchildren both a reward and an obligation, sparing no effort to teach them the folklore of their ancestors and the richness of a heritage which, he averred, could endure only in the life of the reservation. It was thus that Gorse's hopes for the children were somewhat at difference with those of Miss Adley.

Now summer was approaching and with it the First and the Fourth of July. It was the beginning of a period when the bridge would fairly strain under the weight of travellers and holiday-makers whose two-way passings always raised a gratifying jingle in the cash registers of both the southbank and northbank towns-people. Being thus favoured, the townspeople had reason at least once yearly to reflect with satisfaction upon their ways of life which combined to bring freedom and prosperity to a whole continent. It was a freedom and prosperity made all the more precious in these times, threatened as they were by a world stricken with distrust and stockpiles of fearful weapons of war.

For years now, the respective townspeople had gone about their separate and traditional celebrations on the First and the Fourth of July, parading their flags and admiring in turn each other's aerial display of patriotism across the river. But this year was to be different. This year the flags would meet at the centre of the bridge, and there flying together, would witness a clasping of hands across the border. It would be an occasion for speeches of mutual admiration, toasts of good fellowship, and a renewed dedication to the sharing of those treasured values that were a her-itage on both sides of the river. Before a host of television cam-eras, it would set an example and a goal for a watching world.

It was not for want of volunteers that Miss Adley found herself serving on the organizing committee. No. She had supported the idea from the very first. Moreover, when asked to organize the participation of the young people, she was quick to include a place for those on the reservation; for, as she insisted, the affirmation of peace throughout the lands of their ancestors was a blessing for which they, too, could share feelings of gratitude.

Thus did Miss Adley become one of the first to mount the crossed-flags motif on the hood of her convertible to publicize the occasion and spur the growing spirit of participation. But there was more to Miss Adley's method than honouring the facts of history. She saw for her class an early and opportune lesson in the right of free people to make their choice. The obvious choice for the children should lie not in the diversions of the affair, but in the message and the pledge of the flag that would lead the parade — an endowment to be embraced and cherished. She would have the children express it in their own words, and in those words sow the seeds of their future commitment. Indeed, Miss Adley had decided to offer a prize out of her own meagre resources for the best essay. Furthermore, the winning essay would be read by its author at the ceremony, and Miss Adley entertained little doubt that the reader would be Steven Rainmaker. Yes, Steven would bring credit to the school, honour to himself, and inspiration to his classmates.

With the deadline's approach rapidly turning the remaining days into hours, the quiet anticipation of the northbank townspeople had suddenly blossomed into excitement. It was that a large truck, leading a motorcade of lesser vehicles, had drawn its trailer to a halt at the police quarters. There before a cluster of townspeople — and wistful eyes on the reservation — the prancing mounts of a troop of Royal Canadian Mounted Police had been eased down the trailer's ramp, and led by a band playing *The Maple Leaf Forever*, carried their riders through the town to a prepared paddock. On the appointed day, at the appointed hour, they would ride forth in full regalia, so to escort His Honour the Mayor who, in fitting style astride his favourite albino, would lead the townspeople to their rendezvous on the bridge. Moved by the climate of bursting enthusiasm, the organizing committee had called a special meeting, and Miss Adley herself in order to

12

attend had declared an afternoon's holiday for her students. To her surprise, and only then, did she learn of a serious threat to her plans: Steven Rainmaker had said he would not be entering the contest. He had made his decision with reason, saying that a gathering in fellowship and goodwill was not an occasion that inspired an essay to honour flags. Flags, he said, were the very symbols of difference, and more than anything gave cause for uneasiness in a nuclear world.

Miss Adley in her classroom manner had pronounced Steven's reasons as thought-provoking but at the same time, expecting to see them dissolve under her professional guidance, had suggested he remain for awhile after class to talk it over. It was, after all, the kind of situation commonly met by teachers everywhere, to be readily dispatched according to chapter and paragraph of the manual.

Firstly, in the spirit of democracy, one must bend to the right of dissent with grace and equanimity.

(Miss Adley smiled amiably as Steven stepped into the cubicle that was her office.)

Secondly, one must not approach the matter as a dispute over viewpoints, but rather as a misunderstanding between like-minded adults.

(Miss Adley opened the conversation regretting that she had not taken the time to present the virtues of her project more clearly.)

Thirdly, whether at work or at play, who defines the terms sets the rules and may thereby steer a debate in the most favourable direction.

"Yes," said Miss Adley, speaking in terms a peacemaker could not fault, "we have come to accept a world of metes and bounds, hesitating to trespass on each other's territory with so much as proffered hand of friendship. Yet friendship ignored is understanding neglected, and understanding neglected can only become intolerance nursed. Yes, Steven, our hand across the border is our vote to break down the barriers to a true friendship based on understanding and tolerance, and if that is what we believe, that is surely what we must say." Satisfied to have primed the rules,

Miss Adley moved to make her point. "And indeed, Steven, if our proffered hand bears the Maple Leaf, it conveys the wishes of a whole nation, and is it not on the united voices of nations that world peace and fellowship finally hangs?"

Steven's commitment to peace and fellowship was no less keen than Miss Adley's, but if her tutelage had otherwise been an influence on him, it had by no means quenched the inherited spirit of his grandfather. He weighed Miss Adley's words respectfully but impartially, and while her premise had struck the responsive chord intended, her conclusion had not. Here in the privacy of her office, Steven was under no pressure to score a passing grade, and was the more encouraged to respond with what he believed. "Flags divide the world," he calmly reaffirmed. "They are symbols of defiance and conquest. They have always stood between people and the wish for peace."

Miss Adley was disappointed but not dismayed. She nodded her understanding. It was the task of a teacher to reason with students, and she was well able. She contemplated Steven's declaration. "You might certainly say that about Old World symbols," she slowly agreed, noting Steven's satisfaction with her admission. It was a method she often used since, as a rule, by yielding to a general claim, she seldom failed to win agreement for a friendly exception. "But it was here in the New World that the old tyrannies were first cast off, marking the beginning of an end to the conquest of the Old World flags. Yes," she mused, looking out to the bridge, "though who could have dreamed that the Maple Leaf was destined to rise as the very symbol of friendship? That through its goodwill the Maple Leaf would be welcomed by warring factions themselves to carry a world's plea for peace and harmony into their troubled spots?" She beamed an apostolic smile on Steven, inviting his response with a pause.

This time the exception was to Miss Adley's rule, for though impressed, Steven was unswayed. "To speak of peace and fellowship while waving a flag is to speak with a forked tongue, Miss Adley, when the same flag is waved whether to celebrate peace or to wage war."

Miss Adley stiffened. Listening to him, she could now hear

Steven's grandfather speaking, and though disappointing, Steven's words came no longer as a surprise.

Miss Adley had met Gorse only once but could still remember the dreamy look in his eyes — a look that told of a long-ago time when the ancestral home of the Cheechikois was nestled in the hills overlooking the river. It was a time when a Cheechikois alone was welcomed by all the tribes, for a Cheechikois made no war but was a healer and a voice of wisdom to be consulted. They believed in all the spirits, the Cheechikois — the spirits of the mountains, the waters, the skies — seeing in them the unity of creation. To this day still old Gorse kept faith with the spirits, and when Miss Adley had questioned the need for so many, he had simply told her it was to admit that the Hand guiding us prods with many fingers. "Yes," he assured her, "all is the hand of the Great Spirit. Just as what is left in a pool after the sweeping wave has passed is no less water, so what has been left by a sweep of the Great Hand is no less Spirit, whether in the clouds or the heart of man. And is it not the first mark of wisdom to accept all creation as one?" he asked.

Miss Adley would never have disagreed with such sentiments, though she could not agree that the mere acceptance of them would ever turn a nuclear-armed world into an earthly paradise. Yet this was the very question at issue, for through Steven, the passive faith of old Gorse was denying that good holds no primacy and must be wrenched from the hands of evil — was denying that freedom, ever wary, must march on behind its banner of liberation — was denying the very banner Miss Adley revered, visible on its mast in the distance.

She allowed a proprietary eye to linger a moment over the approach to the bridge and its fluttering pennant. "To wave the same flag in peace and war is not to be double-tongued over right and wrong, Steven, and certainly not with such a message as bears the Maple Leaf. It is a message of the New World — not a proclamation of lordship over its domain, nor of menace to a neighbour. No, Steven, not lordship over a people, but a pledge to defend their human worth and values. It is a message to spread hope and courage in both peace and war. It is a message that cannot and will not change no matter the times, for it is a message that finds echo in hearts everywhere. And Steven," she added, easing her voice to a confidential and intimate tone, "no one need tell you that to those who flee oppression and injustice, the Maple Leaf can be the answer to a prayer — yes, a magic charm that grants the wish for freedom and refuge when embraced."

It was a mild display of patriotic fervour on Miss Adley's part, and far short of forbidding contradiction, yet it did narrow the gap between taking an opposite view and being disrespectful. Steven's mind toyed with the privilege of being able to rub a Maple Leaf like an Aladdin's lamp, especially if it were endowed with the power to grant freedom and refuge from Miss Adley's clutch. Her voice reined in his thoughts.

"Could you wish for more?"

Steven pondered an answer to the question, though she had seemed to let it fall more to punctuate her enthusiasm than to ask his opinion of the flag as a magic charm. Nevertheless, he certainly could wish for more, and often had, but not on a flag. Yes, he had also prayed for more, and with equal success. But Miss Adley was really changing the subject, because while she was romanticizing the Maple Leaf with prayers and wishes, freedom and refuge for a few begged the question of peace and fellowship for the many amidst the swirling flags of a nuclear world. Wary of being trapped, he held back, casting about for the politest way of coming to grips with what he saw to be the point at issue.

Reading victory in Steven's hesitation, and preparing to accept his surrender with the utmost grace, Miss Adley encouraged him with a conciliatory smile.

Steven accepted the encouragement. "Those looking for escape from the oppression of the Old World have always found refuge here, Miss Adley, even before there was a Maple Leaf to greet them. The Indian peoples themselves lived in the greatest freedom when there were no flags." His voice was soft and respectful, but the message was clear — there was little tribute to be found in his pen for symbols that divided the world, especially the world of his ancestors.

To Miss Adley the reply was an unexpected blow. Steven was

16

not listening to reason. Had it been any other student the word stubborn might have crossed her mind. She was all the more convinced that Steven's decision was to be blamed on the folklore of old Gorse and the Elders, and forgetting her usual tact, she aimed a barb in their direction. "That is not to say they shared the land in peace and harmony, Steven, for they did not. If flags are a sign of division, no flag at all is most surely not a sign of unity or common cause. It is a sign of everyone for himself. So it was among the tribal allies." Pressing her attack, Miss Adley chose a feigned curtness to give her final words a more telling effect. "In the end," she said, arching her brow, "their divided strength brought them scattered reservations when, through the unity of a common flag, it could have brought them the recognition of a great people who yielded only the field."

Steven's mind quietly covered the field with rows of ghostly crosses, but he was given no time to clothe the vision in words before Miss Adley, regretting the unintended sharpness of her tone, had softened her stand. "What I mean to say," she added, "is that where there is unity, happenings will live on in what is best. So it is that great peoples have been overrun throughout history, yet survived as societies and nations. You see, Steven, the bonds of a flag give to its followers the strength and stature of unity in victory or defeat. Mere allies keep each their own interests and may well fall out even in victory."

Steven was more than ready to accept Miss Adley's amends because they offered a way out of what he knew to be an uneven match. "If they can't hold allies together even in victory, Miss Adley, I don't see how the world can be drawn together in lasting friendship and peace by flags." His eye passed over the distant Maple Leaf as he added, "Especially when they can grant freedom and refuge from each other."

With that Steven made his escape, leaving Miss Adley looking out to the bridge and its guardian flag, wondering where she had gone wrong.

2

Excited over Miss Adley having asked her brother to remain after class, Stella was eager to hear what had been said. She would have been waiting patiently at the schoolyard gate but for a mishap. She had turned her ankle moments before, after running from the classroom, and so had been taken home to have it attended to. Now sitting at the garden table, her amply bandaged foot resting on a stool, she was engaged with grandfather Gorse in his favourite game of odds and evens. Trish, the family's malamute, lay at Stella's injured foot in a show of sympathy for her mistress, quietly chewing on the end of a forked stick which Gorse had cut for a crutch. Aunt Becky was busying herself over the stone fireplace, having taken advantage of the fine weather to prepare lunch in the open air.

Her attention divided between the game and the direction from which Steven would arrive, Stella leaned forward as Gorse, tossing the coloured disks into the air and catching them with dexterous ease, sought to extend his winning streak. As the pieces came to rest, Stella clapped her hands with delight. "Evens again, Grandpa! See, Aunt Becky, how he keeps getting them, Grandpa, evens!"

Gorse beamed and gathered up the disks for another toss. "Today the spirits smile upon me, and the pieces obey my command."

"Then make them disappear. And hurry." Becky stood over Gorse with a steaming serving bowl.

"Aw, Aunt Becky," Stella implored, "can't he try just once more, Grandpa, for evens?"

"We are hot today," Gorse chortled, rattling the pieces vigorously in the plate.

"So is this," said Becky, setting down the bowl.

"What about Steven?" Stella protested.

"We cannot wait any longer for him. The food is ready and I do not want it spoiled. Arrange your places." Becky was emphatic.

"I do wish we could wait," Stella moaned reluctantly.

"Wish something else," said Becky.

"We will abide by Aunt Becky, my little Star," Gorse declared, shoving the disks towards Stella to be put away in the game box. "It is better to eat what we are offered than to risk indigestion from the wrath of an unhappy woman."

At that moment, Trish uttered a low bark. Jumping to her feet, tail wagging, she trotted over to meet Steven who had just rounded the corner of the house.

"Oh, here's Steven!" Stella cried, and unable to contain herself while Steven crossed the yard, called to him in a whispered shout, "What did she say, Miss Adley?"

Trish had already claimed Steven's attention. "Hi, Trish," he cried, and seizing her paws as she leaped towards him, started to romp while Trish playfully chewed at his wrists.

Becky quickly took charge. "Steven, you are late. Hurry and sit down."

"Yes, Lean Bone," Gorse urged, edging his voice with authority, "come and sit down, or you could have us all in deep trouble."

Lean Bone was a name of endearment which Gorse had given to Steven as a small child. The name irked Becky who was afraid it might follow Steven off the reservation and make him a target for mockery. Having scolded Gorse over the matter and forbidden the name to be used, she was now faced with it the more often as a weapon of annoyance. She paused in her bustle between the fireplace and the table long enough to wag a fork in Gorse's direction. "It is not me you are hurting, Grandpa, and if you really wish for your grandson you would do well to remember his name is Steven."

Unconcerned, Steven made his way to the table, teasing Trish as he went.

"What did she say?" Stella insisted.

Becky handed Steven his plate and sat down. "What did who say?" she asked.

"Miss Adley!" Stella's impatience was aimed at Steven.

Steven smiled and shrugged. "Oh, she hoped I would yet change my mind and enter an essay in her contest." Taking his place at the table, he noticed Stella's bandaged ankle. "What did you do to your foot?"

"I twisted it, my ankle, and did you say you would?" Stella's voice posed the question while her eyes appealed for a favourable answer.

"No." Steven's answer drew a nod from Gorse.

Stella frowned her displeasure. "I wish I could write," she said reproachfully.

Over a year Steven's junior, Stella was proud of her brother's honours, and while generally accepting his older judgment, preferred decisions that met with Miss Adley's approval. Gorse watched his granddaughter weighing her loyalty to Steven against sympathy for Miss Adley. She studied her plate for a moment before looking at Steven. "I like her, Miss Adley," she said.

Gorse smiled with satisfaction. "To take a stand without compromising neutrality is the true mark of a Cheechikois."

"If it is homework he will do it," Becky confirmed, "whether or not he likes Miss Adley."

"It isn't homework," Steven said, rising to take his cup to the fireplace where the coffeepot stood simmering. "And anyway, who says I don't like Miss Adley? Of course I like her."

"Then why don't you enter it, the contest?" Stella asked. She cast a sideways glance to make sure Becky was not looking in her direction and slipped a crust to Trish. "After all, it's fifteen dollars, the prize."

Becky raised her brow. "If you can win fifteen dollars we might find the rest for a nice enough bicycle."

"The prize isn't in money," Steven replied. "Anyway, a pony would be better for getting around the reservation. I wish I had one."

"And I wish I had a dollar for every wish I hear around here. You know a horse is out of the question." Becky's burdened sigh discouraged any thought of bargaining, had it been in Steven's mind.

Steven shrugged his resignation. "I know."

"Good," Becky sniffed.

"But that isn't my reason," Steven added for the record.

"They are all doing one, the others, an essay," Stella informed the table.

Becky acknowledged Stella's argument with a nod and emphasized its implications. "You cannot be the only one to refuse, surely."

"Lean Bone has the courage to stand on his own," Gorse asserted. "He has no need to run with a baying pack."

Becky ignored Gorse's remark. "And you always do well with essays, Steven," she finished.

"Sure, when I write them my way." Steven grimaced. "This one would have to say what Miss Adley thinks it should."

"I am sure Miss Adley would find anything you write to be more than satisfactory," Becky declared.

"Oh yes," Steven piped, throwing back his head to imitate Miss Adley. "That is very thought-provoking, Steven, but..." Hovering over the fireplace, Steven's sweeping arm upset a steaming pan, spilling most of its contents over the edge of the fireplace and raising an angry hiss from the fire. "Oops!"

Becky looked over. "Now look what you have done, Steven. And there was hardly enough to begin with."

Steven lifted the coffeepot, testing its weight. "Won't this be enough?"

"Yes, we have lots of coffee, but you have just spilled my pot of witch hazel," said Becky, finally managing to swallow her bite of food.

"Now she tells us," Gorse spluttered, setting his cup down with exaggerated haste.

Steven leaned over what was left of the bubbling concoction and screwed up his nose. "Creepers, what was it for?" he asked disdainfully.

"It was for Stella's sprain," Becky informed him over her shoulder, and then added for Gorse's benefit, "but in the olden days it would probably have been fed to dyspeptic old men."

Stella giggled. "Would they really do that, the tribes, Grandpa, give it to the old men?"

Gorse sucked a tooth and shook his head. "In the olden days the young women respected their elders because if they did not there were other potions that could silence impertinent tongues."

Holding out a crust for Trish, Stella hesitated. "Do you mean, like poison?" she questioned, shaking her head in disapproval.

"Well, my little Star," Gorse replied dryly, "you might say there were some medicines that did not cure as well as others."

Steven regained his seat. "How did the old tribes test their medicines to find out if they might be poison, Grandpa?"

"They tried them on dogs that begged at the table." Becky frowned at Stella. "Stella! You have been told often enough not to feed Trish from the table."

"Aw gee," Stella murmured, "it was only a little piece. And no one would ever do that to a nice dog like Trish, poison her." She extended a protective hand to Trish but quickly drew it back under Becky's disapproving eye. She appealed to Gorse. "Would they, Grandpa, poison a dog?"

"Prisoners of war," Steven concluded in answer to his own question. "Prisoners of war probably."

Stella hunched her shoulders and shuddered. "Oh, Steven. It would be as bad as dogs, that!"

"How do you think then?" Steven demanded, and turned to Gorse. "Am I right, Grandpa?"

Gorse sucked a tooth thoughtfully. "Not the Cheechikois, Lean Bone. In the first place, the Cheechikois held no prisoners — they were healers of the sick and servitors of peace. Sadly, they were actors, not writers, and knowledge of their skills died with the echo of their voice. Yes," he added, searching Becky with the corner of a mischievous eye, "knowledge of the ancient skills has unfortunately been lost in history, and all we have left is herbalist quackery."

If Gorse's remark was intended to provoke an offended riposte from Becky it was unsuccessful, for she knew it was not so much a denunciation of her herbal remedies as it was a criticism of her interpretation of tribal lore, which differed from his. It was that Becky held to the belief that the legendary Star of the Cheechikois was the leafy ingredient of a herbal preparation of great restorative qualities, while Gorse maintained that it was the celestial home of the ancient tribe's guardian spirits. To the tribespeople the matter had long held no more interest than that of a bedtime fairy-tale giving children the whispered hope that some day the spirits might again appear, as they once had done, offering the tribe a miraculous balm that was said could bring the dead to life, holding thereby the secret of a paradise on earth. While in the face of life's realities such a possibility could be expected to influence little more than the dreams of children, Becky, with her passion for natural cures and palliatives, might be forgiven for keeping an eye open for a five-lobed leaf which just might contain unusual healing properties. Indeed, if there was anything at all of the tribal lore Becky could accept and firmly believe in, it was the effectiveness of her herbal remedies — remedies that had been garnered and passed down through the efforts of long-departed generations. So it was she invariably had something simmering on the stove for herself or a neighbour or to be bottled for the winter.

"Herbal medicines are not quackery, Grandpa, and you know it," she replied quietly. "And what is more," she continued, "the old recipes have been passed along perfectly well, and right to this day have performed wonders if not miracles."

Gorse snorted. "Miracles are performed only by the hand of the spirits. Concoctions may raise goose pimples but never the dead."

Becky smiled. "Yes, Grandpa. I remember your attack of lumbago last winter. It was not the spirits you begged for a poultice, and from all the groaning anyone would have thought it the rising of the dead."

"Why don't they come any more, the spirits, Grandpa, with miracles?" Stella asked.

"If they ever did," Becky interjected.

Gorse ignored Becky's scepticism to answer Stella. "It is a matter of faith, my little Star. That there were miracles is of no doubt, for legend could not be all wrong. The faith of the old days has seeped out of the hearts of the tribespeople, and when the people abandon faith, the spirits abandon the people."

"But just think," Steven exclaimed, "if the spirits would really appear with a potion that could raise the dead! The Cheechikois could rule the world!"

"If they blew it once," Becky surmised, passing a critical eye over the surrounding area, "they would probably blow it again."

"The power of kindness and humanity was never a power to attract rulers," Gorse chided, "and if, as you say, the Cheechikois blew it, it is better at least that they be forgotten as ill-fated humanitarians than remembered as successful despots."

"All the same, it would be fun, and it would be already cured with a miraculous balm, my sprain, even if it were broken," Stella concluded.

"Maybe Aunt Becky could try inventing one," Steven suggested.

Becky nodded. "Aunt Becky might certainly have tried if the witch hazel had not been spilled," she replied pointedly.

"Okay, so I'll bring you a heap more," Steven shrugged.

"Good," said Becky. "You were about to be elected anyhow. We need it this afternoon. And I hope you know where to find some because the men cleared out my handy grove when they fixed the road to the wharf."

"No problem," Steven assured her. "I know where there's lots of it."

"Well then, if you are going very far you had better move because there is a promise of rain," Becky warned.

With that the dinner was over, and while Becky collected the dishes, Steven carried Stella piggyback into the house and made ready to leave.

3

"Steven! You had better come back and take your slicker!"

Aunt Becky's words trailed after Steven as he gained the lane leading to the general store where he could expect to thumb a ride in the direction of the next valley. At this time of day, there was usually a pickup truck going one way or another from the store, and Steven could hear the sounds of someone loading. He quickened his pace with barely a turn of his head to answer Becky. "Aw no. I don't need it."

Steven was in luck. A small truck was backing away onto the road as he emerged from behind the store. He managed to catch hold of the tailgate and scramble over it into the open box just as the vehicle started forward in the direction he wanted to go. Pleased with himself, he straddled a sack of potatoes but had scarcely leaned back to make himself comfortable when a sudden bounce all but flipped him clear into the air. As he steadied himself, a face appeared in the cab window, and looking down at him with a taunting grin, as much as told him that the bump had not been entirely unavoidable. From there for the next few minutes it was only a firm grip on the spare tire that saved him from flying over the side of the lurching box. When at length the driver slowed to negotiate a particularly deep hole, Steven quickly jumped free. As he picked himself up, the truck was again gathering speed, and the face reappeared in the window with its taunting grin. Steven grabbed the nearest lump of dirt and let it fly after the receding face. "Dog!"

Steven slowly brushed himself off while he looked around to get his bearings. Here, stemming from an ancient incursion of the river, there was a flat expanse of lowland forest rimmed by a ridge of higher ground. A grove of witch hazel thrived in the moist ground on the far side of a brook which traversed the area, and while the brook could be crossed over by a footbridge not far to one side, Steven knew of a beaver dam closer to the grove. Satisfied, he made off into the trees, turning his steps towards the dam where he could just as easily make his crossing and save time. His chosen course was made easier by a wildlife track, and aside from low-hanging branches, the going was easy enough for an agile boy. Still, it was a warm day, and Steven was encouraged to slow his pace, even stopping now and then to listen to the bird calls or to tease the chattering tree squirrels.

The warning smack of a beaver's tail could be heard in the stillness even before Steven emerged from the overhanging trees, and a widening circle of ripples told where its author had slipped into the depths.

The pond had grown since Steven's last visit. The wide expanse of water now lapped against a tangle of sticks and mud which the beavers had recently thrown up to raise the old level. Steven paused only a moment before starting his way across the rugged structure, hopping the overflowing trickles that sought to open a floodgate for the waters behind. Halfway across, he suddenly stopped and looked up. Yes. He had felt the first drop of rain from low-hanging clouds now taking over the sky.

Steven continued his crossing at a quicker pace, and jumping onto the far bank, set off at a jog towards the grove of witch hazel. Running under the trees, he could hear the raindrops falling against the leaves overhead, but only when he broke out among the smaller witch hazel did he find that it was raining quite in earnest. He knew he was in for a soaking, but plucking the leafy twigs in haste, he soon filled Aunt Becky's bag and was ready to retrace his path.

Steven had scarcely turned to regain the sheltering branches of the forest when a sizzling fork of lightning streaked out of the deepening sky to bury itself among the trees, a mere stone's throw away. Rending the air with an ear-splitting crash, the disturbance reached Steven in a staggering buffet that buckled his knees and left him almost dazed. As if it too had been shattered by the experience, the cloud now emptied its contents in a heavy downpour.

Frightened as he was, Steven was not helpless, for Gorse had schooled him in woodcraft. Refuge from other lightning bolts lay best in lower ground, and that was not difficult to locate. The way was led by many hollows that sloped off towards the brook. Steven bounded into the nearest of them and found it was already gathering a fast-growing rivulet. No matter. That was the way to go, and stooping in a half-crouch that offered a smaller target, he ran to escape the rounds of thunder and lightning, stumbling and staggering over the uneven footing like a commando under fire.

Splashing his way along the descending hollow, he did not stop until at length it spilled into a tree-lined gully. There his eager eyes searched the wooded slopes for a likely cover and came to rest on an uprooted tree which stood halfway up the steep bank. It now lay with its crown pointing up over the rim of the gully. At its lower end, a broad slab of matted roots and soil had clung to the butt and was left tilted over its vacated bed like a half-open oyster. It was a rustic lean-to indeed, but at such a time nothing could have been more inviting. Spurred by a flash of lightning with its crash of thunder, and still clutching the bag of witch hazel, Steven lost no time scrambling up and into the yawning haven.

Crouched in his trench beneath the thick roof of dirt and roots which helped deaden the sounds of the storm, Steven immediately felt less menaced. He wiped the rain from his face and took note of his shelter.

Above his head, a shrivelled bat dangled from a protruding root, its daytime nap undisturbed by the storm. Along the niche where the uprooted slab rested against the ground, a row of small burrows penetrated the hillside. Feeling less alone by their presence, and only too willing to share the accommodation with its little residents, Steven settled back to wait out the storm.

It was like sitting in a balcony overlooking the gully. Below, where he had stood ankle-deep in a rivulet a few minutes earlier, Steven was surprised to see water fast rising under a flow from the opposite direction. Curious, he craned his neck to the side and there saw the open shoulders of the gully where it joined the brook, or at least what used to be the brook. Now it was a spanking river at the height of flood, and rushing past was shedding a swirling backwater into the gully. Steven's view of it was limited by the sloping bank that housed his refuge, but he could see sticks and branches rolling and bobbing past on the lively waters. He stared in fascination. Creepers! Could he be looking at pieces of the beaver dam? But the question had no sooner popped into his mind than his fears were unmistakably answered — a beaver, riding the current atop its lodge, swept past amidst the shattered remains of its labours.

Steven leaned back unhappily. Clearly he was not going to be able to return home the way he had come, but would have to go downstream to the footbridge. He wondered how soon the storm would ease up. Evening was coming on, and with the sky overcast, nightfall would be that much earlier. It meant he would have to start back soon, for he did not relish the thought of stumbling through the forest in the pitch black.

He wished he had listened to Aunt Becky and brought his slicker. Of course, there wasn't much use wishing for his slicker when he was already wet. Wish for the lightning to stop — that would make more sense — or better still, just wish to be home — "I wish I had a dollar for every wish I hear around here." (Aunt Becky's voice) — a dollar a wish — suppose you could get wishes for a dollar — a dollar for the lightning to stop — you pay the lady in charge of wishes, or maybe it's the man — no, everyone knows it's the lady, and men don't hold much with wishing — unless its was like with bombs dropping and guns flashing everywhere around — then they would sure wish — or no, they would more like pray because they would be really meaning it — still, you could mean a wish pretty badly — unless there was a rule that says when to wish and when to pray or you lose — although no one ever really says about the difference or how they are sorted....

A sudden fluttering of wings and the quacking of a wood duck, whose nesting had been disturbed by the invading waters, shook Steven out of his reverie. He watched the bird's uncertain flight to the mouth of the gully, at the same time being conscious of the dwindling thunder in the distance. The dull rumble had subsided some moments before Steven realized he had seen no lightning. He leaned forward to better examine the sky, and could only see the promise of continuing rain. Still, that shouldn't stop the lightning from moving off, he thought. He waited and listened until once more there was a rumbling in the distance. There was little doubt now. The lightning must have moved away, and that was good enough.

Steven crawled from under his shelter and chose a way up the embankment, but then, on the verge of starting off, he turned back to snatch up the bag of witch hazel with a twinge of guilt at having almost forgotten Stella's need. With that he scrambled on up to the higher ground where the going would be easier, and making a headband of his handkerchief to keep the rain out of his eyes, set off through the forest.

There was now as much water dripping through the branches as was tumbling elsewhere about them as Steven jogged along. Descending at length into a slight hollow, he entered a haze of low-hanging smoke which filled his nostrils with its nostalgic pungency. Smoke was particularly so on a rainy day. Unable to rise against the weight of moistened air, it seemed to spread out over the ground as if in search of the wistful past.

For Steven, there was nothing in the whole outdoors to match the comforting aroma of campfire smoke, for it stirred up his fondest memories. It spoke the warmth of comradeship and the essence of togetherness; it was the breath of grandfather Gorse's evening tales and reminded Steven now of the comfortable kitchen. The thoughts sharpened his awareness of the growing discomfort of his clothes which, having soaked up too much rain, now clung to his skin, drawing at the warmth within. Steven quickened his gait the sooner to be home.

The dullness of the overcast was beginning to deepen with the impatient twilight when Steven reached a well-trodden path that could only lead to the footbridge. He turned onto it, enjoying the sudden smoothness under foot, and half running, half slipping, he followed down the slope at the path's prompting. He would not be long reaching home.

Alas, Steven's elation was short-lived, for starting down the last slippery dip, he caught sight only of water instead of the footbridge. Taken by surprise and unable to arrest his forward slide which was carrying him towards the cascading flood, he grabbed at the pathside branches, letting fly the bag of witch hazel as he did so. Finally, clutching onto a willow branch, he lay almost at the water's edge. Turning his head, he saw the witch hazel being swept away and no sign whatsoever of the bridge.

Steven pulled himself up and regained his feet. Staring at the racing current, he stood for a time gripped by the sight of its unrestrained power, imagining himself being carried away like the bag of witch hazel.

"Creepers!"

A slight shudder, prompted less by the thought of his close encounter than by the chilling wetness of his clothes, reminded him that home was on the other side. He cast about for a means to cross, and slowly, as the futility of his search became apparent, his stomach sank with misgivings. Dusk was falling, and he was not going to be home before dark, or perhaps not at all this night.

Thoroughly dejected, Steven pressed against the lee side of the nearest tree for what shelter it offered, captive, yet seemingly ignored by an unfolding world of muffled quiet: the syrupy smooth flow of the swollen brook, sometimes breaking into a low musical ripple; the monotonous fizz of the myriad drops puckering the surface of the brook and the spreading pools; the steady patter of rain on the canopy of leaves above; the passing rustle of a questing breeze, its uncertain breath now sighing in the topmost branches, now quietly brushing a cascade of droplets from a laden bough. Far off, the dull rumble of thunder, almost inaudible, almost apologetic, sounded like an intrusion on the scene rather than a finishing touch.

Steven could not escape the thought of how much better he would have fared had he spent less time teasing the squirrels. He could have crossed back over the beaver dam before the storm and would by now have been well on the road, if not home and out of the rain. He wished he had it to do over again.

Again a twinge of slowly penetrating chill straightened him with an involuntary shiver, interrupting his wishful thoughts and demanding a more practical response to his predicament. He must find a drier place to wait out the rain and flooding. He scanned the near surroundings from his lee-side shelter, but within eye's reach could see nothing with any promise. He would have to look farther afield, though he could scarcely expect to find another fallen tree such as in the gully. Still, it was there waiting even if a good piece back, and on the way he might find something else. That was it then. The gully. It was an instant decision, and his legs were carrying him on his way almost before his mind had given the order.

A fresh peal of thunder, very much closer than before, unhurried and ominous, abandoned its stealthy advance and rolled boldly across the valley. Steven had already sampled one frenzied lightning bolt at close enough range, and the smell of its ozonous fumes remained with him as if it were freshly cracked. He stopped and cocked his ear to gauge the quarter from which the new threat had sounded, but it was echoing from all directions like a predator searching out its quarry. Finally, as if losing the spoor, it sank back into the hills, there to lie in wait.

Steven put his head down and hurried on in the direction of the gully, now favouring the lowest ground for its promise of safety. As the new storm cell drew closer with flickers of light against the gathering shadows, he wished he had stayed as he was in the gully to wait out the storm, at the same time excusing himself, for after all, the fault really lay with the bridge being washed away. And so, while his feet laboured faithfully over the sodden ground, his mind toyed with explanations. The bridge was gone — just like the beaver dam — no amount of wishing can change something that has already happened — even prayers can't do that — or can they? — maybe there could be a rule — like wishes have to be for good things to happen, and prayers have to be for bad things not to happen or they will go to the wrong place —

then even though you are soaked in the rain, you can't get home — you have to run for cover with lightning striking all around — just like you are trying to get away or they will shoot you — "And Steven (Miss Adley's voice), no one need tell you that to those who flee oppression and injustice the Maple Leaf can be the answer to a prayer; yes, a magic charm that grants the wish for freedom and refuge" — well maybe it could be like that when you are someone else and you get away and they can't touch you anymore — but when you are you, and you are trying to save yourself in a storm....

Startled by a blinding flash that cut the gloom and shattered the air with a deafening clap of thunder, Steven missed his footing on the nub of a root. The lightning stroke had not come dangerously close, not nearly as close as the one at the gully, but Steven's legs had by now run a long, difficult course through the forest, and suddenly called upon to catch his balance, they did not quite have the strength to do it. Arms flailing the air, he careened into the bole of a large tree and fell sprawling into the undergrowth at its base.

Thoroughly shaken, Steven lay for a moment as he had fallen, still and panting. It ought to have been no more than a momentary break in his pace, but in the unexpected relaxation he was suddenly conscious of fatigue. Beneath him the ground was cold and damp, but above he could sense the protective cover of spreading branches. His eyes followed a curtain of vines that scaled the tree's rutted bark to mingle with foliage which now loomed dark and impenetrable in the failing light. The massive trunk swelled as it rose, bursting into a crotch of gnarled limbs which reached outwards and upwards to sustain a dense overhead cover. Persuaded by his spent condition, the idea of climbing out of the storm into the comfort of a veritable treehouse was an inviting temptation. Yet, even as he strained his eyes in a tentative search for climbing holds, Steven realized full well that Gorse would never counsel such a thing in such a storm. He allowed the thought to pass unheeded, and feeling all the more tired and dejected, slumped back against the nubbly roots.

"Lean Bone has the courage to stand on his own. He has no need to run with a baying pack."

The words rang in Steven's head as if Gorse were standing over him. Spurred into action by them, Steven rolled stubbornly to his knees, ready to continue. It was thus in a half crouch with his head down that an object shining with a ghostly luminescence amongst the roots caught his eye. He instinctively reached down and explored it with a cautious finger. It was sharp and smooth to the touch, like the tip of an embedded spike. Steven tried jiggling it. It moved easily, for it was not very large, and came free between his fingers. Holding it up curiously in the dim light, his scrutiny was aided by a leisurely flash of lightning. He was holding the long sabre-like tooth of a lynx, pierced with a neat hole for stringing. But even as he beheld the relic, the storm had again moved in close and the lightning flash was punctuated with a deafening crash of thunder.

To Steven's ears where he was already crouched and set to rise, the thunderclap might have been a starting pistol. In a single reflex, he gathered his strength to spring forward, at the same time shooting a glance ahead to guide his direction — but remained motionless, blinking. He thought he could see a glimmer of light. He blinked again and stood erect. Yes, he was looking at a tiny patch of light! It came from a little peep-window in the door of a cabin which nestled for protection against a cliff-like shoulder of the valley, and drifting out from the chimney came the tang of smoke he had earlier breathed.

Heedless now of everything but the beckoning light in the doorway of the waiting haven, Steven left the sheltering tree very much as he had arrived — headlong. Consumed by his single-minded purpose, he ignored the dazzling flashes and swirling downpour, and covering the intervening distance with the spring of a gazelle, gained the overhanging roof of the cabin. He was wet, cold, disheveled, and out of breath. Beating the door vigorously with one fist and grasping the handle with the other, he pressed the latch. The door was unlocked. Without hesitating, he pushed and followed it in, to stand at last in the soothing quiet of a contentingly warm room.

Outside, the marauding storm voiced its resounding disappointment across the valley and made off over the hills still grumbling.

4

It was a surprisingly large room, and much larger than the
cabin itself because it extended into the side of the valley in a
vaulted alcove of stone. The alcove, too, was deepened by a
shallow recess. In the centre of the recess a cavernous fireplace,
rough-hewn by unskilled hands, looked out over the expansive
hearth to command the room. The flanking faces of its recess and
the outstretched walls on either side were hung with tribal artifacts
in colourful array. Reaching to the farthest corners, the memory
of bygone days was embalmed in the display of masks and animal
carvings, headdresses and dancing costumes, drums and rattles,
feathered calumets and medicine bundles, arrows and spears,
woven and painted patterns — the instruments and trappings of a
once great people.

Rocking gently in his creaky chair before the hearth, and
drawing thoughtfully at his pipe, was an old man, his eyes
searching far ahead through the infinite blackness of the sooted
chimney, his mind reaching far behind into the shadowy past.
Only the brightly patterned blanket which rippled against his
shoulders from the draft of the open door, seemed aware of
Steven's intrusion, until the old man turned his head, almost
absently.

No emotion surfaced in the countenance nor in the penetrating
eyes that came to bear upon the bedraggled image in the doorway
— neither surprise, nor approval, nor disapproval. The old man
simply raised a thin, bony hand, as if it were a commonplace to

have one's meditations interrupted by such a figure looking like a castaway risen up on the beach, soiled and dripping as it was. "My son," he said, indicating the hearth.

Steven closed the door, and approaching the hearth, gathered his breath. "I was caught in the storm," he managed. "My grandfather is Gorse."

The old man smiled and nodded, but did not speak.

"My name is Lean Bone … I … I mean, Steven."

The old man's smile broadened. "Let us dry you out and make sure which," he said, and taking up a long stick proceeded to poke the fire while Steven removed his outer clothes and laid them out on the hearth. As he did so, the lynx tooth fell from out the folds. Quickly picking it up, Steven rubbed it clean. "I found it under a tree," he said. The old man paused briefly while his eyes passed from the tooth to Steven and back, though he said nothing.

Sitting back on the sheepskin hearthrobe, Steven turned to look about. Save where he sat, the room was becoming quite dark, and the flickering light cast by the rekindled flames fell just short of illuminating the ring of shadows that fringed the room. He pulled the ends of the robe over his shoulders, and turning towards the fireplace recess, looked up into the sightless eyes of a grotesque face carved in wood. Sprouting from atop its wrinkled forehead, thick black braids of hair hung down to frame two puffy white cheeks streaked with black bars. A droopy red mouth, pierced in each corner by a long sharp tooth, seemed to quiver unhappily in the firelight. Sharing the narrow space as if to counter its depressing friend, there hung a kindred face with bright yellow cheeks, its mouth turned up in a wooden grin. Its thin slotted eyes seemed to squint at Steven with good humour.

On the companion wall of the recess, in contrast with the faces it opposed, there dangled a once proud ceremonial costume now showing the waste of time, its headdress floating above the robe of a long-absent tenant. The headdress, a broad creation of feathers bearing the spreading wings of an owl, was topped with the crown antler of a deer, prong standing erect, crest-like, and trailing down from the back, the brush of a silver fox. The doeskin robe, draping flat against the wall, had been at one time a story-book of pictographs bearing witness to the interests and happenings of another age.

Steven's roving eyes travelled over the faded designs that cluttered the surface of the robe, and came to rest on the figure of a five-lobed leaf, very much the maple — starlike and vermilion. Next to it was a second leaf that lay as if turned partly away, thereby appearing long and narrow. The points and roots of its spurs were accented with tiny stars made the more evident by a faintly visible line which looped the leaf's profile from tip to stem in a rakish ellipse containing a brighter star at its centre. That it was no accident was apparent from a side by side repetition of the elliptic figure, this time enclosing a star on which the two concentric ellipses showed even more clearly. At the sight of such figures, Steven's eyes widened. It was the kind of artistry more to be found in the journals of an atomic age than in the relics of a primitive tribe. If it were in his chemistry book, Steven could have taken the diagrams as atoms in abstract art. As it was, he could only stare, not sure what to make of it.

Having replenished the fire and put down his stick, the old man had by this time returned his attention to his guest, and noting the direction of Steven's interest, broke the silence. "They were great orators, the shamans of old. They chose a costume to hold the attention of an audience, and on it they displayed a record of their encounters, so to intimidate their opponents."

Steven turned to acknowledge the old man's remarks. It was on the tip of his tongue to ask him how an ancient orator might have encountered the atom, or how his opponents would know enough to feel intimidated by it, but the old man had continued to speak.

"Can you read?"

Steven found the old man's question a little surprising — almost offensive — for who would doubt that a boy of his age and intelligence could read? The automatic rise and fall of his head was almost done before he realized the old man was asking about the picture writing on the robe, and quickly changing the 'yes' to a doubtful shake of the head, finished with a somewhat noncommittal hunch of his shoulders.

The old man cocked his head to one side and returned his gaze to the costume, apparently as unperturbed by Steven's silent but sweeping response as he was by his unexpected arrival.

"Miss Adley doesn't teach picture writing," Steven faltered by way of excuse. "I was just wondering about that figure of the leaf."

"The leaf?" The old man's raised brow invited Steven to elaborate his question.

"Has it to do with the Star of the Cheechikois?"

The old man smiled. "Yes, that is so."

Steven relished a deep breath. "I know about the star of the Cheechikois from my grandfather and Aunt Becky, but they disagree over what the star really was. My grandfather says it has to do with the real stars where the spirits lived. Aunt Becky says it was a leaf they used long ago for a balm — maybe even miraculous."

The old man nodded. "There has long been a division of opinion over the star and the balm, and with truth on both sides it seems."

"Like a balm to restore life?" Steven half rose on his knees to squint at the robe with greater excitement, but sank back doubtfully. "But that looks to be only a maple leaf. It couldn't make like a miraculous balm."

The old man cast an affectionate eye over the ancient robe. "That the tribes were visited by the spirits in a great happening, perhaps a miracle, and were counselled on the path to an earthly paradise, is witnessed there in what remains of the record. Unfortunately, the facts of the happening itself can no longer be read. They have come to us by word of mouth, which leaves them without proof and open to preferred interpretations such as you have heard."

In a momentary silence, Steven watched the figures waver under the firelight as if daring to be read. "Pictures are a lot harder to read than writing. It's too bad they didn't know how to write in words," he remarked, partly in commiseration and partly reproachful of ancestors who he now found to be guilty of an important shortcoming.

It was the old man's turn to be offended. "A word written or a word drawn can be no more enduring than the parchment it is committed to, my son, and in the hands of a great ape, no more eloquent. Sadly, it matters little whether a statement is made in words or pictures if there is no one to read them." The old man paused, and his eyes fluttered over the robe. "The voice of the robe that once carried across the hills is now reduced to a whisper. Soon there will be no reader to lend it breath at all; its voice will be stilled forever, and so too the counsel of the spirits, much as it is needed."

Steven was touched by the sadness of the old man's thoughts. He raised himself a little and looked more closely at the figures. Some of them were still clear and crisp for their age, but most showed the work of time. They seemed to derive their strength from the abstract atoms because the pattern faded with distance, finally losing itself in indistinct shadows of what there once had been. Baffled by the unfamiliar language, Steven could readily understand the difficulty of passing on a reader's skill from one generation to the next. "Is it hard to do? I mean read them?"

The old man pursed his lips. "Reading them, just as writing them, is an art to be learned. Try what you see."

Steven concentrated his attention on the figures, and picked on a likely start. His eye was on the caricature of a human form. Its head, covered with vigorous black hair which was gathered in heavy braids reaching down to its hips, was large for the short body. It was draped in something like a magician's cloak. Steven hesitated. "I see a masked dancer, for instance," he concluded, pointing to the figure, "and that would most likely mean about a ceremony, like the visit?"

"He is a spirit, oddly proportioned, but not masked. He is the shaman of the Elder Woman of Lots. He accompanied her."

"The Elder Woman of Lots herself came?"

"Yes, my son. Who better to have brought counsel to us about the path to a paradise on earth, than she who guides the fortunes of us all, be it a hermit or a nation? You see her there beside the tree."

"The tree of the balm?"

"So you may assume."

Steven adjusted his view in response to the old man's nod. What he was calling a tree was indeed a strange one. In a quick glance it might have been taken for a pot of flowers. Its trunk rested on the three prongs of a stylized root and, at mid-height, opened into three convoluted limbs which spread apart and then rejoined like the shreds of a paper lantern. It was topped with a small but billowy cloud of foliage. "The tree looks more like a vase of flowers standing on a crow's foot," Steven chuckled. He rose to the full height of his knees and squinted at the Elder Woman of Lots. "She seems a bit too faded. How can you be sure it is really the Elder Woman of Lots?"

"It is not entirely that she is faded. The faintness is in part because she was fair of hair. It is a feature that in itself helps establish the authenticity of the record because at that time hair other than black was absolutely unknown to the tribes. They would have to have seen it to believe it."

Steven considered the matter. "Where does it say she gave counsel?"

"There in the rest of the row."

Steven studied the detail of the sentence, or paragraph, or whatever the row comprised. It contained seven figures interspaced by a character of two vertical strokes on a horizontal, and it began and ended with the Elder Woman of Lots. The intervening figures included the tree, the abstract star and leaf, a true maple leaf, and a figure in stepped lines. Steven cocked his head dubiously. "I still prefer words. With words you always know the bottom line."

"That is the bottom line," the old man assured him.

"What does it say about the balm then?"

"Both much, and little. It informs us that it holds all things, the home of the spirits, and finishes by saying:

> The spirit is the tree;
> The tree is the star;
> The star is the leaf;
> The leaf is the balm;
> The balm is something;
> Something is the spirit."

Steven frowned in puzzlement. "The balm is something? What is something?"

"Something is the stepped figure, my son ... for need of a better description." The old man's smile was apologetic.

Steven looked at the figure. It was as a perspective of a stairway, its corners being out of square, angled somewhat acutely, as if being compressed. "It looks like a stairway that is being stretched out ... or maybe folded up." Sensing the self-contradiction in his words, Steven almost giggled. "What is it really?"

"It is a symbol I have seen nowhere but here. I have no knowledge of what it represents, and less of its meaning. Both have failed to reach us."

"The balm was something, and something is the spirit?" Steven repeated, more bemused than ever.

"That is so."

"But the spirit is the tree, so it simply goes around in a circle anyway," Steven complained.

"Yes, my son. The mystery of the miraculous balm is an unknown locked in a vicious circle."

"It's a riddle!" Steven's voice reflected his disappointment. "So what we want from the bottom line is missing." He mouthed his annoyance, "Pfft! How do you like that for luck!"

The old man gave a slight shrug of resignation and smiled. "You are dealing with the Elder Woman of Lots, my son."

"But there could be clues," Steven suggested. His eyes wandered over the robe and returned to study the abstract leaf. Its elliptic rings, canted at a jaunty angle as they were, livened his imagination. "It sure does remind me of an atom," he mused, and then on sudden inspiration he spoke his fancy. "Yes, of course, it is an atom for sure. The number of stars in orbit is the clue to what the atom is." He beamed at the old man, and resting his case declared, "Yes, that is what it must be. The leaf has eleven orbital stars. The miraculous balm must have atoms with eleven electrons."

The old man surveyed his young guest. "Whether stars or electrons, they surely are involved in the balm somehow;

40

though," he added somewhat dryly, "if it makes any difference to your atoms, the leaf has twelve orbital stars ... the one at the end of its stem is in fact a double."

"No problem." Steven was pleased with his solution. He would consult his chemistry notes when he got home, and encouraged by such initial success was ready to press on. "And there could be other clues, like in why she came at all, and in what else the story is about."

"Since the Elder Woman of Lots deals only in fortune, and fortune comes only in good and bad, you may take it that, all in all, the story is about good and bad and how to pick sides," the old man replied.

"I mean, tell me it all," Steven begged.

The old man had no mind to hold back. It was as if he had long waited for such an opportunity. He lifted his eyes up over the robe to the headdress and, studying it, silently gathered his thoughts. As though anticipating the coming story, the firelight faded a little, allowing the background shadows to deepen and draw themselves in closer about the hearth, the better to hear.

"It was long before the newcomers arrived," said the old man at length, eyes now fixed upon the time-worn pictographs. "It was a time when, owing to the persuasion of the peacemaker Walking Owl, the warring Montakins and Maliskaps lived in a shaky truce. Neither a Montakin nor a Maliskap, Walking Owl was a Cheechikois shaman who served the Montakins in a little village of Wamwiki, which lay at the foot of a rising bank of hills overlooking the great river. Walking Owl's compelling wisdom and counsel in the cause of peace was drawn from the spirits. To consult the spirits, he had only to trace a ring in the beaten earth before his wigwam and, with a mystic incantation, let fall his divining bones from their pouch, so to read the will of the spirits in the way they came to rest."

While the hypnotic voice flowed on, Steven's attention had wandered from the lifeless figures on the robe to the shifting figures in the glowing bed of coals. Lulled and enchanted by the murmur of words, his languid mind gave substance to the sounds, matching them with phantoms moving on the stage of living embers. Yielding to their shimmering spell, Steven's mind surrendered to fantasy. He followed the ever-retreating forms into the receding twilight and, giving chase, pursued them on through a great stone arch and into a misty gloom that filled his nostrils with its pungency. On he ran, on and on, on and — over a precipice into a void. Tired and aching, his sprawling body could summon no strength to protest. Out he tumbled through space, first resigning himself to its enveloping cushion, but gradually relaxing in its comforting softness. At length losing all resistance, he willed the fall to go on. Then it was the void became filled with pinpricks of light which, growing in size and number, soon filled the eye's reach, dispelling all gloom in a resplendent sweep that was the Milky Way.

Far away a patch of brightness gathered and moved towards him. Its outline sharpened with its approach and, at length taking shape, became a cluster of stars like that of the pictograph, forming two wavering rings that spun slowly, one within the other. Five stars could be counted on the inner ring, and on the outer ring seven, of which two formed a couplet that lost and regained its brightness with a regularity that matched the spin of the rings. When the couplet vanished, a line joining alternate stars of the two rings would trace out the figure of a star; when the couplet had reappeared, the figure would be that of a starry leaf. In the centre, more radiant than the others, was a star with a twinkle of ever-changing colours. As Steven looked on, it grew brighter and brighter until quite suddenly there sprang free of it a gleaming star that shot across the sky in a graceful arc. Persisting long after the star had passed, its shining trail would have given Stella time to wish for the world, and wondering if she had seen it, Steven watched in fascination as yet another star sprang forth.

During this time the little constellation had become very much closer, and a spreading circle of light from the busy star at the centre began to flash with greater intensity until, swirling out like a spinning umbrella, it enveloped Steven in so dazzling a light as to make him bury his face against his knees.

When Steven again looked up, the swirling colours were still there, but now had settled into an iridescent commotion of sun-drenched blossoms, tossing and weaving in a scattering breeze. He was no longer on the fireplace hearth, but was sitting on a flagstone walk in the centre of a beautiful garden. It brimmed with flowers of every kind and shade, stirred into confusion by the breeze — a restless helter-skelter of colour that spread across the garden and over the shrubs. It rose with vines that climbed the trees and dripped back down from their swaying branches, or continued with complete abandon to scale the garden walls and tumble over into the freedom of the countryside. And even there, stirred by the freewheeling gust, the bobbing colours swept along the hillside in a billowing wave, down the valley and on out of its mouth.

With the passing of the wind, all became still and peaceful.

5

Steven rose to his feet and listened intently while his eyes searched for signs of life. He could not see or hear anything. He was alone. He tested the flagstones under foot. They were real and solid enough. They formed a walkway edging an oval-shaped pool with a gurgling fountain in the centre. Lily pads covered with bright yellow flowercups circled the fountain in the now familiar pattern of the star cluster. A large stone bearing an engraved message across its face overlooked the far end of the pool. Tiptoeing around to examine it, he read the inscription:

> *They hold all things, the magic rings,*
> *The wished with unwished twinned and spun,*
> *Wherefrom the least endowment springs,*
> *Not good nor bad, for....*

The rest was overrun by rampant vines, but what was there made Steven pause momentarily, for though the words were new, their sense seemed strangely familiar.

Steven turned from the stone and craned his neck to see what was behind. There he spied a gate buried in a trellis of dangling vines. He approached, and lifting the latch, found it had a spring catch that needed both hands to open. It was only then he realized he was still clutching the lynx tooth, and forgetting he had taken off his jeans, thought to slip it into his pocket. On the point of letting it slide from his hand, he remembered there was no pocket. In a desperate effort to restore his grip on the tooth before it fell free, he only succeeded in sending it flying across the walk, where it bounced onto a lily pad the length of his reach away.

Steven was more than reluctant to lose his lynx tooth, but dared not disturb the lily pad lest his prize slip off and be lost among the roots. He lay flat on his stomach and put out his arm to measure the distance. Yes, it called for a stretch, but he should be able to make it. Balancing himself as far over the edge as he dared, he reached out very carefully, touched the lily pad, felt the lynx tooth, and just as his fingers closed around it, he over-balanced, tumbling headfirst into the water.

As he gained his feet, gasping for breath and standing waist-deep in lily pads, a shadow fell across the water.

"Can you read?"

Startled by the voice, Steven looked up sharply to meet a pair of mild, blue eyes in a face that was weather-beaten from years of service in the garden. Its owner was drawing a red, polka dot handkerchief from his overalls pocket, and while he went on to mop his forehead with one hand, he pointed behind Steven with his battered, straw hat. Steven's eyes turned in the direction of the hat. He beheld a small sign that was competing somewhat ineffectually with the flowers. Nevertheless, there it was in clear, black silhouettes on a white background — two figures, one poised on a diving board, the other holding a fishing rod — and struck across the face of the sign, from corner to corner, was a bright red cross.

Steven was embarrassed and at a loss for words, for the sign left little unsaid, even if he took the figures to be spirits.

"I asked if you can read!" The gardener replaced his hat.

Steven came to life, and clambering out of the pool, "I ... I'm sorry. I wasn't swimming," was all he could manage to say.

The gardener scrutinized him from head to toe. "Where are your clothes?"

Steven was more confused. "I ... I took them off to dry and, well they are...." He hesitated and looked around trying to locate the direction of his arrival, but gave up with a futile jiggle of his shoulders.

The gardener drew a slow, patient breath while surveying the area. "I suppose the others have hidden them on you? You must be from the school," he observed.

The school. He did not say it exactly like it was said at the video store, but to Steven it amounted to the same. Anyway, a school is a school. He nodded and added in a low voice, "Yes sir, I guess so."

"Well, I had better take you to the house. Come," the gardener said, and led the way around through the gate.

With Steven following at the gardener's heels, they emerged from the path into a courtyard, and there the half-naked boy stopped to stare with open mouth. He was standing before a very strange tree — very strange but nevertheless a stately, old maple tree. Brilliant in their autumn hue, its leaves rustled in the delicate breeze, reflecting the sunny day in a shimmering twinkle. And the massive, old trunk that rose out of the ground with a picturesque tilt to one side! That was something else. It branched into three knarled limbs that curled their separate ways upwards in a rugged sweep, to unite again in a sort of rustic arch, whence to continue their rise as one into the tree's majestic crown.

There was little room for doubt. It was exactly like the pictograph.

Missing the patter of feet behind him, the gardener stopped and looked back. "That bird's nest seems to have a mighty fascination for boys," he said, peering aloft, "and the triunium is mighty tempting to climb, but you can forget it." Beckoning Steven impatiently, he stepped onto the cobblestone to lead the way across the wide courtyard, but not without more prodding. Steven had again stopped, this time to admire the elegant splendour of the old chateau to which the gardener had turned their steps. Its vine-covered walls and angle towers with green conical roofs held a romantic touch of olden times, but the tall, central tower which rose over the main hall was furnished with a dome. Except that it was topped with a tall, needlelike spire, the dome looked very much like the newcomers' reactors — and strangely out of place, if not to say mysteriously vigilant.

At the chateau's four corners, from atop the spires of the angle towers, there floated the standards of the chateau's sovereign.

46

They were paired banners, one emblazoned with the leaf red on a white field, the other with the star silver on a field of blue, and always with elliptic rings very like the pictographs. Likewise emblazoned were the caparisons of three high-spirited chargers standing at the foot of the broad entrance steps, their martial trappings gleaming in the sun. A footman in livery of equal taste was too busy holding the horses in check to notice the gardener and Steven cross the yard and mount the steps, though by all counts their passage had been painfully slow, so taken was Steven by the sight of such fine animals.

Inside, the gardener stopped at the first door, and gently pushing it ajar, poked his head around the edge. Steven's roving eye caught a bulletin board on the wall beside the door, and there came to rest on a large poster bearing a sketch of the tree. The poster cited its authority in large letters:

HEAR YE! HEAR YE!
HER ROYAL HIGHNESS FORTUNA CELESTE
OF THE MAGIC RINGS, DAME;
OF QUOTARIS, QUEEN;
AND OF THE TRIUNIUM, GARDINELLE
PROCLAIMS a citizen's holiday and bids all Quotes participate in the Festival of the Wishing Tree, to be held...

Before Steven could get closer to read the fine print, the gardener was guiding him through the door with a firm hand.

Despite its office function, the room into which Steven found himself ushered was furnished with a certain homey touch, and standing behind a large desk, a stout matronly person, her hair drawn back into a tight knob, was in the act of pouring tea. The sudden interruption saw her arrested on the spot, teapot at the cant in one hand, cup and saucer poised under the spout in the other, elbows levelled with her ears. Motionless, she rotated her eyeballs to view the intruders. "Dear me, and what is this?"

"Found him in my pool. Friends hid his clothes, but he don't say. He's from the school," the gardener summed up.

The matron sank into her chair, elbows still cocked, and as she did so, her arms settled gently onto the desk top along with the tea things. "And what am I to do with him?" she questioned.

The gardener shrugged. "Dress him, or send him back, or just hide him," he suggested, turning back to the door.

"All right, Gardener," the matron said, and the door clicked shut behind him while Steven remained motionless before the desk. From the wall behind, the portrait of a young woman of evident charm and grace, regal with or without the tiara, regarded Steven over the matron's head, her eyes welling with an affectionate smile that reached out to put Steven completely at ease. Shielding the portrait, the now-familiar pennants with the leaf and the star hung on either side, cradling it in their crossed staves.

The matron studied Steven pensively for some moments. "You look like a nice enough boy," she finally declared, at the same time raising her eyebrows as if inviting a contrary opinion.

"I fell in," Steven offered apologetically. "I didn't mean to."

"No. It happens with boys," the matron replied. She rolled her head to the side, sharing one eye with the teapot and the other with Steven. "I was about to have my tea. Would you like some?"

Steven shook his head and started to say "No thank you", but at that moment he was caught by an involuntary shiver that chattered his teeth.

"Oh, you poor boy!" the matron cried, jumping to her feet. "Here I am letting you catch cold." Whereupon she snatched up a shawl from the back of her chair, and throwing it around Steven, hurried him through doors and around corners until they came to rest in a room that was heaped with garments of every description. There was everything from peignoirs to evening gowns, doublets to robes, tights to tunics, and buskins to periwigs, all stacked on dollies, draped on mannikins, and hanging in wall-width closets. In the centre of the room, a plump little man, who was leaning over a table snipping cloth with a long pair of scissors, raised his shaggy head at the matron's voice. Eyes widening at the sight of the bedraggled Steven, he shook his head and sniffed, "That boy could do with a bath."

48

Steven retained only a vague impression of spinning back through doors and around corners, into and out of a steaming shower, followed by more doors and corners, before finding himself standing again in front of the plump little man with the scissors. This time the fellow slipped a measuring tape from his neck, and approaching Steven, measured his chest and a leg before disappearing behind a line of clothing. His progress was marked by a disturbance in the garments that moved the length of the closet, and when he emerged at the far end it was only to announce, "I am afraid I have nothing of his size ... except," he paused, "in page boys."

The matron wasted no time considering the matter. "That will have to do. We cannot send the boy back undressed."

And so it was decided.

In no time at all, Steven was standing in his new clothes. They were a good fit and suited him very well indeed. Even the tailor was proud of his job, and the matron was so pleased she saw to brushing Steven's hair carefully. When she was finished she turned him to the mirror, leaving him to stare unhappily at the reflected image of a prim and proper boy in blue velvet jacket fashionably flared from the waist and cut to expose matching knickers that gave way to white-tasseled, knee-high stockings and black shoes. "Creepers!" he gasped.

"That," said the matron proudly, "is the way you should always brush your hair ... what did you say your name was?"

"SSSteven."

"Yes, Steven. Now mind you, go straight back to the school, and don't forget to give my regards to Muster. And when your friends see their little trick didn't work, the laugh will be on them, won't it?"

Steven withheld his reply, but it might well have shown in his eyes, for though he had no idea who Muster might be, he had little doubt on whom the laugh would be if he went near any school in such dress. But being now turned free and given the door, he was quick to take it. Once outside he would find his way home.

Closing the door respectfully behind him, Steven stood looking up and down the corridor for a way out. At the same time, his hand groped for a pocket, for in spite of everything, he had managed to hold onto his lynx tooth. Finding no pockets in his knickers, and even those in the jacket being false, he thought of stuffing it with the handkerchief in his sleeve, but settled on the lace of one shoe for a loop to hang it around his neck. So far it had brought him reasonable luck, he reflected with satisfaction.

Steven had correctly chosen the best direction to find his way out when the door to a stairwell opened, making way for a formless figure that was hurriedly backing out. Gathering his breath from the exertion, the figure turned slowly, and Steven beheld a rather spare man draped in a more than ample toga. A balding pate had left an island of pink flesh on top of his head, while wire-rimmed spectacles riding on the end of his nose might have lent a serious and studious air to a friendly but shy squint, had it not been for an overbite which gave his relaxed countenance a perpetual smile. Collecting himself, he straightened up in time for the door to swing shut on his toga, which tugged on his draping sleeve, spilling a thick bundle of computer printouts onto the floor with a thud.

Steven automatically bent to the man's aid, and picking up the weighty volume of sheets, could read its title as he held it out to the owner:

WAND

THE COMPLEAT RECORD

Compiled by:

KEEP
Chief Clerk
Recording.

The bundle was taken gratefully into the arms that reached out as a mother would reach for her child. And only as a mother could know that the tally was incomplete without counting her brood, the man turned to look anxiously about the floor over his spectacles. "My updates! My updates!" he panted. But there were no updates anywhere to be seen, until Steven noticed a fold of paper dangling from the pinch of the doorcrack. Pulling on it, he started to draw forth what might have been an endless length of sheets had he not by chance pushed open the door and seen the ribbon of paper stretching down over the flight of stairs. Pursuing it and folding as he went, followed closely by the Chief Clerk, Steven was led into the terminal area of a room humming with rank upon rank of computer consoles. The source of the paper was a busy printer that continued to pour out its growing mountain of findings from a sea of spinning disks behind. Standing before the ranks of computing modules, like commanding officers in front of their troops, were three control terminals. Outclassing the others in size, MEGOS laboured under star billing beside its lesser neighbour WAND, and EGOS the smallest. Steven was given no time to question what EGOS, MEGOS, and WAND could be labouring at, or even to be impressed with the size of their operation, for his attention was taken by the Chief Clerk who, with a gasp of "My goodness", had sprung into action. Rushing behind the counter to stop the flow of paper, he collided with a somewhat squat individual who had sprung from nowhere to fly across the room from the opposite direction, his strong nasal voice honking, "I've got it! I've got it!"

As it was, the Chief Clerk was up-ended over the short frame of the heavy-set dwarf, and turning a half somersault in the air, landed on his back in the paperstack. Having escaped from the Chief Clerk's flailing arms, the Compleat Record continued on in full flight, and rising like a comet, unfolded a graceful festoon in its wake before adding its remainder to the heap.

Had the Chief Clerk been a younger person, Steven could not have contained his amusement. Instead, he stood in a slightly tensed posture, undecided as to whether he should drop his armful of paper and go to the man's assistance. However, his indecision quickly turned to total immobility as the dwarf regained his feet, for he was given his first clear view of the fellow's large head with its long, black hair hanging in thick braids on either side. It might have been the strangeness of his surroundings, but it was more likely the fact of having already seen the tree that made Steven's imagination more receptive. Whatever it was, he was completely taken by the dwarf's resemblance to the pictograph on the ceremonial Cheechikois robe, and he could do no more than stare.

By the time the Chief Clerk had scrambled to his feet and was leaning against the counter to catch his breath, the dwarf had halted the runaway printer. Brushing himself off and straightening his cape, the dwarf regarded the Chief Clerk for a moment with mild concern before opening this mouth to vent his strong, nasal voice. "Keep, my good fellow, I said I had it! Are you all right?"

Keep nodded, more disturbed over the state of the Compleat Record than himself. He bent to the task of gathering it in, but the dwarf was more than helpful. Elbowing Keep aside, he took the free end, and encouraging the sheets with a particular twist of his thumbs, watched the returning folds draw themselves in with the snap of an elastic band. With the last page in place, he flattened the pad with an approving tap and handed it to the clerk.

"Thank you, Thalamus," Keep said, scanning the precious bundle for damage.

"No trouble, my good fellow," Thalamus honked. "but given your talent for attracting the unexpected, you had better be more on your toes. Sawni could be under foot again," he warned.

"Sawni?" Keep's response was truly not an echo of joy, though the lines of his countenance had settled back into their habitual smile.

"The gardener caught one of the boys from the school in his lily pond this morning," said Thalamus. "If the boys are about, Sawni will be about with them, and that spells trouble. It might do for ordinary kids, but you cannot straighten out an elf in a reform school. Her Highness should be aware of that even if Muster is not." Thalamus asserted the truth of his statement with a piercing glare that included everyone present.

It was suddenly clear to Steven that the gardener and the matron had established him as an inmate of a correctional school that

52

included trouble-making elves. He shrank a little under the dwarf's glare and dropped his eyes to the floor to gather his composure. He could feel Thalamus looking at him. Could he really be a spirit?

"Her Highness has her own ways," Keep breathed somewhat heavily, "though Sawni does bear a lot of watching. There now," he continued, placing the Compleat Record on the counter, and turning to Steven, indicated a place for him to set his armload. Holding Thalamus in the corner of his eye, Steven put the papers down and backed away. "Thank you, son, thank you," Keep said. "I must remember your name."

"Steven."

"So, Steven, I hope I haven't interrupted you on an errand?" Keep's voice was apologetic.

"No sir," Steven replied, and deciding it was time to put distance between himself and people with reform schools on their mind, added, "but I have to go." He turned towards the stairs.

"If you have nothing important, Steven," Keep hastily suggested, "I could use the help of a page to the Dome."

Steven did not answer. Instead, he hurried to the stairs. In his haste to be out, he stumbled halfway up the flight and lost his unlaced shoe. The shoe clattered back down, and when it ought to have stopped at the bottom, seemed to gather a little speed, rolling towards Thalamus. Steven looked back and hesitated. Thalamus was watching. Steven had half a mind to leave the shoe and make a break for the door.

"The door operates from the counter," Thalamus announced as if reading Steven's mind, but made no effort to demonstrate the working of it.

Steven hobbled down and picked up the shoe.

"What happened to your lace?" Keep asked, a little surprised by its absence.

Steven was not a boy to deceive, and being totally in the hands of strangers, was less encouraged to try. He reached under his neck and displayed the lace with the lynx tooth dangling from it.

"That looks very much like the tooth of a lynx," Thalamus remarked authoritatively. "Roamed the forests of Oulden

Finftroum, the Planet of Five Dreams. I think the Quicks there have left very few of them unkilled."

"It makes a nice one-up piece," said Keep. "It must be the envy of the other boys. Did you fetch it yourself, Steven?"

"I found it."

"I cannot recall seeing any around here outside the museum," Thalamus observed. "Where did you find yours?" he asked pointedly.

The tone of Thalamus' questioning gave Steven an uneasy vision of the reform school. "I found it under a tree." His voice rose defensively. "Before I got here."

"Before you got here?" Thalamus exchanged a glance with Keep. "So, you are new here."

Steven nodded.

"Ah," said Thalamus, letting go a satisfied breath. "I knew it was something." He turned to Keep. "A visiting scholar — one of the Gardinelle's exchange students."

Keep raised his brow and beamed his full smile. "Very good, Steven. A student."

Steven saw blue sky at last. If a visiting student was the alternative to Muster's correctional school, the choice was easy. "Yes," he replied, for he was indeed a student, and to avoid being caught out, he confirmed in a low voice, "Visiting."

"And what are your favourite interests, my boy?" Thalamus inquired.

"I like everything," Steven replied. "Social studies ... science ... writing about things."

The basics of being and communicating," Thalamus summed up. "Here we call it the three S's: Science, Sociology, and Scribbling."

"Well now," Keep exclaimed, "that is excellent, Steven. Participating in the Quotaris exchange was a good choice — and right here on Trovia at the centre of things. Yes, students tend to make out better after seeing for themselves how all the wishing is processed.

"From shooting stars to smiles, as we say," Thalamus put in.

Keep fondled his sheaf of papers and went on. "Yes, you will find the court a rich experience, and we are always on hand to help with the ropes." He interrupted himself. "By the way, my name is Keep. I am Her Highness the Gardinelle's Chief Clerk. This," indicating Thalamus with a flourish, "is Thalamus the Wizard. He sees to the computers, of course, and the routing of incoming wishes."

Steven was encouraged. He relaxed a little more, and acknowledged the introduction with something of a smile.

Thalamus cleared his throat. "You ought to have been shown around, my boy. How long have you been here?"

Steven's heart jumped a little. "Well, just today." He was still uncomfortable with Thalamus, though relieved at being able to utter a few simple truths.

Keep leaned forward. "Just today? That explains it then. Since yesterday, the Gardinelle has been taken up completely with this affair of the stolen trovium, and in the confusion someone has forgotten to look after you. That is too bad. You must have been wondering what was going on."

No words could have offered Steven more comfort and relief. "Yes," he readily admitted, "I have been wondering ... a little ... sir."

Keep nodded. "Just call me Keep." He shuffled his papers absently. "Yes, someone has missed looking after you. All the same, you must never think Her Highness the least unsolicitous. Dear me, no. Granting wishes is not the easiest job, and she is totally committed, Her Highness — totally."

Keep's voice was quiet and matter-of-fact, as though he were speaking to a long-time acquaintance and least of all to a complete stranger suddenly thrust into his presence. Steven could easily guess that Her Highness the Gardinelle must be none other than she of the portrait on the matron's wall. She had certainly looked to be a gracious and caring person, and must indeed be so if it required so much computing power to keep track of all the favours to her subjects. He was on the point of asking about the subjects, but continuing in the defence of his Queen, Keep answered the question.

"Yes," Keep went on, "from the very first she has said that if worlds are to have all the oversights put right and their lots bettered, the Quicks must be given starlight to foster a dream, and shooting stars to resolve the wish. Even now with this investigation hanging over us and the uncertainty of what it might lead to, she has kept the trovium mine at full production, and insists on sending off our quota of stars to keep the wishes coming in just as if nothing had happened." Keep clicked his tongue, marvelling at the doughty Gardinelle's dedication. He cocked an eye in the direction of Thalamus, inviting agreement, but Thalamus' attention at that moment was being diverted to MEGOS. "Missing your arrival was unfortunate, Steven."

If there could have been any doubt left in his mind after what he had seen so far, Steven now put to rest any question of his whereabouts. Keep's Gardinelle was in charge of wishing. The old shaman's pictographs told of the fair-haired Elder Woman of Lots. There couldn't be two of them. The Gardinelle had to be the Elder Woman of Lots. Yes, this was the chateau of the spirits who had visited the ancient Cheechikois. No question. He was on the trail of the Star of the Cheechikois and the riddle of the balm — provided he could steer clear of the reformatory, that was.

Steven's fleeting thoughts left him both elated and sober, and even though Keep seemed truly sorry for his not having been welcomed, Steven was careful to feel his way. "I was watching the shooting stars last night," he said, by way of acknowledging Keep's olive branch. He savoured his recollection of the magnificent display, and formed a mental picture of the blast-off, or rather tried to imagine the mind-splitting equivalent of a hundred or more shuttles lifting off at once. "Can you watch them launch a shooting star from up close?" he asked.

"Why not?" Keep replied. "A tour of the mine and launching silos is open to everyone, but they all find it better to watch from a distance. Not that there is any great danger, mind you, but a trovium-powered booster raises quite a commotion on blast-off."

A nervous question came to Steven's mind. "Do they ever blow up?"

"Not if you mean out of control," said Keep. "The regulations for handling trovium were tightened after the explosion that sprung the Quick Side. I doubt you will ever see such an accident again."

Thalamus had rejoined the conversation just in time. "It was no accident," he asserted. "There is no doubt, in my mind at least, that Fulgor was at the bottom of it, just as he has given Her Highness little cause to relax since. Nor would it surprise me to find his hand somewhere in the present business."

"Even so," Keep argued "there is no danger of him getting enough trovium for another really big bang."

Up to now Steven had only been concerned with the possibility of atom bombs. He had paid little attention to theories of the Big Bang because it was ancient history, and a shade beyond his favourite interests. Besides, he had never heard say of a possible recurrence, but while Keep was putting such a fear to rest he was also leaving open the possibility of something much the same, even if on a lesser scale. Steven preferred to be clear of such a happening. He cast a wary eye at the ceiling as though to weigh its strength under any sudden shock, in case Fulgor were out there now being reckless with a pile of stolen trovium.

Keep considered Steven with a sympathetic eye. "There is no cause whatsoever for concern, Steven." His friendly squint sized Steven up as a thought came to mind. "You will have to watch the other pages, you know. Given that someone has contrived to slip trovium out of the mine against all security, they will have set the rumour mill working in and out of the corridors. Finding a new boy around, they will delight in priming you with all sorts of nonsense." Keep paused. His glance moved to Thalamus and back to Steven. "Under the circumstances, it would perhaps be fair to explain a few things to you now, Steven."

As far as Steven was concerned, the more explaining he could hear, the better it would be. He hastened to approve Keep's suggestion. "Yes sir ... er Keep. I would like that very much."

Keep cast another sideways glance at Thalamus. "We could set Steven even with the others," he suggested. At the same time, his face brightened with an afterthought, and with a gleeful chuckle he rubbed his hands like a mischief-minded schoolboy. "Or maybe put him a little ahead."

"That would not be difficult," Thalamus snorted. "Trovia High turns them out long on history and short on talent for making any. They can tell you the life story of all the great wishers of yesterday out there, and the time and place of every wish they were ever granted. But of tomorrow, when the Quick Side will be stuffed with all else to be wished for, ask the senior class how they will inspire the Quicks to go for the greatest of all wishes!" Allowing the self-evident conclusion to hang unspoken, Thalamus rested his case against modern schooling.

Knowing nothing of Trovia High, Steven was in no position to judge the senior class, but he still had ideas about achieving universal peace. He was of a mind to suggest they could start by inspiring the Quicks to rid themselves of flags, and was the more encouraged to do so by Thalamus' clear indication of where he stood on the matter himself. But having seen the flags flying on high over the chateau's towers, Steven held back. Like Miss Adley, everybody seemed to be in favour of peace, but at the same time raised their warning flags. Deciding in favour of polite silence for the moment, he was nevertheless moved to level a fair question. "If Her Highness wants to correct all the oversights and make worlds better, why not take care of it all at once instead of doing it one wish at a time?"

Keep pursed his lips and shook his head. "That would be considered creative. It would contravene the Covenant, Steven. Creation is strictly reserved to the Remote Side."

"Oh." It was Steven's turn to purse his lips. "Wishing is covered by a special covenant," he repeated, sensing the truth was near at hand.

"Just since the acci... explosion," Keep clarified. "It was only after the explosion that trouble arose between prayers and wishes. Before that time there was no need for wishes, as you know. Since wishes have no religion, they had come to be sent off to wherever the nearest bundle of prayers were going. That slowed down the answers to prayers — which brought grumbling from the devouts. Some right wingers had long taken exception to wishes as rank hand-outs, subsidies to the profane, and an encouragement to creeping communism. They formed a strong

58

lobby to have a new arrangement which would limit wishing to the very needy, or better still, to secularize the estate of wishing and make it self-sufficient — something favoured by the genii who saw an opening for profit-making. In a working compromise, it was agreed that the degree of commitment to a wish should be taken into account — your 'faith of commitment' rule. Soon after, it was decided to separate prayers and wishes altogether, leaving prayers with the Remote Side, and wishes with Her Highness. The choice was obvious since the Milky Way was the Gardinelle's fief, and her extensive deposit of trovium, with its high yield of primordial good and evil, could be used for testing and rewarding the Quicks as well as for shooting-star propellant. With both the mine and a delivery system at her disposal, Her Highness was in an ideal position to communicate the meaning of unity to the Quicks, teach them the advantage of living in fellowship, and generally to oversee their struggle to find the wisdom and faith to reconcile good and evil in a paradise of the Quick Side. The rest is history. The arrangement has so far worked out admirably. I think we Quotes can be proud of our record as honest broker between Quicks and the Remotes."

Steven was delighted to have found so conversant a source of information. He jumped at the opportunity to settle at least one question. "How do you sort wishes from prayers?"

Keep reflected for a moment, and with a twinkling eye that livened his squint, directed his answer more towards Thalamus than to Steven. "When it comes to prayers and wishes, Her Highness the Gardinelle certainly knows the difference between a Remote possibility and a Quick fix." He finished with a chuckle that sobered under Thalamus' blank stare.

Thalmus turned to Steven, for the first time showing genuine approval. "Good question, my boy, and that takes you straight into information processing." He swung around to survey the humming consoles, arms akimbo. "As we say, the computers guide, the Lady decides, and the rings provide. Though," he added, with a sideways glance at Keep, "you may not find computers as interesting as palace gossip."

Steven made answer as eagerly as he dared without offending Keep. "Oh yes, sir."

6

Thalamus was not disposed to answer Steven's question in a single phrase or even in a mere paragraph. "They usually come poorly prepared in computers, and have a good deal of catching up to do," he began. "Have you been grounded?"

"Only a little," Steven acknowledged somewhat shyly. "It was mostly watching computer games."

"Games? Well," Thalamus grunted, "welcome to the biggest computer game in town." He stood for a moment scanning the humming machines, then as if to impress a gathering of adepts, spoke to be heard by the rearmost. "What we have here is a pretty straightforward area-network management. With our fully coordinated stellar satellite coverage, the central processor can access all stores of the Big Computer MEGOS — your Master Evolutionary Galactic Output Synthesizer — which gives us the momentary status of the entire universe and everything in it — and by a small innovation," he concluded, turning a full face on Steven, and lowering his voice to a conversational level, "we have included what the Quicks are thinking." He paused to regard Steven over the flicker of a smile. "Is this what you were expecting?"

"No, I really wasn't," Steven owned quite truthfully.

"It is usually the other way around," Thalamus remarked. "They file in here and expect to see the MEGOS mainframe." For this piece of pleasantry, he permitted himself another thin smile.

Keep added his approval with a boyish titter. "Yes," said Thalamus, "these are only your terminals, of course. The rest," he indicated with a sweep of his arms, "is out there, naturally."

Taken unexpectedly by Thalamus' presentation, Steven could only react with an open-mouthed stare at the array of consoles whose labouring ranks receded into the room's farthest depths.

Thalamus observed the boy in the corner of his eye, and seeing him suitably impressed and struggling to follow, hastened to continue. "Yes, naturally. Here we tap the stores, but MEGOS offers enough work stations out there for Quicks to tap the chronicles, and any who can read should have the wit to temper their wishes accordingly." About to continue, Thalamus relented, and again permitting his thin smile, asked, "Am I going too fast for you, my boy?"

Steven drew a breath to admit that some of the words were bewildering but that he could sense most of the meaning. However, without waiting for Steven to exhale his reply, Thalamus resumed. "Very well, wishes originate with EGOS, your standard thought computer, or more correctly your Encephalo-Gaussian Optativia Signaler. With their EGOS all Quicks are tied into our universal cellular network. Here we gather in their thoughts, though when the signal is of a strength we have been known to gather in a wisher with the wish."

Steven made a mental note of the hazard, wondering at the same time whether it possibly accounted for his own presence.

"And finally," Thalamus went on, "we have WAND, the Gardinelle's Wish and Need Determiner. WAND does all the work analyzing wishful thoughts from EGOS, and cross-checks with MEGOS to see how they would fit into a happening. From there WAND signals whether the Gardinelle may grant a wish one way or another, or at all, but the Gardinelle herself makes the decision." The wizard drew a concluding breath. "So there you have it, my boy, if you like a real game played with three computers, MEGOS holds your facts, EGOS your fancies, and WAND holds the hand of the Lady. Are there any questions?"

Thalamus regarded Steven over his thin smile, while Steven gathered in his scattered thoughts. It was Keep, now standing before a small bulletin board, who made answer. "Being fond of writing, Steven might like to read how Sylvester put it in his prize-winning poem." He motioned Steven to his side, indicating a page which was decorated with a red ribbon. A neatly written composition in three verses bore the title *THE THREE COMPUTERS*, and finding it free of pictures, Steven read aloud:

> *How hath the twilight star traversed by day*
> *The trackless waste, from dawn to dusk, it must*
> *commute,*
> *Nor seen nor seeing as it makes its way,*
> *To take each night its ordered place anew,*
> *Save that the Big Computer MEGOS point its route,*
> *While holding all creation in review.*
>
> *Where to the stars? What be their programmed end?*
> *Why shed they light if not to capture searching eyes?*
> *For in their term doth Truth and Fortune wend,*
> *Which Quicks may know, be they not wanting sight,*
> *Or EGOS wishing them the starlight might, denies*
> *'Twere grant enough that they but see the light.*
>
> *That Quicks may fondle starlight matters not*
> *To MEGOS, counting up the record ray by ray;*
> *It matters not that wilful EGOS ante up —*
> *They gamble with the clay, not with the mould —*
> *For Fortune's WAND both sorts and deals, and*
> *waits the day*
> *The greatest of all wishes to unfold.*

Steven turned from the board. "It's nice, and I guess I see what they do, all right, but I still don't see how you sort prayers from wishes."

Steven's words were boldly put, but went unheard because they were drowned out by the raucous sound of a computer horn which not only made Keep jump, but changed his quasi-smile to a clear expression of anguish. "Oh, dear me," he gasped, "I have clean forgotten Her Highness. We must hurry." Springing into action he tossed a bundle of printouts into Steven's arms, and himself clutching the Compleat Record, hurried off up the stairs.

His question remaining unanswered, Steven was obliged to race after the flying toga, and close on its heels lost his shoe while rounding the first corner. Though he quickly recovered it, and continued with one foot unshod, he was unable to overtake Keep until the man had reached the elevator foyer. The foyer served a choice of shafts which were identified as LOCAL and REMOTE. In less hustling circumstances, Steven could not have contained his curiosity over the destination of REMOTE, but at the moment he had found a better and more pressing use for the string that bound his parcel. In fact he barely finished lacing his shoe with it when the door to LOCAL sprang open, and he was hurried into the cage by the anxious Keep.

With time at last to catch his breath, Steven found himself standing opposite two white-smocked individuals. The one was a pleasant, young woman who smiled at him while passing the time of day with Keep. The other was a young man, remarkable for a shock of very red hair, who passed a preoccupied glance over Steven, raising his eyes to watch the indicator. He had not long to watch, for the cage had scarcely started to rise when it again came to rest. The opening door gave Steven a view of what was clearly a scientific laboratory, but his glimpse was encumbered by the departing couple, and quickly eclipsed as the door snapped shut on their heels. As the cage again began to rise, Keep spoke. "The young lady is Resal, the Gardinelle's favourite scientist. The young man is Kwah, Resal's half-brother."

What with Thalamus and the computers helping the Gardinelle, Steven had least expected to hear of any need for scientists. "What do they do?" he asked.

"They research ways to satisfy wishes."

"Ways?" Steven's surprise came from his long adjustment to the fact that wishes seemed simply to be granted or not granted, and usually not.

"Well, Steven, a wish cannot be granted with a snap of the finger — at least not any more. In earlier times the Quicks understood little of what was involved, and cared less as long as they got their wishes. With growing populations and a burgeoning need for staff, both the qualifications and supervision of our agents suffered. Misconduct began with some agents demanding kickbacks from the gullible Quicks. Others started diverting wishes into a black market. We suspected the genii of complicity, and had the matter in hand when we finally caught one gating wishes through a lamp, if you can believe it. Unfortunately the talebearers moved in with all their minstral hype and blew it into the famous lamp gate affair. That brought out the scientific methodists, and nowadays nothing can be sent out if the magic shows."

"Still, I can't imagine scientists wishing, at least not really," Steven replied.

"Why not?" Keep raised his brow. "What else are they to do? After all, everything has to start with a wish, if just to blow your nose. And scientists want to do a lot more than that. But if you like science you will enjoy seeing how Professor Remspruk handles the problems. We will make a point of taking you in."

The cage came to a halt on Keep's promise, and the door slid aside, giving way to a spacious room. Keep lost no time resuming his lead, and stepping from the elevator, Steven knew where they were the moment he looked up into the immense Dome.

The whole Dome area was divided across its centre by a low wall which housed the elevators and supported a mezzanine floor above. A solid bannister completed the top of the wall, and extending across the width of the room, followed scroll-like along descending stairs on either side. The furnishings were those of a conference room with seating arranged to favour a long table, at the head of which stood an elegantly carved, tall-backed chair.

"This part of the Dome is the council chamber," said Keep, setting his course for the nearest stairs, which were posted: TO COSMOSCOPE.

Taking to the stairs on Keep's heels, Steven was hard pressed to look around while holding the toga in the corner of his eye and trying to keep pace. From where he climbed the stairs he was given a wide view of the countryside through the Dome's transparency. It was as he reached the top that a giant fireball rose out of the ground not far distant, and gathering speed, vaulted into the sky, leaving behind a streaming tail of scintillating vapour. So sudden and distracting was the spectacle that Steven failed to notice Keep who, arriving at the head of the stairs, had stopped in his tracks to admire the event. Colliding with him, Steven momentarily lost balance and almost fell back down.

"It is always something to see," Keep marvelled as he straightened himself. "Some of them have a long distance to go by nightfall, and must be started early. The launching silos are over there," he said, pointing far out to a broad circular depression containing a number of volcano-like mounds. "Beneath the mounds is the trovium mine."

Steven looked out on a breathtaking view. Below him to the rear of the chateau, he could see the garden and fountain. A cobbled area surrounded by a massive stone wall that was shared on one side by the chateau's courtyard, contained what was clearly the barracks quarters of a legion of knights. It included stables with more fine horses such as he had seen in the courtyard on his arrival. To the front, there was a spacious town square fringed with trees, plots of grass and flower beds. Set well back from a broad walkway circumscribing the square, the pillared facades of buildings in granite and marble ringed the area. In the centre of the square before the admiring eyes of basking onlookers, a group of knights astride their well-groomed steeds, were rehearsing rhythmic movements to the strains of *The Maple Leaf Forever*. Farther away a semicircular stadium, strategically placed on top of a knoll, commanded not only its grassy sports grounds, but looked out over the launching mounds and off towards the horizon. The rolling countryside was dotted with lakes and crisscrossed with tree-lined lanes that wound their way past picturesque cottages and their flower-laden gardens. It was Steven's first full view of Trovia and his introduction to the other planets of Quotaris, for hanging in space above the horizon, he caught sight of first one planet, then another, and yet another. Turning his head he found more of them, all circling low over the Trovian hills. "Say! Look at all the moons!" he exclaimed in awe. "Like soap bubbles all around us."

"Yes," Keep agreed, sharing Steven's rapture and forgetting his hurry, "you can see the whole of Quotaris from the Dome. I never tire of the view."

"Are they inhabited?" Steven asked.

"Oh yes. Gom over there is the homeland of the giants," Keep pointed out. "Nubibia there is where the Gardinelle's knights are at home. The gnomes who work the trovium mine come from Trollium yonder, and so on."

Steven stared at the floating orbs. "How can you tell which is which?"

"It is easy. There are only twelve of them, and the five on the inner ring are easy to distinguish, being the larger. To identify each, you first locate the binary twins Vanitas and Fastus there on the outer ring to the south, just above Fatania." Keep indicated a planet in the nearer distance with two smaller ones floating above it in the farther distance. "Behind us, directly opposite Fatania and the binary, you will see Mutaria on the outer ring. With those aligned north and south you have eight left, four on each side — Gom, Teratica, Nubibia, and Minoria to the east, with Nisus, Jinnia, Arborus and Trollium to the west. The distance between them changes a little though they keep the same order, but Fatania never moves relative to Vanitas and Fastus."

It was a large mouthful to swallow at once, but Steven offered his best. "And Fatania never moves from its spot just below the binary twins," he repeated, locating the key orb on the horizon.

"Or just below where the binary ought to be," Keep confirmed.

Steven blinked. "If Fatania never moves relative to the binary, the binary shouldn't move relative to Fatania."

"Of course not," Keep replied, "but the binary brightens and fades with the seasons, and disappears completely in the spring."

"What makes it do that?"

"It is a legacy of the explosion," Keep explained. "Vanitas and Fastus glow in the reflection of each other. They tarnish with space dust and fade, then brighten again like a self-cleaning oven. The regularity of it measures the aspects of Quotaris. With the

66

spring fading we enter the star aspect, and that is when we are busiest mining the trovium and moulding shooting star boosters. When the binary brightens again we enter the leaf aspect, and at its brightest the leaves of the triunium also reach the peak of their autumn hue. That is when we hold the Festival of the Wishing Tree, to foretaste the day when the Quicks will have been left only to choose the greatest of all wishes."

"Oh," said Steven, "now I understand why you have the two flags — like, one for each aspect."

"No," Keep corrected, "it is just one flag with two sides. The star and the leaf are one in the unity of all and, of course, signify the unity of creation — your first Complement of Being."

The unity of creation was something the Cheechikois and everyone else seemed to believe in, but to Steven's mind it was the last thing anyone would symbolize with flags. And calling it a complement of being! Gorse always spoke of the unity of creation in the same breath as faith and brotherhood, but without numbers. Suspecting the answer to his question, Steven nevertheless asked it. "Keep! What are the Complements of Being?" ... Keep made no reply. "Keep?" Still hearing no reply, Steven turned, only to see that the toga had again taken flight. Hurrying after it, Steven entered the Dome's mezzanine and saw Keep round what had to be the cosmoscope which stood pointing into space. He continued on after the toga, and gaining the far side of the cosmoscope, entered an area ringed with an array of electronic consoles. Surrounded by control panels and monitors from which there issued now and then the eerie sounds of outer space, a large video screen flickered. At a comfortable distance from it was a tall-backed chair, a twin to the one at the council table. Standing beside the chair was Keep, and in the chair was the golden-haired lady of the portrait.

Steven came to an abrupt halt and started to back away. Turning her head at that moment to accept a paper from Keep's outstretched hand, the lady caught sight of Steven with his armload of printouts, and smiled a welcome. Her expression was just as in the portrait, bearing an aura of friendliness and affection. The sincerity of it was rendered the more reassuring by the faintest of telltale wrinkles in the corners of her eyes, confessing to an unaffected appreciation of life.

"This is Steven, Your Highness," Keep informed her. "His arrival unfortunately coincided with the trovium affair and found you occupied."

The Gardinelle smiled, "How nice to have you, Steven."

Bowing was not among Steven's accomplishments, but faced with the need, he managed to bend his neck and one knee in an exercise that showed better intentions than taste. "I am pleased to meet Your Highness."

The Gardinelle accepted the gesture with a gracious nod, and passing an approving eye over his dress, hesitated only the briefest instant before accepting that one shoelace was indeed a piece of string. "I see someone has been looking after you," she concluded with an even more disarming smile.

"Yes, Your Highness," Steven answered with the utmost politeness. He even reinforced his reply with an energetic nod to make sure there was no question of his satisfaction with the reception he had received. Being then offered a plush stool to sit on until he was needed further, Steven took his place in sight of the screen which was presenting something of a travelogue of everchanging mountains, rivers, and forests, with the occasional appearance of familiar animals. But Steven had little interest in television — his eyes were on the Gardinelle.

"As I was about to say, my dear Keep," the Gardinelle took up, "the growing difference between the number of wishes received and the number granted leaves me uneasy. It seems not to follow the old rule of thumb."

"That is true, Your Highness," Keep verified, leafing through the Compleat Record. "I thought at first we could be out of line, but going over the updates I find the imbalance between fruitful and unfruitful wishes is not that we are granting fewer, but that WAND and EGOS disagree over the number being received."

"If WAND and EGOS disagree over the count, it sounds very much like a problem for Thalamus," the Gardinelle observed. "I wish you had thought to bring him. But what have you found exactly?"

"I am afraid it is a problem of screening, Your Highness," Keep replied, lifting his eyes from the Compleat Record to peer at the Gardinelle over the top of his spectacles. "The count fails reconciliation because much that EGOS has been offering as wishes, WAND has been rejecting as fribbles. It seems to be a matter of things falling between two stools."

"If they are neither wishes nor fribbles, what must they be then?" the Gardinelle questioned.

"Wibbles, My Lady," a voice honked.

Raising her eyes at the sound, the Gardinelle beheld Thalamus who seemed to have appeared from nowhere.

"You wished Keep had thought to bring me, Your Highness," Thalamus announced.

The Gardinelle nodded and elevated a questioning brow. "Did you say wibbles, my dear Thalamus?"

"Yes, My Lady. I am afraid the Quicks out there have taken to wibbling — ignoring the protocol for Propers, and choosing instead self-indulgent and casual appeals totally wanting in any commitment."

"And how would they have come to that?"

"It seems to have started with parents," Thalamus replied. He canted his head to one side with the air of an harassed mother. "I wish you wouldn't do this. I wish you wouldn't do that. I wish you could be like the Jones children." He straightened up. "Wibbles! Rejecting commitments of any kind and ignoring the Three Complements of Being."

"But surely no one expects to be granted model children for wibbles," the Gardinelle exclaimed.

"My Lady, they seem not to realize that just as Quick computers are governed by Gin-Go, so computers of the First Kind are governed by Win-Wo."

"Win-Wo, my dear Thalamus?"

"Wibbles in — Wibbles out, My Lady. As long as EGOS loads WAND with wibbles, WAND will respond in kind. It is simply Win-Wo."

The Gardinelle nodded agreement. "That seems as it should be, my dear Thalamus. Wishes that ignore the Complements of

Being and lack the faith of commitment, ought not to count in any amount."

"Fair enough!" Keep voiced his approval from the folds of the Compleat Record. "If we accept that wibbles don't count in any amount, the disagreement between EGOS and WAND is easily settled."

The Gardinelle hesitated. "That may clear up the discrepancy, my dear Keep, but does it resolve the problem? If wibble-wishing is so common, it must be at the expense of ambitions for the betterment of the Quick Side. That being so, it must be that not only Regulars but," and here the Gardinelle winced, "Propers as well as Perfects must be suffering. What does the record show?"

Keep was pursing his lips as he resumed leafing through the sheets. "Your Highness has always been more than fair with Regulars, being guided as much by compassion as by merit, though," he quickly interposed to avoid any appearance of criticism, "you would expect it to have encouraged the Quicks to try for the more rewarding Propers and Perfects. Unfortunately," and here Keep paused to look up sadly, "unfortunately, that has not been the case. We have received instead only a few Propers in recent times — and those mostly from humanitarians, doctors, and scientists — and no Perfects in many Quick years."

"In many Quick years?" the Gardinelle repeated unhappily. "But why? Proper wishes have always carried their own reward, and Perfects the recognition of a transcendental favour." Her troubled gaze scanned the faces of her chief clerk and the wizard.

Listening intently, Steven was surprised to hear that wishes were not to be a simple handout, and were not only to be sorted from prayers, but were themselves sorted on some kind of merit. More curious than ever about the process, he leaned forward, ready to make use of the first polite opening to put his question to the Gardinelle herself.

"It is not a problem of computers, My Lady," Thalamus was being quick to declare.

"Nor of the Compleat Record," Keep as quickly vouched.

"Then," concluded the Gardinelle, "something has quite definitely gone wrong, and if it is not here, it must be out there among the Quicks. It is unfortunate that wibbles have displaced Regulars, but the loss in Propers and Perfects is most disheartening. It cannot be that the Quicks are satisfied with their lot — at least not when so many deficiencies remain to be corrected. And yet we seem to have lost touch. Could it be a new scepticism has overtaken them? Could it be that the genii are again tempting them with false dreams of a life of wealth and power? Might they," and here her voice trailed off in anguish at such a devastating possibility "might they even despair of achieving the greatest of all wishes?" While thus thinking aloud, the Gardinelle had risen, and walking to the transparency, now stood looking out in silent contemplation.

Waiting for the Gardinelle to conclude her reflections, the quietness of the room weighed heavy with her disappointment. Steven leaned back, saddened by the Gardinelle's apparent sorrow, and resigned himself to waiting for a later time to raise his own question. At length an eerie discord from the space monitor broke the silence, and Keep, who could no longer contain his sympathy for his unhappy Queen, intruded upon her thoughts. "Could we not send out the Knights Courier to investigate?" he ventured apologetically.

"A commendable idea," Thalamus honked, and as the Gardinelle turned to face the room, he continued. "The problem calls for a tour of the Quick Side such as would challenge the best. I can see the gallant Sirgal and Breach vying with each other for the honour of such a task. You would need only choose between them."

The Gardinelle inclined her head in a tentative approval of the idea, but weighed it carefully. "The dauntless Breach? No. This would not call for the audacity of a Breach. He much prefers to scout the untravelled paths of adventure, sounding out the threats to our realm. No," she continued slowly, "travelling among the Quicks will require rather a knight with the courtesy, sensitivity and compassion of a Sirgal. Yes, the Knight Courier Sirgal would be the one to send," she concluded with satisfaction.

The Gardinelle had no sooner reached her decision than an insistent high-pitched dissonance of the space monitors drew all eyes to the cosmoscreen.

7

The Gardinelle regained her chair, and making herself comfortable, touched a button on the armrest. Immediately the cosmoscreen began to grow in size, bulging out to meet the transparency which shrank to meet it, the one diffusing into the other. At the same time, the tone of the space monitors softened, and changing their quality, melted into the shrill voices of young people screaming cheers of delight and shouts of encouragement. Interrupting its meandering progress to search out the voices, the unfolding scene continued its evolution on through the wooded banks of a winding river, at length merging with a haze that overhung the orderly-ranked wigwams of a little Indian village.

With the last rays of sunshine peeking over the sheltering hills, the figure of a boy carrying a lesser form piggyback, made its way through the lengthening shadows towards the voices, a dog trotting faithfully at heel. Reaching a group of shouting children who lined the side of a shinny field in the village compound, the boy lowered his burden. It was a slight girl, little more than a year his junior, clothed very much like himself in a beaded shirt and leggings, her hair in tight braids tied with coloured tassels.

"Falling Star!"

"Lean Bone!"

The greetings rose from many lips, and making room, the welcomers saw the girl settled comfortably on her knees in an habitual posture, leaning halfway back against the afflicted limbs that would not let her stand like other children. As well from habit, and responding to the simple word "Trish", the dog took its place beside its mistress.

From the stick-wielding shinny players on the field the welcome continued more urgently. "Lean Bone! Lean Bone! Our side needs you. Hurry!" With no more urging, the boy took up a proffered stick, and racing onto the field, joined the chase after a gnarl of wood that was the ball.

Not far distant an elderly man sat cross-legged by his fire in front of his wigwam, his attention riveted on the ground at his knees. He wore the costume of a shaman, the robe figured with pictographs testifying to his oratory in treaty and counsel. The headdress, a broad bonnet of feathers bearing the outspread wings of an owl, was topped with the crown antler of a deer, its prong standing erect, crestlike, and from the back there trailed the brush of a silver fox. Interrupted by the motionless figure, the rays from a setting sun formed an oddly distorted silhouette on the wall of the wigwam.

At this instant the shaman's knitted brow was bent over a circle drawn in the dust, for in that circle a clutch of little bones lay as they had fallen from his hands moments earlier. In their scatter the bones held a puzzling message which was to be drawn from a talon curled about the wishbone.

From the doorway behind, a lavishly woven blanket covering her shoulders, her head of unruly locks held in check by a beaded headband, a young woman of unpampered but striking beauty studied the shaman's mood with disapproving eyes. Drawing a breath as if to speak, she changed her mind, then biting her lip with resolution, drew another breath and spoke. "And what does the shaman read in his tattling bones tonight? The signs seem to be no more pleasing than ever."

As if unhearing, the shaman remained motionless, his head bent over the dusty circle of scrambled bones.

"I know it concerns the children," the young woman declared, "for the bones brought that look into your eyes the night Falling Star was born, and many times since. What portents do the spirits reveal that disturb the great Walking Owl, Shaman of the

Cheechikois, Voice of Wisdom, Leader in Peace? What were the portents that puzzled him the night Falling Star was born, and continue to puzzle him to this day? I have a right to know. She may be your grandchild, but it was with her dying breath that Redwing placed her children in my care."

Walking Owl stirred. "Your tongue disturbs the spirits, Alabak. That they have taken an interest in Falling Star is of little doubt, but whether she will come to live her mother's wish is yet too soon to tell."

"Yet too soon?" Alabak scoffed. "Too soon to see that when a child is sent into the world crippled and useless to the tribe, the name that was wished upon her must surely be at fault? Too soon to see a shameful charm at work when first her father falls to an arrow of the hateful Maliskaps, and then her mother is taken before the child scarcely draws breath? Too soon? Ha!"

"The ways of the spirits are not for us to question," Walking Owl replied. "It is enough that on the very night the child was to be born, Redwing was sent the sign, and not only did the star cast its trail wide across the heavens, but vanished into the waters before her very eyes. Fortune smiles upon one who receives such a sign, and to the wishes of such a one the spirits are bound to listen."

"And more is the pity," Alabak retorted, "for she, stupid girl, favoured with such a sign, wasted it wishing on her unborn child a luckless name and the call to follow in the peacemaker's steps. Forgive the past and lead the tribes along the path of peace," she sneered. "Peace with such as the Maliskaps, indeed! While my brother — yes, the child's own father — lies unavenged!" Alabak paused only to catch her breath. "The name Falling Star carries an evil charm. It must be changed!"

"According to the law of the tribe," Walking Owl replied calmly, "Falling Star will keep the name her mother gave her for yet twelve moons, and only then will it be changed if she prefers to choose another. She likes the name and it pleases her to be called by it. What the spirits were witness to is not for Alabak to alter."

"And that Redwing left the children in my hands the spirits also witnessed," Alabak was quick to answer. "It is time to put things

74

right. I will choose a new name for her. A new name invites a new guardian spirit, and I will wager a new one will make more sense than those you have been courting."

"Your tongue is disrespectful of the spirits, Alabak," Walking Owl warned. "Take care lest their displeasure see misfortune brought upon yourself, if not upon the whole of Wamwiki."

"Nevertheless," Alabak snapped, "the naming ceremony is not far off, and when that day arrives she will choose a more suitable name." She threw back her head defiantly. "I will forbid her to keep the name Falling Star, for it is truly a name of ill omen.

"She will keep the name, and with it the faith to face her lot, however difficult," Walking Owl replied, "for I will school her well in the paths of wisdom, that her life may be crowned with the happiness of serving the goal her mother wished."

"The children are my responsibility," Alabak hurled back. "I can take them from this wigwam if I must, and raise them my way and with the names I please." With that she stormed off into the evening shadows.

Walking Owl shook his head sorrowfully, and taking up a beaded doeskin pouch that lay at his side, gathered the bones into it, while from the compound, the strains of song reached his ears.

O starlight is teasing,
With magic so pleasing,
That leads you to grieving,
Too late you will know.

In the compound the shinny game had long since ended, and now encircling a blazing bonfire, the children were engaged in their evening singsong. The aches and pains of life as yet untasted, and true to their age, the children were seeing humour in everything, and even the very sadness of life was something to be mocked in song. No less than the others, Falling Star laughed and chanted as the ring of bodies swayed in rhythm with their voices. When the verse was ended, Falling Star clapped her hands and pressed for more. "Again. Again. Lets everybody sing it once more, Starlight!"

With little ado the chorus was raised anew.

The magic of starlight
The night skies adorning,
Slip off with my dreams in
The cold gray of morning,
And shadows deceiving
Unseen for the glitter,
Emerging with daylight
Turn sweet into bitter.

O starlight is teasing,
With magic so pleasing,
That leads you to grieving,
Too late you will know.

Walking Owl sat listening to the voices. After a time he shook his head sadly, and taking up the beaded doeskin pouch, held it above the circle. Closing his eyes so as not to influence the cast, he slipped the drawstring, allowing the contents of the pouch to tumble as they would. As they fell, his face gave no clue to his thoughts, though had his lips moved they would have been heard to say,

Bones whose spirits, now departed,
Wander freely seeing all
Secrets, schemes, and plots unseemly,
Bare them in the way you fall.

Opening his eyes, an almost imperceptible widening was all that gave any hint of the ominous message they beheld — for there was the sign as it had appeared before — the talon lay curled about the wishbone!

"YOUR HIGHNESS!"

The scene crumbled into its silent monitor, and Steven shook his head as if waking from a dream. All eyes in the Dome had turned from the screen to identify the voice which, though robbed of air by lungs that had mounted the stairs too hurriedly, could not be robbed of its excitement. "Your Highness! Breach has been caught with the stolen trovium!"

The gasping messenger was a tall, thin-faced fellow, his eyes circled with dark rings that brought to mind a raccoon. He halted, his little potbelly bobbing up and down in rhythm with his adam's apple, awaiting the Gardinelle's response. Her response was to be no more than a painful expression of incredulity.

"The Knight Courier Breach, Your Highness," the man repeated.

The Gardinelle's expression remained one of astonishment as she pressed a button on her armrest, shutting off the cosmoscreen altogether. "Surely not, my dear Reefer," she finally murmured.

"Yes," Reefer expanded, "the Knight Courier Sirgal himself stumbled upon the place where the trovium had been hidden. As Chief of Security, I authorized a trap to be set, and in it Sirgal caught Breach returning for the stolen material."

"Then there can be no mistake?" the Gardinelle sighed.

"I am afraid not, Your Highness. We are bringing him in. It is indeed a regrettable end to the affair," Reefer added sympathetically.

"My, oh my!" exclaimed Keep under his breath, turning to Thalamus. "The favourite Knight Courier Breach caught in the act by the favourite Knight Courier Sirgal."

"Less a case of knight catching knight as of day catching night," Thalamus offered in reply. "And mark my word," he whispered, "if Reefer thinks that could be an end to the affair he is badly mistaken. Such a turn of events must prove to be only the beginning."

Accepting the unhappy news, the Gardinelle rose from her chair. "Very well, my dear Reefer. In the council chamber." She thereupon led the way to the floor below where the fast-spreading word was already bringing councillors and knights together in hushed voices.

With the Gardinelle's entry the room quieted, while everyone quickly seated themselves in the place of their rank. The air of expectancy heightened when someone announced, "The Knight Courier Sirgal is on his way up."

Attracted by the growing hum from the rising cage, Steven watched the flashing annunciator. When the safety door slid aside, the lightly-mailed form of a fair-haired knight stood framed in the opening, his headpiece held in the crook of one arm, the other arm loosely brushing the silver scabbard at his side. His bearing relaxed and assured, he made the slightest of hesitations while his earnest blue eyes swept the room to find and rest upon the Gardinelle. Then, rippling the curls across his shoulders with a courteous inclination of his head, he approached with measured step to make a courtly bow and caress the hand of his Queen. "Your Highness," was all he said, or needed to say, for the richness of his voice was at once modulated with sorrow, respect, and devotion.

"My dear Sirgal," the Gardinelle greeted him affectionately, "how sad a day for us all and for you who must denounce a comrade knight with whom you have shared such feats of honour in the service of Quotaris."

"I would readily denounce myself should my heart ever falter before the least sacrifice in the cause of Your Highness," Sirgal made answer.

"Thank you, my dear Sirgal," the Gardinelle breathed gratefully.

Taking his leave with a bow, Sirgal withdrew to the side, because another murmur of anticipation had circled the room. Almost immediately the swish of a sliding door could be heard, and the knightly prisoner was ushered into the room, an armed escort at his elbows. Bereft of his sword, he carried himself with scornful dignity. There was a boyish softness in the lines of his face, its pallor the more evident against the ebon sheen of his hair which, as he removed his headpiece, fell in curls about a bandage covering his temple. The cloth was faintly stained, its mute appeal capable of stirring compassion in the most insensitive breast. Surveying the room as he walked, the man's liquid black eyes settled briefly on Sirgal in a defiant glare, and moving on, he stopped a respectful distance before the Gardinelle. The shadow of a smile playing the corners of his eyes, part contrite, part mocking, he made an elegant bow. "Your Highness," he said in a voice that could scarcely soften its metallic ring.

The Gardinelle looked at him sorrowfully, acknowledging his bow with just a hint of a nod before turning to Reefer. "And how does the Chief Security Officer state the charge that thus brings our distinguished Knight Courier Breach before us?"

"Your Highness, he is charged not only with the theft of trovium, but with the intent to use it to commit an act of violence."

The Gardinelle raised her brow. "An act of violence?"

"Counting on its high yield in evil when shocked by a detonator, he planned to make an engine of destruction with the stolen trovium and explode it amidst the Dogtrolytes, Your Highness."

The Gardinelle turned to Breach. "And how do you plead, Sir Knight?"

"Guilty, My Queen," Breach replied with another respectful bow, while an excited buzz ran through the audience.

The Gardinelle studied the knight for a moment and sighed. "You have at least the gallantry to spare your comrade Sirgal from having to bear witness." She paused. "It is scarcely a few days since you returned to us from your last mission, suffering wounds from a brush with the Dogtrolytes — with whom, if I recall, your mission ought not to have had the least affair."

"We were by way of taking a shortcut home, Your Highness," Breach assured her with an easy shrug, his boyish charm needing little pretense. "Seeking passage in the name of Her Highness, Queen of Quotaris, our peaceful troop displayed the flag of the realm clearly as we rode. The Dogtrolytes fell upon us in force, and trampled it."

There was an exchange of knowing glances among the knights, while Reefer, with obvious difficulty, overcame the desire to speak.

"And now," the Gardinelle suggested, "you plead guilty to the theft of trovium which you would put to use punishing those witless anti-beings."

"The honour of our flag could demand nothing less than a lesson that even a Dogtrolyte can understand," Breach replied.

An affair of flags! Steven listened more intently.

Reefer was shaking his head angrily. "Your Highness, the Knight Courier's reputation for audacity speaks much clearer than his words. The men of his troop admit he led a provocative charge through the home of the Dogtrolytes who have never wanted more than to haunt their canyons and be left alone. Having been soundly beaten for his foolishness, Breach would now seek Your Highness' indulgence over a questionable point of honour, and hides a cowardly revenge behind the flag. Where is the honour in that?"

Reefer's intervention left Steven feeling less detached and indifferent, and although he was sorry to see the Gardinelle thus upset, he also could have told her so. Yes, he thought, without a flag to egg him on, Breach would probably have behaved more sensibly. Flags are all alike, and people with peace on their mind would do well to get rid of them.

The Gardinelle held views of her own. "Thank you, my dear Reefer," she said, "we are well aware of the Knight Courier's reputation, for which I fear he may not be entirely to blame. No. It was the rashness of a dashing young gallant we too readily forgave that became the imprudent valour of a devoted arm. I am afraid his valour has blinded us to the danger of his devotion falling victim to the love of danger itself — and to the making of a knight errant." She studied the bandaged head thoughtfully. "The wound you now display reminds us of other wounds you have more honourably received in our cause." Breach acknowledged the favourable words with a modest inclination of his head. "Not the least of them," the Gardinelle went on, "received beside your comrade the Knight Courier Sirgal, courageously defending Quotaris against the treachery of our arch-enemy Fulgor. If the Quicks have wished themselves a lot beyond their mindless cowering before the mastery of Fulgor's thunder and lightning, thanks are largely owed to the exemplary spirit of the Knights

Courier of the Wishing Tree. There are few who are endowed with the qualities to carry the flag of Quotaris, dispensing the bounties of creation, correcting its oversights, and inspiring the Quicks everywhere to put their faith in the fulfillment of dreams and not in a sheeplike submission to demons. Nor can a knight bear greater trust than the flag and its message, for they who ride ahead with the flag colour it, and all who follow behind are coloured by it. To sacrifice oneself defending the flag is to show the greatest devotion; to sacrifice the flag defending oneself is to betray not only knighthood and its trust but those for whom the flag is held to measure loftier values and the promise of fulfilling more laudable dreams and wishes."

While the Gardinelle spoke, the mockery had drained from Breach's eyes, and his expression had slowly sobered. Nor were the Gardinelle's words missed by Steven, to whom, however, they brought a fleeting vision of Miss Adley who seemed to share much in common with the Gardinelle when it came to mixing flags with wishes.

"Your faithful service," the Gardinelle concluded, "cannot be allowed to blind us now to a duty which I regret to have poorly served in the past — the unpleasant duty of discipline. The Knight Courier Breach will therefore be confined to barracks until further notice."

The Gardinelle's final words brought a stir among the knights present, though many exchanged whispered smiles as Breach was led away. Choosing to be alone, the Gardinelle rose, dismissing her staff, and left by her private entrance.

In the stir of departing knights and councillors, Steven found himself separated from Keep and Thalamus, and passing the stairs, was reminded of the drama in Wamwiki. He needed no one to tell him it was a replay of the old shaman's story, and he determined to miss none of it. On impulse, he stopped with his foot on the first step, pretending to tie his shoelace. With the corner of his eye alert, he seized the opportunity, and slipping under the stairs, concealed himself to await everyone's departure. From his hiding place he could hear the passing voices quite clearly.

"That will go down hard with the likes of Breach," said one.

"Have no fear," said a second. "I will wager the rascal soon worms his way back into the Gardinelle's good graces."

"Any punishment is more than Breach can take," a third put in. "But he could not have done it alone, you know. Yet nothing was said of an accomplice."

The voices faded and were gone, and peeking out, Steven found himself alone. He lost no time running up the stairs, and once in the Gardinelle's chair, found the button on the armrest. He pressed it and watched the screen spring to life — just in time to catch Alabak.

The young woman had traversed a narrow strip of forest, and now emerged beside a dilapidated little hut that stood in a clearing distant from the village. A grotesque old tree, the nesting place for a band of raucous crows, rose over the hut, and in the twilight shadow under its spreading branches, an old woman was throwing grains of corn to the grateful birds. She talked to them as they scratched and pecked.

"He was a good hunter and a good husband, you know. I told him not to go to the river that day. Not with the spirits moaning in the trees as they were. But you know how men are."

"Chikchik."

Alabak's voice startled the crows. In a flurry of flapping wings and a clamour of hoarse cries, they rose into the cover of the branches overhead, while above the noise Chikchik's shrill voice called after them. "When you visit the spirit world tonight don't forget to look for him and bring me back his tidings."

Taking a stool by the side of Chikchik's smouldering fire, Alabak chided the woman. "Why do you waste your time and your precious corn on those foolish birds? They can tell you nothing, though the unseen world of spirits lurks about your miserable hut the livelong night. But I can see them. They are all there in the coals of your fire. Do you see how the spirits of the dead writhe and twist among the embers there, trying to speak and finding no one who can hear? But I can hear them, and perhaps your dear husband among them."

82

Chikchik stepped closer, and as she leaned over to peer into the flickering coals, Alabak passed her hand through a curl of smoke, and letting fall a sprinkle of powder, caused a crimson flash to burst from the smouldering bed. Chikchik straightened with a start. "There, you see," Alabak purred. "Waiting to be freed they are."

Chikchik stood for a moment, drawn back, fearful yet curious. "What do they say?" she asked. "Did my husband speak?"

"Tomorrow night, he said, and that was all," Alabak confided.

"Tomorrow night?" Chikchik drew closer, looking into the coals hopefully, anxiously. "Tomorrow night," she repeated. "But ... but how am I to speak to him? I cannot hear the voices."

"You have only to help me, and I will help you pass your messages," Alabak offered. "Tomorrow and as long as you do me faithful service."

Chikchik nodded her head in vigorous agreement. "Yes, yes. What can I do?"

"You must speak of this to no one, not even the crows," Alabak replied, and added menacingly, "lest you be turned into a rabbit and be eaten by the village dogs."

Chikchik nodded.

If you breathe a word, I will know, for no one else knows my secrets, not even Walking Owl. They can be learned only from the Sisters of the Five Dreams. So beware!"

"Oh, I swear," Chikchik piped, raising a shaky hand over her heart.

"Good," said Alabak. "In the old man's place and mastering the tribes, I will reward you greatly. But first there is the matter of a smart-aleck boy who must not inherit his doting grandfather's powers, and the boy's useless little sister who promises to be a meddling nuisance like her mother, the more so since her name bears a charm and her grandfather's blessing."

Chikchik kneeled, listening attentively.

"First, let us see some better embers in your fire," Alabak ordered.

Chikchik hurriedly threw a handful of chips onto the coals, and stood waiting for further orders.

"Tomorrow," Alabak continued, "you will collect the herbs and barks that I tell you of. We will need them to make potions, for we must prepare to cast some dream spells. They are five in number, and we may need to cast them all. And now," she finished sternly, as the darkness quickened, "be off into your hut, and leave me be, for I must consult with the spirits."

With Chikchik gone, Alabak turned to the fire, and first casting upon it a sprinkle of her crimson powders, stirred the dying embers. Gazing into the limitless depths of the awakening coals, she surrendered herself to the spell of their wavering glow, seeing there the mystic forms of a writhing spirit world whence would come the guidance for her secret schemes.

Motionless save for the flickering light that played about her entranced stare, only the spirits could hear in the moaning sounds escaping her lips, a wailing cry to coax their ear:

> *O spirits thread my smouldering loom,*
> *To spin a web to seal a doom;*
> *Of one whose name repels all harm,*
> *Reveal the key to break that charm.*

Possessed and overcome, Alabak thereupon sank into a deep trance, and while the night deepened around her, a far-off brightening in the sky heralded the resplendent glitter of the Milky Way.

In the silence, Steven heard the footfall of someone mounting the stairs. He quickly pressed the button to switch off the screen, and slipping out of the Gardinelle's chair, backed quietly away towards the opposite staircase. Ducking behind a cabinet that would cover his retreat, he listened as the footsteps rounded the cosmoscope, and peeking out, saw a white smock topped with a shock of red hair. It was the young scientist he had seen in the elevator — Kwah — and he seemed in a hurry. Going directly to one of the consoles, he drew on a set of earphones, and adjusting a dial, uttered a single word, "Eks". Steven watched, gathering himself ready to steal away as soon as Kwah would be well enough occupied. He had not long to wait. The screen began to take in the heavens as Kwah busied himself over the switches and dials. At first but a sprinkle of stars, the scene quickly cleared as the Big Dipper took shape and began to close in, faster and faster. The rushing approach reminded Steven of his arrival in the garden, and deciding it was high time to leave, he tiptoed away and down the stairs.

8

Steven watched the pointer spin as the cage carried him down after his stealthy departure from the Dome. Still holding onto Keep's printouts, he arranged them under his arm, preparing for the door to open.

"Oh, there you are, Steven!" Hugging the Compleat Record to his bosom, Keep had been standing with Thalamus waiting for the cage. Steven halted in the doorway, surprised to have found his friends so easily. "And you remembered the updates," Keep exclaimed happily on catching sight of the bundle.

Thalamus crowded Steven back into the cage. "The boy promises to be a second Keep what with the latest printouts trailing about his person."

Keep followed in behind Thalamus. "We were looking for you in the page's lounge. Among her visits today, the Gardinelle is going to the laboratory. I remember promising to take you there."

"I was in the Dome," Steven replied, and having reason to make sure of the rules, ventured his question. "I was wondering, Keep, does the Gardinelle mind anyone watching her cosmo-screen?"

"Oh, certainly not," Keep chuckled. "After all, watching the Quicks is the business of Quotaris, is it not?"

"Like, I could watch when she isn't there?" Steven asked more precisely.

Keep nodded, and Thalamus chortled, "Heaven knows the Quicks bear watching."

Once again the door slid open, and this time Steven stepped out among the white smocks that were busying about in the electrified atmosphere of the laboratory. Ushered forward between Keep and Thalamus, he was in time to join the tail end of the visiting party.

As the Gardinelle moved ahead exchanging words with the staff, Keep left Thalamus and Steven to take his place making notes at her side. Relaxed and at ease among the strange glass creations of bubbling liquids and sputtering electrical contrivances, the Gardinelle's example was reassuring, though the fizz of incandescent tubes sent a tingle through Steven much as the near miss of a lightning bolt. An involuntary reflex drew him closer to the wizard.

"This stuff bothers you, my boy?" Thalamus asked.

"It depends," Steven replied, somewhat dubiously. "I know it has to do with granting wishes, but I don't know just how."

"Delivery systems, my boy. A granted wish has to be delivered. Here we research the messenger magic."

"Messenger magic?" Steven raised his brow. Now there were different kinds of magic. "Is that different from ordinary magic?"

"Some," said Thalamus. "Messenger magic reflects logic."

Steven's inquiring eye passed over the buzzing laboratory. "I know what things look like when they reflect light, but what do they look like when they reflect logic?"

"The same," replied Thalamus. "You see them, but you cannot see through them." He allowed his thin smile and added, "So to speak."

"But how can you hide the magic from scientists?"

"With logic, my boy. Logic is time, but time stands still at the magic boundary, you see — a Quick mind cannot cross."

"But scientists always ask why, until they have the truth."

"Truth, my boy, is a chameleon that changes colour with every point of view, except from the Remote Side. Messenger magic will provide Quicks with answers to 'when', 'where', and 'how'. In the end, logic holds them prisoners of time, but 'why' being timeless must be viewed from the Remote Side and, thus, will forever lie beyond the grasp of Quicks. No, my boy, with all their probing of messenger magic, the Quicks can only wish for more logic, and when they do, the Gardinelle nudges them closer to the greatest of all wishes, though getting there in Quick time is so painfully slow that she sometimes has to call for a miracle."

"A miracle?" The idea of miracles had escaped Steven's mind completely. "Why doesn't she go for miracles all the way?" he questioned in surprise.

"Well, of course, we are responsible only for the magic," Thalamus confided. "Miracles are the responsibility of the Remote Side, and under the rules, they set the limit at only one in a million."

"I know miracles are only one in a million, but I didn't know it had to be a rule," Steven replied.

"Oh yes, quite," Thalamus assured him. "A singleton is luck; two out of three is good; three out of five is tops; four out of seven is gospel — and one in a million is a miracle." He pursed his lips. "It spells logic to the Quicks, so why not?"

At that moment Steven's wandering gaze passed over the entrance door, and there caught sight of Kwah who had left the elevator and was skirting the far side of the laboratory. Steven watched the red hair lose itself along the way. Returning his attention to Thalamus, he found the wizard's interest was directed to the party ahead, where the Gardinelle had stopped before an alcove that was draped and overflowing with assemblages of coloured balls. They were in all shapes and sizes, some dangling from the ceiling in grapelike clusters, some festooned in chainlike catkins. Others hung in twisted and deformed patterns, while yet others stood like Tinkertoys, their nodules joined by slender stalks.

"There you are, my boy," said Thalamus. "Professor Remspruk's magic works without smoke or sparks. That should please you."

"I know those," Steven declared knowledgeably. "All the laboratories have them. They are, like, models of molecules."

"Oh?" Thalamus arched his brow as with profound admiration. "You read molecules!"

"Well," Steven faltered and sighed. People seemed to be reading everything but books. "I just sort of know about them, but not exactly what those ones mean."

"I see." Thalamus allowed his thin smile. "Professor Remspruk has revolutionized the chemistry of messenger magic," he offered by comparison. "What you see, my boy, are his idea enzymes. The Professor makes the pills, and a courier slips them into your bowl of soup, your cup of coffee — or even into your tub of bathwater, like the Eureka classic over there," said Thalamus, inviting Steven to admire a nubbly creation hanging over a blackboard.

Steven looked in the direction of Thalamus' finger, but was more taken by a shaggy-haired gentleman who was fast covering the blackboard with lines of chemical intelligence. The rhythm of his arm, accompanied by the high-pitched complaints of his long stick of chalk, produced the air of a virtuoso in recital. Having covered the length of one wall and two-thirds of its neighbour, he finished with a tattoo of flying chalk that came up with a concluding symbol shaped like a star.

"Professor Remspruk himself," Thalamus honked in Steven's ear.

Begrudging himself no more than a moment to stand back and admire the result, Remspruk hurriedly sorted through his bottles, placing the chosen ones beside an apparatus in elements of blown glass and tubing. Inserting a funnel into the topmost opening, and taking his cue from the blackboard, he introduced the vital liquors one after the other, erasing each completed step from the blackboard before proceeding to the next. As its volume gathered in the bottom of a large globe, the mixture grew livelier with succeeding additions — to Remspruk's mounting satisfaction — until at length bubbling vigorously, it burst forth to spiral in and about the maze of passageways. Beaming with delight and anticipation of impending success, Remspruk turned to the blackboard for his next instruction only to see it disappear under the swipe of a dusty brush.

The culprit was a little lady under a broad-brimmed hat. She stood on a stool, and matching the Professor line for line, had erased his text from the conclusion backwards to meet him in the corner. Angry beyond measure, Remspruk snatched up the nearest model cluster, and giving vent to his rage, hurled it in the lady's direction. It was then that the lady turned from the blackboard, and to Steven's surprise he saw that she was a chimpanzee who, with a toothy grin, calmly offered up her brush to the Professor.

The chimpanzee's gesture did little to placate the irate Professor. Crying "Sima!" and voicing unintelligible sounds, he rushed at her, and raising his hands to inflict due punishment, he found himself at the receiving end of a choking cloud of chalk as Sima blew lustily across the laden brush. While the Professor convulsed in sneezes, she dodged his flailing arms, and scurrying to the Gardinelle's side, there defied pursuit.

For the first time since setting out for the witch hazel, Steven found himself not only entertained, but screaming with delight, and even Thalamus' thin smile deepened its crease.

Having scampered out to greet her friends, Sima now peeked at Steven from behind Keep's toga. It was Steven's first encounter with a monkey of any kind, and the novelty of Sima's humanlike behaviour was irresistibly engaging. "Sima, Sima," he called, inviting her friendship with outstretched arms. But Steven's entreaties were quite unnecessary. The affectionate Sima accepted his overtures without hesitation, returning them in an avalanche of hugs and kisses. Tickled beyond measure, Steven was almost too weak with laughter to impose more fitting decorum on his new friend.

During the diversion, Kwah had suddenly appeared on the scene, and avoiding Steven and Sima with the aloofness he had shown in the elevator, approached the Gardinelle. "Your Highness, I beg a thousand pardons for not having met you at the door. My work chose an awkward time to demand attention."

"Not at all, my dear Kwah," the Gardinelle assured him pleasantly. "Duty must come first, and confidentially," she added in a lower voice, "guided tours tend to be stuffy, do you not think?"

90

Kwah raised a protesting hand. "I know of no way a visit from Your Highness could become stuffy, and if I might be permitted to see you around...."

"That is very thoughtful of you," the Gardinelle replied, "but as it happens, I have little more than the time to find Resal, and then I must be on my way."

Kwah nodded towards a nearby door. "I believe Resal is still playing with her little trovium particles." His words were not impolite, though he could have said "little paper dolls" with equal voice.

"Then," the Gardinelle observed approvingly, "the dear girl has not yet given up her search for a way to create microstars."

"Or a star scientist," Kwah suggested. While the remark fell again lightly from his lips, his eyes reflected little if any sign of humour.

Thalamus turned to Keep, and shielding his words with the back of his hand, asked, "Do I detect a trace of jealousy in Kwah's voice, my good fellow?"

Keep cocked his head judiciously. "He might well feel some resentment at having to work in the shadow of his sister's accomplishments," he admitted in a whisper. "Her concept of the microstar seems very creditworthy, and envy could perhaps be at the root of Kwah's sometimes difficult humour."

If the Gardinelle had drawn as much from the young man's utterances it was not apparent, neither in her voice nor by her graciously offered hand as she thanked him and turned towards Resal's door. Having anticipated the Gardinelle's move, Keep had already spoken into a microphone on the wall, and now standing aside for Her Highness, watched the door slowly draw aside. "My dear Resal," said the Gardinelle as she stepped ahead over the threshold.

With Sima holding his hand, Steven followed the others into a high-ceilinged room that was filled with the acrid smell of heated insulation. The odour rose from a huge doughnut-shaped machine that stood on porcelain legs in a shallow pit. From openings in its shielding case of metal — through which heavy wire coils and clamped laminations could be glimpsed — a flood of cables issued and converged into the rear of an electronic control console. Nestling close over the doughnut's core, a globular structure, resembling an exotic fibrillated creature fished up out of the deep, was barely accommodated within the height of the ceiling. Its exterior was an open array of finely drawn filaments whose slender loops encircled a large transparent globe, crisscrossing each other in every direction like a loosely wound ball of string.

At the sound of the Gardinelle's voice, Resal had turned from her assistants who were grouped around the apparatus. She greeed the Gardinelle in a lively voice. "Your Highness! Do come in!"

"A happy face reveals a granted wish," said the Gardinelle. "I hope it means well for your project."

"Well, yes and no," Resal replied, though she was unable to suppress a quaver of excitement. "We made some changes to the condenser," she went on, indicating the strange looking ball. "We seem close to producing a microstar, but what we are getting breaks down so quickly we are unable to tell much about it."

At that moment an imperious beep sounded from the console, and the assistants instantly rushed to their instruments.

"The condenser is clear and ready," a voice called.

"And the trovium proplasma?" Resal asked.

"The plasma generator is charged and holding."

"All right," Resal instructed, "start the cycle."

In an instant the doughnut crackled and began to buzz with constrained energy, while at the same time the metallic click of a switch threw the room into darkness. Bright spots could now be seen moving slowly through the filaments around the globe. They gradually gained speed, lengthened, and catching up with their tails, traced their paths in incandescent loops. Accentuated as it was by the surrounding darkness, the contrasting light and shadow produced the effect of three-dimensional glasses. Steven was beginning to feel an hypnosis creeping over him before the snap of another switch saw the big globe start to loom forth in a glimmer of its own, gray and ghostly, like a full moon breaking through the mist. With a sudden crackle the glowing filaments gave up their store to the globe, which flashed brighter. The exchange filled the room with a new, vibrant hum which grew in intensity as the contents of the globe began to shrink. With its diminishing size the globe cast an increasing brightness over the room, and as it receded to a point and vanished, the room became bathed in a rapturous shimmering kind of daylight.

Following the event on their instruments, the assistants drew a single breath. "This time we have a perfect microstar!" But alas, before the exclamation was free of their lips, a murky red flash enveloped the globe. For a fleeting instant the motionless watchers were cast as stark and fleshless skeletons under the stygian glimmer whose source dissolved in a swarm of afterglows that lost themselves among the filaments.

The room was left dark and quiet, save for an exhausted buzzing of the doughnut. With the clack of a switch the buzzing stopped, and there was complete silence.

The Gardinelle's voice broke the hush. "Incredibly effective, my dear Resal. It seems a perfect packaging of good and evil."

"But as Your Highness can see, there is a problem. It is far from stable," Resal lamented as the room was restored with light. "They will do little to satisfy the coming wishes of Quicks unless we can find a way to stop them from flying apart."

"Why bother?" Thalamus asked dryly. "The Quicks have a liking for things that explode. One way or another they blow up everything we send them."

The Gardinelle's thoughtful expression acknowledged Thalamus' remark. "Yes, it is very impressive, my dear Resal," she said, "and the Quicks will surely be wishing for such a thing. Still, there would seem to be time enough to overcome your difficulties, for as Thalamus warns us, the Quicks are far from ready to be granted such wishes."

"Oh, I quite agree, Your Highness," Resal was quick to voice. "All the same, they have come a long way since the days they wished only for a castle and a handsome prince."

"Indeed they have, and more is the pity," the Gardinelle admitted wistfully. "When the honour of a shining knight stood between good and evil the choice was clear — and paradise seemed very near a wish away. What with pollsters taking over the call, a happy ending now seems less a wish and more a prayer away."

Steven could easily have added his grandfather's views on the fashion-makers of morality, but hearing the mention of wishes and prayers in the same breath, his ears pricked up. He had let the last opportunity to put his question to the Gardinelle slip away. He seized this one without hesitation. "Your Highness? How do you sort wishes from prayers?"

On hearing the question the Gardinelle smiled with pleasure, and as all good teacher do, first repeated the question to make sure that none of the class would be caught at sea. "How do we sort wishes from prayers?" Then as all good teachers do, she started her answer at the very beginning. "Well now, Steven, first we must ask ourselves: Why must we know the difference?" She paused, just long enough for Steven to reply if he could, but short enough to sound rhetorical if he could not. He could not. "Because," the Gardinelle continued, "they must be answered wishes with magic, and prayers with miracles." Allowing the wisdom to seep in, she went on. "And what is the difference between magic and miracles?"

This time, having had the benefit of Thalamus' coaching, Steven offered an answer. "Magic works all the time but miracles only once in a million?"

The Gardinelle darted an accusing glance in the direction of Thalamus. "That seems often the case, Steven, because most prayers are not Devouts, just as most wishes are not Propers. But it is always the case that miracles reveal the truth, while magic conceals it. That is why the separation of wishes and prayers is so very important, and the most reliable way of doing it is simply to......"

"SIMA! BRING THAT BACK!"

The interruption was Resal's. She had turned too late to grab Sima, who having rummaged through her desk and found her mirror, was making for the door on the run.

Steven, hanging on the Gardinelle's exposition for the crucial words, and unaware of Sima slipping from his hand, was slow to react.

94

"Steven!" Resal's cry was both a reprimand and an alert. "Stop her! A broken mirror brings bad luck!"

Shaken from his stupor, Steven sprang up in pursuit. "Sima! Sima!" he called, rushing out of the room after the chimpanzee.

All of which left the Gardinelle holding her conclusion like the icing for an unfinished cake.

Sima huddled at the end of the corridor waving the mirror, and quietly waited while Steven ran towards her. Just as he reached out to take her hand, she slipped through the door into the tower and began to romp up the spiral stairway. Laughing and calling as he stumbled after her, Steven found the chase exhilarating and more fun than he had enjoyed in a long time. So did Sima. She now and then took a turn at rolling up the stairs backwards, heels over head, and now and then she mounted the bannister to teeter over its edge for the benefit of her pursuer whose hysterical screams were multiplied by every stone and cranny in the tower's walls.

Breathless, Steven arrived at the top, and pushing through the still-swinging door, entered the familiar council chamber. Sima was sitting on the bannister above the elevator doors, but only while Steven climbed the nearest stairs. As soon as he arrived at the top, she fled around past the cosmoscope, scaled the back of the Gardinelle's chair, and plopped into the seat. Pressing the button on the armrest, she sat back, and showing not the least concern as Steven joined her, watched the cosmoscreen spring to life.

9

The sight of Wamwiki on the cosmoscreen was enough to divert Steven's purpose. He sank beside Sima into the welcome comfort of the Gardinelle's chair, and was quickly lost to the rustic scene.

Wielding his knife and hatchet, Walking Owl sat by his campfire making the bark and chips fly from what had been two stout hickory saplings. That the sticks concerned Falling Star was evident from their forked ends, if not from the joy that was setting her face aglow. Supervising the fashioning of his sister's crutches, Lean Bone was down on one knee leaning over his bow, now and then throwing a chip in the air for Trish to catch.

Having touched up the shape of his workpieces, Walking Owl went on to smooth the forked ends with a rough stone. He stopped to hold one of them at arm's length, squinting along it with a professional eye to judge his progress. "I am not a master craftsman, and these may not be the nicest legs in Wamwiki, but they will be among the stoutest."

"But Grandpa," Falling Star exclaimed, "they look perfect!" She passed her hand over the surface. "Just feel how nice. And am I ever going to make them go!"

"Of that I have no doubt, my little Star. And while they may not level the playing field for you, you will get to see it at least."

"And I can be less bother to her, Aunt Alabak, I mean."

Walking Owl grimaced. "Tut tut, now. You are no bother to anyone, and we could never do without our Falling Star."

"Well, she doesn't seem to be too pleased with me sometimes, Aunt Alabak." Falling Star thought for a moment. "Why does she want me to change it, my name?" she asked sadly.

Walking Owl shrugged and took up the second crutch. "Bothered people are not always the ones without fault. Aunt Alabak has her superstitions, and she still harbours ill will over the loss of your father. Some day she will be over it. But you take Lean Bone here. He is what you might call real trouble. Does he let it bother him? No sir. He concentrates on what he wants to be good at. Very soon he will be a leader in woodcraft and hunting, and we shall never go hungry."

Lean Bone was prepared to confirm his grandfather's observation. "I found deer tracks on the far side of the cornfield this morning. He will have to be kept away."

"He?" Walking Owl mused.

"It was a big buck," Lean Bone asserted.

"And how would you know that?" Walking Owl wondered.

"I tracked him to the south ridge. He left deep prints in the ground, and I saw where he had reached up high to nibble off a tasty twig," Lean Bone explained knowledgeably.

"But you did not see him?"

"No, but the tracks were getting fresher, and I would have caught up with him if the stones along the foot of the cliff hadn't veiled them."

Walking Owl smiled at the boy's self-assurance. "The big ones always get away," he bantered.

Quick to defend his prowess in front of his sister, Lean Bone rose to his knees, and fitting an arrow into his bow, slowly drew his arm back full length. "Had I got there two minutes earlier I would surely have seen him, and then, zing! I could have got him."

"I daresay it would take a more powerful bow than yours to down such an animal," Walking Owl teased.

"Not with a flint-tipped venata," Lean Bone was quick to contend. "I could easily have bagged him from as far away as that crooked elm, if I only had one," he said, pointing to a distant tree.

"With a venata?" exclaimed Walking Owl. "You do not use a

venata to kill food, unless you would poison yourself. Only warriors and other such idiots ever use venatas. Fortunately the yellow and black feathers of the venata have not been seen around here for a long time — not since the old hag Belo pricked her finger making one. No, my son, you have no need for arrows of that kind," he concluded, sizing up a piece of fur for padding.

"But Aunt Alabak says a good warrior should always have a trick in his quiver," Lean Bone insisted.

"A good warrior?" Walking Owl gasped, putting down his work. "What nonsense is the girl talking? You are a Cheechikois. The Cheechikois are healers, and you will be a healer too. You need only practise the skills of a hunter so you will not starve on the pay you receive."

"But, Aunt Alabak...."

Lean Bone got no further, because Walking Owl had cut him short. "Never mind the 'buts'. We will talk to Aunt Alabak about your future before it has come and gone."

"Well, Grandpa," Falling Star put in, "I don't want to see him be one, a warrior, Lean Bone, and go off somewhere to be killed. Just the same, I don't see why he should learn to kill them either, the forest creatures."

"Oh sure," Lean Bone retorted. "Maybe I need not be a warrior, but if the deer are not to be killed, where will we get furs for the winter? And perhaps you would like to eat corn three times a day. Not me!"

"There are lots of other things to eat," Falling Star protested. "And it is wrong to kill them, things that do no harm to anyone. Isn't it, Grandpa, wrong?"

"The answer to that, my little Star, is that it is not wrong to live, and to live one must have nourishing food."

"All the same, an arrow is an arrow," Falling Star declared. "If it is wrong to kill with one, it must be wrong to kill with another."

"The Great Spirit made no living thing to go without food, and He would be unhappy to see us refuse the food He has so thoughtfully put here for us," Walking Owl replied. "But a venata is made only to take the life of a fellow being. Not only that, whatever other life it may take is laid to waste, for even a carrion creature dare not eat it. Killing for food is a different matter. I remember the first time my father took me hunting. While we were hiding near a water hole waiting for dinner to arrive, I asked if it was really proper for a Cheechikois to prey on other creatures. 'Indeed it is,' he said, 'unless you envy the unhappy Dermamolter,' and fitting an arrow into his bow, he recited a little rhyme: "

> *I am a born protectionist,*
> *It is a special calling,*
> *Because the thought of killing things,*
> *To me is most appalling.*
> *To shame the nasty human race,*
> *For eating things that cuddle,*
> *I searched about the universe,*
> *For nature's perfect model.*
>
> *The Dermamolter of them all,*
> *Most satisfied our purpose,*
> *He sheds himself in spring and fall,*
> *And eats his epidermis.*
> *'So thin and unextraneous,*
> *I'm doomed,' he sobbed, 'and cannot win —*
> *A diet so cutaneous,*
> *Will never save my skin!'*

Falling Star found it difficult not to laugh. "But it is only a rhyme, that," she said.

"Ha!" Lean Bone exulted. "But it shows how silly you can get. So if you want to save your skin, you will have to eat like the rest of us."

"Hold on, now," Walking Owl cautioned. "It does not mean that your sister is wrong. It is a way of reminding us of the unity of nature — with its forest creatures and all — and that we are not intended to live independently."

"I think they would like us to leave them live by themselves though, the forest creatures," Falling Star suggested, levelling a disapproving frown at Lean Bone.

"And Trish would live with the wolves, of course," Lean Bone countered.

"No, not her!" Falling Star stroked Trish affectionately. "She is one of us, Trish."

"Indeed she is," Walking Owl agreed, "and we and Trish will continue to look to each other. So you see, everyone is right. Lean Bone should not become a warrior, because instead of killing his brothers he should be sharing their friendship. And he should kill only for food and warm furs to satisfy our needs, because satisfied stomachs and warm bodies make contented souls, and contented souls please the Great Spirit." Walking Owl searched the two young faces. "Are we all in favour of that?"

Lean Bone was more than willing, and quickly agreed. Falling Star hesitated before giving a reluctant nod — to make it clear she really was not pleased with killing, not even for food.

"Good!" Walking Owl heaved a laboured sigh by way of confessing that the argument had been well and fairly contested on both sides. He bent his head thoughtfully. "Still," he said reflectively, watching the children through the corner of his eyes, "it is remarkable how, quite in our own way this morning, we have come up with the three paths of wisdom."

"We have?" Lean Bone queried.

Falling Star screwed up her nose quizzically. "The three paths of wisdom?"

Walking Owl smiled with satisfaction. "They are the ancient code of the Cheechikois: honour the unity of this great habitat the Great Spirit has given us; trust the wisdom in the lot we receive; live in peace and fellowship with our brothers. So our ancestors taught, saying that if all the tribes would abide by those rules, then our world would be as a happy hunting ground, and we would at last enjoy complete happiness."

"Oh, Grandpa," Falling Star demurred, "I couldn't be happier than I am with you and Lean Bone. And, of course, Trish," she added, planting a kiss on Trish's head.

Walking Owl nodded. "Yet, the greatest happiness can grow even more when it is shared with others."

"We have always shared our fun," Lean Bone hastened to put on record.

"Sharing fun is a good thing," Walking Owl agreed, "and can be done without much pain. The test comes when there is need to share something greater. Your mother would share anything she had, and when she had little else she would simply wish nice things for people, and would be pleased if fortune smiled on them."

"And do wishes come true when you follow them then, the three paths of wisdom?" Falling Star asked.

"Special wishes, like for a pony," Lean Bone added more precisely.

"I am not much of an expert on special wishes," Walking Owl admitted, "though of course your mother was a great believer, and she seemed happy enough."

"All right then," Falling Star demanded, "which is best — following them, the three paths of wisdom, or wishing on a star?"

Walking Owl drew a meditative breath. "Well now, that is not exactly a fair question, because if you follow the three paths, there is less need for most ordinary wishes. On the other hand, if you do not follow them, it leaves so much to be desired that some of it is bound to happen no matter how you wish."

Falling Star's eyes widened, and she studied her grandfather for a moment in silence. "Does that mean you don't believe in wishing on one then, a star?"

Walking Owl was quick to deny such heresy. "Goodness no, but when you are looking for favours it is wise to know what might be expected. As a boy, I was told that after He got things going, the Great Spirit put out a suggestion box where people could post good ideas that had been overlooked. To begin with, the suggestions were equally divided between people wanting it warmer, cooler, wetter, and drier. Deciding it was fairer to please all the people some of the time rather than a few of them all the time, the Great Spirit invented seasons. But people being what they are, they continued to disagree on what was good or bad, since what was good for one was usually bad for another. To escape the difficulties of compromise, they began going each his or her own way, and when faced with the consequences, would be waiting to suggest concessions when the courier arrived to clear the box. By this time the Great Spirit had decided they should develop their faculties for managing good and bad, so He took the box in. By this time too, the people had formed a habit of calling for favours whenever the likes of a courier was seen on his way across the sky. So that is how people came to continue wishing on stars, and that is why they do not always get their wish, especially if they are avoiding responsibilities or being greedy."

"Everybody knows not to be greedy even if they were allowed to be," Lean Bone conceded with a shrug. "So that is one path we already cross often enough."

"You do not cross them, you follow them," Walking Owl corrected. He tested the final thickness of padding and declared the crutches finished. "There," he said, holding them out to Falling Star, "let us see if they will work."

"Of course they will!" she exclaimed, rising to her knees and eagerly accepting her grandfather's modest achievement. "They are just perfect!"

With help on both sides, Falling Star raised herself erect, and balancing uncertainly over her splayed feet, looked about for a moment, beaming. Sensing the importance of the occasion, Trish bounded about in circles, barking joyfully. But freedom by any name was never the reward of those who falter. Biting her lip resolutely, Falling Star ventured, easing the crutches ahead, and slowly adjusting her weight, cautiously drew her body even.

"That's it!" Lean Bone encouraged. "Keep on!" Afraid she might fall, he stood facing her while his arms, outstretched to make the catch, fluttered like a young bird on the verge of trying its wings. "And when you learn to manage real well, I will show you the hidden pool where the deer drinks."

Falling Star was much too taxed to reply, but the silent look she sent her brother in return was enough to seal the bargain. Her face pinched with concentration, and jaws set for the effort, she teetered forward again, and when at length she had moved a pace or two, she stopped to look up, panting but ecstatic, with only the breath to call, "See!"

Walking Owl patted her head affectionately. "Yes, my little Star, I see. But it will take time to build up your strength, so you must be careful and not overdo it." With that he bent to recover his tools and, as he slowly gathered them in, noticed the bow and quiver where Lean Bone had let them fall. Pausing, his eyes hovered in momentary concern over the discarded weapons, as if they themselves lay slain by the deadly venata.

It was Sima with her sharp ears who caught the sound of voices below, and slipping from the chair to steal off and peak over the bannister, roused Steven with her disturbance. Steven switched off the monitor and scrambled to his feet ready to follow, at the same time spying the mirror which Sima had left lying on the cushion. He quickly retrieved it as the Gardinelle's voice rose up over the bannister.

"So, my dear Sirgal, we must know what it is that has affected the wishing among the Quicks. We hope for your success and shall look forward to your return with a full report."

"I shall not keep Your Highness waiting longer than necessary," Sirgal's voice sounded in reply. "I shall be as thorough and as quick as possible."

Steven hastened to the head of the stairs, while Sima, seeing him on the move, and taking for granted that the merry chase was on again, scampered off into the tower. Steven hurried down the stairs with all haste, only to reach the floor of the council chamber as the elevator closed on the departing Knight Courier.

Seeing Steven approach with the mirror, the Gardinelle commended him with a smile. "Oh, how nice, my dear Steven," she said, accepting it and passing it on to an attendant, "you managed to get it back without a scratch. Resal will be relieved. And now," she announced, turning to Keep and her entourage, "we must attend to the day's visits."

10

The Gardinelle's party emerged from the chateau into the square, and from there set off along an outer walkway which circled to the far side. It was a model sunny day with just the right breeze to spread the fragrance of scattered flowerbeds. The sound of high-pitched laughter, drifting across the square from a group of children who were enjoying a dancing lesson on the open grass, revealed the Gardinelle's destination. With a nod and a smile for the passersby, she led her little party in that direction, Keep at her side with Steven following in the swirl of his toga.

"It is always a pleasure to meet with the students," the Gardinelle remarked. "You have perhaps noticed that though the schooling may be different in unlike societies, students are much the same no matter where you find them."

"That is very true, Your Highness." Keep agreed. "It is sometimes not evident in their classroom humour, but the young generations everywhere do seem to share a common vision of peace and goodwill no different from our students at Trovia High."

"Yes," said the Gardinelle, "I am sure our senior class will do themselves honour. I have chosen today for a visit because it is today they study practical wish management. Perhaps," she ventured as they mounted the steps, "these fresh minds can help us with new ideas to make Proper wishes more popular among the Quicks."

Inside, the tall marble walls of a deserted foyer radiated the hushed tension of a school at work. Greeting the visitors from its niche in the facing wall as they entered, was an elegantly mounted plaque in gold and silver, its illuminated lines declaring Trovia High's guiding precept.

"I can never pass without stopping to read these inspiring words of the school's founder," the Gardinelle admitted, "though I have known them by heart from childhood."

Steven, too, scanned the lines, though on this occasion no one thought to ask him if he could read.

The Democracy of MEGOS

There is a great democracy,
Whose limits are the skies,
It reaches past the Milky Way,
Beyond all enterprise.
And every atom has its word,
All parts howe'er remote,
And every single voice is heard,
Mere actions are a vote.

No act can you from MEGOS hide,
Abuses weak or brave,
For ones may from the living cry,
Or zeros from the grave.
And naught the counting interrupts,
No wish will change the way,
The zeros and the ones add up,
With how you vote today.

The Gardinelle finished reading. "It makes a nice postscript to the Three Complements of Being," she observed, "don't you think?" But without waiting for a reply she left her attendants to the revelations of the foyer, and followed by Keep and Steven, moved quietly through the swinging doors into a long hallway. There the hush of the foyer gave way to a subdued buzz, and coming to the senior class door, the Gardinelle stood for a moment with her hand on the knob, trying to divine the nature of the lesson within. Then, announcing herself with a gentle tap on the door, she turned the knob and entered.

Peering through thick lenses at the upturned faces of his class, the teacher was not immediately aware of the royal entrance behind him. He was left to puzzle the meaning of the suddenly-drawn breaths which were released in smiles, a few giggles, and here and there an exchange of knowing winks, all of which became submerged in a spontaneous clapping. Following the diverted eyes of his class, the teacher turned to find the Gardinelle at his shoulder, acknowledging the welcome of his students with a regal smile.

"Your Highness!" the teacher exclaimed, adjusting his mortar-board and gown in self-conscious but flattered embarrassment.

The Gardinelle bathed him in her cordial smile. "My dear Stock. Please do not let the lesson be disturbed. If you would just continue, perhaps we might all take part?"

"But of course, Your Highness," Stock exclaimed. "Splendid!" He inclined his head respectfully. "This afternoon we are looking into some of the problems of wish management — spec-ifically, considerations prior to the granting of Regular wishes."

"Oh, how very nice. It is my favourite subject," the Gardinelle replied. "Do go on with it," she urged, moving to take up a posi-tion to the side of the class.

Steven was not sure what to do. He began to follow Keep with an obedient step or two, but feeling the eyes of the class upon him, shied against the wall and remained near the door where he felt less conspicuous. There he found himself standing beside the desk of a friendly girl, her lively blond ponytail tied with a blue ribbon to match her eyes. She looked up at Steven. "You seem to be new," she whispered. "What is your name?"

"Steven."

"I'm Marcie. Do you stay at the chateau?"

"Yes," Steven replied, and as an afterthought, "I think."

That Steven seemed unsure where he lived tickled Marcie's funny centre. Her cheeks bulged under the pressure of a con-tained giggle, and covering her mouth, she lowered her head. For a moment or two her shoulders bobbled.

Stock was meanwhile gathering up the thread of the day's lesson for the Gardinelle's benefit. "Each student has jotted down a Regular wish," he explained, holding up a sheaf of papers. "I am ready to read them in turn, and the class is to weigh their merits by accounting for the near and the far-reaching effects of the wish if it were to be granted." He surveyed the class with a professional eye. "As an example, the wish that winter be a month longer would be good for a winter sportsperson, but would increase the cost of snow removal and home heating — and further down the line it would pose for farmers a problem of late seeding."

"Excellent!" the Gardinelle applauded. "The ripple effect. One cannot place too much importance upon how one event influences another. The game can be played many different ways. In my school-days, as I remember, we actually called it RIPPLES."

"We call it wibbles!" came a harsh whisper. "Useless wishes!"

Marcie's head went down, and again her shoulders began to bobble. One or two other shoulders followed suit, and some cheeks puffed out as if they would burst. Steven's eyes opened with alarm, for he recognized the symptoms of a schoolroom fever which Miss Adley referred to as "cachinitis". It often broke out at the end of a long term, starting with giddiness and suppressed giggles. In such a frame of mind almost anything could spook a whole class into a prolonged and uncontrollable fit of laughter. Standing at the Gardinelle's elbow, Keep too seemed to have sensed the possibility, but breathed easier when the shoulders steadied as Stock read from the slip of paper, "I wish the Festival of the Wishing Tree could be held twice a year."

"That seems a pleasant wish," the Gardinelle commented.

Stock smiled happily, and looking down the aisle, made a choice. "Let us lead off with Kevin," he suggested.

Rising to respond, the curly-haired Kevin stood tall and handsome, every inch an athlete, the fullness of his frame draped in a thick woolen pullover. "The sporting activities of an extra festival would give athletes a greater chance to compete," he offered, and sat down, while Stock turned to make notes on the blackboard.

"That there Kevin is a heel!" Marcie muttered the words for Steven's ear. "He knew the eighth dance was mine, not Beth's. Said he forgot. Well, I haven't, and did I ever remember to put in a wish for him today!" Marcie chuckled over the thought, then her shoulders started to bobble, and she quickly put her hand over her mouth to contain a giggle. The girl across the aisle shared a confidential glance, and did the same.

Steven watched the ponytail quiver. He found it more intriguing than braids, and pondered the idea of ponytails for a tribal fashion. When his mind returned to the classroom, Stock was adding to the list of pros and cons for holding the Festival of the Wishing Tree twice a year. "A holiday for one is extra work for another," he wrote, and taking his cue from the voices behind him, continued. "Parades bring everyone together. Parades are one occasion when the young have a chance to carry the flag and take part."

Stock stood back, and considering the list with satisfaction, invited the Gardinelle's opinion.

"Very refreshing, my dear Stock," the Gardinelle beamed. "The students have developed a clear perception of the problem, and I can see little to add. But I must say this," she went on, speaking to the class, "it is true that holiday parades are a particular occasion when our young citizens have a chance to carry the flag, but that should not be taken to say that they do not otherwise carry it, for they most certainly do. And though you may not gallop with the flag at the head of a cavalcade of knights, the meaning of the flag gallops ahead of you, and that meaning springs from the goals you set and the way you strive for them. And remember that such is the truth whether you are at work or at play, because you cannot be seen for more than your conduct, just as your flag cannot be seen for more than you. Indeed, a flag and its nationals are both the object and the image, both the source and the reflection of each other. It is the citizens who make their flag, and it is the message of those citizens it symbolizes — young citizens as yourselves. Yes, a parade does give you a chance to carry the flag above your head, but the pride you feel can be no greater than the respect your flag commands through the message you have given it to carry for you."

When the Gardinelle had finished speaking, a deep silence momentarily blanketed the room, and then without the need for encouragement from Stock, was broken by an enthusiastic round of clapping. This time the Gardinelle's words had also drawn a small but reluctant concession from Steven, who admitted to himself that until flags could be outlawed altogether, they would surely be safer in the hands of young people.

Allowing the applause to run its course, Stock spoke. "Your Highness," he said, "those words will surely inspire us all to greater effort."

"Then," replied the Gardinelle, catching her breath with a smile, "let us by all means resume our study."

With that, Stock drew the next wish. Marcie looked at her friend, and holding her breath in anticipation of her special wish for Kevin being drawn, seemed ready to burst.

"I wish the price of ice cream could be reduced to one dollar a barrel," Stock read, at the same time casting a satisfied glance in the direction of the Gardinelle, who nodded her approval.

Marcie and her friend relaxed.

Stock's eye toured the faces in front of him for the one who could most safely be entrusted with the honour of the school, and came to rest upon Sylvester. It was a meeting of minds as well as of eyes, for though Stock made no sound, Sylvester rose to his feet, and hesitating only to finish polishing his glasses, launched into an account of the good and bad effects that the granting of such a wish would have on the health and earnings of the farmers, vendors, and consumers in the community.

Pleased with the boy's performance under the Gardinelle's scrutiny, Stock could not resist the urge to pose an easy supplement. "One might also consider in the same vein a wish for the price of ice cream to be forty dollars a barrel," he challenged.

Again rising to carry the honours, Sylvester pointed out that although some people would stand to turn a handsome profit on the sale of ice cream, the less well-to-do children would find themselves deprived.

The Gardinelle nodded vigorously. "In short," she summed up for the class, "we must think of a wish as being someone's idea of how creation, or some small part of it, could be improved. And while it is true the Quick Side is made better if even one person's lot is made easier, a purely selfish wish cannot be considered much of a step forward. Now suppose," she continued, looking toward Sylvester and narrowing her eyes shrewdly, "suppose I wished the price were forty dollars a barrel so I could give the profits to the poor?"

The room became bathed in silence. Clearly the Gardinelle had thrown the cat among the pigeons, and a number of winks were exchanged behind Sylvester's back by some who were glad to see 'mister-know-it-all' squirm a little. Stock, too, was taken by surprise, and seemed in fact just a little put out that the Gardinelle would ask a question which she knew would require at least a small computer, if not the big one over at the chateau. As he struggled in his mind for some way to throw his favourite student a lifeline, Sylvester calmly rose to his feet and faced the Gardinelle. Everyone held their breath, and a few shoulders bobbled under the pressure of suppressed giggles. Something bounced off the back of Sylvester's head, but he remained unperturbed.

"By phrasing it in that way, Your Highness, the wish reflects a deep concern for your fellow beings, thus drawing upon one of the Three Complements of Being. It therefore becomes a Proper wish. In this class we have not yet completed the study of Proper wishes." He turned to sweep his classmates with a cold and defiant glare, then sat down.

Stock, regaining his poise, smiled with a glow of pride and relief.

"That is truly excellent!" the Gardinelle exclaimed, clapping her hands with delight. "A wish that draws upon a Complement of Being is a Proper wish. And what is a wish that draws at once upon all three of the Complements of Being?"

This time Sylvester did not rise to answer because he was not even listening. He had slipped an elastic band from his wrist and was intent on rolling a tight little wad of paper which he gleefully compacted between his teeth.

Pausing only briefly, for a good teacher must keep the momentum of her class alive, the Gardinelle cried enthusiastically, "A Perfect wish! Drawing upon all three Complements of Being at the same time in a single wish makes a Perfect wish!" Her eyes sparkled. "Studying the Perfect wish is something you can all look forward to, and I am sure you will find nothing more exciting than contemplating the award of a transcendental favour."

"I think they may already have found something," Keep muttered to himself, one nervous eye on Sylvester and the other on his watch. Failing to catch the Gardinelle's attention with a warning signal, he instinctively shifted to a more secure position behind her.

"I must say this has been a lovely visit," the Gardinelle continued, and noticing Keep's interest in his watch, sighed, "and I would like to stay much longer." Then changing her mind from an immediate departure, gave a reckless toss of her head. "But perhaps we could squeeze in just one more example before I take leave."

Keep's expression was a model of uncertainty.

Still beaming with delight, Stock reached for the next wish and read it without hesitation. He was no less surprised than the others to hear his voice announce, "I wish Kevin could count to eight."

There was a momentary silence punctuated with a harshly whispered "Ouch" as Sylvester's wad found its mark. Turning to enjoy Kevin's embarrassment, Marcie spluttered and released an infectious giggle that swept across the room like a grass fire.

"Counting to eight would be a strain for Kevin," someone called out.

"Or counting to even seven and a half," another voice added.

"Seven and a half is not even!" cried another.

Over Stock's mild protestations the giggling warmed up into laughter. But now the class had taken up the challenge, and jocular voices joined in from every corner.

"Mind your vulgar fractions!"

"What was the wish?"

"I wish I knew!"

"Somebody wibbled!"

By this time the laughter had mounted beyond control as other paper wads flew in reprisal, while Stock found himself waving his arms wildly but in vain for order.

Having nothing to learn about the art of governing, the Gardinelle bowed gracefully to the will of her people, and following the line of retreat which Steven needed no counselling to prepare, slipped through the open door in a discreet but hurried departure.

When they had gained the peaceful outdoors, the Gardinelle, in her characteristic fashion, was inclined to look upon the positive side of the incident. "Well, my dear Keep," she observed, "that last wish would have to be classed as a Proper since it reflected one person's concern for another."

"And it did seem quite popular," Keep smiled wryly, recalling the Gardinelle's hopes as they were entering the school a few minutes earlier.

Stimulated by the agreeable weather, the Gardinelle chose the long way around for her party's return to the chateau, but they had not taken many steps when Keep faltered and slowed his pace. Unblinking and intent, his eyes were trained on the scene ahead. "Muster!" he gasped with evident annoyance, more to himself than to Steven.

Muster? Steven experienced a twinge of apprehension, for he had almost forgotten his close call with the reformatory, and following Keep's line of sight, distinguished what had to be the plump figure of the reformatory's mistress. She was holding a freshly-made sign in her hand, and stood on the walk, studying the wall near the doorway of the grey stone museum. Behind her, on a side of the walk opposite a spreading triunium, was a group of workers who were busying themselves in a hole beside a pile of dirt and stones.

With the prospect of at last running into the sinister Muster face to face, Steven instinctively drew closer to Keep, all the more since he now sensed Keep to be an ally, and Muster a common threat.

112

Not so the Gardinelle. Her smile broadened, and turning her head to speak, found Keep lagging. "Come, my dear Keep," she urged, quickening her pace, "I do believe Muster has something new going."

Keep responded by breathing harder, but his pace remained unchanged. "Muster!" he repeated. "The woman is a nuisance," he confided with Steven. "Cannot mind her business."

Muster turned her head to acknowledge Keep's tardy arrival with a nod, and though the friendly twinkle in her eye said more, she continued speaking to the Gardinelle without interruption. "And since I moved the school to the rear of the museum the boys make too much traffic through the front." She held up her sign to gauge its appearance by the door.

> ## SCHOOL
>
> ## REAR DOOR ONLY

"Your generosity and diligence is an example to the community, my dear Muster," the Gardinelle observed, "but perhaps it is asking too much of you to take care of the school as well as the museum."

Muster shook her head with a good-natured laugh. "No, I really would miss my guests, Your Highness. They are very useful at restoring old wishing charms, and helping around the museum keeps them out of mischief. Especially the likes of him," she added, nodding in the direction of the workers where an elfin figure sat working underneath the triunium, helping the masons chip stones.

Steven was surprised to behold in Muster this affable woman, so outgoing and of such good humour. He stole a look at Keep, who seemed uncomfortable and was fidgeting as one who would rather be continuing his way home.

The Gardinelle's curious eye having turned to the workers, the hint was enough for Muster. "We have just acquired an exquisite old Arabian wishing well from Oulden Finftroum," she announced. "Most Quicks believe that throwing a penny into the well will see their wish granted. That would be considered a Regular bargain these days, would it not?" she asked Keep. Stabbing at the Compleat Record with her finger to make her little joke clear, she burst into a fit of laughter.

As if not having heard, the Gardinelle's attention was still turned to the workers.

"I am having it set out here opposite the wishing tree as a reminder of the difference between a Regular wish and a Proper," Muster explained.

"That is a nice thought, my dear Muster," the Gardinelle conceded slowly, while her gaze shifted from the hole to settle affectionately on the stately old triunium which had clearly occupied its position of honour in the square for generations past. "Still, ever since Thalamus conjured the triunium maple out of my dream for a popular guide, it has always been a truly compelling symbol of the Three Complements of Being and the proper form of wishing."

Keep darted a look at Muster. "And without the need for a hole in the ground," he agreed, wholeheartedly.

Steven stared at the old tree. "So," he mused, "it is more than a strange looking tree — it's good for a miraculous balm out of the leaf, and the tree itself is a kind of wishing charm." He was allowed only the time to register his thought, because with no more than a smile to acknowledge Keep's 'tit for tat', Muster was drawing the party into her gallery of other charms.

Inside, Steven found himself looking across an immense room that was fairly stuffed with an exhibition of things wishful and magical such as had served Quick Side fancies over the ages. He was surprised to see many things that were still commonly accepted among the newcomers, and mingled with them in a display that shared them equal prominence and authority, were the relics of tribal days, including many things from the old shaman's cabin. There were medicine bundles displayed next to rabbit feet for gamblers, four-leaf clovers for inveterate wishers, as well as coloured beads and jeweled amulets for everyday wear. Steven had never before given the matter any thought, and was now intrigued to find that as far as wishing and magic were concerned, his own people had long shared much in common with the newcomers, although it scarcely seemed appropriate to have a conjuror's robe and mask hanging next a stuffed black cat for a stroke of good luck. But there were things he knew Aunt Becky still looked for, like seamless garments with no embarrassing inside-outs, and lording over the display in an eye-catching pose stood a statue of The Archer, bow at the ready and a smoking star skewered to the point of his arrow.

"We have not used The Archer for quite some time now," Keep explained. "As the universe expanded and filled up, we had to switch to the present trovium motors for the power and speed to meet tighter schedules. The Archer was getting old and his arrows were much too slow, you see, and we were receiving an overflow of demands for riches from Quicks who claimed to have repeated "money" seven times during a star's passing. Not that we have ever offered wealth to anyone who could accomplish such a feat. Spreading that idea was the work of a certain Quote by the name of Sawni, who is always up to tricks of the sort."

"Is that the same Sawni who is in the reformatory?" Steven asked, making an effort to keep his voice casual.

"Yes, that was the little fellow we saw out front," Keep replied. "Some say he is a small dwarf and others say he is a large elf, but those who have been the butt of his pranks claim his parents must have been one of each, and they mince no words saying so. But we have to admit that his "money, money" prank was not all that bad. No. It gave the Choral Society an idea for fundraising, and they have since made an annual event of their contest to see who can chant "money" the fastest — with prizes too for duos, trios, and even choruses. Yes, they come up with some excellent harmony, but the sopranos seem always to win. In the Festival of the Wishing Tree the contest is open to challengers from the audience, and that can be very entertaining."

Coming to a display of exotic teapots, Steven stopped to read the explanatory note:

IT IS A COMMON BELIEF AMONG
QUICKS THAT TEAPOTS SUCH AS
THESE CAN GRANT WISHES WHEN
RUBBED.

The reliability of this assertion carried the endorsement of:

MUSTER
CURATOR

Steven sensed a shadow across his shoulder, and looking up
found the Gardinelle beside him. He ventured a comment. "I
think there are not many who still believe in magic teapots, Your
Highness — at least not on Oulden Finftroum."

"Perhaps not, Steven," was the Gardinelle's noncommittal
reply. She took up the teapot, and slowly lifting the lid, peeked
inside. She set the pot down again with a disdainful sniff.
"Although you would think everyone would have known it for a
trick the moment they saw the genie."

Muster waited for the Gardinelle to finish and then motioned
that she had something special to show. Curious over the
Gardinelle's remark, Steven lagged behind, and taking up the
teapot himself, tried to peek inside, but was quite unable to raise
the lid. Meanwhile, Muster had led the way past a collection of
rare wishbones towards a display of children's treasures. As she
did so there stole into her eyes a mischievous twinkle which was
directed towards Keep. It warned of something embarrassing to
come, and it was not wasted on Keep, for everyone could see a
slight blush of apprehension creep into his normally colourless
cheeks. Steven noticed it immediately, and to her obvious delight, so did Muster as she stopped before a solitary glass case.
Her broad smile was enough to excite the curiosity of her guests
in the case's contents, or rather the case's content, for it contained
only one item — a child's tooth resting on a large gilt cushion.

Muster looked up and clasped her hands in mock ecstasy.
"This was an exciting find. We believe it to be the first tooth that

was returned under the Chief Clerk's moneyback guarantee." Muster had difficulty swallowing a gurgle of laughter, and while Keep's blush deepened, Steven noticed that the Gardinelle had slipped away from her attendants, pretending to be satisfying her interest in other exhibits.

"Yes," Muster continued, regaining control of her voice, "Quick youngsters who couldn't say "money" fast enough were invited to leave their faulty teeth under their pillow for a generous cash refund."

Keep snorted. "Made more sense than old maids and their piece of wedding cake. And it was for only a trove — worth less than pennies Quick."

"For shame," Muster gasped, "the Chief Clerk himself admitting he broke the Covenant, buying and selling like a genie in a teapot." She rolled her eyes towards the heavens imploring compassion for one so guilty. At that the blush on Keep's face turned so bright a scarlet Muster could no longer contain herself, and bursting into a peel of laughter, she could be heard clear into the street.

At this point the choralists, who were gathered in the adjacent building to practise for the competition, chose to warm up their voices, and Muster's laughter was almost lost in an overwhelming wave of "money, money, money". At this point too, Sawni's curious endowment for timing brought some much-needed relief to the cringing Keep. Having volunteered to find water for the Arabian wishing well, Sawni had slipped in and taken over the fire hose. Opening the tap to its fullest as he grabbed the nozzle, he now found himself being propelled forward by the rapidly expanding coils of hose behind him.

It was not cowardice but his apparent concern for the Compleat Record that saw Keep disappear for safe cover (and not much ahead of the agile Steven) in the face of the advancing threat. Muster, however, whose back had been turned, received no such warning before Sawni and the thrashing hose were upon her. Having no choice but to add her weight to Sawni's futile struggle, Muster and her energetic little charge were swept out of the door under the astonished gaze of the Gardinelle.

In the lull that followed, Keep crept out of his hiding with Steven peeking from behind him, and cautiously reached the door to see how the matter had resolved itself. From there the pair beheld the dripping Muster who at last stood speechless in the shallow pit, scanning her low horizon for the whereabouts of Sawni, who had seen fit to vanish.

Anticipating the Gardinelle's signal to assist the curator out of her new exhibit, helpful bystanders were attending to the rescue by the time Keep had followed the now lifeless hose out to join them. By this time too, the Gardinelle had decided to postpone a visit to the reformatory for a less adventurous day, and bidding Muster a sympathetic good day, redirected her steps along the walk. Keep, prompted by the dying strains of "money, money, money", tossed a trove over his shoulder as he passed the well, at the same time muttering a fervent wish under his breath.

11

Leaving the citizens of Quotaris to their own devices, the Gardinelle had returned to the Dome, and there with Keep and Thalamus at her side, once more turned her attention to the state of wishing on the Quick Side. For Steven it was a chance to collect his thoughts and digest what had been a hectic introduction to the court of the Elder Woman of Lots. He could now agree with one of Keep's first remarks — that she was a doughty woman. Indeed, the granting of fortune was far from the child's play of a magic wand — it was a challenge and a burden which she carried with dedication and vigour. But one thing was already clear: the Gardinelle was the very same Elder Woman of Lots who had visited the ancient Cheechikois. Since she was responsible for wishing as well as granting fortune, it made sense that she would counsel on the greatest of all wishes. No question. It also made sense that she would have considered that a miraculous balm with the power to restore life would be a force for good in the hands of the peace-loving Cheechikois — like giving them an invisible sword to see them win their way to the greatest of all wishes. Yet, in the Gardinelle's laboratory, Steven had neither seen nor heard anything of the lost balm or how it was prepared from the leaf. No matter, it would turn up. What made least sense to him, though, was the Gardinelle's passion for her flag. It was a reminder of Miss Adley, and although he could readily applaud the principles of which the Gardinelle so eloquently spoke, he could not forget that, with the Quicks, flags fed the evils of chauvinism, and chauvinism stood in the way of the greatest of all wishes.

Steven was roused by the cosmoscreen from which an eerie beep had sounded as it returned to life where he had left it — surveying a small wigwam nestled beneath a grotesquely shaped old tree full of roosting crows.

Motionless before a crackling campfire in front of Chikchik's hut, Alabak stood looking pensively into the flames, the folds of her blanket drawn about her like the robe of a high priestess before an altar. Her richly beaded headband danced with the firelight, reflecting it in a crimson halo whence from the centre a single feather rose like a sentinel peering into the encircling shadows.

"How very striking!" the Gardinelle exclaimed. "But so young to be a witch."

Alabak was stirring the coals of her fire and watching the sparks spiral upwards like tiny spirits enjoying a brief but scintillating freedom. Carried into the room with the eerie sounds of outer space, a honeyed voice (which brought the word "Fulgor" to Keep's lips) was coaxing Alabak's thoughts.

> *Oulden Finftroum, world of fancy,*
> *Self deceit and necromancy,*
> *Living but a dream awakened —*
> *Visions through a glass misshapen,*
> *Sounds to soothe, with fragrance mingle,*
> *Taste for sweets, and touch to tingle.*
> *Windows five reveal creation,*
> *Seeking truth through clues mistaken,*
> *Oulden Finftroum, ripe for reaping,*
> *Bides its windowed hold asleeping,*
> *Willing prize for witching schemes,*
> *Calls the Sisters of Five Dreams —*
> *She whose web can snare the gull,*
> *Wins ascendance over all.*

With sudden resolve, Alabak turned and went to a corner from which she brought out a tightly woven willow basket. Taking three small leather pouches from the folds of its quilted lining, she sprinkled a pinch of their powdery contents into a clay pot. After adding liquid from a thin-necked jug, she set the pot on the fire to steam, and throwing her coloured powders into the flames, called upon the spirits to help with her newly made plans.

As, with a final moan, Alabak gave herself up to the revelations of a trance, Steven stirred thoughtfully, and looking to Thalamus, posed a question. "Is it that wishes come to WAND and witch's incantations go to Fulgor?" he asked, fully expecting such to be the case.

"No," Thalamus replied, "they all come to WAND."

"All to WAND?"

"A wish is a wish, my boy, and WAND is an open door if the Sisters of the Five Dreams should wish to repent." Thalamus offered his thin smile. "Sides make a contest, but the rules are the game."

Steven had by now learned that Thalamus' thin smile usually signified an obscure joke. He turned a questioning face to the Gardinelle who made answer only in the fullness of her customary style. "Just as it is not in the number of voices that the oratorio consummates its splendour but in its division of parts, so the grandeur of democracy cannot be rendered through an infinity of voices chanting a mere unison. And so, too, with MEGOS," she reminded Steven in the measured delivery of Trovia High's plaque, "every atom has its word, and every single voice is heard. Yes," she assured him, "black wishes are heard and examined by WAND just as all wishes are."

That WAND and, by inference, a nice lady like the Gardinelle could be the grantor of both good and evil came as a disturbing revelation to Steven. "And WAND sees to them just like any other wish?" Steven gulped, incredulously.

"It is the rule," the Gardinelle replied soothingly. "Nevertheless, although black wishes are sometimes used, they are never granted as such. You see, Steven, it is only after a destination is chosen that roads take on a right or wrong direction for the traveller. So it is that to begin with, things are created not of good or evil, but only of opposites — in equal measure. After that the presence of one measure can only be increased by reducing the other. The proportion of good and bad is for us to decide, and that is where we find a use for black wishes."

"But black wishes are only wished to do evil," Steven resisted. "How can you make more good out of that?"

"It is not easy, naturally," the Gardinelle replied. "It takes the Big Computer MEGOS to conduct so complex a transformation, and it can be a time-consuming process — even when supervised by Thalamus." It was the Gardinelle's turn for a thin smile, or rather a twinkle in her eye. "You could say the magic rings grant all things, but it is MEGOS that tests your faith."

Some of the Gardinelle's words rang familiar, and in their sense Steven recognized the epigraph in the chateau's garden. Up to the present he had had little time to think on its message, though he had not read its finish. Even so, he was intrigued with the thought of MEGOS turning evil into good, and wondered over the possibility of seeing it done. Turning to Thalamus he cleared his throat to inquire about it, but was upstaged by the melancholy bay of a wolf. The sound drew all eyes to Alabak and brought the witch out of her trance with a start.

Quickly regaining the thread of her enterprise, Alabak lifted the pot from the dying embers. It had now boiled dry, and under the first streaks of dawn the young witch could be seen scraping a white scaly substance from the bottom. Collecting the scales on a flat stone, she ground them into a fine powder which she carefully poured into a vial. That done, she smashed the pot with a heavy rock, and gathering the pieces into a sack, sent Chikchik off to throw them far out into the river. And to make sure the woman did not throw in the whole sack where it might be fished out by someone, she ordered her to bring it back empty.

When Chikchik had completed her duty and returned with the empty sack, Alabak gave her some instructions which she told and repeated several times so no error would be made.

Today, she said, would be the day Sun Dog, the Chief's eldest son, would pass through the ceremony of becoming a young warrior. It would end with a blood ritual when Sun Dog would suffer a flesh wound above his heart to prove his manhood. It would be Walking Owl's duty to dust the wound with ceremonial salt which was believed to ward off evil and protect the young man from the harm of other injuries.

Alabak's plan was simple. She would draw Walking Owl from his wigwam on a pretext. While he was out, Chikchik would sneak in, find the sachet exactly where Alabak said it would be, and would mix with the ceremonial salt the contents of the tiny vial. And if anyone saw her come or go, or if she breathed a word of the matter to anyone, she would immediately turn into a helpless rabbit and fall prey to the village dogs.

Chikchik listened attentively, nodding agreement all the while, then accepting the vial, concealed it in her garment.

As it happened, no pretext was necessary to get Walking Owl out of his wigwam because an early caller had summoned him to the assistance of an ailing child. While he was gone it took Chikchik no time at all to carry out her instructions and return to Alabak with the empty vial. Casting it into the fire, Alabak watched with satisfaction as it was consumed in a brilliant flame.

Soon the tribespeople were gathered for Sun Dog's initiation which in itself promised to be a short ceremony, but according to custom would be followed by hours of merrymaking.

Starting off with a wrestling match in which Sun Dog threw his opponent with little difficulty, there followed a warrior dance. Head held high, Sun Dog stood against a post while painted warriors and costumed spirits danced in a circle around him, thrusting their spears towards him as they passed. When the dance was finished and Sun Dog had not flinched, the Chief entered the circle holding the ceremonial knife. Approaching Sun Dog, he called upon the spirits of tribal ancestors to witness the act, and drew the blade across Sun Dog's heart. It was necessary for only a drop of blood to touch the knife which the Chief then raised high in the air, and with a bloodcurdling howl, led the others in a wild ecstatic dance.

Meanwhile, dressed in his robes of office, Walking Owl approached the boy, and while repeating incantations calling upon the boy's guardian spirit to protect him, dusted the wound with the contents of the ceremonial sachet.

When the dance was finished, Sun Dog received many gifts, the most exciting of all being a lively piebald pony. While the children thronged about to admire it, the tribespeople began their celebration which would last into the night with dancing, singing, feasting, and story telling.

Alabak was looking on from the side, pleased with the way things were going, when she caught sight of Lean Bone. He was among the other children whose attentions were centred on Sun Dog's pony. Moving into their midst, Alabak spoke to him.

"Did you ever see such a nice horse, Lean Bone? And fit only for a warrior, eh boy?"

"Yes, Aunt Alabak," Lean Bone replied, stroking the animal's head.

"I guess a boy would give just about anything for a horse like that! How would you like to own one like him?"

"Oh, very much, Aunt Alabak," Lean Bone breathed longingly, without taking his eyes from the pony.

"Well, when you become a warrior we will have to find you one, won't we?" Alabak smiled. Lean Bone looked at her wistfully but managed no answer. As she turned to leave she let slip, "Or maybe we could find a way of getting one sooner. Yes," she repeated more confidentially, "maybe we can find a way of getting one a little sooner." With that she moved into the evening's gathering shadows, deep in thought.

Alabak had scarcely left when Falling Star hobbled up. "See how well I make them go, my crutches?"

His mind having followed Alabak, Lean Bone made no reply.

"And you know what you promised," Falling Star informed him. "To show me the pool where the deer drinks."

This time Lean Bone heard, but his sister's suggestion found him more surprised than enthusiastic. He shook his head. "It would be too far for you yet."

"I can do it," Falling Star insisted. "Please!"

It was clear that Falling Star was in a determined mood, and would not take 'no' for an answer. Lean Bone reflected for a moment and offered a safe compromise. "We would have to ask Grandpa." Without waiting to argue, he turned and led the way.

124

Arriving at the wigwam, the children were about to enter when they were forced aside by an excited servant of the Chief. She rushed past them crying, "Come quickly, Walking Owl! Come quickly! The Chief sends for you!"

Walking Owl had retired early, and being awakened from a sound sleep, asked groggily, "What is the matter?"

"The evil spirits have entered Sun Dog and sickened him. He lies desperately ill. Come! Come!" With no more ado the servant hurried back to tell the Chief she had delivered his message promptly so as not to be found at fault should the worst happen.

When Walking Owl arrived at the Chief's wigwam he found the spirit dancers already formed in a ring with tomtoms in the centre beating a fast rhythm. Robed dancers, chanting and rattling noisemakers to scare off the evil ones, allowed Walking Owl to make his way inside where he was met by an angry Chief. "My boy is dying," the Chief cried, "if not dead. Is this how your magic protects our young warriors against harm and shields them from evil spirits?"

Walking Owl said nothing. Instead, he went directly to Sun Dog's bedside to see what could be the matter.

The boy lay deathly still, and over his heart a leaf poultice had been placed. Lifting it off, Walking Owl was surprised to see that the ceremonial wound was neither swollen nor inflamed. Still, he had expected nothing else. It had really been nothing more than a scratch such as would have been ignored by a child at play. It should give no trouble even if it had not been treated with the cleansing salt. Moreover, when a harmful spirit entered a wound it was perfectly obvious, for Walking Owl had seen the effect often enough.

Walking Owl was puzzled. The more so since the boy lay as if preserved in a frozen sleep. Even when it did enter a wound, a noxious spirit would not produce such an effect as that. "What is in this poultice, and why did you apply it?" Walking Owl demanded of the old woman who was tending the bedside. Rocking back and forth, she was murmuring supplications to the spirits.

"It is of the healing yarrow. The evil spirits have entered there," she said, and convinced there was nothing more that could be done, resumed her moaning.

"Walking Owl," cried the Chief, who had stood by wringing his hands while Walking Owl made his inspection, "it is your responsibility to see that such a thing could not happen."

"An evil spirit could not have entered the wound against the ceremonial salt," Walking Owl replied calmly. "It must have been through something else. He has eaten or drunk something to take him in this unusual manner."

"Why should he alone be affected by the food and drink?" the Chief demanded. "No one else is suffering from such an illness. It is you who are at fault!"

Try as he would, Walking Owl could not fathom the nature of the visitation, and so had no idea whether he would risk even greater harm applying his simple medicines to try and bring the boy out of his coma. Nor could he satisfy the Chief that his part in the ceremony was beyond reproach. The Chief insisted that the evil spirits had entered the wound that Walking Owl's magic was supposed to have closed against them. Either that or Walking Owl's ritual had not pleased the good spirits. Either way, the Chief argued, Walking Owl had failed in his responsibility. "If the boy does not recover," the Chief finally warned, "there will be an accounting."

The Chief's words drew no reply, for Walking Owl's mind was too occupied with the boy's condition. It was clear an evil spirit had entered him and taken possession, and if it was not through the ceremonial wound or the food, then what else? It was a mystery.

Walking Owl slowly drew forth the beaded pouch and sank to the floor. Inscribing the ritual circle and closing his eyes in total concentration, he let the bones fall free.

When he opened his eyes to read the message, a cold shadow seemed to settle over him, and with it a faint shudder passed over his spare frame. The talon lay curled about the wishbone!

126

When their grandfather failed to return, the children settled down to a sleepless night, what with the sound of tomtoms and the coming and goings of a disturbed village. Still holding Lean Bone to his promise, Falling Star gave him no peace until he finally agreed to take her to the pool. So it was that with the breaking of day they set off into the forest, taking a satchel of corn and berries for themselves and a bone for Trish.

As Lean Bone had warned, the trip was more than Falling Star had bargained for, and though he found the easiest pathways, they had to stop often for her to rest. There were places where she had to be carried piggyback, and by the time they emerged from the dense forest growth to stand at the edge of the pool, the sun was mounting high overhead.

It was a spacious clearing. At one end a gurgling brook entered, and at the other end a beaver dam closed off its escape. The children's arrival surprised a beaver who slid into the depths with a slap of his tail. A mother duck waddling off the far side of the dam lost no time entering the undergrowth ahead of her scurrying brood. Lying at their feet, the remains of a long-fallen tree reached into the water, and from a skeleton branch, a saucy kingfisher, who had been sitting motionless waiting for some luckless minnow to swim by, flew off at the disturbance. Lily pads decked with yellow blooms covered a dainty cove, and with the kingfisher gone, a chorus of little green frogs came out of hiding to sit and catch flies. Looking from the fallen tree into the water's crystal depths, lazy fish could be seen hovering over a bed of gently swaying weeds, and looking up, flowering vines were to be seen climbing into the lofty home of songbirds whose voices rang clear on the summer air and echoed off a nearby cliff.

Whatever had been the labour and pain of reaching these idyllic surroundings, Falling Star immediately forgot them. "What a beautiful sanctuary!" she exclaimed. "This will be our very own." She looked down to admire the deer tracks that came out of the forest and led to the water's edge. "We will keep this a secret — with the deer," she announced.

"He swims across," Lean Bone explained authoritatively, pointing to the opposite side where the tracks reappeared.

"Behind the trees there is the cliff where I lost his tracks in the hard stones. At the bottom of the cliff, I found the entrance to a cave where we can take shelter from the rain."

"A real cave? Oh, show me!"

Lean Bone led the way to the far side of the pool, and following the deer tracks through the trees, emerged at the foot of the cliff. Tumbling over the face of the cliff was a thin column of water. It fell splashing into a hollow slab of stone where it gathered itself before continuing headlong into the forest in the direction of the pool. A few paces further on, Lean Bone stopped beside a clump of junipers, and there behind them was the opening of a cave.

If the pool had its fascinations, the cave held even more. Looking in from the entrance it seemed not to penetrate very far, but exploring further, the children found a surprise. Instead of a blank wall, the tunnel widened into a room at one side, its ceiling giving rise to a chimney-like shaft that opened to the sky above. It might well have been the waterfall's escape at one time, and now remained an abandoned course.

Falling Star was the first to notice something, and she could scarcely contain her excitement over the discovery. If she looked up through the opening, she could see the stars in broad daylight. "It's enchanted, the cave," she cried out. "Lean Bone! Come and see them, the stars."

Lean Bone joined her, and the two sat in silence for some time looking up at the stars. Falling Star was the first to speak. "Do you think they could be enchanted, really, the stars? Ones that could grant a wish, no matter what?"

"Maybe," Lean Bone conceded doubtfully.

"What would you wish for?"

"That's easy," Lean Bone replied. "I would wish for a pony — a pure white pony who could skim over the ground like the wind over a cornfield. What would you wish?"

"Maybe to be a beautiful dancer," said Falling Star dreamily, "who could pirouette like moonbeams over a rippling pool. Then every night I would dance right across it, the sanctuary — if it could be even a hundred pools across."

128

With that they fell into silence again, and after allowing their imaginations to run free for a time, came at length to feel their hunger. Making their way back to the entrance of the cave, they were glad to rest and eat their meal.

While they were thus talking and planning their future visits to the sanctuary, Trish stood up suddenly, sniffing the air with her sensitive nose. Falling Star put a restraining hand on her collar, and then Lean Bone, who was resting on his knees and could see more clearly, motioned excitedly for silence. He pointed in the direction from which they themselves had left the forest, and whispered, "It's him. It's my big buck."

And sure enough it was. Just emerging from the thicket and coming in the direction of the cave was a beautiful white-tail. He stepped high, his head proudly erect, eyes bright and alert, antlers glistening in the sun. Falling Star held her breath. Never had she been so excitingly close to such a magnificent animal.

Without taking his eyes off the deer, Lean Bone reached out slowly, furtively, for his bow. As if guided by a sixth sense, the buck stopped dead in his tracks, and stood poised and motionless as if cast in stone. Though motionless, his every muscle was drawn taut and ready, all his energy held as in the draw of a bow. As he stood, he was more than a proud and beguiling prey. He was a symbol, an epitome of the wild — the whispering forest, the starry night, the cry of the loon, the bay of the wolf, the west wind — all rolled into one waiting bundle of energy.

Lean Bone's fingers curled around the stave of his bow, and then he started to draw it gently towards him. Suddenly realizing what her brother was about to do, Falling Star drew a sharp breath. "No!"

The effect was like a pistol shot. The dam broke, unleashing a torrent of energy. There was a flash of white from his tail and the buck was gone.

Lean Bone, still kneeling with his arm outstretched, was caught with scarcely a half-hold on his bow. He had been cheated, and his disappointment erupted in an angry burst. "You spoiled my chance!" he cried.

"But I don't want you to kill him, the deer," said Falling Star. "You must not touch him."

"Why? He is mine! I am going to surprise Grandpa. We will have a real celebration on my first kill."

"No. You must not kill anything here. It would not be right. I could never come back." Falling Star was beside herself with emotion.

"But Grandpa said it is right to kill for food, and you had to agree," wailed Lean Bone.

"But not here," insisted his sister.

"What is the difference, here or somewhere else?"

Though she found no words to describe them, the thoughts that were turning over in Falling Star's mind were clear. A day would come when the white-tail would have his customary swim through the pool and would follow his path to the cliff. Stepping out from the trees, head high, antlers tossing defiantly, he would suddenly feel the sharp sting of a swift unseen arrow as it pierced his heart. Bright eyes clouding in bewilderment, he looks in vain for his hidden assailant as he sinks to the ground. The blood that coursed through his veins but a brief moment ago now stains the ground he trod. Then, as with a final shudder his spirit takes leave, weary eyelids close over his last beseeching question, "Why?" Now there is whispering among the spirits. The cliff whispers to the brook, "It was the brother of Falling Star. Why?" And the brook whispers to the crystal pool, "Why?" And the pool whispers into the rising mist, and the rising mist into the treetops, and the treetops into the passing wind. And the wind whispers throughout the forest, "It was the brother of Falling Star. Why?"

As Falling Star thus agonized, searching for words to describe a sacrilege against the creation she loved, a coldness seized her heart and choked whatever words might have come. At length, in utter despair, the tears she could not hold back welled up to voice the sadness in her heart.

"And if everyone joins in the celebration of a first kill," Lean Bone was summing up, "it is because it is right; and what is right for the whole tribe, including Grandpa, must be right for Falling

130

Star." With this final telling argument, he turned to accept Falling Star's surrender, and saw only the tears.

He loved his little sister, admired her courage, and marvelled at the goodness that was her charm. Although he took advantage of any opportunity to correct her or to overcome her in debate, it was not to make her less, but to raise himself that she could look to him, for he was her protector. It was not in him to inflict any injury or sadness, or to be the least unkind, and confounded by the eloquence of tears, his overwhelming arguments dissolved in sorrow, for she had never cried but when the hurt was deep.

Words no longer held any account in the discussion. The bow fell from his hand, and with an involuntary gesture he grasped her limp hands in his with no thought but to comfort her. And so it came about that on that day Lean Bone made his promise never to kill a living thing within Falling Star's sanctuary. To prove his sincerity he took the sharp point of an arrow, and with clenched teeth, pierced his arm. Then from the wound he squeezed three drops of blood onto the ground. It was the solemn oath of the Cheechikois — to be broken only on pain of death.

Meanwhile, back at Sun Dog's sickbed, Walking Owl had met with difficulties. After reading the portents, he had gathered up the bones, and regaining his feet, spoke to himself. "The spirit has entered by an evil hand to work its spell, and the way could be one of many."

He thereupon set about trying all the ways he knew to seek out the nature of the spell and to overcome it. Tirelessly and determined, he worked through the day and on into the night, allowing himself only an occasional sip of thin soup from the clay cup set down for him by the old squaw. And so as the shades of night crept over the sickbed for the second time, Walking Owl's weary eyes did not see the hand that reached out from the shadows to cast a colourless drop into his cup. Then, after sipping of its contents once more, he could only think to chide himself for a weak and tired old man as he sank to the floor to be overcome by sleep.

While Walking Owl slept, Alabak was very much awake. Going to the Chief, she said, "I brought the shaman a little food and found him asleep from exhaustion, poor man. He is getting old and is neither as strong nor as capable as he once was. But I have learned much from him, and I am sure I could cure Sun Dog if you would allow me the chance."

The Chief, angry that Walking Owl had not only failed to cure the boy but slept while death was left to have its way, would at first have nothing to do with her. Then out of his great love for his son, and realizing that to try anything would be better than trying nothing, he gave in.

Alabak lost no time working her magic, and as the first rays of dawn sprang out of the east, Sun Dog opened his eyes and sat up as if coming out of a pleasant sleep.

So it was that when Walking Owl awoke, it was to see the Chief hugging his boy and congratulating Alabak. He could not at first believe his eyes, and had to be told that as he lay exhausted and asleep, the worthy Alabak had wrought a miraculous cure. She would be well repaid, the Chief said, dismissing Walking Owl with a wave of his hand.

Steven's rapt attention was broken by the voice of Thalamus. "There you are, my boy!" he honked, favouring Steven with his thin smile. "The scene is set for a witch's evil, but only when the wishes are all in will we know whether good can find a role to steal the show."

12

Steven stood with the Gardinelle and Keep before the chateau's elevator doors. The arrival of a cage would see them whisked up to the council chamber where, returning from his hurried tour of the Quick Side, Sirgal would report on what he had found there.

As the tinkle of a bell sounded and the elevator door opened in front of them, the Gardinelle noticed a smudge of soot on Keep's face. Taking the handkerchief of the nearest attendant, she gave the spot a motherly rub, while Keep, his arms wrapped about the Compleat Record, did little more than blink under the royal ministration.

Steven studied them in the corner of his eye. He admired their composure, if not his own, because they were returning from what had been a harrowing visit to the reformatory — harrowing even by the standards he had come to accept as normal for the Gardinelle's sorties among her subjects. But, Steven reflected, it could have been truly serious this time had it not been for the intrepid Vroomers. The Vroomers had turned out to be an aerial squad of acrobatic witches — or so they were billed — though having now seen them in action, Steven was ready to believe whispers that they were, in fact, retired astronauts escaping boredom. Having exchanged besoms for vacuum cleaners, which were equipped with powerful trovium miniturbines, their displays of plain and fancy flying were in much demand. Thinking to enhance the Gardinelle's visit of encouragement for those who were plodding the road to rehabilitation, Muster had invited the

Vroomers to entertain the school and invited guests with an indoor performance.

That Muster had chosen a popular entertainment was evident from the applause that brought the Vroomers into the hall. They stepped forward at a lively pace, handles sloped over their shoulders, bags tucked under their arms, squeezing forth an agonizing wail of bagpipes. A round of marching had brought them before the Gardinelle where, after a succession of movements with crisp military precision, they acknowledged the royal presence with a bow. At this the Gardinelle clapped briskly, believing the act was finished, but the Vroomers had scarcely warmed up.

Mounting their machines, the Vroomers motored over the floor with ease. After carrying out a routine of intricate figures and criss-crossings, they formed a vee, and rising vertically into the air, hovered briefly before putting on a display of close-formation flying. This had proven all the more breathtaking in the limited space of the reformatory's hall.

Needless to say, the act was thoroughly enjoyed by the packed audience whose willing and noisy approval marked every turn. Muster, too, had been enjoying the show. She had taken the opportunity to squeeze in beside Keep who, with the Gardinelle at his other side, was caught without room to retreat. Thus occupied, Muster had allowed Sawni out of her sight. Not Steven. Reminded of his own delicate position, and wanting to avoid the possibility of any guilt by association, Steven was anxious to keep distance between himself and such a troublemaker. So it was that while necks were craned to follow the Vroomers, Steven, from his customary stand by the door, could not miss noticing Sawni recover a cigar butt and disappear behind the draperies. So, too, he was the first to see the ominous curl of smoke when the fabric took light, and though he cried a warning, it was only to accompany a rampant billow of smoke and licking flames. Instantly the room was filled with screams of "Fire!" and shrieks of terror, while everyone joined in a wild stampede towards the door. Everyone, that is, except the royal party, which was left deserted — though not by Steven. Caught by the unexpected speed of the evacuation, Steven found himself pinned against the wall behind the door, where he could only look on in helpless horror. Then, just as the gathering flames were reaching out beyond the draperies and it seemed that all would be enveloped, the Vroomers swooped down upon the scene. Dismounting, they deployed their vacuum hoses, and sucking in the flames and all, ended the incident as quickly as it had begun.

Keenly interested and not having moved from her seat, the Gardinelle cried "Bravo!" and applauded as if it were all part of the act. Meanwhile, Keep tidied up the Compleat Record, leaving Muster, as usual, to search out the missing Sawni.

The elevator came to a stop, and being shaken from his reverie, Steven followed the Gardinelle's party into the council chamber. She had timed her arrival well, for she had no more than greeted the waiting councillors when the flashing annunciator drew attention to "REMOTE". Sirgal, too, had arrived.

Eager to hear Sirgal's report, the Gardinelle lost no time in taking her place in the Great Chair — Keep on his tall stool at her elbow, the Compleat Record on his lap and a long pencil behind his ear. From his position behind Keep, Steven's interested gaze scanned the array of councillors, among them some now familiar faces from Breach's arraignment. All seemed alive with expectation except perhaps Thalamus who seemed to be dozing, and Resal whose attention was centred on a patch of mathematical symbols on her note pad.

He had travelled the length and breadth of the Quick Side, Sirgal informed his listeners, visiting the worlds of Quicks wherever they were to be found. "And wherever and however I found them," he reported, "whether backward or progressive, exemplary or imperfect, ancient or more recently come, they share a common talent for doing the opposite of what they preach, and a mind for seeing only what serves their immediate purpose. It makes of the Quick Side a wonderland of contradiction where the pursuit of destruction is carried out with the utmost discipline, while those in pursuit of a peaceful and harmonious society demand unbounded freedom. Thus it is they live an endless struggle that sees peace emerge out of conflict, and conflict out of peace."

The Gardinelle, as was her way, seized upon the bright side. "But you do say, my dear Sirgal, there are those at least who are mindful of building an harmonious society, if not a paradise."

"Building a paradise is the goal of all Quicks, Your Highness, but as to the form it should take, there is little agreement between those who would manage the paradise and those who would be managed by it. When I questioned why they were burning down forests, burying the fragrant countryside under concrete, and building chimney stacks to pollute the environment, I was told it was to improve the quality of life. They see no contradiction in striving to create a paradise in this way because to most Quicks, good is simply the absence of evil. Arranging evil to be elsewhere makes it sufficiently absent for entrepreneurial purposes."

"Are they totally without ethics then?" a voice inquired.

"Unfortunately not. They ardently uphold the work ethic — so much so that creating jobs is a virtue that sees resources expended with abandon and bled to extinction. Indeed, any who oppose such progress and try to blunt the tools of destruction are like to be judged the vandals."

"Are they blind to their direction?" asked a voice in pity.

"Or have they not yet learned to read?" piped a derisive voice.

"They read dinosaur bones quite well, and the weather somewhat," Sirgal replied, "but the ravages of progress, being widely scattered, leave much more to read between the lines than does the devastation of war. Yet even those who were hotly engaged in war and were laying waste one another's lands assured me they were doing it for their children."

"Indeed?" the Gardinelle gasped. "And what is it they hold against their children?"

"Strangely, Your Highness, it is not a lack of parental concern. On the contrary, most Quicks lavish great care and attention on their children. They have unfortunately been overtaken by a belief that the formative years of young Quicks should be spent in learning how to laugh and cry and to be contrary, rather than how to wish properly."

"Are the children taught nothing of wishing then?" the Gardinelle asked. "Is that what has gone wrong?"

136

"What with their contrariness, it is difficult to lay blame on any single fault, Your Highness. Since learning to distinguish between the rewards of Your Highness and a genie's humbug, it has become a ritual among the Quicks to withhold their acceptance of a granted wish until they have searched it well for evidence of a genie's trick, as we knew. So, too, they have come to remember the great wishers among them, and to honour their contributions to the welfare of the Quick Side. I found the children to be well schooled in the lore, particularly of wishes granted to doctors and scientists where the faith of commitment is extolled, and the Complements of Being are clearly evident in the benefits to all. Yet the children seem to be leaving their schools quite without appreciating that the very effort itself of striving for a goal can make all the difference between a Proper wish and a wibble."

Sirgal's words awakened in Steven's ears the distant echo of Miss Adley's voice crying, "Wish for the moon, and strive with faith!" Miss Adley, at least, seemed to be an exception to Sirgal's complaint, Steven thought. In fact, Miss Adley and the Gardinelle were turning out to be surprisingly like-minded in many respects. He turned his eyes to study the Gardinelle. She had taken up Sirgal's point and was drawing conclusions.

"With that being the case, my dear Sirgal," the Gardinelle observed, "there is little wonder that wibbling has grown out of proportion, and young Quicks are in danger of becoming ... of becoming ..."

"Wibble-wishing Win-Woers, My Lady."

It was the dryly honked prompting of Thalamus that interrupted the Gardinelle's search for a word to describe the children's imminent peril. Her compressed lips formed a tiny "o" of distress. "Well, yes, perhaps even the danger of becoming wibble-wishing Win-Woers. And yet, my dear Sirgal, there on Oulden Finftroum where I have watched the tribespeople of Wamwiki who have no great history of wishing, there is a refreshing show of reverence for nature at least, and even their mischief stops short of destroying their habitat."

"That is true, Your Highness, and just as well, because the landscape of Oulden Finftroum is regularly reshaped by everything from earthquakes to hurricanes, and tidal waves to volcanoes," Sirgal replied. "Indeed, the hand of Fulgor is always in evidence and he misses no opportunity to demonstrate his power. Unless we can somehow meet his challenge, I fear that the most extravagantly granted wish will hold the Quicks on Oulden Finftroum in much less awe than a single visitation by Fulgor."

"Dear me," the Gardinelle sighed, "then we must by all means find a way of matching his presence and of encouraging the Quicks there to strive for the greatest of all wishes. But how?"

Having listened too long in silence, the councillors welcomed the Gardinelle's question with a clamour of advice and proposals. It was with difficulty that she at length prevailed upon order, and inviting them one at a time, allowed their suggestions to be weighed.

"The primitives seem to be the least at fault," observed one.

"If from what Sirgal has told us, the situation on Oulden Finftroum could set the test for other planets," a second put in, "it might well be most profitable to turn our attention there."

"Yes," another lent her support. "The success of a special effort on Oulden Finftroum could be a stepping stone."

"That seems reasonable enough," the Gardinelle agreed. "What kind of special effort would you have us make?"

If up to now Steven had been carried along in a dreamlike awareness that he was retracing the ancient Cheechikois legend, he was suddenly jolted into acute wakefulness by the Gardinelle's question. This was it! His subconscious expectation was about to be satisfied. This was where the miraculous balm would come to light. Steven held his breath.

"Perhaps," the councillor replied reflectively, "we could encourage interest by offering more for Propers."

"That could be dangerous," the Gardinelle cautioned. "We dare not risk encroaching upon the transcendental value of Perfects."

The Gardinelle's flight of ecstasy over the mere thought of Perfects was still fresh in Steven's mind. He observed the back of her head, relieved that she was not persuaded to risk her precious Perfects, and silently urged her to suggest instead the miraculous balm. Alas, even if it were in the back of her mind, the enthusiastic councillors seemed bent on other solutions.

"Perhaps we could follow Fulgor's example and reveal to them a sign of some kind," a new voice was urging. "We have never tried signs before, and one cannot deny Fulgor's success with them."

"Signs are usually too scary," the first councillor came back. "We do not want to send the Quicks scurrying for shelter. Symbols are better. Symbols can fire the imagination and rally support for a cause."

"That could be it!" another cried. "A symbol to be seen everywhere like a candle to light the way for those who dream of a paradise."

Others took up the thought. "A symbol to give guidance and lend heart."

"Especially to the young!"

Voices grew in excitement and intensity. "A veritable emblem to lead their common cause, spread courage, and sweep them along!"

"From planet to planet!"

"In a great crusade for the greatest of all wishes!"

Words could no longer vie for hearing in the din. Sharing the mood, the Gardinelle clapped her hands, and in a momentary lull there could be seen, rather than heard, to fall from her lips the words, "wishing tree". It was more than enough to rekindle a crescendo of triumphant applause mixed with cries of "The tree! The tree! The wishing tree!"

When quiet had been restored once more, the Gardinelle nodded approvingly. "The tree itself then — our symbol of the Three Complements of Being and their guide to proper wishing. Yes, that could become the inspiration for young Quicks everywhere. That will be our resolve."

And the miraculous balm! Steven cried to himself, jubilantly.

"Well, don't rush off to bell a cat."

The caution came from Thalamus.

"What do you say, my dear Thalamus?" the Gardinelle questioned the wizard with surprise.

The voice of Thalamus would have been heard clearly enough in the prevailing mood, but in the hush that now fell it fairly echoed back out of the ceiling. "How will you introduce this symbol to such contrary beings without achieving a result opposite to what you want?"

"How can that be?" an offended councillor quickly demanded. "We are, after all, offering them the key to a meaningful future."

"They will take it to be a trap," said Thalamus.

"The alternative is to withhold all bounties until they mend their ways," the councillor chided.

"They would label you a hypocrite and a dictator," Thalamus countered.

The Gardinelle interrupted the exchange. "What do you suggest then, my dear Thalamus?"

"I suggest only that you restrain from any overzealous haste," Thalamus replied. "You would be better advised to look for an opportunity that cannot be fouled by the perversity of Quicks or the wiles of Fulgor."

"Then let us add that to our resolution," the Gardinelle concluded, turning to Keep who, with an appropriate flourish of his hand, noted the council's momentous resolve for the Compleat Record.

The councillors were given little time to enjoy their round of self-congratulations, for Sirgal had again risen to his feet. "While at a rendezvous in the Big Dipper," he announced in a voice that could not conceal his misgivings, "I was told that scouts from the Fiendom of Roth have been seen in the area on more than one occasion recently."

Sirgal's words, falling upon the room without warning, jolted Reefer bolt upright and turned questioning faces towards the Gardinelle.

"Fulgor's scouts around the Big Dipper?" the Gardinelle exclaimed mechanically. "The Big Dipper is a long way from where his scouts can claim any rightful business."

Reefer cleared his throat. "It bodes no good. Fulgor's ambitions travel with his scouts, and where they go trouble is seldom very far behind."

The Gardinelle studied her favourite knight as if to read his unspoken thoughts. "Well, my dear Sirgal, what do you suppose has brought them to this end?"

Sirgal shook his head apologetically. "There is little to go on. They were seen very briefly on each occasion and were not heard to break their silence, though at the rendezvous strange signals were overheard coming from Quotaris."

"Strange signals?" The voiced reaction came from many throats in unison.

"From Quotaris?" The astonished Reefer exchanged a glance over raised eyebrows with Garth, Captain of the Quotaris Guard. "What kind of signals?"

Sirgal again shook his head in apology. I can only repeat what I was told. The signals were thought to be some kind of code."

"But they were intended for Fulgor's scouts, you think?" Garth pressed.

"That was the feeling," Sirgal nodded.

"It would seem then," Reefer reasoned, "that Fulgor's scouts were not just passing by. They were around on business, and someone in our midst was in touch with them."

"That could account for a small problem we had with our cosmophone yesterday," said Garth. "We thought it was sunspots, but I see now it could have been interference with our beam."

"It is safe to assume their interest was more in Quotaris than in the Big Dipper," Reefer concluded. Then moved by second thoughts, he cast a glance in Resal's direction and added, "and more than likely in something special we might have."

"If you are thinking of the work on microstars," Resal replied, "I doubt whether any member of the staff would have passed information along — nor have we conducted the kind of test that might be detected beyond the laboratory."

Everyone looked at each other confidently, but there was no denying a deep uneasiness that had gripped the room. Breaking the tension quite suddenly — as much to his own surprise as to the surprise of the councillors — Steven's high-pitched voice blurted, "Kwah!" His involuntary cry was enough to make Steven himself shrink back in embarrassment, but the astonishment and shock in which all eyes turned upon him almost staggered the boy against Keep's dangling legs. Catching himself, and feeling at a disadvantage but not cornered, he turned to Resal to explain, for he was after all a forthright and respectful boy. "I didn't know it was all right to watch the cosmoscreen, so I hid when Kwah came. He put on the earphones and then I saw the Big Dipper on the screen. While he was busy I left."

Now the councillors looked at Resal, who for a stunned moment sat motionless before seeming to grasp the full meaning of Steven's story. Half rising in her seat, her usual composure very much shaken, she wagged a cautioning finger at Steven saying, "I know my stepbrother is at times not entirely happy, but that is no excuse for a snooping page boy to suggest he could be dealing with…"

Before she could finish, and as the abashed Steven cringed before the unexpected attack, the Gardinelle interrupted. "My dear Resal, my dear Steven. Let us not jump to conclusions on either side. It is very likely not what it seems, but where the security of Quotaris is at stake, we must seek an explanation of everything." So saying, she turned to an assistant and instructed him to send out an officer to question Kwah on the matter.

Without further ado, the Gardinelle turned her attention to the security of Quotaris. "My dear Garth," she half declared and half questioned, "there is surely no reason for us to be caught off guard by any sudden move on Fulgor's part."

"Certainly not, Your Highness," Garth replied, "but we may not be entirely ready to fend him off. Our success in the last encounter came because he had concentrated the Roths for the attack. In that formation they offered a perfect target for our starballs, and with such heavy losses they were forced to withdraw. With his improved charge-augmented bolts he would be free to spread his strength over a wider area. Our starballs would be no match against such dispersed cabolts."

Sirgal knew as well as anyone the power of Fulgor's devastating cabolts, but he was quick to respond. "Your Highness need have no fear. The Knights Courier will stand fast against any assault."

142

The Gardinelle nodded her confidence in Sirgal's pledge, and all those present knew that Fulgor would taste the valour of the Knights Courier once again if he dared strike. But Reefer shared the sober thoughts of Garth, agreeing that Fulgor may have learned something from the last encounter. "And if he has," he cautioned, "it could explain his new-found boldness."

"Then we must find ways to meet any move on his part," the Gardinelle responded with determination. "Perhaps a few more starball launchers would do."

Garth was far from willing to rely on starball launchers. "They are much too cumbersome," he argued. "It would take too many to cover all possible angles. But," he added with a knowing look in Resal's direction, "perhaps we could prepare a special surprise for him."

Resal drew a thoughtful breath. She directed her reply to the Gardinelle. "Garth has raised with me the possibility of fitting our lances with particle beams generated by microstars," she explained. "You might call them 'micropars'. I have not yet given it much thought, but micropars could be an answer to Fulgor's cabolts. Still, it would take time to prove out microstars in such an application."

"That is not exactly what I am suggesting," Garth interjected. "I am thinking of a megamicropar with the power to rip the Fiendom of Roth to shreds. It need never bother anyone again."

"Really, my dear Garth!" the Gardinelle protested. "We must not be carried away with ideas of the like. It is just such thinking that led poor Breach astray over the Dogtrolytes. Wisdom tells us that if it is wrong for evil to destroy good, then it is equally wrong to waste good destroying evil, for the good is just as much lost in either case. It is for the Big Computer MEGOS to convert evil to good. It is not for us to waste good doing the work of evil. Trovium is a bounty we are bound to use for its benefits to creation — to satisfy the dreams and wishes of all. We shall therefore sacrifice only what is needed to counter Fulgor's evil, and preserve the greater amount for those who would make a paradise of the Quick Side.

"But, my dear Resal," she continued, turning her attention to the young scientist, "you were saying you could fit our lances with micropars which would be less wasteful of good, and still offer us protection enough. How soon could our forces be equipped?"

"Of that I am not certain, Your Highness. The instability of microstars still poses a problem, though I have now found a way out of the difficulty. I have been planning a test that would take advantage of the orbiter race during the Festival of the Wishing Tree. My procedure would be to seed the rocket fuel with microstar power, but with Fulgor's scouts around...." Her voice trailed off uncertainly, and she finished with a questioning glance towards Reefer.

While Reefer hesitated over a reply, Garth struck the table with his fist. "Say the word and we will have them out of there!"

The Captain's firm stand moved Reefer to agree. "Perhaps it would be well to show the flag, and set an example that will convince travellers they should give Quotaris the same wide berth they have long been persuaded to give the Fiendom of Roth."

"My dear gentlemen," the Gardinelle admonished, "protecting Quotaris is by all means necessary and honourable, but if the flag is to be shown, it will be shown for what it is — a symbol of fellowship. Do remember that our flag is first and foremost a symbol of the fellowship of those who have gathered in a cause, and then of the greater fellowship of those who would share in its message. Mark you, therefore, that if our flag ceases to invite the greater fellowship and signifies a haven only for its nationals, it becomes a contradiction of itself, for it is then but a symbol of exclusion. Let it never be that a traveller have reason to steer a wide berth at the sight of our flag."

A chorus of voices rejoined with "Here! Here!"

Steven, still somewhat shaken from his exchange with Resal and freshly reminded that he was himself a stranger, found a measure of comfort in the Gardinelle's assertion that the leaf of the triunium maple was a friendly flag, and there to bid welcome. In fact, he mused, it would be a step forward if countries could be

144

persuaded to turn all their flags into coloured welcome mats. His musings were arrested by the voice of Thalamus.

"Well said, Your Highness." Thalamus hoisted himself to his elbows and cleared his throat. "However, there should be no need to show the flag one way or the other, because as far as Fulgor's scouts are concerned, we are in the habit of launching stars. A mere orbiter should hold little interest for them. What would there be to suspect?"

"Why, I suppose there is really nothing," the Gardinelle observed.

"So who cares if they even watch the race?"

"Then you think it safe to go ahead?" Resal asked.

Reefer exulted. "Why not? A proof test right under their very nose. How appropriate!" He beamed over the table.

The Gardinelle nodded agreement. "It would be unwise to put the test off in any case." Questioning her councillors with a raised brow, she received a unanimous shout of approval. "Well then," she concluded, "the future of Quotaris may well hinge upon the outcome of the orbiter race. We shall all be looking forward to the Festival with more eagerness than usual."

The councillors being now dismissed, Steven thought to avoid another encounter with Resal, and seeing her start towards the far door, sought the one nearest for himself. As he approached his escape, Reefer caught sight of him from across the room and signalled that he would like a word. Pretending to be on an urgent errand, Steven scurried away through the milling councillors, and finding his only safe line of retreat was the mezzanine stairs, ducked behind the bannister and followed it aloft.

13

While the hum of conversation among the lingering councillors rose from below, Steven seized upon the opportunity to wait out their departure in the comfort of the Gardinelle's chair, watching the drama of Wamwiki. He recognized the voice of Alabak even before the screen brought first her silhouette to life.

Alabak's words seemed to be for Chikchik's ears, but her attention was devoted to a small piece of meat which she was dipping into a simmering pot. "When children are keeping quiet and whispering to each other," she was saying, "you can be sure they are up to something, and I intend to find out where they are going. I could have followed them yesterday but for that stupid dog running about in circles and giving me away. Well, that dog might as well enjoy this meal because it will be her last."

Alabak interrupted her complaining to turn to Chikchik who sat nodding agreement. "The fire needs another stick!"

The order sent Chikchik scrambling for firewood.

With the fire taken care of, Alabak continued to review her grievances. "And their grandfather is not making things any easier with his old-fashioned ideas. I have been too lenient with those children," she muttered, squeezing a twisted root into the pot and stirring. "I thought time would pass more quickly. You hear those stupid mothers complaining that their dear children have grown up and gone away before they could be enjoyed. Huh! You could say that about mumps!"

146

Spearing the meat with a sharp stick, Alabak drew it from the pot and stood swinging it back and forth to cool it off. "Here we are, still waiting for the day when a spell can be cast to separate the children from their guardian spirits — the day of Lean Bone's first kill, and the day of Falling Star's naming ceremony. And while I wait, Walking Owl uses the time to fill their heads full of more nonsense as if he knows he is working against time. What have the bones told him? Could he have read in them my plans? Those eternal bones! If ever I lay my hands on that pouch he will never see it again!"

By now the meat had cooled off, and cutting a tiny corner, Alabak tossed it up to a roosting crow. The bird caught the crumb in its beak and toppled from the branch — dead.

Satisfied, Alabak held out the skewered remains to Chikchik. "Take this over to the wigwam," she instructed, "and place it in the hollow against the wall where Trish always lies. I saw them all going towards the cornfield, but they might soon be back, so hurry. And make sure you are not seen!"

The old woman nodded, and with a last anguished glance at the dead crow, took the stick and was quickly on her way.

With the sun high overhead, it was warm and there were few villagers about, so making her way to Walking Owl's wigwam without meeting anyone, Chikchik left the meat as Alabak had directed. Wasting no more time than it took to drop the deadly bait, she turned to retrace her steps and was gone without noticing a small inquisitive dog who came from nearby.

Always hungry, dogs living in the old tribal villages never took the time to consider the quality of food or even to taste it. Whatever they got their teeth into was quickly swallowed, lest it be snatched by another half-starved animal. And so it was to be expected. The hungry little fellow seized the tainted morsel and devoured it in a single gulp, only to fall instantly in his tracks.

The deed had closely missed its mark, for at this moment the voices of the children and Walking Owl could be heard returning from the woods. Moving slowly to suit Falling Star's laboured pace, Walking Owl carried a bundle of willow boughs and spruce roots.

Falling Star stopped long enough to draw the necessary breath. "Lean Bone! You are letting it drag in the dirt, my cape!"

Lean Bone who was walking ahead, his bow and quiver over one shoulder and his grandfather's tool bag over the other, turned and gathered up the abused garment.

"Boys!" Falling Star sighed, and renewed her gait. "Can you make it this afternoon, Grandpa, the travois?"

Walking Owl adjusted his bundle and nodded. "We have all that we need here. From now on, Trish will be able to carry your things with no trouble."

Panting with the heat, Trish trotted ahead, anxious to reach her shady niche where she could quench her thirst, and rounding the corner, stopped abruptly on seeing an intruder in her place. Offended by its cheek, she made ready to do battle, but immediately recognized her little friend and sensed the truth. As she raised her head to the sky, there escaped from her throat a weird and mournful note which ended in a distressed sob that carried across the quiet village. If Alabak heard the sound she must have brightened, thinking it to have been Trish's departing cry. The strangeness of it caught Falling Star's ear, and shocked that her pet had met with an accident, she cried out, "Lean Bone!" But Lean Bone was already on his way without sparing the time to shed himself of his burdens.

"It is not Trish," Lean Bone puffed with relief as Walking Owl arrived close on his heels and bent over to examine the unfortunate dog.

When Walking Owl straightened up he was clearly perturbed, but he said nothing while Falling Star hobbled up with amazing speed to fall upon Trish with endearments. By now, too, some neighbours had appeared, and after satisfying their curiosity, took the dead animal away with Walking Owl's instructions to see that it was well buried. That done, Walking Owl set the children to work sorting out the material they had brought from the forest, and then returned to the niche. Drawing forth the beaded pouch, he knelt and made a circle in the dust, and mumbling his incantation, let the bones tumble. During a long moment he sat motionless, staring at the pattern, for the talon lay curled about the wishbone!

At length Walking Owl swept the bones back into their pouch, and still thoughtful, rejoined the children.

"Hurry, Grandpa," Falling Star urged, making room for him to sit next to her as she unravelled the last of the spruce roots. "Everything is ready."

Walking Owl accepted his place, and reaching over, took from Lean Bone the sharp flint knife he was whittling with.

"Aw," Lean Bone grumbled, "I wish I had a sharp one like that."

"All in good time," Walking Owl replied as he set about trimming the slender willows.

"What is it for, everything?" Falling Star asked, eager to imagine the finished product.

"With these we will make the frame," Walking Owl explained as he worked, "and then we will weave the roots into a bag-net."

"Make it good and strong," Lean Bone instructed, "so we can see if Trish can pull me."

"No," Falling Star objected, fondling the dog, "she is not to be a horse, Trish."

"Those with the strongest legs are usually the laziest," Walking Owl philosophized over his work.

"She can just bring my things and carry what I say, eh Grandpa?"

"She is your dog, my little Star, and in your care," Walking Owl conceded.

Falling Star taunted Lean Bone with a grimace. "See!"

"No matter," Lean Bone shrugged in return, looking for the last word, "I'm going to have a nice riding pony, and I'll pass you like a whirlwind."

"And I will have a fine mare who will run even faster," Falling Star pouted in reply.

Lean Bone could not resist the challenge. "Except," he mocked, "you don't approve of hunting, so you won't have a first kill."

"What in the world has a first kill to do with it?" Walking Owl asked absently, eyes intent on his weaving.

"Only that when I bring the heart of my first kill to Aunt Alabak, she will exchange it for a pony of my very own," Lean Bone replied.

Walking Owl's head jerked erect. "I beg your pardon, young man?" he exclaimed, almost dropping his work.

"Well, that is what she promised," said Lean Bone hesitantly, as if remembering too late it was supposed to have been a secret.

Walking Owl was more than disturbed, and controlled himself with great difficulty. His brow drawn in thoughtful concentration, he slowly resumed his work. Finally he looked squarely at Lean Bone and in the sternest voice said, "My son, the spirits are very serious about a man's first kill, for it guides the success of his lifetime. And every first kill must be brought to the village to be shared and celebrated with everyone, however small it be. Not to do so will see you end in starvation or under the fangs of a wild beast." His face reflecting the deep affection and concern he held for the boy, Walking Owl paused, drawing Lean Bone's eyes from their study of the ground. "You will remember?"

"Yes, Grandpa," Lean Bone answered contritely.

Looking upon the young face for yet a moment, Walking Owl removed from about his neck a lightly beaded thong with a pendant lynx tooth. "This amulet will help you remember — and more. It will shield your path and your fortunes," he said, slipping the thong over Lean Bone's head.

"To keep?" exclaimed Lean Bone, fondling the treasure.

"Wear it always," replied Walking Owl, returning his attention to the travois. "Now," he said with renewed vigour, "you can hold Trish while we fit the harness."

Only with great difficulty was the task finished, because Trish, wanting to share in the excitement behind her, insisted on turning around in the shafts and had to be held. But at length the final thongs had been tied, and Trish stood as ready and eager as was Falling Star to be taken for a walk. So it was that the children went off to tour the village and display the new travois. But it was not long before Lean Bone thought of a way to put the outing to much better use. They should go to the hazelnut grove, he suggested, and fill the bag-net.

It was in passing near Chikchik's hut that the children's attention was arrested by the familiar voices of Alabak and Walking Owl. Hesitating, the children could hear Walking Owl speaking with great emotion. They had never before heard him raise his voice in such a manner, and the sound of it fairly took their breath away in surprise and alarm. In the silence, they could overhear a bitter exchange.

"And," Walking Owl was saying, "with the heart of his first kill you would trap his spirit. You have become an evil person and are unfit to guide the lives of those children. I will not stand by and see you destroy them to feed your evil and ambitious schemes."

"You have no choice," replied Alabak. "I have told you before and I will tell you for the last time. Redwing gave the children to my care, and they will be raised by me as I see fit. Now go. And mind your own business."

"Yes, I will go, but it will be to the Chief since I cannot get satisfaction from you. May the Great Spirit forgive me that I must denounce the children's aunt."

"Go to the Chief and show him the fool you are," Alabak snapped back. "You of all people should know that not even the Chief can alter the wishes of the dead. And did I not make his boy Sun Dog well when you failed? Without me the lad would have died, and it would have been on your hands."

There was a momentary silence before Walking Owl's voice resumed. "I see it all now," he cried, to the horror of the listening children. "You have worked a vicious trick to discredit me and open your way to the Chief's confidence. Without you the boy would never have fallen ill!"

"Without me," Alabak replied, and her voice was icy cold, "the boy might well die the next time, and I doubt whether anyone could save you from an equal fate for failing a second time with the cure!"

That many a shaman had met with an untimely end when his magic failed with the life of the Chief's favourite, was known to everyone, and the open and shameless threat against Walking Owl was apparent even to the children who stood transfixed.

"Now that I am warned and know what I am facing," replied Walking Owl more evenly, "I will gladly pit my magic against yours to save the children from your hands, though it risk my life."

"Then risk your life!" Alabak sneered. "Falling Star will change her name or there will be Satan to pay, for the name 'Falling Star' is doomed to raise nothing but trouble."

Frightened now and not wanting to hear more, the children fled the scene, nor did they stop until they were well away under the cover of a nearby thicket.

Lean Bone was the first to speak, because Falling Star was still too breathless. "Do you know what?" he asked.

"No," panted Falling Star, "what?"

"I think Aunt Alabak is a witch."

Falling Star's eyes popped wide at the revelation, and she could only stare back at her brother while she regained her breath. Then at length she said, "I think we should go to the pool and think about it."

Lean Bone agreed, so that is what they did.

When they neared the pool, Lean Bone stopped and turned to his sister. "My buck should be there. Wait here while I see if I can get the drop on him again."

"Why do you always want to scare him, the nice buck? You are mean," Falling Star complained.

"Would you rather I shot him?" Lean Bone retorted, and without waiting for an answer, moved ahead steathily, his movements becoming more cautious as he approached a thicket bordering the pool. Then he dropped to the ground, and crawling to the edge of his cover, spread the leaves and peeked out. He smiled with delight because the buck was there on the grassy margin of the pool, savouring the lush growth. Lean Bone slipped off his sash, and holding one end, allowed its length to fall free. Then gathering himself, he sprang from cover waving the sash wildly and screaming, "Wolf! Wolf!" Taken by surprise the buck's head came round with a start, and with a frenzied bound into the undergrowth, he raced off, his rapid departure mocked by Lean Bone's victorious fit of laughter.

After sitting by the pool for awhile, things seemed no better than before, and now having thought and rethought the matter, Falling Star finally wiped a tear from her eye and resolved to give up her name for one that would please Alabak. Afterwards, she suggested, Walking Owl would be free and could tell them what to do.

Feeling only slightly better for the decision, Falling Star was ready to go back to the village, but just then a shooting star streaked across the clearing and off into the distance. There was nothing for it but the invitation should be accepted, and kneeling there beside the pool, despaired of keeping her special name and fearful for her grandfather, Falling Star wished. "I wish," she said, "when I give up my name it could be changed into an invisible mantle that could cover Grandpa with the greatest wisdom for healing the sick." Then looking to Lean Bone for help, hurriedly added, "Especially those who are sick from evil spells."

No one would have to be a Keep to record that wish as a Proper, which drew upon at least one of the Complements of Being. But it was also a strange wish, and since Keep was now under strict orders to investigate such things, no time was wasted. Scarcely had Falling Star hoisted her small frame onto her crutches than an auroral glow danced across the northern sky, casting a ghostly light about.

The shimmering light seemed to gather overhead and then subside, only to reappear amidst the surrounding trees. It grew brighter and brighter, turning the gathering night into brightest day. As the children fought to keep their eyes open against the blinding dazzle, it shrank into a gleaming mass on the far side of the pool. Then suddenly it evaporated, leaving in its afterglow a lone horseman who rode slowly into view from behind the trees. He drew up at the edge of the water and stopped. It was Sirgal.

To the children, he rode with a proud bearing, the horseman. The nobly cast lines of his face were heightened under the frame of a headpiece that was topped with quivering red and white plumes. A gleaming breastplate, seemingly too small to offer any protection, was emblazoned with the triunium. The elliptic-leaf pennant of Quotaris draped the silver lance in his right hand, while his left hand lightly clasped the reins of his stately white charger. Noble, too, with its flowing mane rippling in the light breeze, the charger like its master was sparingly protected, bearing only a silver breastplate and adornments to its shanks.

The children could only look upon the vision spellbound, while Trish stood her ground, hair bristling.

Sirgal broke the silence. "Hello, Falling Star. I was looking for you." His rich melodious voice was so soothing and reassuring that it banished the spell of awe, and replaced it with one of serenity.

Falling Star's natural friendliness was quick to recover from the stranger's astonishing arrival. She responded in pleasant surprise. "You know my name!"

"And I am Lean Bone," said Lean Bone, who was kneeling protectively beside his sister. His bow was over his shoulder as he had been taught to carry it within easy grasp should the need arise.

Sirgal regarded the boy with a twinkle in his eye. "Yes, I know that too," he said. Then, under an almost imperceptible movement of the reins, the charger gathered himself and glided across the pool in a single effortless leap which brought him to a stop so close to the children that they could feel the warmth of his breath.

Dismounting, Sirgal dropped to one knee in front of Falling Star and, removing his headpiece, announced, "I am Sirgal. I come from the Queen of Quotaris." As he spoke, Trish came forward first to sniff his hand and then to look up and meet the charger's equally curious sniff. Now everyone knew each other.

"The Queen of Quotaris?" Falling Star cast a sideways glance at Lean Bone.

"Quotaris is where the shooting stars are made, and the Queen is in charge of wishes everywhere." A gesture of his hand took in the entire heavens. Then he went on to tell them about the Gardinelle and how she was very interested in the way people were wishing these days. "And so," he concluded, "I came to learn more about your very strange wish."

Meanwhile Lean Bone, who could not turn his eyes from the charger, had stood up to move a little closer. "May I stroke him?" he interrupted. As Sirgal nodded, the charger lowered his head to receive the boy's admiring touch. "What is his name?" asked Lean Bone, marvelling at so fine a beast.

"His name is Welkin," replied Sirgal whose attention was being demanded again by Falling Star.

"How did you know about it, my wish and all that?" she asked, for though the horse was a beauty, she much preferred to hear more of this strange warrior's story.

"I was told by Keep who looks after these things," was the reply. Then Sirgal's eyes sparkled teasingly, and he added, "Keep said to me, Sirgal, there is a young person out there who certainly knows how to make a Proper wish. See if she learned it from her fairy godmother."

"No," Falling Star replied sadly. "I made my wish because I have to give up my name." Then she related to Sirgal her whole story, leaving out nothing and allowing Lean Bone to express his opinion of Aunt Alabak.

When the children were quite finished, Sirgal stroked his chin thoughtfully. "It would be a pity to give up such a pretty name," he said. "I think you should keep it. I am sure the Gardinelle would agree."

"Do you really think so?" Falling Star almost shouted for joy but checked herself on second thought. "And would it mean they could not touch him, spells, my grandfather?"

Sirgal pursed his lips. "I am sure that if WAND sees nothing wrong, the Gardinelle would agree to a package."

"WAND? Who is WAND?" Falling Star asked.

"WAND is the Gardinelle's wish computer," Sirgal replied.

"Wish computer?" Falling Star shook her head, greatly perplexed.

"A computer remembers things and can tell you how they add up," Sirgal explained. "WAND sorts out all the reasons for and against a wish, and says whether it can be wisely granted."

"Oh, I see. That is your shaman, WAND. You call him a wish computer." Falling Star narrowed her eyes with concentration and weighed the information.

"You might look at it that way," Sirgal replied with a chuckle. "WAND is like a shaman but remembers much much more. WAND can tell how things will work out in a twinkling and, most important, never makes a mistake."

"He is a shaman, my grandfather, and he is always right," Falling Star informed Sirgal in return.

"Except he never grants wishes," Lean Bone observed with a wistful eye on Welkin.

"I did not mean to criticize your grandfather," Sirgal hastened to say, "but thought computers sometimes cannot separate fact from fancy."

"Thought computers? Do you call him a thought computer, my grandfather?"

"Anyone who sends out thoughts is a thought computer," Sirgal replied. "That is the only way wishes can reach WAND."

"Then if WAND heard my wish, I would be a thought computer too." Falling Star waited politely in case Sirgal might want to reconsider his sweeping statement.

Sirgal nodded agreeably, but gave no sign he would be changing his mind.

Falling Star was not sure what to say next. She could remember things and add them up, but she could not say wise things like a shaman. She looked at Lean Bone and giggled, thinking Sirgal was putting them on, but quickly caught hold of herself. Finally she remarked more to herself than to Sirgal, "WAND can hear my thoughts, but I cannot hear him."

"WAND is not a person," Sirgal corrected.

Falling Star looked puzzled. Lean Bone nodded with a flash of understanding, and turned to his sister's aid. "WAND must be where they keep the bones," he whispered hoarsely.

"Oh!" Falling Star exclaimed. "He keeps them in his pouch, the bones, my grandfather."

"He does?" Sirgal raised his brow.

"Yes. It is made with lovely beaded doeskin, my grandfather's pouch. No one is allowed to touch it because it would not please the spirits. I suppose they will tell him if my wish is granted — the spirits, my grandfather?" Falling Star ventured.

"WAND speaks only through the granted wish, I am afraid," Sirgal explained.

Falling Star studied him thoughtfully. "Then I would always hear if the answer is 'Yes'," she reasoned, "but when the answer is 'No' I will hear nothing."

"That is usually the way with children," Sirgal sighed, his eyes atwinkle.

Falling Star ignored his banter. "All the same, that doesn't say when it's time to quit waiting, silence."

Silence is only what you do not hear," Sirgal smiled. "That is why important messages are usually written in signs. Signs can speak louder than words, if you read them."

"A good hunter knows how to read signs, but not girls," Lean Bone remarked for the record. "I have learned to read the forest and how to track animals," he informed Sirgal with pride.

"And how to kill them," Falling Star retorted.

"Only for food," Lean Bone reminded her.

Falling Star appealed to Sirgal. "He should learn to respect them and be kind to them, creatures that do him no harm."

Sirgal nodded agreement. "That is a commendable attitude for young people."

"It is a path of wisdom," Falling Star confided.

"Indeed?" Sirgal inclined his head with interest.

"Do you know them, the paths of wisdom?" Falling Star asked. "There are three of them, you know."

"Three paths of wisdom?" Sirgal searched his memory. "No, I do not recall them. But I do know that all important things come in threes."

"We learned them from my grandfather," said Falling Star. "They are like paths that can lead everyone towards happiness on earth."

"And it is right to kill for food," Lean Bone added.

"It is not a path, that," Falling Star objected, momentarily forgetting Sirgal while she took pains to refresh her brother's memory, though there was less help needed than Lean Bone pretended. Very much taken, Sirgal was content to listen, giving Falling Star an approving smile when, with her patience strained after doing her best, she turned to him for support.

"I like them your way, Falling Star," Sirgal declared. "Yes, your paths of wisdom are very nice. They are so very like the Three Complements of Being, the Gardinelle will be delighted to hear about them." He rose to his feet.

Falling Star straightened. "You are going?"

"But what about killing for food?" Lean Bone challenged. "Grandpa says it is right."

Sirgal took up Welkin's reins. "We will just have to take your grandfather's word for it, Lean Bone."

Falling Star leaned forward anxiously. "My wish! And how will I know if I can keep it, my name?"

Sirgal rose smoothly into the saddle. "When the day of the naming ceremony comes, you will see a full moon and a shooting star. If the star passes under the moon, the answer is 'No'. If it passes over the moon, the answer is 'Yes'." With those words he flicked the reins, and Welkin shot up over the trees, disappearing in an auroral glow that faded into the northern sky.

Finding themselves alone again, the children looked at each other. "We must hurry back and tell Grandpa," Falling Star suggested, taking up her crutches.

As they prepared to retrace their steps home, Lean Bone sensed an oppressive stillness in the air that made him stop and take note. Looking up from the pool, he could see against the fading sky a dark mass of clouds swirling into view over the cliff. "There is a storm coming," he cried to Falling Star who was already hobbling off. "We had better run for the cave."

No sooner had Lean Bone spoken than the sky became threaded with the veins of a sizzling fork of lightning. Shedding a blinding flash that penetrated into the very undergrowth of the dense forest, it signalled a crash of thunder that bounced from the face of the cliff to echo on and away down the valley.

Taken by surprise, Falling Star sank to her knees, and even Trish crouched almost flat on her stomach to steady herself against the trembling ground. Himself shaken and near blinded, Lean Bone was too intent on reaching his sister to pay much attention. Moved by the single thought to reach the safety of the cave as quickly as they could, he took Falling Star on his back and stumbled off through the trees.

The distance to be covered was not great, but with the rough ground under foot and the weight of his burden, Lean Bone found himself heavily taxed. Nor with his back arched and head bent down against the rain could he see more than a pace or two ahead. So it was that Falling Star's warning came too late. They collided with a fallen tree and tumbled in a heap under its levelled trunk while the lightning crackled all about. Almost spent, Lean Bone was willing to stay where they lay, when Falling Star shook his shoulder and pointed. There, not many paces ahead, the opening of the cave loomed out of the cliff's face, beckoning. It was enough for Lean Bone. Sliding under the tree after his sister, he raised her once more on his back, and tottering up the rocky apron of the refuge, fell sprawling onto its powdery dry floor.

Outside, the streaking tentacles of the storm had reached out over the valley, and even now illuminated Alabak's face as she leaned over the flickering hearth in Chikchik's hut. "We must have some laurel," she murmured to Chikchik, "and immediately, while the spirits are restless about."

Chikchik looked out fearfully into the storm and back into Alabak's tortured eyes. If she were weighing the wrath of the stormy spirits against Alabak's wrath if her command were to go unheeded, Chikchik must have reckoned the storm to be the lesser threat. Drawing a shawl over her head she slipped into the night, and keeping to the cover of the trees as best she could, made her way to the laurel thicket.

Chikchik spent little time judging the twigs for quality, but muttering entreaties to the spirits at every flash and distant rumble, hastily gathered a spray. It was only while retracing her steps with but a short distance to go that a soaking squall sent her scurrying for refuge under the spreading limbs of a tall tree. As she crouched against the massive bole to draw a breath, misfortune struck. At that moment the tree received a lightning stroke that streaked down its trunk, splitting it asunder and flinging Chikchik to the rain-soaked ground. It all happened so quickly the old woman was laid out unconscious without having drawn a gasp.

Waiting and impatient over the length of time it was taking Chikchik to complete a simple errand, Alabak at length snatched up her cape and went herself in search of the necessary laurel. Hurrying in the darkness, she did not see Chikchik's inert form where it lay at the foot of the blackened tree until she tripped over it. As she scrambled to her feet Alabak could not contain a stifled cry, for a distant flash of lightning momentarily exposed Chikchik's deathly face. Believing her dead, Alabak was reaching to take the spray of twigs when the hand that clutched it twitched ever so slightly, revealing a breath of life. So it was that the young witch dragged her faithful servant back to the hut, and there wrapped her in warm dry skins before turning her attention to the purpose of the twigs.

It was while Alabak busied herself over a steaming pot that an unearthly moan filled the hut. So hollow and melancholy was it that Alabak at first thought it came from beyond the grave, and all but froze to the spot where she knelt, when she realized it was Chikchik come to life.

In moments the old woman's delirious voice could be heard above the sounds of the abating storm. Sometimes groaning senseless and confused ramblings, but at other times speaking clear and lucid phrases, Chikchik began to repeat the confidences and spells of her mistress — among them the telltale phrases of Sun Dog's mysterious illness.

Alabak remained motionless, listening. Only her eyes revealed a growing concern that someone might overhear, and as they narrowed, all but spoke her evil decision. She rose and went to a far corner, returning with the familiar twisted root. "There can be no

160

place for a loose tongue," she muttered, and squeezing the root into a bowl, prepared her deadly potion, all the time eyeing Chikchik as she stirred it.

Ready at last, Alabak approached the old woman, and lifting her head, had almost pressed the potion to her lips when she paused. "Still," she muttered, "who will I find to take your place and carry out your tasks?" She remained thus thoughtful for some moments, and reluctantly setting the bowl aside, looked towards the door and sighed, "I will have to care for you myself and see that no one enters the hut until you are again well."

"Steven."

Keep's voice drew Steven's presence back from Wamwaki. "I thought you might be here. It is almost time for the Gardinelle to open the Festival of the Wishing Tree. We must hurry."

14

Embracing the Compleat Record, the tag end of a loose print-out dangling from the folds of his toga, Keep led the way to the rear entrance through which Steven had first been ushered by the gardener. This time a gleaming coach-and-four, captained by a polished coachman who looked resolutely ahead while an attendant held open the door, waited at the foot of the steps.

Even without the appearance of the Gardinelle's coach, Steven would have known this was not to be an ordinary day. Even had Keep not told him that this day was the Festival of the Wishing Tree, he would have known there was something special in store. The moment he stepped outside into the early morning, he could scent a vibrant excitement in the clear crisp air. And there across the court to whet his expectation, its rustic limbs clothed in shimmering leaves of crimson hue, stood the triunium, breath-taking in its autumn splendour.

Savouring the experience, Steven followed Keep into the plush interior of the coach, and being assigned his place by a professional bob of the attendant's head, sat backwards facing Keep.

"Her Highness expects you at the front entrance, and will go directly to the arch to start the marathon," the attendant informed them as he closed the door with noiseless ease.

The coach rocked gently as it slid into motion behind a clatter of hooves against the cobblestones, and swinging wide within the court, turned a full semicircle to make its exit alongside the stone wall.

162

"This is the big celebration," Keep said thoughtfully, as if sorting through cherished memories, "when the tree is at the height of its beauty and the binary twins are at their brightest. Yes, they will be here from all the planets of Quotaris today to compete in the contests — or to cheer their favourites who are competing. Sports, stage entertainment, orbiter racing, jousting — you will see it all," he chortled in anticipation. Then, surveying the passing wall, he sobered a little. "Confined to barracks there, Breach will have to watch it on television this time. It will not be the same in the lists though." There was a touch of disappointment in his voice. "It has always been Breach leading the blues against Sirgal leading the reds."

"Well gee," Steven exclaimed, "you would think they might let him out of jail for the celebration then."

"Not jail," Keep corrected. "Confined to barracks is not like being in jail exactly. He can do whatever he wants but may not leave the grounds. Still, it is hard punishment for a knight such as Breach, and no ranking knight has ever before been denied the right to defend his position in the lists on a festival day — at least not since Eks, that is."

However Keep might spell it, Eks sounded like Eks, and it turned Steven's mind back to the moment in the Dome when Kwah had uttered that very sound into the microphone. It was a coincidence, to be sure, but it made Steven wonder. "What happened to Kwah?" he asked.

"Kwah would not deny you had seen him in the Dome, but he refused to answer any questions." Keep jerked his head in the direction of the wall. "He is being held in the barracks guardhouse while they investigate him further."

Steven thought for a moment. "Who was Eks?"

"Eks? Oh, he was a real swashbuckler." Keep smiled over the recollection. "Yes, Eks was a mite older than Breach, and I daresay something of a hero to the young man at the time because Eks lived for the thrill of danger, and believe me he could set a young knight's imagination running. They say he committed an offence against the code, and young Breach happened to witness it, though the matter was not properly brought to light because

Breach held a comradely silence. Eks afterwards saw fit to leave Quotaris as a free lance. Some say he entered the service of Fulgor for want of a place, but no one seems to know for sure."

Steven pondered the story. Breach admired Eks. Eks left Quotaris under a cloud. Kwah was calling an Eks from the Dome. And from under the stairs he had heard someone say Breach must have had an accomplice. "Are Kwah and Breach friends?" The question popped out involuntarily.

Keep pursed his lips. "I would doubt they have too much in common, Steven. Why do you ask?"

Steven wanted to tell Keep what was on his mind, but the thought of upsetting everyone again and making himself unpopular made him hold back. Regretting he had asked the question, he answered Keep with a shrug. "I just wondered."

At that moment the coach made a sharp turn, and entering the coachway, rolled on under the marquee at the entrance to the chateau.

Sounding from the inside the Gardinelle's voice could be heard approaching, and hastening to be prepared for the royal arrival, the attendant opened the coach door. Again no word was spoken, but drawn from his seat by the attendant's body language which made easy reading, Steven found himself standing respectfully on the walk. He had not long to stand, however, for the Gardinelle was prepared to start this of all days with her customary zeal. In no time the coach was again on the move, swaying to the cadence of clacking hooves.

The Gardinelle was in high spirits, happy in the thought that this was the day of the festival, but happier still over Sirgal's visit to the little village of Wamwiki on Oulden Finftroum where a simple tribal child knew the Three Complements of Being, and had made a Proper wish. "As soon as WAND has compiled the outlook for Falling Star's wish, you must bring it to me immediately," she instructed.

Keep nodded. "I had hoped to have something by this morning, Your Highness, but there seems to be a slight holdup."

"Oh?" the Gardinelle murmured. "And how is that I wonder?"

"I find it difficult to say at the moment," was Keep's reply, "but I expect the delay will not be for long."

At the arch, the Gardinelle's coach was greeted by an enthusiastic gathering of shivering runners and sports fans who clapped a welcome as Her Highness alighted. While she made her way to the foot of the arch, Steven clambered up onto the coachman's bench to better observe the proceedings.

As might be expected at such an early hour, the Gardinelle faced an audience that could only reflect a population of early risers, confirmed runners and outdoor zealots, although she seemed not perturbed in the least by the number of fishing poles and golf bags that made up the group — nor for that matter by a few homeward-bound party-goers. Being there to encourage the marathoners in the coming test, she did so, speaking of the virtues of an exhilarating run and its rewards in added years of vigour. Then, after pausing for the wholehearted applause of the anglers to abate, she declared the day's activities to be officially opened, and reaching out, tugged at a hanging ribbon. Her effort launched a rocket from atop the arch, and at the same time released the marathoners who poured out of the starting gate and down a long road that was to end hours later at the stadium.

Rising like a lark into the morning sky, the rocket burst into the form of a maple leaf, but lingering overhead only briefly, it was wafted away to tatter slowly in the breeze. While it thus floated off in freedom, Steven again thought of Kwah and Breach, wondering whether he ought to have confided his suspicions to Keep. He continued to turn the matter over in his mind while the coach picked its way through the livening streets to the parade rendezvous, and by the time they reached the appointed spot, he had resolved to speak up the next time Kwah's name was mentioned.

The gathering point for the parade was a scene of confusion in the midst of last-minute preparations, what with marchers seeking their fellows, and other entrants milling about the decorated floats or scurrying to complete a finishing touch.

The Gardinelle's feet had scarcely touched the ground when the exuberant Muster rushed forward to bid her welcome. "Oh, how nice!" the Gardinelle exclaimed happily over her shoulder for the benefit of Keep. "Muster is looking after the children's entry again this year."

The good tidings were wasted on an empty seat, because Keep had vanished, or at least had sought to vanish by means of the opposite door. Instead he collided with the passing Thalamus, and fell against the half-opened door. Needing few facts with which to sort out cause and effect, Thalamus, supporting himself against the coach with an outstretched arm, calmly accepted Keep's stuttered apologies before wagging a finger under his nose. "Escape, my dear fellow, can be no more than the dead spot in a blink," he said, shaking his head in pity. "It is a word that is ill suited to reality." So saying, he straightened the blushing Keep's spectacles, recovered the Compleat Record from the ground, and pressing it into the unhappy man's bosom, continued on his way.

The Gardinelle had meanwhile hastened over to see the children's entry which was being prepared next to her ceremonial landau, for as always, the tots were to precede her in a position of honour. At this point the children had long been ready and impatient to be started, and some were eagerly holding the coloured ribbons of their triunium Maypole around which they would dance. As the Gardinelle approached, two were fighting over one of the ribbons.

"My, my," the Gardinelle teased, "are there not enough of them to go round?"

"The red one is mine!" cried the little girl.

"She always wants the red one!" the boy countered.

"Red is nice," said the Gardinelle, taking up an unclaimed ribbon, "but I must say yellow is very attractive. It reminds me of gold and sunshine and all that is happy and gay on such a day as this." She sighed, and caressing her cheek with the ribbon, allowed it to fall. Her back was no sooner turned than the fallen ribbon was seized by avid little hands, and while the red now lay ignored on the ground, the dispute had resumed over the yellow.

Muster had now caught up with the Gardinelle, the reluctant Keep at her side. Having failed to make his escape, Keep had accepted the penalty, and summoning what dignity he could, was

166

allowing himself to be pulled along. It was at this moment that a pandemonium had broken out beyond the royal party. Steven had seen what was about to happen, and was already on his way to join the fun. He had spied Sima who, in affording amusement for a group of knights, had just leaped into the saddle of one of their chargers. With everyone now scattering to safety, Sima clung to the frightened animal, fanning the air with her hat while two mounted knights attempted to seize the flailing bridle. Doubling with laughter, Steven gained the scene screaming cries of encouragement. "Sima! Sima!"

It required some moments for the knights to collar the horse and quiet it down. Sima, who wanted more, continued to jump up and down in the saddle until she was finally grabbed from behind and deposited on the ground. It was then she heard Steven's familiar voice, and being delighted to meet an appreciative friend, ran to hug him. By this time, too, the Gardinelle had arrived.

"Naughty Sima," the Gardinelle murmured, raising a scolding finger, only to receive an affectionate welcome from the chimpanzee in return. "Who is supposed to be looking after you?" she asked, looking around. "Where is Professor Remspruk? Sima is his charge."

No one had seen the Professor, but Steven was certain he had caught sight of Sawni beating a hasty retreat during the to-do, and wondered whether he should mention the fact, but decided it was of no account when Keep provided the Gardinelle with what seemed to be a satisfactory explanation.

"The excitement in the streets would have been enough to lure her out, Your Highness."

The Gardinelle contemplated the situation. "Someone must take her back to the chateau," she declared, and turning to Steven, put the chimpanzee in his care, saying, "Please, return her to the chateau, Steven. The coachman will see you there and back."

As Steven hurried away with his charge, Keep called after him, "I will meet you here, Steven. Tell the coachman to hurry so you will not miss anything." He cast a furtive glance at Muster, hoping she had heard his commitment.

At the chateau, Steven left the coach standing at the rear entrance while he took Sima up to the laboratory in search of Professor Remspruk. The Professor, absorbed in his work, had not even missed her, and Steven wasted no time with explanations. He was fond of Sima, but the waiting parade, jousting knights and all, was for the moment a much greater attraction. He closed the door behind him and hurried back to the elevator, just in time to see it drop out of sight. He pressed the return button, and pacing impatiently, looked out of the window.

From where he stood, Steven could see over the barracks and across the town. To his right, some distance down a side street running along one wall of the barracks compound, he could see the cluster of marathoners approaching. In the compound, a group of recruits had gathered around a television screen in the window of their headquarters building. Steven guessed they were watching the marathon, and as he looked on, one of the group consulted his watch, and ceding his place to a young recruit behind him, quietly deserted the spot. Even at that distance, Steven had no difficulty now recognizing Breach by his jaunty step and flowing curls. He watched Breach turn and make his way past the guardhouse. Drawing even with the guard, he raised a friendly hand, or so it seemed, but at that moment Steven caught sight of a shock of red hair in the barred window behind the guard, and surmised that Breach had given a signal.

Continuing without a pause, Breach made his way straight to the stable and disappeared inside. Save for the group watching television, all was quiet and peaceful in the barracks. Suddenly the stable doors flew open and a stampede of frenzied horses emerged. They galloped out of the paddock and into the alleyways, raising dust and commotion — rearing, pitching, and whinnying with fright.

In moments the guards and recruits were fully occupied in an effort to round up and corral the milling animals. While everyone was thus taken up, a shock of red hair appeared on the roof of the guardhouse, and reaching down from a stable window, Breach pulled Kwah up out of sight. Seconds later, two marathoners slipped out of the stable onto the stone wall and dropped down

168

among the passing plodders. It all happened so smoothly no one in the barracks saw the pair make their escape.

Steven watched the marathoners continue along their course for a moment or two before quite realizing what had happened, and he stared a moment or two longer before realizing that he had undoubtedly been a privileged onlooker. And there they were, Breach and Kwah, trotting along in their stolen freedom with no one around being any wiser, except for Steven himself.

Steven's initial impulse was to run and tell someone, but he hesitated, the sting of Resal's sharp tongue still being with him. His desire to help turned to annoyance with Kwah for again making him privy to his secret, and his irritation found measurable satisfaction in the thought that the two renegades would be punished when they were caught. When they were caught? The question prompted Steven to ponder his role in the matter. The Cheechikois teachings — embracing as they did the values of universal brotherhood and the rules of conduct they prescribed — placed him squarely on the Gardinelle's side, but still thinking of Resal, he contemplated the unhappy result of crossing the ill-defined line between fraternal help and unwelcomed interference. Still, if he had told Keep that Kwah could be linked to Breach through Eks, precautions could well have been taken to prevent this new dilemma. The thought nudged Steven with a twinge of guilt — a realization of having let the Gardinelle and Keep down. He owed more loyalty to his friends!

The thoughts had raced through Steven's mind, and the conclusion reached in much less time than it takes to tell. But seconds had ticked by. Without waiting for the elevator, Steven ran to the stairs and followed their downward spiral in such haste that on reaching the bottom his head continued to spin. Unable to gauge the door, he reeled drunkenly into the wall and was brought up with a thud. It was a bad start, but if nothing else the effect was to clear his head and make him think. Judging that Breach and Kwah must soon be missed, he concluded that rather than look for help, his best plan would be to take after them and not let them out of his sight.

Thus it was that Steven left the coach where it stood at the rear of the chateau, and flew out of the front entrance in pursuit of the marathoners, making a generous shortcut across the square to intercept their course in the next street. Taking up a position well behind, he was able to hold Breach and Kwah in sight without being noticed. Having never run with a marathon before, he found the pace a little awkward, but being fresh he had no difficulty holding it. Anyway, he thought to himself, Breach and Kwah will break off as soon as they are well away from the barracks.

The run was steady and uneventful as it wound through the streets, but before long Steven was feeling the disadvantage of his unsuitable shoes and close-fitting garments. He was hoping Breach and Kwah would soon make their break, when a roar of applause broke out ahead. As Steven neared the spot, he discovered that the applause was for two reasons. First of all the marathoners had just crossed the main boulevard with its ranks of parade onlookers, and along with that, the parade itself had just reached the intersection and was waiting for the marathoners to pass.

Steven realized only too well what was about to happen, for he saw the supervisors raising their arms ready to close off the flow behind the marathoners and so let the parade move on. He drew upon his unspent resources in a dash to cross the intersection, and with success in sight, reached it almost on the heels of the last contestant. Too late! A burly individual stood in his path, feet planted far apart and arms stretched wide to control the surge of fans and onlookers. Steven tried to duck around but was caught, and against his struggle, was forced back into the crowd.

"They are getting away!" Steven cried. "Breach and Kwah! We have to stop them!"

Steven's entreaties were drowned in the clarion call of trumpets accompanied by shouts and cheers. Immediately the receding runners were eclipsed by an array of knights in ceremonial dress, who trotted forward on their caparisoned mounts, lances adorned with fluttering pennants. In their lead, Sirgal, borne on the high-stepping Welkin, carried the flag of Quotaris proud and high.

170

Now surrounded by eager viewers and being crowded back, Steven jumped up and down, waving and calling out for attention. "Sirgal! Sirgal! Breach is getting away!" Alas, even those around him could not make out his words amidst the cheers and shouts, let alone Sirgal.

Steven turned and did his best to keep pace with Sirgal through the crowd, but losing ground, was overtaken by the following entry in the procession.

It was Trovia's float, decorated with golden wheat sheaves and orange pumpkins in a brilliant harvest scene. A giant, shimmering silver star rose upright in the centre, and marking the points and recesses of its five spurs, the lambent stars of Quotaris glowed. From its skyward pointing tip the great star launched a rocket that soared aloft to explode in a dazzling maple leaf of every hue. While the flickering form evaporated overhead, its parent on the float faded before the eyes of the onlookers, leaving behind only the stars of Quotaris to hover in space, whereupon the magic rings appeared, capturing the stars on their ghostly filaments which pulsed with unhurried regularity from round to oval. In turn the rings dissolved, leaving the brightening binary twins and their shifting sister planets to engage the emerging outline of a maple leaf. Then continuing the sequence, the leaf disappeared, and with a return of the shimmering silver star, a zooming rocket again flashed into the sky to begin another repetition of the phases of Quotaris.

By now compelled to stop and look, Steven watched the Phantom Express of Nisus roll into view. It was a stage coach drawn by four black horses, all adorned with coloured leaves, pentacles, and fluttering pennants. Atop the coach a masked driver dressed in black to match the horses — as were two armed guards who clung behind — was held half erect by the pull of the reins. Shades were drawn over the coach windows, but a large baggage tag hanging from the roof rack bore the word *Resolutions*. As the coach glided along, parts of the theme vanished alternately. At one moment the group would be driverless, and in the next would have regained the driver, only to lose the coach, the horses, the guards, or the wheels. But whatever was missing, it was never the pennants and garlands.

So the parade unfolded with Quotarians from all the planets — Fatania, Gom, Nubibia and the rest — all competing for the best display with the specialities of their home planets.

Along the boulevard, lines of cheering spectators jostled and craned to take in the show, while every few minutes all eyes were drawn to the sky to watch another rocket from Trovia's float burst over their heads, or to watch the Vroomers flit about with flawless precision.

Coming from the distance, the sound of youthful voices raised in laughter and song drew attention to the approach of the senior class. They were enjoying a rollicking hayride in a wagon dripping with fresh yellow straw, crimson maple leaves, and coloured pentacles. The students had somehow tricked Keep into climbing aboard, and unable to escape, he was now sitting in the straw surrounded and tightly held in place by the entwined arms of the gleeful class and by Muster's head on his shoulder. Hugging the Compleat Record in a tight embrace, he was being swayed by the bodies around him. They were singing verses to the song Steven had heard at the campfire of Wamwiki.

> *The magic of starlight*
> *All down through the ages,*
> *Romancing the dreamers,*
> *Entrancing the sages,*
> *Yet hides in its gleaming,*
> *A menace infernal,*
> *An end unredeeming,*
> *Though it be eternal.*
>
> *O starlight is charming,*
> *With sweetness disarming,*
> *Its throes so alarming,*
> *Too late you will know!*

O starlight is charming,
With sweetness disarming,
Its throes so alarming,
Too late you will know!

The unexpected appearance of Keep reminded Steven of his interrupted mission, and he responded with vigour. "Keep! Keep!" he cried, jumping up and down with arms upstretched. But Keep had little interest in the outside world. His attention was directed inwards, pondering the insensitivity of youth while longing for an early end to his ordeal.

Steven saw his chance passing away. He tried to elbow forward with a mind to slip through the barricade and reach the float. "I have to get through," he pleaded. "I have to see Keep. Keep is expecting me!" But those in front were not about to yield their places, and seeing the float distancing itself, Steven made a desperate effort to hoist himself between the shoulders in front. He succeeded only in raising himself for a better view, and peering between the heads, was in time to catch the eye of Marcie who happened to look his way. Swaying and laughing with the others, she gave a friendly wave as Steven fell back exhausted.

Behind the students, the children had all found coloured ribbons to suit their taste and were now making them ripple in the breeze as they danced around their tree.

At last came the Gardinelle's honour guard of Knights Courier, romantically clad in sparkling but scant armour. They formed a flowing tableau of rippling white capes and caparisons bearing shimmering crimson maple leaves, while above them, rising from a bed of elegantly plumed headpieces, pennants streamed from silver-tipped lances, flaunting the realm's elliptic emblem.

Drawn by four faultlessly-groomed dappled grays, the Gardinelle's ivory landau now appeared, covered with trembling crimson maple leaves. Two footmen in court attire rode the rear stirrups, their composure being sorely tried by a milling throng of youngsters who followed along, all but jostling each other under the carriage wheels. A flurry of applause traced the passage of the royal carriage as it moved down the boulevard while the

Gardinelle, radiant in a misty blue gown and sparkling tiara, acknowledged the acclaim with her winning smile and graciously raised hand.

Steven wriggled to the rear where he could more easily make his way in the direction of the parade, and hurrying as best he could, determined to catch Keep or the Gardinelle when they broke away at the finish.

His progress was at first painfully slow. After a few laboured paces he feared to be again thwarted, but soon other spectators were moving with him, and presently he was being carried along in a flood of bodies all moving in the same direction. He could see the tip of the children's tree not far off, and keeping it in view, drew reassurance knowing that Keep was just ahead of it and the Gardinelle was just behind.

Where everyone was going soon became apparent, because turning a corner, Steven perceived the silhouette of Trovia's stadium. It loomed like a half moon above the sea of heads, and was declaring a welcome to all with streaming festive banners.

Now the surge of bodies slowed and began to move with mixed purpose, some continuing towards the stadium and some milling about with less resolve. Still guided by the children's tree and favouring that direction, Steven at length found himself deposited on an incline overlooking the entrance to the stadium. Stretching from the doors to the boulevard a broad carpeted walkway waited in readiness — surrounded and isolated by an impenetrable mass of spectators. Even as Steven contemplated the scene the royal carriage arrived, to be greeted at the curbside by the Gardinelle's councillors and palace attendants.

It was the knightly Sirgal whom the Gardinelle favoured with her hand — to be assisted down — and as her feet touched the carpet, waiting children gathered in her wake to take up her train and follow primly along.

Steven reluctantly accepted the impossibility of reaching the Gardinelle's side through the packed spectators. He would have to wait until the royal party was settled inside before he would be able to join it. He turned to the stadium without waiting, thinking to gain entry while others were still absorbed in the Gardinelle's

174

arrival, but to his dismay the broad lobby was already jammed, as were all the doors going into it. He fitted himself into a waiting line with a sigh, and prepared to be patient, but just as quickly relinquished his place. Far down the side of the stadium an exit had opened, and through it the senior class was being spirited inside. Dodging and weaving, Steven covered the distance in record time, and melting into the cluster of frisky students who were being urged along by schoolmaster Stock, heard the metal door bang closed behind him. He was inside, and it would be no problem finding the royal box, he thought.

15

Steven looked around to get his bearings. He was in a vast semicircular theatre erected on a broad promontory that over-looked a clear horizon. Embracing a performing stage at their feet, the tiered rows of spectators could view, in the grassy sportsfield beyond, the open lists and tilting fences of the jousting area. Farther afield, hanging in space across the horizon, Steven could see several of the ring planets, one directly in front of the stadium and, closer in, two others, one on each side of his field of vision. As he looked, a spacecraft shot into view and streaked across the horizon while overhead a giant viewscreen, relieving the boredom of the waiting spectators, brought a close-up view of the strange craft into the stadium. Other craft like it, resting on a ramp to the side of the sportsfield, looked like stars that had been stretched out of shape, giving them a long slender nose, stubby wings, and twin-thruster tails.

Across the semicircle of seats, Steven's eye located the royal box, and searching for a connecting aisle, he started to worm his way through the standing-room crush. His shuffling progress was slowed by a group of visitors whose hostess had stopped to recite her commentary. "From the stadium you have the best view of the racing orbiters," she declared. "The planet opposite us is Mutaria, on the outer ring. Those to the side are the inner-ring planets, Nisus on your left, and Minoria on your right. The orbiters must stay in the spacetrack lanes between the two rings all the way around or they will be disqualified. At this time, of course, the outer ring of planets has shifted south, which brings Mutaria nearer and narrows the spacetrack in front of us like a lopsided doughnut. We call this narrowest section the waist. Here the orbiter lanes are crowded closer together. To lessen the chance of accidents the lanes are staggered above and below the track, and while we cannot see the lanes ourselves, the orbiter computers can identify them and signal their claims to each other. It is in jockeying for the best lanes that computer speed and pilot daring can give the fans their greatest thrills."

As the hostess finished speaking, a round of cheers from the main entrance announced the Gardinelle's entry, bringing all to their feet. Making her way to the royal box, she took her place, and in a hush that fell over the assembly, the orchestra struck up a stirring round of the *Maple Leaf Forever*. That concluded, and knowing him eager to join his fellow knights on the jousting field, the Gardinelle gave Sirgal leave, bidding him good fortune and honour. Being now given its cue, the orchestra swung into *Twinkle Twinkle Little Star*, which raised a pandemonium of applause as the Choral Society marched onto the stage chanting "Money, money, money". And the show was on!

Free again to move about, Steven renewed his course towards the royal box when on the point of turning into an aisle he was confronted by an official.

"Ticket please," the official demanded.

Steven paused, unprepared for such a challenge, then faltered, "I ... I was with the Gardinelle."

The official surveyed the figure before him, somewhat soiled and worn from the day's trial, his hair badly in need of combing. "With the Gardinelle?" He smiled, barring Steven's path with his hip while making way for an elderly couple to pass by.

"Why, I do believe it is Steven again," said the woman, stopping to examine Steven.

Steven looked up in relief at the sound of the familiar voice. It was the matron. "And still wearing our fitting," she smiled. "But look at you," she clucked, "and your hair!"

"You can vouch for the boy?" the official asked.

Steven quickly vouched for himself. "I ... I'm a visiting student ... with the Gardinelle."

"That's right," said the gardener. "He's from the school. Had a run in with him the other day."

"Oh," said the official with a wink.

"But I don't think he is such a bad boy," said the matron, cocking her head to one side with a kindly squint.

Steven drew back in alarm. He thought to call out to the Gardinelle but was too far away to be heard above the noise of the "Money, money" competition. He decided to make a run for her instead, and thinking to draw the official off balance, started with a jog to one side then sprang to pass on the other side. The official was experienced and ready. He pinned Steven against a seat with his hip. "Oh no, you don't," he cooed.

Steven squirmed. "I have to be with the Gardinelle! Tell her I'm here and you will see!"

The official took him by the arm. "Shall we tell the truant officer instead?" He looked about for someone to take Steven in hand.

Steven had visions of being questioned and unable to explain his presence — of being thrown into a reform school and held while no one bothered to tell Keep, supposing Keep still cared after hearing Steven had withheld facts from him. He wrenched free and dove into the standing line of spectators, and wriggling through them, easily eluded his pursuer.

Steven had no idea where he was going, but keeping his head down, slipped in and out, following the path of least resistance. It led him along the outer wall and down towards a front corner. Stopping behind a cluster of happy celebrants, he peered about to take stock of his position. He was to one side of the stage, opposite the royal box and a long distance away.

On the stage the search for the fastest mouth in the "Money, money" contest was promising an early completion. The solos had finished in a dead heat between a fast-talking auctioneer who could chant "money" without moving his lips, and a mountaineer who harmonized with his own echoes in a rainbarrel. Taking their cue from the passage of shooting stars across the viewscreen, quartets were now filling the stadium with harmonies in perfect unison as they chanted against time. Meanwhile, stirring everyone's anticipation while waiting for their cue to take the stage, the Vroomers were circling outside above the jousting field.

Steven gauged the distance to the royal box and pondered his chances of making a run for it. The greatest obstacle was an official whose gaze was sweeping the spectators as if looking for someone. Steven, suspecting who the someone must be, kept his head down and prepared to wait. When the Vroomers took over the stadium and necks were craned to follow their antics, he would easily slip across.

At that moment, Steven spied Resal. Clothed in a G-suit, she had just left the royal box. She was looking at her watch, and hurrying down the aisle, turned in Steven's direction to cross in front of the stage.

Resal would vouch for him even if she were still angry. The thought and the decision were as one. Steven left his cover and ran to meet her. In the corner of his eye he saw the official start towards him. Good. Resal would put everything right. But alas, in an instant Resal turned sharply, and reaching a door in the corner, disappeared through it.

Steven was committed and had no choice. Bent on overtaking Resal, he ran for the door with the official in hot pursuit.

Through the door a flight of stairs led down to a tunnel that branched to right and left. Steven hesitated, crossed his fingers, and took the left branch, arriving at the first corner in time to see Resal's heels disappearing around a bend. Conscious of the door slamming and footsteps tripping down the stairs behind, he took after Resal with all speed.

It was not a very long tunnel — no more perhaps than fifty running paces — and when Steven caught sight of Resal, she was already mounting the stairs to an exit door. Steven had drawn a breath to shout her name when he realized he would be telling the official which direction he had taken. He used the breath instead for a burst of speed, and darting up the stairs to push open the door, found himself on the orbiter ramp.

A few paces away, five orbiters were standing in a line abreast. A muffled rumble sounded from the glowing tailpipes of their twin trovium thrusters, while some distance in front, standing waist high in his pit, a controller dropped a red flag and raised an amber. Holding up three fingers to signal for time, Resal clambered through the entry port of Number Three while a mechanic ducked under the orbiter's belly to detach a cable.

Steven heard a shout just behind in the tunnel. It was all that was needed. Slamming the door behind him, he flew the last few paces and leaped through the port after Resal.

Bent over his final ground duty, the mechanic had not seen Steven's entry. He finished his task quickly, and straightening up, slipped into the port. Inside, he secured the cover, at the same time calling out to Resal, "All clear!"

Resal, intent over the instrument panel, signalled thumbs up. She touched a control, and Steven, lying breathless on the floor, felt the vibrations intensify. At the same time, the mechanic completed his entry with a single continuous swing and turned to gain his place beside Resal. Instead, he tripped over Steven and fell face forward between the cockpit seats.

Resal looked down. "Good heavens Kit!" she cried. "We are on amber and counting down. Get ready!" As the surprised Kit lifted himself up by the seat arm, Resal spied Steven underneath. "Steven! Kit! What in Trovia is that boy doing here?" She drew an impatient breath. "Never mind! Strap him in the jump seat. We have only seconds to zero."

For Steven they were the fastest-moving seconds of his life, and their passing left him sitting behind Resal and Kit, having been lifted without a word, dumped into the jump seat and strapped down like a sack of potatoes. Before he knew it, a green light had flashed and Resal's hand had swept across the control panel. The orbiter shook. Steven felt the pressure against his back, while outside a swirling cloud of vapour billowed up as the glowing tailpipes burst into streaming infernos. It sent the orbiters rocketing side by side up the ramp and out into space, leaving behind a long sweeping arc of vapour, and then they were in the spacetrack jockeying for position.

"We will fly a wide orbit to stay clear of the others," Resal instructed. "Set the guidance control to track by the outer ring."

Kit raised his brow. "That will make our circuits much longer than the others. It will call for a lot more speed to beat them."

"Whether we win or lose the race is of little account," Resal replied. "The important thing is to prove we have stable microstars and can control the energy of their disintegration."

"You are the doctor," Kit grunted, bending over the guidance computer.

In their concentration over the flight displays and control knobs, Resal and Kit ignored Steven as though he didn't exist. Steven watched the spinning indicators and flicking readouts on the instrument panel, and felt himself sinking tighter and tighter against the seat. Through a viewport in the belly, the grayish ball of a planet appeared below and drifted back out of sight.

"Jinnia falling behind already!" Kit exclaimed, looking down.

Resal made no response. She continued her study of the monitors and made entries in her flight computer, while the orbiter, its cabin disturbed by no more than a deep muffled rumble to break the silence, sped on. Ahead, another of the grayish planets hove into view and began to sink down below the orbiter's nose to pass underneath. It was all so smooth and peaceful Steven would have had no notion of hurtling along through space were it not for the ring of planets passing under his viewport. Save for his weight against the seat, it could have been more exciting to watch from the ground.

Kit's voice broke the silence. "The binaries are coming up," he called out. Steven came out of his reverie in time to see a grayish ball slide into view below, and while he watched, its twin floated out from behind.

Resal raised her head. "We are leaving the others well back," she smiled. "Hold our velocity steady as it is."

Kit busied himself over the control panel while yet another planet passed below. "We will be starting our approach to the waist in a minute. We should be reducing speed for the tighter arc unless you don't mind having the forces build up."

"Let them build up," Resal replied. "That should keep the lift jets working at maximum cruise thrust. It will make a better test of our fuel stability."

For the next while, Steven could see the needles and dials spinning about on the control panel, and felt himself growing heavier and heavier. Just when he began to wonder nervously when it would stop, Kit called out, "Passing the stadium — Trovia overhead and Mutaria below!"

Steven could picture himself in the spacetrack, streaking past the stadium as he had seen the orbiter earlier, but could not get used to the idea that here in the orbiter 'up' was 'in', and 'down' was 'out', because rocketing around the spacetrack was like being whirled on the end of a string. He remembered reading about a spinning space station, and imagined what it would be like to live in a hollow world. Looking down he saw Mutaria slide past under the orbiter's belly, and almost immediately the force on his body began to ease off ever so little. Resal held her thumbs up, and laughed with delight. "I think our souped-up fuel is working just fine. We should easily win by more than a lap."

While Kit attended the controls, Resal turned to Steven as if noticing him for the first time. "So! What are you doing here?"

"I needed you to tell the officials who I was," Steven summed up.

Resal stared at him as if not hearing properly.

"I saw Breach escape." Steven hesitated, anxious not to upset her further over Kwah, and decided it was best to leave him out. "I ran to tell the Gardinelle, but the official wouldn't let me by."

Resal drew a breath. She studied the instrument panel and spoke to Kit. "That boy and trouble seem to attract each other." After a thoughtful moment she added, "The Gardinelle heard that Breach and my brother were missing just before I came away. It held me up."

Kit's mouth opened to reply, but at that moment a crackling noise issued from the radio monitor and filled the cabin. It was followed by the controller's voice. "Number Four, you are out of your lane. Acknowledge and correct."

The controller's message was met with silence. Resal turned to Kit again. "Who is Number Four?"

182

Kit shook his head. "I have no idea."

The controller's voice sounded again. "Number Four! Number Four! Do you read me?"

Still there was no reply.

The controller's voice once again came through, this time with urgency. "Number Three! Number Three! We have lost contact with Four. Four is swinging wide of his orbit. He is in danger of crossing your path in the waist. Come in and take action."

Resal leaned towards the microphone. "Three to Control. Roger. Watching for Number Four." She turned to Kit and frowned. "His computer doesn't acknowledge our claim to this lane. He seems to be in some kind of trouble."

"If we are going to overtake anyone in the waist, our forward scanner should pick him up ahead of us just about now." Kit reached out to touch a button and watched while a ghostly outline of the spacetrack formed on the scanner display. "Yes," he confirmed, indicating a bright spot, "that must be Four. He's drifting across from his inner lane and wobbling into our fast track. Should I resolve him and take a look?"

Resal shrugged. "It wouldn't help much."

"We are overtaking him, but fast," Kit warned.

"Right," Resal agreed. "At our speed it is just as bad as head on. We had better set a wider orbit," she concluded, entering an instruction in the guidance control. "I think we can slip by."

Kit's eyes were glued to the scanner display. "At the rate he is drifting into our lane we are still on a collision course!" he exclaimed. He leaned forward. "We have to cut inside!"

"No!" Resal put out a restraining hand. "That would make too tight a turn for our speed. We should black out at the least!"

"All right!" Kit shouted. "We can revert to manual and break from the track!" His arm shot out again, this time to engage a switch.

"No!" Resal screamed, grabbing his arm. "We are too close to the outer ring planets. The gravity field is destabilizing. If you disengage our auto-guidance, we will be tumbled out of control into the asteroid belt out there!"

"What is the difference, colliding with an asteroid or him? He's zig-zagging right into our path!" Kit choked.

"Our only chance is to hold our orbit and try to zig when he zags, with a kick from our microstars," Resal panted, letting go of Kit's arm.

The distance between the spots on the display was fast diminishing. Hurriedly keying in her instructions, Resal reached for the throttles, her eyes steady on the forward scanner.

The monitor crackled again. The controllers' voice had taken on a high pitch. "Number Three! You are going out too far!"

Resal gave no sign of hearing. "Ready," she warned, and as she punched the throttles hard against the stops, shouted, "Cross your fingers!"

Steven felt a greater thrust against the seat, and in seconds saw the briefest flash of orange zip past the overhead viewport.

Kit let go a deep breath. "Missed his tailpipes by a mile!" He started to laugh almost hysterically, but the laughter was cut short. A large gray planet loomed up over the orbiter's nose, and this time remained hanging there — growing larger and larger. "Mutaria!" Kit shrieked. "Pull out!"

Resal was frantically punching buttons. The voice in the monitor was screaming unintelligibly. Already pinned to his seat, Steven felt the pressure increase even more.

"Creepers!" Steven was being crushed into his seat. Everything began to lose colour and blur. He could barely make out Resal and Kit who were both reaching for something — reaching and yet seeming unable. The orbiter began to tremble. A sheet of flames swept from the nose to blanket the viewports, and the monitor died with an unearthly squawk. Steven could no longer make any sense of things — the surroundings became unreal, detached themselves and drew farther and farther away, leaving him to sink into oblivion.

16

An awareness seeped into Steven's mind. As it grew, he began to feel the rest of his body and the now familiar pressure against the seat. He opened his eyes to the overhead viewport which was streaked and smudged with a sooty black deposit. His gaze slowly wandered over the interior of the orbiter. Resal and Kit were calmly working over the controls while the orbiter moved serenely along. Resal spoke into the microphone. "Three to Control. We are coming in." She turned to Kit. "Set the lift jets for landing."

The pressure he had become accustomed to gradually eased, leaving Steven with a feeling of weightlessness. Turning her head to look at Steven, Resal spoke to Kit. "See if the boy is all right."

Kit swung round. "How are you, boy?"

Steven nodded. "Okay, I guess. What happened?"

"We brushed Mutaria's outer atmosphere." He smiled ruefully. "Orbiters are designed for it some, but it gave us a fright." He encouraged Steven with a thin but friendly smile. "Next time you hitch a ride in an orbiter, bring your G-suit."

By the time the orbiter had settled onto the ramp, Steven was feeling back to normal. Resal herself was in high spirits. "I think the experiment was a success, but it remains to be seen what the instruments say," she confided with Kit as they climbed out to examine the scorched shell.

Steven was relieved over Resal's good humour, but could not read her intentions. He stood somewhat anxiously, wondering whether she would see him past the official. Although there were many watchers in the stadium still tingling over the excitement of a near tragedy, to Steven the experience in the orbiter seemed little compared to the unknown threat ahead. He cast his eye about for an alternative route in case he should have to make a run for it, heedless of the lingering trail of vapour which marked the orbiter's comet-like flight past Mutaria and to which most other eyes were still turned.

Kit, who was already poking around under the spacecraft, crawled out. "Our machine doesn't seem much the worse for wear," he announced cheerfully. "The panel covering your instrument package is a little glazed though. I will have to go and find some tools to get it open."

A blare of trumpets from the jousting lists, mingling with waves of applause from the stadium, reminded Steven of his interrupted errand. Across the field a victorious knight was unhorsing his last opponent, while with perfect timing, the first of the marathoners were entering the grounds. Spurred by the new clamour of encouragement to the runners, Steven, anxious to join the Gardinelle, looked at Resal. Mellowed by success, she was satisfied to wait for Kit to recover the record, and turning to the tunnel door, led the way without the need for urging.

So it was that the orbiter was left to cool off. Meanwhile more weary runners were staggering into the grounds, and mopping their heads with towels, passed over the finish line to collapse on the cool grass in the shadow of the stadium.

Emerging from the tunnel, Steven was surprised by a change in the atmosphere of the stadium. The shouting had ceased, and in its place an expectant hush had settled over the mass of spectators while they became engulfed in darkness as a course of shades was lowered to shut out the daylight.

"The festival dancers are getting ready to perform The Unfolding," Resal whispered in the gloom. "Follow me. We will have to hurry."

186

Her counsel was unnecessary, for having been caught once, Steven was now to be twice shy, and slipping his fingers under Resal's belt, took no chance of falling into the hands of the officious staff.

They barely reached the royal box when the stage brightened, and before a breathless house, a chorus of thirteen dancers pirouetted across its surface to ring their leaders in two circles, one within the other. Steven would have recognized the figuration to be that of Quotaris with no other clue than the binary Vanitas and Fastus. They were circling with the outer ring, spinning toe to toe in an embrace that opened and closed rhythmically as they rocked back over their heels to the full stretch of their arms. Illuminated by an enchanting sparkle of miniature stars that regularly fell to twinkling in unison, the costumes flared out as whirling disks which, being brought momentarily to rest while reversing their spin under the singular effect of the starlight, quivered transiently as motionless stars — except of course for Vanitas and Fastus. At such moments as the motion of the pirouetting troupe was held arrested, the twins would be seen only to rock slowly back and forth on their heels, like lovers kissing and falling away.

In a stillness that throbbed with the eerie pulse of orchestral strings, the rings slowed, stopped turning, and left the dancers spinning where they stood. Now while the flaring costumes were captured under the twinkling light to hold their stars motionless and shimmering, with the binary twins slowly rocking back and forth, a solitary figure dressed in a magician's top hat, cape and cane, mounted to the front of the stage. It was Thalamus.

Taking his position in front of the twins who began to fade and reappear on the touch and separation of their noses, Thalamus bowed, and in the penetrating nasal tones of a hawker, delivered his introduction to the dance:

> *That we are here is probable,*
> *And all about is chancy;*
> *Our blinking eyes, if synchronized,*
> *Could prove our facts are fancy;*
> *Now you who always put things off,*

And choose procrastination,
Should contemplate what might have been,
Had chance detained creation,
    Or had a bathroom-call delayed
Your sire a tick or two,
    Could you be here in someone's place,
And are you really you?

What sound could warn, what means forsee,
The Bang that loosed creation?
What signs alert eternity,
To prime our destination?
If nature's key was unity,
The Bang made faulty coining,
    For opposites alone persist,
And disappear, rejoining;
    Such wily tricks with opposites,
Defeating their detection,
    Sprung Evil forth, entwined with Good,
Confounding both inflections.

Now Good and Bad hold equal sway
In nature's rare democracy,
    For choice forsooth without the truth,
Would make of it hypocrisy;
    So Truth enlightens Right and Wrong,
As each in turn the franchise guides,
    To draw from every Quick Side tongue,
The wish that peace with them abide.
    Thus may the magic rings unfold,
A paradise delicious,
    Where Quicks in brotherhood behold,
The greatest of all wishes.

Having uttered the last line, Thalamus raised his cane, doffed
his hat, and faded away. As he did so, there again sounded a
clash of cymbals, and the dancers, regaining their spin in the

twinkling light, were overtaken by a flood of others who invaded the stage to play out the history and life of Quotaris. In the extravaganza of colour that followed, the phases of Quotaris were alternated with scenes and dances of the little constellation's planetary inhabitants. Only after tracing and retracing the star, the magic rings, and the leaf, did the spectacle reach its finale. In a flourish that saw the dancers hold the star and the magic rings in their pose, a display of exploding novas and shooting stars filled the screen overhead. Then rising as one, the audience stood in silence, while from the wings, in a grand finale, the orchestra filled the stadium again with strains of the *Maple Leaf Forever*.

With the ending of the hymn the festival had run its course. Shutters were raised and doors hurriedly opened to allow the exodus of the satisfied spectators. Any who chanced to look out to the field would have seen two of the runners sauntering towards the launching ramp like curious sightseers. Steven saw them — still with towels over their heads — and recognized them as Breach and Kwah. At last free to convey his message, he cried out to the Gardinelle, "Your Highness! Your Highness! There they go! Breach and Kwah!"

For a moment the day appeared to have been saved without Steven's intervention, for a knight who was riding by stopped to accost the runaway pair. He had clearly recognized Breach, but as it was, merely raised a friendly hand as if passing the time of day, unaware that Breach was enjoying unauthorized freedom. Taking him by surprise, Breach grabbed the fellow's lance and dragged him down from his horse with lightning speed, laying him out unconscious on the ground. At that, Kwah made a dash for the orbiters — the nearest of which stood somewhat scorched but nevertheless ready — and would have been followed by Breach had Sirgal not witnessed the affair from a distance. Charging down upon Breach, he shouted a warning. Alas, the knight in Breach gave him no choice but to mount the standing horse and prepare to defend himself, though Sirgal would have had no intention of riding against a horseless man without armour. Indeed, he had not even raised his jousting lance to the ready as he galloped up to Breach demanding surrender and expecting Breach to comply. Breach instead, handling the fallen knight's lance like a javelin, hurled it with all his might.

It was more the surprise than the force of the blow against his breastplate that unhorsed Sirgal, and before he could recover, Breach had turned away at a full gallop. Running down Kit who was hard after Kwah, he pulled his mount up sharply on its rump, and leaping off, dove into the orbiter after his accomplice. In seconds the powerful thrusters had erupted into life, sending the craft off the end of the ramp and into a long swoop that carried it far out and away.

17

Steven found himself beside Keep. They were climbing the spiral stairs up to the Dome.

"It is today they hold the naming ceremony for the children in Wamwiki over on Oulden Finftroum," Keep was saying. "It promises to be a big day for little Falling Star. Yes, a name can have a much greater effect on a person's life than is generally appreciated. Among the Quicks it is the primitives who seem to be most aware of that."

The importance of a name to the tribespeople was known to Steven, and though mothers still searched for a nice name, it was no longer with the same concern. The choosing of a name, and its effect on the life of a maid or brave, was the theme of many of Grandfather Gorse's stories. Mothers would lie awake at night fretting over a name that might displease her daughter's guardian spirit, or later on discourage the attentions of an eligible husband, or even affect the child's children yet to come. Steven wondered whether the ancient attentions would be much different.

"Of course, our own day is not too clear," Keep went on. He fondled his sheaf of printouts. "We are still waiting to hear of WAND's clearance before sending the sign that Sirgal has promised. Not that the Gardinelle is short of problems, what with the state of wishing all over the Quick Side."

"And the orbiter, too," Steven put in regretfully.

"Yes," Keep nodded. "Still missing. Though the tower

tracked it straight to the Dipper and into an area where Fulgor's scouts were thought to be hanging about."

They arrived at the Dome to find Reefer engaged in earnest conversation with the Gardinelle.

"Resal is working long hours to prepare a new test," Reefer was saying. "Everyone was too busy watching Resal to see what happened to Number Four, so it is missing too. Until Resal's orbiter is located, or until Breach and Kwah can be collared, we just won't know whether it was all planned to steal the experiment."

"But so elaborate," the Gardinelle demurred. "Who could have foreseen that the orbiter would have to be left sitting on the ramp as it was? It may be that Breach simply took the orbiter to express displeasure. They could have lost control and become helpless passengers."

"I think not," replied Reefer, shaking his head. Breach is foolhardy enough to do anything without much question, but not Kwah. He is a knowledgeable technician and knew what he was doing."

"Then you do not think they could be lost in either the orbiter or its wreckage — wherever it may be?" The Gardinelle shuddered at the thought.

"The course to the Dipper was well set. It was no doubt their firm intention to get there — taking the experiment with them," was Reefer's confident reply.

The Gardinelle drew a breath and sighed.

Keep, who had been standing quietly, took advantage of the lull to clear his throat respectfully. "You asked for me, Your Highness?"

"Oh, my dear Keep," she exclaimed eagerly. "I know you need no prodding, but I was wondering about the child Falling Star who wants to keep her name. I would like to have that much settled for now, at least."

"Yes," Keep replied, "I knew that was it. I brought the latest update."

The Gardinelle accepted WAND's record, and reading aloud, raised her brow questioningly.

192

```
UPDATE TENTATIVE
INDICATIONS FAVOURABLE BUT ERRATIC
FINALIZED SCAN TO FOLLOW
```

She set the paper aside. "But this means we cannot yet send out the sign that Sirgal has asked for."

"Not yet, Your Highness, I am afraid," Keep apologized.

The Gardinelle knitted her brow. "That could be cutting things rather fine, my dear Keep. Have you any idea where the trouble lies?"

"It may be only my imagination, Your Highness," Keep said thoughtfully, "but since this affair with Breach and Kwah started, WAND has been taking longer than usual with scenarios for the wishing on Oulden Finftroum."

Steven shifted self-consciously, and Reefer raised his unease. "It sounds to me like Fulgor," the Chief of Security interjected.

The Gardinelle nodded. "It seems to me that Fulgor's growing presence must be taken as an indication he is planning to challenge us more seriously than we first thought. You must redouble your efforts to locate the orbiter, my dear Reefer, so we might know whether Breach and Kwah have gone over to him, and especially whether the microstars could be involved." She returned her attention to Keep. "It would be well to program Sirgal's sign for automatic release if WAND's final scan proves favourable," she instructed. "Sirgal has already left and will be available in case anything goes wrong." She reached for the cosmoscreen control, and pressing the button, brought Wamwiki into the room.

The screen brightened in time to catch Walking Owl mounting a hillside, behind the children. Aided by a tall staff that was banded with many colours and tipped with ribbons, he was shepherding the children single file up the side of a small hill at the edge of the village. Well in the lead, Lean Bone arrived at the top first, and without stopping, ran across the bald crown to hop-skip atop an old vine-covered stump. He stood looking down towards the village with one eye on his sister's progress. Breathing hard from the climb, Falling Star emerged from the path and drew aside, leaving Walking Owl to pass by while she rested on her crutches.

Walking Owl continued to the centre of the clearing where he halted, and leaning over his staff, looked down on an arrangement of flat, coloured stones. They were set in a rough semi-circular pattern about a tilted stake, and in the bright sunshine, the stake's shadow lay in a sharp line across the centre of a white stone. Walking Owl dropped to one knee, and first measuring the stones with his eye, laid the staff across them, being careful to match the touching colours of the staff and the stones.

"The neighbours are arriving from all over, Grandpa!" Lean Bone called out. He was shading his eyes from the sun. "I see two canoes on the river, and a file of Maliskaps following the south bluff."

"Yes, my son," said Walking Owl without looking up, "the ceremony offers a chance to see a truce crowned with friendship."

Having joined her grandfather, Falling Star knelt beside him. She passed her hand back and forth through the shadow. "It comes back to the very same spot every year, Grandpa, the shadow?"

"Every year, my little Star. When it cuts the green stone I know it is time to lead the villagers into the field for seeding; when it cuts the red it is again time to bring in the harvest. Yes, each stone marks a day of importance when the spirits are to be consulted, and the shadow faithfully picks each one out in turn as the year passes."

"Unless someone has moved a stone." Lean Bone had jumped down from the stump to tease Falling Star with his comment.

Falling Star looked at Lean Bone with alarm, and turning back to Walking Owl, quickly asked, "Can it be wrong, the shadow?"

"Have no fear," Walking Owl assured her, leaning over to remove an unwanted weed. "This is the right day. The staff will always verify the stones in their places."

Falling Star screwed up her nose at Lean Bone. "See! Grandpa knows a lot more than you. And it will be full for sure, Grandpa, tonight, the moon?"

"Unless there is a cloud," Lean Bone teased, and jumping back onto the stump cried, "I think I see a big cloud coming up already."

"When a spirit appears before you as Sirgal did, and tells you you will see a full moon," Walking Owl said quietly, "you will see a full moon." He patted Falling Star's head. "And I am sure he will send the sign," he added encouragingly.

"She wants to call me Moonchild," Falling Star murmured with a wry face. "Should we have told her about him, Aunt Alabak, Sirgal?"

Walking Owl sucked his tooth and reflected for a moment. "When the sign comes should be time enough," he suggested. "And now we must get back or the sun will be set."

Falling Star needed no coaxing. She struggled onto her crutches and started for the path. "Beat you down, Lean Bone!" she cried.

Lean Bone hitched his bow over his shoulder and allowed his sister to very nearly gain the head of the path before he shouted, "No you won't!" Quickly nipping past her, he slid to a halt in front. "Grandpa says I always have to go ahead in case you fall," he reminded her, and began to lead the way down.

In the village the bustle had been mounting with the arrival of neighbouring tribespeople, and now the sounds of talk and laughter carried afar. Those with a passion for gambling had already formed a circle and were wagering such valuables as they had over their favourite guessing game, which was to guess the number of sticks that were hidden in the clenched hand of the one who was the keeper. A din of whoops and shouts rang out from the group each time a successful guess saw the sticks change hands, and leading off with the cry "How many? How many?" the new keeper would start a fresh round of guessing while the pile of wagers grew in front of him.

The children had gathered together. They were singing and sharing with each other the account of their search for an adult name, but for once Falling Star did not join her friends. Instead she had long chosen a place where she could sit with Lean Bone and watch across the compound for the rising moon. "Bring us the bearskin to sit on," she persuaded Lean Bone. "He said from here we will be able to see it rise between the hills, Grandpa, the moon."

That Falling Star was beginning to feel the strain of her wait as the afternoon drew towards its close, was evident in the more frequent turn of her head in the direction of the moon's expected arrival. On each occasion, she would close her eyes and cross her fingers, and her lips moved ever so slightly without making a sound.

When the sun had dropped close towards the hilltops, two large bonfires were built at the edge of the compound while around them many hands lent themselves to preparing pots of steaming food. Amidst the aroma of the festivities and the clamour of happy revellers, an area between the fires was made ready for the attractions to come, for after the sun touched the hilltops darkness would follow quickly, and the naming ceremony would be held by firelight. In the meantime the villagers and guests were encouraged to take over the empty stage and exercise their talents for singing, dancing, and pantomime. With everyone eager to perform, there was no shortage of entertainment, and whatever was offered was received with cheers and jocular catcalls, to the enjoyment of all.

A momentary lull was filled with a chorus of shouts from one side, and moving across the stage to a rhythmic drumbeat, a group of masked dancers shuffled and twisted through a ritual dance paying tribute to the spirit of renewal and growth. Their gaily fashioned costumes were decked with the leaves and flowering sprigs of familiar plants, but their masks, draped with clusters of long stringy hair and faced with brightly painted features carved with toothy grins, were more hideous than humorous.

Their dance finished, the group formed a semicircle. One dancer, whose robe and headdress were fashioned with the seasonal foliage of the maple, separated from the line. To a quickening drumbeat, he executed a lively dance, and for the benefit of a boisterous group of young people, demonstrated an intricate step rarely seen by the villagers. The young people took up the beat, clapping and chanting, but their words were scarcely those of the ritual chant.

> *The faces in a crowd can be*
> *Amusing things to gaze upon,*
> *Depending on your point of view,*
> *Or where you might be looking from.*
> *Though many faces are a front,*
> *Pretending to be stern or kind,*
> *At times they are a happy mask,*
> *That covers up a bear behind.*

The song was met with smiles and chuckles from most of the villagers, but the elders exchanged scandalized glances and made signs of disapproval for what they saw as disrespect for the spirits.

By now the twilight shadows had emerged with the darkening night, and while everyone made themselves comfortable facing the stage area, the bonfires on either side were heaped with logs to spread more light and cheer over the proceedings.

By now too, the moon had brightened the horizon and was slowly emerging from the hilltop. Watching it rise, Falling Star found herself facing the moment of truth. Suddenly all the possibilities that had been so easily hidden behind a cheerful smile loomed large and real, and her anxiety grew in bounds. As if seeing the moon for the first time, her eyes widened. She covered her mouth to keep the doubts inside but could not contain them.

"What if he has been too busy to talk to her about sending it, Sirgal, the Gardinelle, the sign?" she gulped.

Lean Bone could see that teasing was no longer enough to keep her lively imagination in check, but at a loss for better encouragement, could only take his sister's hand in silence.

"What if he has mistaken the day? Or maybe he could just have forgotten," Falling Star murmured.

Lean Bone remembered Walking Owl's reassurance. "When a spirit says he will send a sign, he will send one," he repeated with conviction.

With all else approaching readiness, Walking Owl appeared out of the shadows. In the flickering light the spreading wings of his headdress seemed to flutter with life. A feathered mantle which he had thrown over his figured doeskin robe for the occasion gave an indistinctness to his outline, allowing him to invest the affair with the mystique of his calling. Shaking his rattles to drive away the evil ones and encourage the children's guardian spirits to smile upon them, he circled the stage with a slow shuffling gait. As he took his place on the threshold of the stage in front of the Elder Women, the masked dancers snaked once more into the light, stepping high to a lively beat in anticipation of the happy event.

Patiently holding vigil and daring not to blink, Falling Star's eyes were sore from staring, and still no sign had come. She was now beginning to believe her worst fears, and adding to them she could see Alabak looking about her with growing impatience. Disappointment and resignation creeping over her drawn face, she rose slowly and reluctantly, preparing to join the group of parents as if to attend her doom. At that moment, the masked troupe ended its dance, and while his colleagues drew back from the firelight to make way for the ceremony, the Maple Dancer pirouetted across the stage, coming to a finish in a pose with both hands pointing to the sky. All eyes turned in the direction of his imperative gesture, to behold the silent moon hovering over the hills in its radiant fullness. At that very instant, a star broke over the horizon and shot straight towards it.

Clinging to her crutches, or rather hanging from them, Falling Star stopped and held her breath to look on the phenomenon, spellbound. Before her riveted gaze the star seemed to hesitate for an eternity as if unsure whether to go over or under the moon's gleaming orb, but finally careening over the top, it swept on across the trees and disappeared over the hills. No one could have missed the unusual spectacle, and certainly no one in Wamwiki's compound. The whole gathering drew a single breath and allowed it to escape in a long enthralled "Ooooh!" without anyone having the presence of mind to make a wish.

With the star gone, the memory of its passage seemed unreal, and as the tribespeople turned to look at each other for reassurance, the scene became bathed momentarily in a stunned silence. Then in the rear a round of clapping could be heard, and gathering strength, swept over the compound to reach the Maple Dancer in a wave of cries and applause for his superb timing, if not for his authorship of the happening.

Now Falling Star breathed again, and her relief was apparent in a happy smile as she quickly hobbled off to face the ceremony.

While everyone was thus getting settled again, the masked dancers renewed their dance, shuffling about the stage to a rapid drumbeat. It was while Falling Star was working her way around them that the Maple Dancer brushed past her. As he did so, she heard a voice say, "Take heart, Falling Star."

There was something strangely familiar about the voice — especially its friendly reassuring tone — that made Falling Star pause and wonder. But by the time she overcame her surprise and had turned on her crutches to look one way and another for the owner of the voice, there was no one close by. She looked for the Maple Dancer but could only see that he had taken up his position with his fellows. Puzzled, she bent over her crutches and continued on her way to join the other girls.

Completing the last detail, the parents and children were assembled on opposite sides of the stage, the parents around one bonfire, the children around the other. Satisfied that all was now in readiness, Walking Owl rose before the Elder Women, and raising his arms, sounded his rattles for attention. For a moment all was still as the participants gathered themselves expectantly for the start of the ceremony, but before a nod could be given, there was a movement among the masked dancers. Once more the Maple Dancer stepped forward, and turning to the children, broke into song in so rich and clear a voice as to compel a hush over the assembly.

What word did call upon this earth the orchid's bloom?
What word invoked the starlit sky, the lover's moon?
What trembling lips did gasp before those prospects rare,
Inventing sounds that could such silent charm declare?

What hearts upon their cradled blessings cannot gaze,
But searching deep, find only beggared words of praise
To clothe those thoughts that love alone can testify,
And failing words, discover names to say them by?

Wherefore the ardent poet by a maid enrapt,
Would in the smithing of impassioned lines entrap
The sounds, that lyric words will ever seek in vain,
To speak his heart as does the breathing of her name.

When the sound of the Maple Dancer's voice had died away, Walking Owl motioned the first child to approach him. As she joined him in the centre of the stage he raised his arms, and with a dexterous quiver of his frame, made the rattles fairly buzz. Having so warned off the evil ones he stood over the child while her mother spoke in praise of her and her chosen name. All eyes turned then to the spokeswoman for the Elders, who after first consulting her council, gave a nod of approval. Once again making the rattles buzz, Walking Owl pronounced the chosen name in a voice for all to hear, and then calling for the benediction of the child's guardian spirit, allowed her to cross and rejoin her mother, to the applause of the well-wishing audience.

Last in line, Falling Star at length made her way slowly towards her grandfather, amidst shouts and cheers of encouragement from all sides. When quiet had again fallen, it was Alabak's turn to speak. She first moved closer to the fireside, and looking into the flames, made an obscure sign before turning to face the Elder Women. In a strong voice that rang with victory she declared, "This unfortunate child, who was sent into the world stricken and orphaned by an insensitive Fate, and who has been forced to bear a luckless name, may now look forward to being smiled upon by more favourable fortunes with the new name Moonchild."

There was another burst of applause because everyone wished Falling Star well, and the Elders, too, took little time to nod their agreement. Walking Owl turned without a word and looked with affection into the eyes of his little granddaughter. She needed no other encouragement. "No!" she cried. "I am Falling Star. I want to keep the name she wished me to have, my mother."

At first stunned, Alabak's temper quickly rose to the occasion. "That is not the child's idea. That is the idea of this meddler," she hurled at Walking Owl. "As guardian by her mother's dying wish, I must act to set the child's life on a proper course. I demand the name Moonchild be pronounced!"

"Is this true?" the spokeswoman of the Elders asked Walking Owl.

"It is true my daughter Redwing put the care of her children in the hands of their aunt Alabak. It is not true that I have influenced the child in the choice of her name," Walking Owl replied.

"Do you not think it best to accept the guidance of your guardian aunt who cares for your welfare?" the Elder spokeswoman asked Falling Star.

"He came out of the sky on a white horse, my guardian spirit Sirgal, and told me I should keep my name," was the polite but firm response, "and that is what I want."

"Your guardian spirit appeared and told you that?"

"Well," replied Falling Star, "he said he would tell the queen, my guardian spirit, and if the shaman of the spirits said it would be all right, he would send a sign. It would be a star that passes over the moon, the sign. Now it has happened. Everyone saw it happen."

"Nonsense!" Alabak interrupted. "The child has been very disturbed lately and is carried away by a mere coincidence. Her grandfather puts ideas into her little head and she imagines them to be real. She is in great need of my care and attention." She glared at Walking Owl. "And without interference!"

"Did Walking Owl bring you the guardian spirit?" the Elder spokeswoman questioned Falling Star.

"No. My grandfather taught me the three paths of wisdom, and my guardian spirit said the shaman of the spirits would be pleased with that."

The Elder spokeswoman showed no surprise at Falling Star's story because she knew from long experience that children of

Falling Star's age often came to be visited by their guardian spirits. "How did he come to you?" she pressed.

"I made a wish because I was afraid."

"You were afraid? What were you afraid of?"

"I was afraid of Aunt Alabak. Of what she might do."

The Elder spokeswoman studied Falling Star in silence before calling her council to put their heads together. After a moment's deliberation they beckoned Walking Owl to join them, and continued their consultation. There was disagreement, because Walking Owl could be seen to shake his head several times. A murmur of impatience began to rise from the gathering, and grew with the delay. At length the Elder spokeswoman raised her hands for silence, and waiting for everyone's undivided attention, delivered her verdict.

"It is our conclusion," she declared, "that the child is being pulled between her aunt and her grandfather. It is our ruling that Alabak should be left to guide the child without interference."

Confusion showed in Falling Star's face as she realized what the words meant. She quickly turned her face away from the spectators to hide her bitter disappointment. Alabak, smiling triumphantly, made another of her curious signs, and flung out her hands to say, "That's that!"

Not knowing which side to favour, all eyes moved back and forth between Alabak and Walking Owl. But the Elder spokeswoman had not quite finished. "We accept that the child, being afflicted as she is, has made ardent prayers to her guardian spirit who has answered her. She will, therefore, keep the name of her choosing and will be called Falling Star."

Pleased with such a fair solution, everyone cheered the Elder spokeswoman, but Alabak's smile quickly changed to a scowl. "If I am to raise the child it is my right to say what is best for her," she cried. "I cannot accept the name her mother gave because it was ill chosen and has brought the child nothing but ill fortune!"

"What the spirits have set their hands to cannot be questioned," the Elder spokeswoman replied. She looked at Walking Owl. "Pronounce the name," she instructed.

Walking Owl turned to his little granddaughter who had all this while remained hanging from her crutches awaiting the verdict. Though her face was pale and somewhat pinched from a day of anxiety and the enervation of having her hopes raised and dashed, the trial was already forgotten in a cheerful smile. Walking Owl raised the rattles above his head, and making them buzz as never before, called out the name Falling Star in a voice that carried over the shouts and cheers of the villagers. The masked dancers, rejoicing in the outcome, leaped forward to thread their way in and out with a lively rhythm.

Angered beyond measure, Alabak had no intention of seeing things rest as they were now. With no thought but to reach Chikchik's hut where she could consult her omniscient flames on a plan of action, she spun on her heel and broke away from the milling crush of parents. Hurrying across the stage, she bumped against a masked dancer and drew back with an impatient snarl. She stepped aside to go around him, but whichever way she moved he continued to block her path. With mounting anger she looked about and could only see a ring of grinning masks. Caught in their circle, she turned to find herself looking into the mask of the Maple Dancer. She could not divine what or who was behind the mask, but the voice that issued from it was soft and mocking as it lent words to the rhythmic chant of the dancers.

Lies so white from little misses,
Not repaired by timely stitches,
Turning dark in thoughts capricious
Grow beyond the cure of switches,
Spinning dreams of crowns and riches,
Thread the mules of busy nixes;
Mystic words and rites pernicious,
Waxing dark in schemes ambitious,
Weaving webs in covert niches,
Yield at last to hidden glitches:
Little white lies, then black wishes,
Changes pretty girls to witches!

Their chant finished, the dancers opened a path for Alabak to escape. She swept out of the ring in a fury, but once free, turned to face the Maple Dancer, for she was not to be intimidated, and lashed him with a torrent of angry words.

A cowering face gives ought for fright,
Nor saucy words that have no bite,
But sauce I'll give in wordsabout,
The sharper seasoned inside out,
For flames behind that mask will peek,
And you'll pay dearly for your cheek;
Before the glowing coals shall die
And spelling words their mystics cry,
Beware a web discretely hides,
Partakes a trap, and veils a lie,
And sleep in peels from potion's pot,
Brings dreams to seal a meddler's lot!
I'll mend white lies and wishes black —
With stitches from a witch's sack!

The final line was flung back over her shoulder as she wheeled away. Fleeing into the darkness, she muttered curses and threats of dire punishment on the heads of those who stood in her way.

Happy that she had kept her name, but concerned over Alabak's anger, Falling Star was thoughtfully making her way to rejoin Lean Bone. So taken up with her worries over Sirgal's tardy sign, she had not stopped to consider what might be the consequences of Alabak's disappointment. Now the question could not be ignored. She had not taken many steps when she met Lean Bone coming towards her with the bearskin over his shoulder. "She was not at all pleased, Aunt Alabak," she reported.

"I know," Lean Bone agreed.

Falling Star expressed her new fear. "Do you think she will blame Grandpa?"

Lean Bone shrugged. "Maybe. Or maybe she will blame the Elder Women."

"Well, what should we do now?" Falling Star asked hopelessly.

As if to answer her question, the masked dancers, who were doing a final circuit of the stage, shuffled by. As they passed, acknowledging Falling Star with friendly gestures, she heard the familiar voice again. This time it said, "See you at the pool when the shadow touches blue."

Falling Star looked up and laughed. Now she knew the voice. "It's him!" she cried. "It is Sirgal." But before she could reply with an enthusiastic "Yes", the dancers had left the stage and were melting into the shadows beyond the firelight.

18

Sitting quietly at the fireside in front of her hut, Chikchik had let the flames die down and was nodding dreamily when Alabak arrived. Continuing in her fury, Alabak snatched the poking stick from Chikchik's listless hand, and stirring the fire with a stroke that sent sparks sailing off into the night sky, shook the old woman out of her reverie with a start.

"They won't long hide from me behind those masks!" Alabak raged. "And that Maple Dancer! I'll give him white lies and black wishes!"

Not having seen Alabak in such a mood before, Chikchik pulled her shawl tighter over her head and ducked into the hut, retreating to the farthest and darkest corner to be well away from any stray bursts of her storming mistress.

Churning the coals with a final impetuous thrust of her stick, Alabak drew a handful of grains from her pocket. She tossed them over the coals and watched a cloud of angry black smoke rise and swirl off into the darkness. From far distant the bay of a wolf wafted back in an eerie lingering answer. Moved by the sound, Alabak began to dance slowly around the flames. Growing more and more excited she gave rein to her feelings until finally, wild eyed and carried away, she flung up her arms, and throwing back her head, hissed the most witchful words she could summon.

Vengeful thoughts and blackest wishes,
Writhing brutes in fires perditious,
Coals that hold the smouldering answer,
Now unmask the Maple Dancer.

Her emotions exhausted she sank to her knees, and preparing to receive whatever guidance was forthcoming, fixed her eyes on the coals, offering up her mind to the hypnotic spell of their magnetic glimmer. And what came was quite beyond anything she had hitherto invited of her ritual incantations, let alone conjured up. For even though the night had long since fallen, a greater and deeper shadow now fell across the scene, bringing down a chilling air that congealed the dancing flames into a weird quiescent glow. The sombre aura that descended with it had scarcely claimed the stillness before a spine-tingling wail, half screech and half whinny, shattered the night.

Shocked back to her senses by the piercing cry and a bedlam from the frightened crows above, Alabak started to rise but instead became rooted to the spot, an involuntary scream lodging unuttered in her throat. For sweeping out of nowhere, there suddenly loomed over her what seemed to be a monstrous apparition with bloodshot eyes and fuming nostrils. Mounting it, a lesser form sat motionless, peering at her with eyes that were set in a pallid ghostly visage. Under the mute scrutiny, Alabak had neither the power to move nor the will to speak, but as her eyes grew to penetrate the gloom, she could distinguish more clearly the form of an armed rider on a spirited black horse.

A cold grating voice that welled out of the rider at length broke the uncanny silence. "Hello, Alabak," it said, "it seems to be high time we got acquainted."

"Who are you?" Alabak managed to stammer when her pounding heart slowed to a less violent beat.

"I am Breach, serving Fulgor."

"Breach? Fulgor? I do not know you. What do you want?" Alabak demanded.

"I was under the impression it was you who wanted something," replied Breach. "We are always available for vengeful thoughts and blackest wishes, Spy and me," he said with a mirthless laugh and a twitch of the reins that made Spy rear.

"Oh," gasped Alabak, scarcely knowing what to make of the situation. "You were snooping."

"Yes, of course. I came to hear your proposition." The words were followed by what could have been a chuckle.

"I have no proposition. I was seeking the name of a masked dancer who I would make to answer for his cheek," said Alabak who was now recovering from her initial shock.

"And what would you give to see this masked one suitably punished?" Breach asked.

"What would I give? What would I give?" Alabak spat, and then not knowing in precisely what values the stranger dealt, she could not think what would be an attractive offer, so could only finish by muttering, "What wouldn't I give!"

"In that case," Breach returned, "we can probably be of service to each other." Then after a pause, "Your masked dancer is a person for whom I too have little use. He goes by the name of Sirgal."

"Sirgal?" Alabak fairly leaped to her feet. "Sirgal? I know that name. It was spoken by my charge Falling Star as her guardian spirit."

"No!" Breach's tone exulted with disbelief. "Falling Star's guardian spirit. What incredible luck!" As if to rejoice with him, the fire regained its cheery brilliance.

"How do you say that?" Alabak demanded. "He is a cheek," she added, feeling her old self.

"Oh yes," Breach added, "oh yes. He is always butting into people's affairs, that one. Perhaps this time we can singe his nose."

"I want more than a nose! And more than a singe!" Alabak cried. "And if you have found him such a nuisance, why have you not done something before?"

Breach scowled unpleasantly at the rising tone of Alabak's voice. He might have tried to explain how easy it was for Sirgal to skip around unseen, but he chose not to. Instead he rasped, "Watch your tongue young woman, or I will take it and leave you

208

with only the voice of your pet crows." At the same time, his great steed reared nervously, causing Alabak to draw back so sharply she stumbled to one knee.

Alabak had never met the man who could truly instill her with fear. Breach's opening words, indeed the fact he spoke at all, had eased the initial fright of his strange arrival. But there was something about him that stirred her with uneasiness. His voice and his laugh raised visions of phantoms in a stony graveyard. She could see the glint of his lance in the firelight, and his shield was unlike the leather bucklers of tribal warriors. Still, he was only a man, and her anger accepted the challenge. Without bothering to regain her feet, she flung a handful of dirt and followed it with a volley of words.

"And you can watch what you are doing, or I will turn you into a...." The words were cut short, for Breach, with a quickness that mocked the eye, twirled his lance in a flashing spin than sent Alabak flying backwards into the dust.

For a moment Alabak lay sprawled in confusion, and as her senses again took charge she was conscious of her tingling flesh. Yet the lance had certainly not touched her. The stranger had tricks up his sleeve, and it brought back her initial dismay. From where she was looking up, it was all again much as when Breach had arrived. He sat pale-faced looking down from the back of his wild-eyed steed, surveying her silently with unblinking eyes as if from behind a mask. And again he was the first to break the silence, but this time the voice was colder, if anything, and had lost its hint of sardonic humour.

"I warned you about your tongue, angel. But since we have decided to work together, we'll say no more about it this time." He paused, imparting a veiled menace for the next time.

Alabak stared back without speaking.

"Now, I will tell you what you are to do," Breach continued. "First you will find out where and when Falling Star gets to meet our friend the guardian spirit. Then I will tell you what to do next."

Alabak remained silent.

"Is that clear?" Breach's mount reflected his impatience.

Alabak slowly swallowed a rebellious answer. She met his gaze with mixed feelings of anger and respect. The evil glint in the eyes that peered at her from an expressionless face left no room for evasion. Yet he was to be her ally, and the question of who would become the master and who the slave could wait. She drew a breath and nodded. "How will I find you?" she asked grudgingly.

"Just light a fire," he replied, turning his dancing mount, "and call for your guardian, angel!" The last words were thrown back over his shoulder with laughter that was left echoing derisively as he swept away into the night.

Alabak rose to her knees and spat defiantly in his wake.

Suddenly the image of Wamwiki vanished. Steven blinked and emerged from his dreamlike concentration. Looking about he saw the Gardinelle's hand draw away from her remote control.

"So, Your Highness," Keep observed, leaning back to look at the Gardinelle unhappily, "now we know."

"Yes, Breach seems to have gone over to Fulgor," the Gardinelle sighed, accepting the fact with reluctance. "Council will have to be informed of this turn of events."

The sound of Breach's departing laughter was still ringing in Steven's ears. It was a chilling sound, the more so because coming from Breach it lent strength to Alabak's threat of revenge — a threat that menaced not only Sirgal and the efforts of Falling Star and Lean Bone to save their grandfather from staking his life against Alabak's secret potions, but a threat that could derail what Steven had taken to be a replay of the legend with its coming revelation of the miraculous balm. Breach had, in fact, added a whole new dimension to the contest between Walking Owl and Alabak. It left Steven at a loss to comprehend how a trampled flag and the trespass of an adventurous knight against the celestial home of the wispish Dogtrolytes could become a struggle between the forces of good and evil in a far-off Cheechikois village. That Breach could so invade Wamwiki , and on the side of a scheming witch, filled Steven with indignation in any case. It was true he had frowned on Breach at the very start rather for his having disappointed the Gardinelle than for the quality of his crime even though the Gardinelle had more than justified her censure. But upset now by Breach's lengthening shadow over the whole story, Steven was given reason to stop and think more seriously on the knight's faculty for wrongdoing. All in all he found himself faced with the simple truth that Breach was lacking in moral virtue and would be at odds with right-minded people wherever he went. He was a menace to Wamwiki and everyone's purpose, and as Steven thought about it, Breach's unwarranted interference now filled him with more anger than dread. He was no longer a mere sympathiser of the Gardinelle, and no longer a mere spectator of an ancient legend — he was, if anything, a player. "We must warn Sirgal!" he blurted.

Steven's exhortation was lost in the reverberations of a door that had slammed shut behind a clatter of hurried feet on the stairs. A voice carried above the noise. "We have word on the orbiter!"

The source of the commotion, Reefer, immediately burst upon the Gardinelle's group. "Your Highness," he wheezed, "we have word on the orbiter!" He stood with his potbelly palpitating from the climb.

The Gardinelle turned from Keep and looked at Reefer without speaking. Her silence invited the details of what was almost an anticlimax to the scene she had just witnessed.

Reefer fumbled his notebook out of a breast pocket while catching his breath. "It was abandoned not far from where our tower lost touch," he announced.

"Abandoned?" Resal, drawn along in Reefer's wake, had appeared quietly behind him.

Reefer half turned towards the sound of Resal's voice. "Fortunately our watch on Mizar caught its signature during the time it circled and landed on Alpha."

Now fully resigned to her brother's defection, Resal was more concerned about her experiment. "And did the patrol go after my instruments then?"

"They were too late. They say that one signature made a landing, and immediately afterwards two made a departure — one heading in the direction of Roth, the other straight into the sun. There was nothing to see by the time our patrol got there. Clearly Fulgor's people picked up our men, accessed the orbiter's computer, and fired it into the sun to cover their tracks and...."

"And the theft of my work," Resal concluded.

"That seems very much it," Reefer agreed. "It is rumoured that Breach is already armed and riding for Fulgor!"

"It is more than a rumour," the Gardinelle confirmed. "I am afraid the Knight Courier Breach has found the discipline of knighthood too punishing for his taste. He has found escape in Fulgor's free rein instead."

"Then you have already heard something?"

"Yes, my dear Reefer. He shortly declared himself to the young witch, Alabak."

Reefer shook his head. "And at a time when Fulgor seems to be planning trouble for us." He knitted his brow. "Your Highness, it is of vital importance to have the micropar ready for our forces on the shortest notice." He shared his appeal between the Gardinelle and Resal.

Resal bit her lip thoughtfully. "Judging by the orbiter's performance, I am quite sure the microstars will give us a particle ray of unequalled strength, but how dependable it will be in the field cannot be said until we see the results of our new tests."

"Or unless we try it in the field," Reefer pressed.

"If you can accept the risk," Resal added.

"Once again we seem to have little choice," the Gardinelle observed. "You must prepare our forces for the micropar in any case, my dear Resal, and we will hope for the best. And let us hope especially that Fulgor gives us the time we need."

At last given an opening, Steven again unburdened his concern. "But what about Sirgal?" he cried, eyeing the screen. "We have to warn him!"

The Gardinelle gave Steven a reassuring smile. "We will keep an eye on the Knight Courier Sirgal. He is to meet the children

212

when the shadow touches blue, is he not?" She brought the screen to life with a light sweep of her hand.

Dawn was breaking, and Alabak, already busy at the fire in front of Chikchik's hut, was humming contendedly about her work over a steaming pot. Chikchik's head appeared in the doorway, and she slowly emerged with a deep yawn. Seeing Alabak at work, the old woman drew her shawl tighter about her head and ears as if to protect herself before venturing towards her mistress. Looking up, Alabak beamed a "Good morning" and continued with her chore. Surprised by Alabak's cheerful mood, Chikchik stopped and eyed her warily.

"I hope you slept well, Chikchik," Alabak said agreeably. "We have a big day ahead." Scooping a handful of corn from her pocket, she held it out. "Here, feed your crows, and then come and sit at the fire. I will tell you what is needed."

At a loss to understand what had come over the young witch, Chikchik hastily took the corn and retreated to the tree, keeping one eye on Alabak as she called to the crows. After testing a grain on the first bird, she slowly sprinkled the rest at her feet. At length, apparently satisfied that Alabak was not out of her mind, Chikchik took her place by the fire.

Alabak finished kneading a bowl of dough and began working it into small cakes. "Today the girls are to pretty themselves for a party to celebrate their new names. Walking Owl will be with them, as usual, to tell them nice little stories that will teach them to be good girls." Alabak snickered and formed a patty with great care. "But guess who won't be there? Little Miss Falling Star who never passes up a chance to enjoy the pleasure of her friends. Isn't that a surprise? And why won't she be there? Because she doesn't want to hurt Aunt Alabak's feelings? Huh! Not likely! But ask her grandfather. He knows. Oh yes, he's in on the secret, or he wouldn't let her forego his goody-goody lessons. Yes, he knows." Alabak paused and looked up at the sky while a satisfied smirk curled her lips. "And so do I." Her eyes fairly sparkled with pleasure. She looked at Chikchik.

"When children whisper in the corner and change their plans, and are allowed to miss sermons, you know something important is afoot. Something important — like meeting a guardian spirit. And when I find out where they are meeting him...." Alabak shook her head, relishing her thoughts. Hurriedly adding the finishing touches to her patties she arranged them on a woven platter. "Now," she said, turning to Chikchik, "you will take these to the party. When it comes time to spread the table, you will slip one of these treats in each place — and above all don't miss the Maliskap children." Alabak could not restrain a smile. "This will put the tribes at Walking Owl's throat — if not at each other's. Yes, we may get two birds with one stone," she gurgled as her smile gave way to a chuckle. "And with any luck the Maple Dancer will make three!" Unable to contain herself any longer, Alabak lay back her head and laughed so deliriously that Chikchik was moved to join in. Then having thus nourished her soul, Alabak dried her eyes, and taking up the platter, handed it to Chikchik.

Chikchik examined the attractive delicacies with approval.

"And don't be tempted to nibble," Alabak warned in a stern voice. "If you do you will enter a dream, and I will let you stay there forever — far from your husband!" With that, Alabak hurried off, and concealing herself in a thicket where she could see the comings and goings of the village, prepared to wait.

It was not long before the children appeared, and harnessing Trish to the travois, loaded it with what small things they needed for an outing. They were quick to complete their arrangements, and once ready, quietly slipped off into the forest, Falling Star in the lead and Lean Bone bringing up the rear. Intent on scanning the way ahead while calling instructions to his sister, Lean Bone was unaware of the figure that fell in behind and flitted from tree to tree as it followed.

It was when they neared the pool that Falling Star's eye caught a flash through the trees and then saw Sirgal gliding forward on his mount to meet them, the silken pennant of Quotaris floating from his staff. "Hello, Sirgal," she cried, stopping to gather her breath. "I hope we aren't late," she puffed.

"Late? I think not, Falling Star. Perhaps you could say cutting it close," Sirgal replied, and cocking his head with a rueful smile, added, "but not as close as your wish." He leaned down, and lifting her, crutches and all, sat her in front of him on Welkin's shoulder."

Falling Star managed an anguished pant, "No, eh!", which was almost lost against Lean Bone's shout.

"Hey! Don't forget me!"

Sirgal twisted in the saddle to catch the outstretched hands, and hoisted the boy up behind him. At that, Welkin gave Trish a friendly sniff and turned towards the pool, encouraged by a gentle pat from Falling Star. Riding high on the charger's rump, Lean Bone stretched his neck proudly to survey the surroundings. Within a blink of catching Alabak slipping between the trees, his attention was captured by the rippling pennant. "Can I hold the flag?" he begged.

Sirgal released the staff into Lean Bone's hand while Falling Star, now settled and breathing easier, took up the thread of their greeting. "Yes. I almost died when she won at first, Aunt Alabak. I was sure she was forgetting to tell them, the Gardinelle, the Elder Women, that it was for my wish, the sign."

"No, the Gardinelle had not forgotten," Sirgal assured her, "but it happens sometimes that for all of MEGOS and a willing WAND, she can only wait until time runs out for EGOS."

"EGOS is the thought computer," Falling Star recalled.

"So," Sirgal exclaimed with delight, "you remembered!"

"And did you hear me tell them, the Elder Women, what you said? That the shaman of the spirits would be pleased to hear he teaches them, Grandpa, the three paths of wisdom?"

"Except it is the Gardinelle herself who is pleased, not the computer," Sirgal corrected.

"Oh, yes! Maybe for the excitement I didn't say it quite right, but I thought it was important to let them know, the Elder Women," she confessed apologetically.

By now they had reached the pool, and reluctant to vacate his throne, Lean Bone flirted the pennant overhead. "I wish I had a flag."

"Oh?" Sirgal responded. "And what would you have it say?"

Surprised by the question, Lean Bone looked at the pennant with amusement. "A flag can't talk."

"Oh yes, it can. Everything speaks in its way, and anything can be a flag. A flag can be the way you cut your hair."

"Except that haircuts don't bring wishes," Lean Bone countered.

"Right, Lean Bone, nor can a flag — not without the stand of those it speaks for. And while nothing speaks its message more eloquently than a flag, it is you who must be the knight courier of its bounties, just as I am Knight Courier of the Gardinelle's."

Lean Bone seemed clear on at least part of the Knight Courier's message. "I wished for a pony, a white pony, and nothing happened," he said accusingly.

"That is most often the case," Sirgal admitted.

"How is that when Falling Star made a wish you came right away to take care of it?"

"That was because your sister made a Proper wish, and as it was also rather unusual, I was asked to look into it."

"A wish is a wish," Lean Bone declared.

"Not exactly. Yours was a Regular. Falling Star's was a Proper. And without the faith of commitment, Regulars are wibbles."

"Well, what is the difference?" Lean Bone demanded.

"A Regular asks favours for the wisher; a Proper — like Falling Star's — asks benefits for others. That is why Propers come first. As far as the Gardinelle is concerned, wibbles don't count in any amount, while Regulars might, and Propers delight. Always remember that," he smiled.

"Where is it fair if you can only wish for things you don't get?" Lean Bone complained.

"Falling Star shook her head, disappointed in her brother. "Lean Bone!" she scolded him, "you only half listen, and you don't remember what he said when he made my crutches, Grandpa — like when you have nothing else to give you should wish nice things for people."

216

"All right," Lean Bone agreed. "I will wish something for you if you will wish I had a pony."

Falling Star looked at Sirgal. "All he thinks of is a pony."

"And Aunt Alabak would have given me one," Lean Bone rejoined with an accusing look at Falling Star.

"Why do you look at me like that?" she asked.

"Well, you made me take the oath." Lean Bone grumbled.

"So what was wrong with that?"

"So I could have got my buck. Maybe I should wish away my oath," he threatened.

"You can't. An oath is an oath. And anyway, Grandpa said you couldn't have it, Aunt Alabak's horse," Falling Star reminded him.

"Just for the heart!" Lean Bone retorted. "Maybe Aunt Alabak has other ways."

Sirgal became curious. "What is all this about?"

"He always wants to kill things," Falling Star replied. Then she told of the oath and what Walking Owl had said about Lean Bone trading the heart of his first kill for a pony. "Can you do that?" she asked with a negative shake of her head.

"Not if you know what is good for you," Sirgal counselled. "We call it black magic, or fool's magic. It looks good for awhile but soon crumbles into nothing and worse. You see, it is the best Fulgor can manage, and it suits witches who just want to trap a victim. Fulgor would like to have the Gardinelle's magic, and he has been her all-time enemy for it."

Behind the clump of cedar where she had worked her way within earshot and lay listening, Alabak's ears pricked up. "So that is where Breach enters the picture," she said to herself. "It pays to listen around."

"But he can't go back on his promise, Lean Bone, and he can't wish away an oath can he?" Falling Star asked anxiously.

"No, of course not," Sirgal assured her, "unless perhaps you forgive him. But I am sure he would not mean to break his oath anyway, would you, Lean Bone?"

"I only meant suppose," Lean Bone admitted a little sheepishly, but still hating to lose an argument. "It would have been better if I hadn't told about Aunt Alabak's horse."

"It would have been worse to keep it a secret," said Falling Star.

"How about that!" Lean Bone retorted, and taking in the sanctuary with a sweep of his arms, "It was your idea to keep all this secret."

"Only from Aunt Alabak," Falling Star objected.

Alabak raised her brow. "That little brat is going to get more than a new name before I'm through," she muttered, and deciding she had heard enough, made ready to sneak off. At that moment too, Sirgal rose to his feet, saying it was time to be on his way. Not knowing which direction he might take, Alabak saw fit to remain hidden.

"When will you be back?" Falling Star asked anxiously.

"Well," Sirgal replied slowly and regretfully, "now that you have your name there is little need for me here, and there are others to be taken care of in worlds everywhere."

"Oh," Falling Star sighed, "I wish you could please come back more."

Pausing in his preparations, Sirgal looked down at the pathetic little figure hanging from her crutches, her dark entreating eyes asking so little — neither for pity nor care, but little more than the warmth of friendship, which those more blessedly endowed than she seemed not to need yet indulged to the full.

There are times when the patience of a saint cannot tarry while Justice balances her scales, and there are times when the devotion of a Knight Courier cannot attend the sortings of Fortuna. This was such a time.

"What in all the world would you like most for a Regular wish?" Sirgal asked.

Saddened but accepting the fact that she could not ask Sirgal to turn his attention from the needs of others, Falling Star summoned the most cheerful smile she could under the circumstances and searched her mind for some pleasurable consolation. But stirred by the deep and manifest compassion in Sirgal's eyes, she paused. Her smile at first wavered, then vanished as her leaping heart seized upon the unspoken message. Wide-eyed, she could for a moment only return his gaze, then stealing a furtive glance towards her feet, quickly turned her eyes back to Sirgal's, not daring to voice so cherished a thought.

Sirgal nodded. "Watch for the day the shadow touches red. On the instant it is halfway across the red, there will be a star — an enchanted star." He smiled, and his eyes flickered significantly towards the cave. "You know how to see an enchanted star in broad daylight, don't you?"

Falling Star nodded.

"When you see it, make your wish."

Falling Star's thinly pressed lips opened and silently formed the word "How?", for she still dared not speak lest the spell be broken.

"Let me see," said Sirgal thoughtfully. "Yes, WAND will be listening for the wishwords: "

> *I wish with might*
> *On this one's plight,*
> *Kind pneumatypes*
> *Could shine their light.*

"But," Sirgal finished lightly to ease the child's tension, "if you should change your mind and would rather see me, just say instead: "

> *The wish is strong,*
> *The flesh is weak,*
> *Let Sirgal come*
> *Of faith to speak.*

So saying, he leapt upon Welkin's back and was gone.

Being unable to see what was going on, Alabak was not immediately aware that Sirgal had left, and she lay congratulating herself on having waited to learn of the signal and the wishwords. But with Welkin's strong scent out of the way, Trish soon detected Alabak's presence, and giving a bark of recognition, started towards her hiding place.

219

"Blood and fires!" Alabak muttered under her breath. "That miserable pest." What she had learned this day was not to be forfeited by letting her presence become known. With no time to work a spell, Alabak drew a wicked-looking knife from her person. She clenched her teeth. "This time I will make sure of the job," she muttered. But as Trish gathered herself to plunge through the branches, the travois became caught on a root, arresting Trish's leap so abruptly that Alabak's knife fell short and buried itself harmlessly among the roots. No matter. The immediate need was satisfied, and while Trish struggled to get free, Alabak made use of the opportunity to slip quietly away. And just as well, because Lean Bone, thinking Trish was chasing after some forest creature, quickly ran over to take her in charge.

In the Dome, Steven scarcely noticed Alabak's departure, so caught up was he in the thought of Sirgal's promise of the wish. Falling Star's wish to keep her name had not quite met his expectations of magic, but this would have to be different — this was something undreamed of — something almost unimaginable — that he could be witness to the granting of a really fabulous wish! It was true that things people wish will oftentimes come about, and people will often smile and tell you their wish came true. Yet, like Falling Star keeping her name, how could you say for sure that things would not have turned out just as they had without anyone wishing it? But this time the wish would have to be truly granted — just like that — with the snap of a finger! Yes, Steven told himself with anticipation, it is always nice to see things turn out the way people want. And although a butterfly is a beautiful thing to behold, to be there watching it emerge from a cocoon to slowly unfold its delicate wings and fly away — that is something else! He paused and gasped. Could this reveal the miraculous balm?

The Gardinelle, too, was pleased. "That is a perfectly splendid idea of Sirgal's!" she exclaimed. "And Falling Star is such a deserving child."

"Yes, Your Highness," Keep agreed. "Shall I call Thalamus to have it programmed in a star?"

"Indeed, my dear Keep. Please do that. It is to be cleared well in advance. This time we must spare any suspense."

19

With the affairs of Wamwiki having taken a new and important turn, the Gardinelle was remaining in the Dome where she could keep herself informed of developments.

By now too, the tribespeople of Wamwiki were in a turmoil. The morning party had gone well, but as the afternoon drew on, one parent after another was running to Walking Owl for help, saying that a strange malady had come over their child. Before long it was apparent that all of the children who had attended the party were stricken in the same way. To make it easier for Walking Owl to administer to them, the long house was being taken over for a hospital, and there the victims were being brought together.

Completing the examination of his patients, Walking Owl rose from the last bedside and stroked his chin thoughtfully. "The symptoms are very much the same as those of Sun Dog," he muttered to himself. "Alabak!"

Though Walking Owl was certain of his conclusion, he nevertheless drew forth his beaded pouch, and tracing the ritual circle in the dust before the long house door, cast the bones into it. The result was just as he had expected. The talon lay curled about the wishbone! There was no room for doubt. The talon was Alabak. The bones had warned him all this time, and he had failed to read their message.

Walking Owl remained motionless for some time, contemplating the bones and wondering over a decision. Finally looking up to meet the silent stare of the parents who had gathered around, he said, "It is a dream spell that Alabak has cast upon them, and not a sickness."

"Then cast it off!" cried the parents in unison.

"It is not so easy," Walking Owl replied, "for there are many ways in which such a spell may be cast, and only one way it can be safely broken. To try others would invite death."

At this, some of the parents hurried off to seek out Alabak, but returned almost as quickly saying she was not to be found anywhere in the village. On hearing this report some of the parents became moody, and one of them spoke out saying, "He cannot cure the children so charges an innocent woman with sorcery. Yet he is supposed to be a great shaman!"

"That is true," cried another. "Alabak cured Sun Dog when Walking Owl could not, and he has since then hounded her with jealousy. Now he has driven her away."

"Yes," added a third. "He tried to set the child Falling Star against her even at the naming ceremony."

Others now chimed in. "How can he accuse Alabak of such a thing when everyone knows how well she nursed Chikchik when the old woman was so badly ill. And has she not even accepted to be the guardian of her dead brother's children? Are these the deeds of a bad woman?"

"The bones do not lie," warned Walking Owl, who had gathered in the bones and was now standing by the door. "We must go and find Alabak so the spell may be undone."

In answer, the spokesman Two Bears approached him and said, "Walking Owl, you will go nowhere. You are a shaman who speaks with the spirits and claims to know all things. You have denounced the poor girl Alabak, yet we know hers to be a good hand. But you it is who call upon your spirits to work their influence upon our lives and the lives of our children. A spirit and a man are to be known by the company they keep. Now, in the treatment of our children, let your spirits show their hand and the hand that is yours — be it benevolent or malevolent. Your life will ride with the outcome."

Having thus spoken, Two Bears pushed Walking Owl inside saying, "You will come out when the children come out, and just as they do." Whereupon a guard was appointed to make sure Walking Owl could not leave until the spirits had rendered judgment.

On returning to the village, Lean Bone and Falling Star were surprised to find that the parents were speaking out against their grandfather. On learning where he was, they hurried to talk with him, but at the long house the guard turned them away saying that only parents could enter.

"Now what are we going to do?" Lean Bone wondered. "Grandpa could be in deep trouble."

"You should sneak inside and talk to him," Falling Star replied without hesitation.

Lean Bone looked first at the tall guard who filled the doorway, and then at Falling Star. "And how am I supposed to sneak past him?" he asked with little hope in his voice.

"I know how we can do it," Falling Star whispered, drawing her brother farther away. When she had finished telling her plan the two could be seen approaching the long house again. This time Falling Star made her way towards the group of parents who had gathered to hold council, but short of reaching them she lost her balance, and falling forward onto the ground, lay as if stunned. The concerned parents quickly ran to the child's aid calling out advice to each other. Craning his neck to see and calling out advice of his own, the guard also pressed forward, and during the instant his attention was diverted, Lean Bone slipped behind him and through the door.

Inside, Walking Owl had watched the ruse, and smiling broadly, praised Lean Bone for his skill. "But," he added, "you will be called upon to show even greater skill. I must know where Alabak is hiding if I am to learn the secret of her potion. Let us see how well you have learned your woodcraft, and when you discover where she is, come straight away and tell me. Be very careful she does not see you first, and above all watch out for tricks — you are to be the cat, not the mouse. The lives of these children could depend on you."

Promising to do as directed, Lean Bone returned to the door, and leaping out, fell into the arms of the astonished guard. "Here now, I told you you could not go in. Now get along and stay away from that old faker," he growled, shoving Lean Bone away so roughly the boy would have fallen had not a parent caught him in time.

"My grandfather is not an old faker," Lean Bone cried back. "I am going to find Aunt Alabak, and then you will see!"

Meanwhile, Falling Star had regained her crutches, and after a dusting off, appeared to be none the worse for her fall. As the two moved away, Lean Bone told her of the task Walking Owl had given him. Anxious to be of help, Falling Star was determined to go along, and it was only after a stiff argument that Lean Bone agreed to let her go with him as far as Chikchik's hut, "but no farther," he declared. "Besides," he reminded her, "tomorrow is the day for your special wish. It would be better for you to rest and be ready for the long walk to the cave."

With the argument settled, and arming himself with his flint knife and bow, Lean Bone led the way to Chikchik's hut in search of the first clues. There they found the place thoroughly deserted and the ashes of the fire dead cold. "They have been long gone," Lean Bone concluded upon reading the signs. "They must have gone to their hideout together. But which way?"

"Maybe down along the river," Falling Star suggested.

"I don't think so," said Lean Bone, looking in that direction. "There are always too many children around and people fishing. There is really no place to hide."

Falling Star drew an anxious breath. "Do you suppose she might have a secret place near the sanctuary, Aunt Alabak?" she quavered.

"No." Lean Bone was emphatic. "I know through there like the back of my hand."

Having eliminated those two directions, Lean Bone about-faced and contemplated the trees. "The far side of the forest is bordered by a big swamp, and over there," he said, indicating the remaining possibility, "the forest never ends."

While Lean Bone was trying to decide in which direction to start off, the two children stood in silence. Suddenly Lean Bone straightened up and cocked his head. He looked at Falling Star. "Do you hear anything?"

Falling Star listened intently for a moment. "No, why?"

Lean Bone pointed up into the old tree. "There are no crows. They have gone!"

"Not all of them," Falling Star corrected, pointing skyward. "There is one."

And to be sure, a large black bird wheeled silently above them, and descending in a lazy spiral, came to rest on the tip of a high branch. Pausing only long enough to fold and unfold its wings, the bird rose in the air and flew leisurely off over the trees.

Lean Bone watched for a moment. "Aha!" He rubbed his hands together with satisfaction. "He is heading towards the swamp."

"So?" Falling Star questioned.

"That is where the others must be. Don't you see? Like Grandpa says, birds of a feather flock together. And the crows would go with Chikchik. I will look for them in the direction the crow has taken."

So it was that after promising his sister he would be back by sundown, Lean Bone hitched his bow over his shoulder and trotted off through the underbrush.

Far ahead, Alabak had stirred the coals of her fire in front of a giant hollow tree that was her shelter. With the blaze well kindled she drew a handful of grains from her pocket, and sprinkling them over the flames, brought forth a black swirl of smoke. Slowly starting to dance, she repeated her performance of the previous night precisely, and having uttered the incantation, had no sooner sank to the ground than presto! — there was Breach. Holding the prancing wild-eyed Spy with a mean grip on the bridle, his long curls flying in the breeze, Breach surveyed Alabak, his smile coldly mocking. "What is it, angel?"

Alabak gathered herself from the ground. "My name is Alabak, and I will thank you to call me by it."

"All right, Alabak, or whatever," Breach replied with a smirk.

Alabak narrowed her eyes with resentment, but turned to the business at hand. "I have found out where the children meet Sirgal," she said, concealing her exultation with difficulty.

Breach arched his brow in surprise. "Well! Good girl!" he exclaimed. "Tell me."

Sitting back, Breach listened to Alabak's account without interruption, his expression reflecting more and more pleasure as she continued until, hearing about the sign and the wishwords, he burst into spirited laughter. At length containing himself, he thought for a moment before coming to a decision. "I will see you before then," he said, "and will tell you what is to be done." Still overjoyed, he wheeled Spy around to be on his way, but hesitated over an afterthought. "A girl like you could have a great future," he cried. Then with a boisterous whoop and a wild sweep of his incredible lance, he uprooted a small tree at thirty paces, and leaving it a charred reminder of his visit, melted into the forest.

"Yes," Alabak muttered after him, "I could have a great future. With Walking Owl out of the way, and with your spear, I could rule the tribes from here to the great waters." She turned and stood looking into the fire thoughtfully.

At this point, Chikchik burst from the forest and hurried to Alabak's side. Bubbling over with the excitement of the village, she could not wait to tell Alabak the news. "Lean Bone says he is coming to look for you," she reported.

"Coming to look for me is he? The boy is coming to look for me?" she repeated, rubbing her hands with glee. "Well, well. We will have to make sure he finds us, won't we?" With that she laughed again; she could not have planned things better.

When Alabak's mirth subsided, Chikchik told her the details of Walking Owl's predicament. On reaching the point where Walking Owl had denounced her, saying the bones do not lie, Alabak scowled and then became very angry.

"Those eternal bones!" she exclaimed, and spat into the fire. "I must have them before they make us more trouble." So saying, she drew Chikchik closer and said, "You must go into the village and steal the bones while he sleeps, and it must be done this very night, for tomorrow there is much at stake."

At this, Chikchik drew back. She looked at her hands, and her eyes filled with terror.

"Have no fear, Chikchik. The spirits hold no anger while the bones are in the pouch," Alabak assured her. She went on with her plan. "He places them at his head while he sleeps. It will be easy," she said, and repeated soothingly, "very easy. The bones are harmless and will not burn you while they lay charmed within the pouch, but when we have them the power will be ours. And who knows,' she added, striking at Chikchik's weakness, "your husband could be among the spirits who speak through the bones. How he could speak to you when the bones are mine!"

Huddled over and embracing her knees with misgivings, Chikchik nodded a timorous agreement.

Not far off, Lean Bone was jogging his way through the trees, stopping now and then to listen and examine the ground for signs. At length he came upon a small clearing on the banks of a sparkling stream, and first quenching his thirst, sat back against the bole of a tree to rest. His upended quiver surrendered a handful of corn which was not much for his growing hunger, but he quietly munched it while casting his eye over the surroundings. Suddenly he stopped chewing and listened. His attentive ear had caught the sound of crackling branches, and while he listened, the sound drew closer. Something was smashing towards him with reckless speed.

Taken by surprise, Lean Bone jumped to his feet and stood with his back pressed against the tree. At the same time, a deer leaped out of the near trees and, in a giant bound, sailed over the brook and into the clearing. In another flying bound, it had reached the far side to disappear amidst the trees as quickly as it had come. Just as abruptly, two wolves broke from the underbrush, their tongues hanging out hungrily over a row of ferocious-looking teeth. With nothing but their quarry in mind, they splashed through the stream and past Lean Bone in hot pursuit.

So swiftly had the happening taken place, Lean Bone had neither the time nor the thought to reach for his bow — not that it could have mattered. Instead, he stood like a statue clutching his lynx tooth when yet a third wolf splashed through the stream in pursuit of the others. But catching either sight or the scent of Lean Bone, he veered off sideways and slid to a stop, eyeing the hapless boy over his shoulder, more in wariness than in menace. Deciding it was safe to turn his back, and anxious to join in the kill, the wolf resumed his chase, making off at a furious pace to regain lost ground.

With the return of peace and quiet to the forest, the look of bewilderment faded from Lean Bone's eyes. He began to breath again, and as he regained himself, a smile slowly spread across his face. And why not? He had stood eye to eye with a savage wolf — and it had shied away! No matter that the tree had prevented an equal reflex on Lean Bone's part, which might well have invited a less desirable response from the wolf. Instead, Lean Bone let the amulet fall free from his hand, and taking up his bow, prepared to be on his way, a whole head taller.

The afternoon shadows were now melting into the softness of early evening, and with a last look around, Lean Bone started back the way he had come. He had only taken a step or two when he stopped and peered through the trees ahead. That was the way the wolves had gone! He turned about, and taking fresh bearings, began a wide detour of the chase area. Now set on returning to the village, he started to move more quickly, but he had not gone far before his ears detected a familiar sound. Stopping to cup his ears and listen, he heard it again. Yes. It was the crows, but they were a good distance off. Still, anyone could guess they were near the edge of the swamp because the ground was already dank and softening underfoot.

The boy was elated. He started to move cautiously back in the direction of the faint sound of cawing, then hesitated. Reconsidering his rash intentions, he quickly turned and set off again at a fast trot in the direction of the village. Walking Owl himself could not have counselled a wiser decision.

It had been a day for Lean Bone such as any boy would long remember, what with his having cleverly reasoned Alabak's whereabouts from the trail of the missing crows, and on top of that a tale to tell about his encounter with the wolves. He trotted through the trees looking pleased with himself, and with the air of a proven woodsman whose day's work was well done. And his good fortune was not yet ended, for directly in his path the heavily laden branches of a wild plum tree swayed and nodded to him invitingly. There could not have been a more welcome sight for a stomach that had been dealt little more than a handful of corn for some hours, and Lean Bone lost no time partaking of the well-deserved feast. Smacking his lips over the intoxicating succulence, he allowed the evening shadows to gather while he satisfied his craving.

At length, having eaten his fill and being refreshed from the delicious meal, Lean Bone turned his attention once more to the journey home. It was at this moment he beheld a sight that made him rub his disbelieving eyes. When he looked again, his face brightened and his heart leaped for joy, because what he thought at first to be a curious deer standing in the shadows, was not a deer at all, but a pony. Yes, a beautiful white pony.

Lean Bone stood without moving. The pony stood and stared back. He wore no halter, nor did he carry any sign that he could belong to anyone. Shaking his head playfully as though beckoning to the boy, he turned and started to walk slowly away as if Lean Bone were not there.

Lean Bone came to life and fell in behind. Stepping along stealthily, he quickened his pace as much as he dared without frightening the animal. Totally absorbed as the distance between him and the pony slowly diminished, Lean Bone paid no attention to the narrow trail they were following, nor to the fact it led away from the village and towards the swamp.

Still ignoring his pursuer, the pony stopped to nibble at some tender shoots. This was his chance. Lean Bone slipped his bow from his shoulder and grasped it firmly in both hands. He had seen the braves do it often enough. A quick flip over the animal's head, a twist of the stave, and the pony would be mastered. Of course, success rarely comes without practice, but Lean Bone was not to be denied. He gathered his every ounce of strength and determination, and….

230

"Gotcha!"

Alabak's icy fingers dug into his arms with a vice-like grip, turning them behind his back and rendering him quite helpless to struggle. And worse still, Lean Bone's head came up to see that the pony was gone.

Without loosening her grip, Alabak pushed her captive half stumbling along the narrow path ahead of her. Nor did she speak while she forced him into the hollow tree, and there not only bound him securely but lashed him to a sturdy root so he could scarcely squirm. Only then did she speak.

"And has your grandfather, the great shaman, discovered what is ailing the children yet?" she asked, though it was only to mock.

Lean Bone made no effort to reply.

"So you are not very talkative," Alabak shrugged. "No matter. Chikchik will go and find out soon enough." With that she went away.

Through the opening, Lean Bone could see Alabak busying herself over the fire. Presently the savoury odour of venison wafted in to deepen his growing pangs of hunger, and he could glimpse the sizzling meat on its spit. Taking her time, Alabak ate with relish. After finishing, she smacked her lips, and placing a juicy cut on a woven platter, took it into the shelter and placed it at Lean Bone's elbow. Then turning her attention to his bindings, she said very pleasantly, "I was thinking how nice it must be to have a guardian spirit like Sirgal. Of course, the Chief's boy Sun Dog would probably rate one even better."

Lean Bone said nothing, but looked with hungry anticipation at the delicious meat. "Yes," Alabak continued, "Sun Dog is not a Cheechikois though, and does not make stupid oaths. He will be a great warrior. He is not afraid to die, Sun Dog. His guardian spirit would have to be the best." Then busying herself with the knots, Alabak observed almost casually, "Yes, I would think his guardian spirit could show you a star in broad daylight. I doubt whether Sirgal could do that."

"Oh yes, he could," Lean Bone blurted out, and then caught his tongue, because the words had popped out unintentionally.

"He could?" exclaimed Alabak, feigning disbelief. "And how could you say that?"

Lean Bone remained quiet. Walking Owl had told him to watch out for tricks, and he had fallen into her very first trap out in the forest. Now she was asking questions, and it was plain the knots were not loosening any. She was only pretending to untie him.

"Come boy," Alabak pressed amiably. "You can tell me."

Lean Bone held his tongue.

"And then," Alabak continued, "you can eat a good meal. You must be about starved."

Hungry as he was, Lean Bone was on the defensive, and it became clear to Alabak that he was not going to talk. "All right," she finally concluded, "no talk, no food. When you are hungry enough just call out." With no more ado she went away, leaving the tantalizing platter under his nose.

20

Arriving at the long house in the darkness, Chikchik found the guard sitting at his fire drinking a hot tea. Glad to have Chikchik's company in his lonely vigil, the guard encouraged her to stop and talk, and taking advantage of the offer, the old woman disarmed him with her memories of old warriors. But the moment he turned his back to reach for fresh firewood, she slipped a sleeping potion into his cup. Presently only the murmuring voice of Chikchik could be heard, and overcome by sleep the guard sank back drunkenly against the long house wall. As he did so, his sprawling arm dislodged a spear that leaned against the wall beside him, and falling across the back of a village dog who had curled up in the warmth, it sent the animal scampering away with a surprised yelp. Chikchik, too, scampered for cover lest anyone had been awakened by the noise.

As it was, the dog's cry brought Walking Owl out of his sleep and bolt upright in his cot. "Lean Bone?" he called out in a hoarse whisper, and sat listening. Receiving no reply, he rose and went to the door to peer outside. Seeing only the guard slumped against the wall in the dim firelight, he turned back, but paused, because the unmistakable sound of deep snoring was clearly audible. Cautiously leaning out of the door for a better look, Walking Owl could see that the guard was indeed enjoying a sound sleep. It offered Walking Owl an unexpected opportunity, and seizing it without stopping to don his feathered bonnet, he tiptoed past the guard. Once safely around the corner, he broke into a fast pace towards the far end of the village.

Chikchik had seen it all, but without his bonnet Walking Owl looked no different to her than a visiting parent. For that reason she could be forgiven for leaning back patiently to allow Walking Owl, inside, time to bed himself and fall asleep now that he was free of visitors.

Falling Star, too, was active for that time of night. Lean Bone had promised to return by sundown, and with his return long overdue, her wakefulness was understandable. She passed much of the time practising Sirgal's wishwords with her eyes closed and fingers crossed. When at length Lean bone had still not come, and the village was bathed in the stillness of sleep, she crept out of the wigwam, straining her eyes in the direction of the long house. Curled up dreaming one instant and wide awake the next, Trish wagged her tail and nuzzled her mistress happily, overjoyed at the prospect of a nocturnal prowl. But Falling Star was of a different mind. "I am going to sneak over to see him, Grandpa. You have to stay here." So saying, she tied Trish securely and hobbled off in the direction of the long house.

So it was that while Falling Star made her way slowly through the darkness, another figure was hurrying furtively towards her from the other direction. Rounding a corner, they came upon each other so unexpectedly as to collide and knock each other to the ground. Falling Star was the more easily recognized, and Walking Owl was quick to shush her involuntary gasp of surprise before it gained the strength of a frightened cry.

Falling Star was not long telling Walking Owl of Lean Bone's sally into the forest and his failure to return as promised. For his part, Walking Owl was pleased to hear that Chikchik had left her camp because his destination at this very moment was the hut, where he intended to search for clues to Alabak's mysterious potion. Together they made their way to the old woman's place, and having it to themselves, Walking Owl searched every nick and cranny for leftovers, sniffing every pot and pan for telltale aromas. It was all to no avail, and sadly admitting defeat, he decided to return to the long house and continue to do what he could for the children while waiting for Lean Bone.

Having made herself comfortable for a short wait, Chikchik had meanwhile become drowsy, and before she knew it, had allowed herself to doze off. When she awakened with a start it was getting on towards dawn, but fortunately for her the guard was still sleeping soundly. And so, too, must Walking Owl by now, she could expect. Calling on her aching muscles, she slowly got to her feet and cautiously approached the long house entrance. Inside all was quiet, and in the dim light Chikchik could make out what must be Walking Owl's bed nearest the door. The rumpled furs remained motionless as she stole closer.

Reaching the head of the cot, Chikchik slid a tentative hand under the pillow and gingerly searched for the pouch where Alabak had said it would be. And as usual Alabak was right, for Chikchik stiffened with a shiver as her fingers brushed against the beaded doeskin. Holding her breath, she brought both hands to bear upon the pouch, and slowly, ever so slowly, eased it towards her. Not a sound nor a stir came from the bed. Then, unbelievably, she had it! With this sudden realization she was almost too frightened to hang onto the pouch as it balanced in her trembling hands, but finding her hands did not burn, she gained reassurance that the bones lay well and truly charmed within.

For their part, Walking Owl and Falling Star had by now re-entered the village, and passing a tepee halfway back to the long house, were arrested by a voice from within. "You there, the faker!" It was the voice of Two Bears who had awakened, and looking out had recognized Walking Owl, for though the old shaman may not have been easily identified in the dim light, Falling Star could not be mistaken. "What are you doing out of the long house?" The words were loud and angry, and following them, Two Bears jumped out of his entrance.

At first turning to stand his ground, Walking Owl felt for the beaded pouch, and to his chagrin, realized he had come away without it. As Two Bears bore down upon him at a fast run, other forms appeared in doorways to find out what the clamour was about. Menaced on all sides, Walking Owl turned and ran for the long house and the protection of his beaded pouch, while a hue and cry went up from the aroused villagers.

Two Bears was young and fast. He was passing Falling Star before Walking Owl had turned the first corner, and would have overtaken and collared him in a few strides but for Falling Star. As the racing brave came even with her, she thrust a crutch between his flying feet. Losing all control of his limbs, Two Bears plunged headlong into the dust, and before he could collect himself, Walking Owl was out of sight and well on his way to the long house.

Meanwhile Chikchik, clutching the beaded pouch, had not paused to savour her success, but turned towards the door with the haste of one who could not be quickly enough gone. Throwing all caution to the wind, she darted towards the opening which now beckoned to her in the gray light of early dawn. But alas, her careless fingers caused the knotted drawstring to slip its restraint, and in an instant the contents had slipped to the floor to lie menacingly between her and the door. She stopped in her tracks and stood staring, her face lined with horror, and shrinking back, fell onto the bed. Only then was she aware that Walking Owl had not been in it.

It was at this point that Walking Owl gained the home stretch and made for the long house entrance. The sight of yet another threat coming towards her out of the murky dawn shook Chikchik out of her dilemma. Dropping the empty pouch, she sprang for the nearest cover, burying herself in a heap of furs behind the cot just as Walking Owl stumbled over the threshold. No longer driven by dire necessity, Walking Owl's old legs buckled under him, and he fell sprawling on top of the scattered portents. As he lay panting eye to eye with a tiny skull, it dawned on him slowly that he was looking at one of his precious diviners. Shocked, he sat up to find the beaded pouch and its contents strewn about him. He quickly gathered them in, with an accusing eye on his tormenters outside, before turning his attention to the motionless children.

At her hideout, Alabak, who had been sitting by the fire, rose and entered the tree. "Well boy," she asked, looking down at Lean Bone, "are you ready to talk?"

In answer to his defiant stare, Alabak turned and went out.

236

This time she picked up her poker, and first stirring the fire angrily, stood in apparent indecision. The mood was short-lived, for with her mind made up, she began her ritual call for Breach, which by now was well perfected. Thinking himself the subject of Alabak's dance, Lean Bone writhed at the spectacle, for though he had been witness to wild dances around a fiery stake, he had then been only an onlooker. That was a far cry from being the one who was trussed up and waiting to be dragged out.

Lean Bone tried to moisten his parched tongue. If he was on the verge of calling out in surrender, he was saved, because at that moment Alabak uttered her wild incantation and sank to the ground. At the same time Breach arrived on the prancing Spy, and in his customary fashion set the forest ringing with his wild laughter.

By now it was clear that Breach could have spared Alabak the elaborate and precise repetition of her ritual, and merely waited to enjoy her entire performance before making his appearance. This time he could not resist the impulse to deal her a playful tap on the backside with the shaft of his lance. The impertinence so infuriated her that she snatched up a firebrand and went for him with it, much to his amusement, for with little guidance Spy moved about like a ballet dancer, always out of reach. The sounds reached Lean Bone's ears as if they were at his elbow, because the walls of his prison gathered them in and enlivened them like a giant soundbox.

At length having had enough of it, Breach sent Alabak's firebrand flying with a wave of his lance, a jest Alabak had learned not to challenge. "Now," he chided while Alabak glared up at him, "I thought we had this business settled perfectly well. What else could you be wanting at this hour, unless of course you have forgotten the wishwords?"

"I can remember the wishwords," she snapped, "but I cannot get the boy to talk."

"So?" Breach shrugged. "He won't be bothering you with questions."

"We must find out how that idiot Sirgal expects them to see a star in broad daylight!" cried the exasperated Alabak.

"Who cares?" asked Breach acidly. "If the children can see it, you should see it too. I expect you are as bright as a child."

"And I expect you to be bright enough to make sure there are no problems," Alabak snapped.

"I am not a stupid earthbound Quick," Breach reminded her, his voice stiffening. "Your job is to remember the wishwords and get the children out of the way so they cannot warn Sirgal off. Mine," he rasped, drawing his finger across his throat, "is to take care of him when he shows."

"And I hope he knocks you off your fat horse!" Alabak shouted, "and what is more...."

"You," Breach cut in sharply with a warning quiver of his lance that made Alabak draw back, "will simply take your position by the pool and watch me for your cue. When the star appears, I will signal you with my lance from my place on the escarpment. Surely that and a child's wish should not be too difficult for you to manage. In the meantime I have other things to do." Without another word he swept off.

"And if I ever get my hands on that spear you will have other things to do, I can promise you that!" Alabak screamed, shaking her fist after him.

Having thus relieved her feelings, she calmed down and walked back to the tree muttering. "Time is passing and I have to make sure there is only me around to make a wish for little Miss Falling Star. Still, it should not be hard to catch that little cripple." With those words she blocked the opening of the tree with a big root, leaving Lean Bone alone with his thoughts while she took herself off down the path towards the village.

In the village the light of day had spread over the sky when Falling Star hobbled to a vantage point behind the villagers who were crowding in front of the long house. Walking Owl's escape had enraged the handful of visiting Maliskaps who were ready to believe the Montakins guilty of an act of treachery against their children.

As the morning developed, many of the Montakins themselves, seeing the danger of renewed hostility with the Maliskaps, were willing to trade Walking Owl for peace. Others were won over, and by the time the sun had risen it was clear that Walking Owl's little pouch of bones might not protect him much longer. The behaviour of the gathering took a turn for the worse when the Maliskaps dispatched one of their number for reinforcements. Then it was that a handful of the more vociferous young braves drew aside and put their heads together. Presently they separated to go different ways, and when they returned some carried a long sturdy pole while others had found digging tools. Setting to work in front of the long house, they made a deep hole in the ground, and planting the post, danced joyfully on the fresh earth to pack it firmly. On seeing this, a lusty shout of approval went out from many lungs, and some ran off to fetch bundles of twigs.

It was only too clear what was being planned, and at the sight of it, Falling Star was beside herself with fear for her grandfather's fate. Taking up her crutches, she picked her way hastily through the crowd to stand beside him, but seeing her intentions, the young braves turned her back. Resisting with all her strength, she sank to the ground on her knees, and striking out with her crutches, sobbed, "You must not! You must not!"

In the end, a kindly neighbour picked her up and carried her away saying, "This is not a place for children. Stay out of the way and give them time to think better about what they are doing."

As it was, the young tribesmen were not ones to kill in cold blood. Instead they much preferred to dance and work themselves into a proper frame of mind before turning their attention to the victim. They now commenced a pow-wow around the post, but how long it would take before they would feel the time ripe and ready to drag Walking Owl out, despite his pouch of intimidating bones, was a matter for guessing.

Faced with this frightening turn of events, alone and helpless, and with no sign whatever of Lean Bone, Falling Star put her arms around Trish's neck for what comfort she could find. By now the sun had moved higher in the sky, and with its warming rays striking her, Falling Star looked up. Suddenly she remembered. Smothering a sob, she hugged Trish and whispered, "The wish. I can make it for him, Grandpa, my wish. Sirgal will help." She looked at the rising sun and then at the chanting braves, and now having a plan to claim her attention, she harnessed Trish to the travois as fast as her shaking hands would allow. "Please let there be time," she murmured, and wiping back the tears with her shoulder, led the way into the forest with an anxious eye on the rapidly climbing sun.

Meanwhile, at Alabak's hideout, Lean Bone was far from discouraged because he was on the way to being free. The hunger and cold he had suffered throughout the dark night had drawn the tone from his muscles, and leaving them less than full, had eased the discomfort of his bonds. Now there was a slackness in the thongs which he could work to his advantage, and doing so he felt the knots loosen. The sun had not climbed far above the horizon when he slipped his hands free with a final wriggle, and in no time he sat rubbing warmth into his stiffened joints.

Faced with the prospect of Alabak reappearing at any moment, Lean Bone quickly turned his attention to the scraggy stump she had jammed into the doorway. It resisted his first tentative shove, and only when he leaned against it with his back, heaving with all his might, did he manage to dislodge the jagged knobs that clung tenaciously to the rim of the opening. When they did relent, it was with a suddenness that caught him quite unprepared. As a flood of daylight burst past him into his prison, he was unbalanced, and falling back with a thud, found himself sitting in the doorway facing Alabak's platter. Illuminated by a golden shaft of sunlight that reached over his shoulder, the meat remained as Alabak had placed it, and although now cold and without aroma, drew Lean Bone as would a king's table. For an instant the meat and freedom pulled in opposite directions, but in a single movement Lean Bone assured himself of both. He seized the cut of venison, and diving out into the open air, ducked behind the tree. He was free.

Crouching between the claw-like roots of the big tree, Lean Bone nibbled his breakfast and listened. There was no sound coming from any direction, and only one or two crows hunched disconsolately in the branches overhead, waiting for Chikchik's

240

corn. Lean Bone relaxed a little then and continued to nibble thoughtfully.

In the Dome, Steven understood the thoughtfulness and was himself wondering what would be the right thing to do. Walking Owl wanted to know the location of Alabak's hiding place, and Lean Bone could go straightaway and tell him. But what of Falling Star?

As if sharing Steven's thoughts, Lean Bone suddenly jumped to his feet. "It is Falling Star's wishday!" he exclaimed to the crows.

And that is what had just crossed Steven's mind, because Alabak had gone to the village after Falling Star, and as she had muttered, it would not be difficult to catch the little cripple. So what if Falling Star fell into Alabak's hands? If Alabak went to the pool with the wishwords that would bring Sirgal instead of Falling Star's wish, Breach would be waiting ready to fall upon him. But though Falling Star might not get to the cave to await the star and make her wish, Lean Bone could wish for her. So what should be done? Hurry to Walking Owl first and then to the sanctuary? The day was wearing on, and the sun was climbing higher in the sky. There might not be time to do both. Whose need was greatest, Falling Star's or Walking Owl's?

Steven stole a glance at the Gardinelle, wondering whether he could make a suggestion. The Gardinelle was watching Lean Bone, and Lean Bone was looking up at the sun. The boy could not know of his grandfather's peril.

Lean Bone was, in fact, stroking his chin thoughtfully as though searching his memory, and at length the words he sought came out. "I wish with might, on this one's plight, kind pneumatypes could shed their light." He pursed his lips doubtfully and tried again. "I wish with might, on Falling Star's plight, kind pneumatypes...." He jumped to his feet without finishing, and shaking his fist at the crows, cried out, "Yes, you stupid crows, I can make the wish for her!"

"Oh, how nice!" exclaimed the Gardinelle, "that would make it a Proper."

Without further ado, Lean Bone turned his back on Alabak's path and started off towards the sanctuary. Alas, after scarcely a dozen strides, he was brought up suddenly by the howl of a wolf. The sound broke the morning stillness from the bushes not far off, and Lean Bone's hand reached to his shoulder for the comfort of his bow. He had forgotten it.

Casting a hesitant glance in the direction of Alabak's path and first cupping his ears to catch any distant sound, Lean Bone ran back to the tree. He listened again, and hearing nothing, darted inside. It did not require much of a search to find his bow, for it lay with his quiver and knife where they had been carelessly thrown to one side. Retrieving them, he made ready for a hasty departure when his busy eye caught sight of something hanging on the wall. He took a second look and there was no mistaking it. What he saw was the yellow and black feathers and the sharp tip of a deadly venata!

For a moment Lean Bone was completely distracted by the sight. He took the shaft gingerly between his fingers and examined it, but spurning the temptation, returned it to its cradle and turned to the door. He reached it just as the ominous bay of the wolf carried once again out of the nearby thicket. The melancholy tone resounded within the hollow tree, gathered strength, then gradually subsided into a lingering threat. It was all the boy needed to decide his hesitant mind. Taking down the venata once again, he placed it carefully in his quiver, and with first a reassuring touch of his pendant lynx tooth, he trotted off in the direction of the sanctuary, keeping a wary eye over his shoulder.

Alabak, meanwhile, had been approaching the village cautiously, and skirting its outer wigwams, went directly to

Chikchik's hut. Entering the clearing, she called to Chikchik in a low voice. If she had expected an answer she was disappointed for Chikchik was nowhere to be seen.

Alabak retraced her steps to the head of the path that led to the village and stood looking for a moment waiting and listening. Finally, looking up at the sun with impatience, she started along the path, craning her neck as she went, careful not to be seen first. It was then that the commotion around the long house carried to her ears. Being so warned that the village was very much alive, she slipped from the path and made her way to her favourite place of concealment, there to watch. She could hear the shouts of the young braves, and listening to their taunts of "faker, faker", surmised Walking Owl's plight. Her lips curled in a satisfied smile — but only for a moment, because her searching eyes had come to rest on Trish's night leash, one end attached to the wall, the other end lying free and loose in the dust.

"Blood and fires!" Alabak spat to herself. "The little pest has already gone!" Cursing her luck as she went, Alabak hurried around to the place where the children usually entered the forest, and there scoured the ground for tracks. Sure enough, the marks of Falling Star's crutches and the shafts of the travois were plain to see in the dust.

Now Alabak, too, raced off in the direction of the sanctuary on the trail of her quarry, anxiously watching the sun as it soared towards the appointed hour.

In the long house, Walking Owl seemed unaware of the mounting ferment outside as he occupied himself with his patients, when at length someone hurled a stone through the door. It was a brave's way of calling upon the courage of all to follow in after it and claim the intended victim. Angered by the act because the stone came close to striking a child, Walking Owl took up the missile and threw it back more vigorously than it had come. As luck would have it, the ringleader had chosen that very instant to lead an assault towards the door, and being caught on the temple by the full force of the stone, fell back into the arms of his comrades, insensible.

Stretching their leader out on the ground and seeing to his revival, the braves interrupted their assault for the time being.

At this juncture, Walking Owl's attention was drawn by the sound of a loud sneeze that had emanated from behind the cot. He turned in time to see Chikchik who, having thus given herself away, stood up thinking to make a run for the door. It was instantly clear to Walking Owl what had been going on. As the old woman sprang for the door he caught her by the wrist which he twisted with little mercy until the truth was forced out of her clenched teeth. Only then did he release his grip, and just enough to lead her to the door where she confessed, before everyone present, the extent of Alabak's cunning and deceitful schemes.

As quickly as it had mounted against Walking Owl, the wrath of the villagers now evaporated to renew itself with greater intensity against Alabak. On hearing of her intentions to advance her evil ambitions still further at the expense of Falling Star's chance to be cured of her affliction, their outrage grew beyond measure. Turning as one towards the forest, the entire village of Wamwiki surged forward with a single cry — overtake the culprit, thwart her evil intentions, and deal out justice!

"Wait!" Walking Owl cried after them. "We must take the children! Alabak alone knows the cure!"

So it was that while the braves ran on ahead, other villagers took up the children's litters and followed on their trail. And thus it came about that everyone was at one and the same time hurrying towards the sanctuary: Falling Star bent on saving her grandfather; Alabak bent on destroying Sirgal; the villagers bent on destroying Alabak; and Lean Bone, trotting doggedly over fallen trees and through streams, determined to make his sister's wish for her, unaware of the others save for the knowledge that Alabak intended to put Falling Star's alternative wish to her own ends. And already at his post in the distance ahead, was Breach. Sitting astride his ebon mount in a lofty niche, his armed figure dark and sinister in a rippling cape, he surveyed the sanctuary with a cold and pitiless eye — waiting.

21

Lean Bone was making by far the better time in the race to the sanctuary and would easily arrive there first. In the direction he was running, the ground began to fall off along one side of his path. With each step the drop became more pronounced until he was moving along the shoulder of a high terrace that rose from the forest flat. It was not long before he slowed and stopped, because there was a decision to be made. Spreading out from the lower side, the verdant forest flat was dense with undergrowth and brambles that gave difficult passage. On the higher side the growth was sparse, but the shoulder on which he was running continued to rise. As it rose it grew steeper, mounting in the distance to a promontory whose face broke into the escarpment that overshadowed the sanctuary. It would be there at the foot of the escarpment that the entrance to the cave lay.

Clearly, the higher ground offered the easiest passage — if there would be a way down — and, after taking careful note, it was along the rise that Lean Bone chose to make his approach. Resuming his way, he allowed his pace to slow with the climb, for he was soon at eye-level with the treetops in the flat, and then above them. When at last the ground relented its ascent and levelled off, the panting boy stopped to look across the outstretched forest. He had judged his position well and could see the pool not far to one side.

About to move back, something drew Lean Bone's eye for a second look. Beside the pool, to his delight, he saw the flag of a white-tail standing out against the forest green. A smile spread across his face. His old friend the buck was browsing in his favourite spot. With the prudence of a veteran hunter, he stealthily retraced his steps to a tall tree that stood on the brow of the escarpment. Around its base the beaten ground was imprinted with animal tracks, and its exposed roots were worn and scarred by the passage of cloven hooves.

It did not require the eye of a woodsman to interpret the signs. In the Dome, Steven read them aloud. "That would be a stag's lookout," he observed. "Probably the buck's."

From where Lean Bone stood, there was an easy drop to a shelf. The shelf gave way to a narrow track that angled down across the rocky face, and reaching the forest flat, turned towards the pool to lose itself among the trees. Brimming with light-hearted anticipation, Lean Bone unfastened his sash.

Steven frowned, not too pleased that, at a time like this, Lean Bone was allowing his attention to be diverted from the task at hand. Vague recollections of teasing the squirrels instead of hurrying after the witch hazel passed through his mind, along with the misfortunes it had set in train, though in Lean Bone's case the fault seemed less forgivable. Steven voiced his irritation. "Surely he doesn't intend to stop and play with the deer! He won't reach the cave in time!"

Steven's comment went unacknowledged, if not unnoticed, because the others were watching expectantly as with the ease of having done it before, Lean Bone dropped to one knee, and preparing to gain the shelf below, reached for a handhold to steady himself. He had scarcely commenced the move when he stopped and jerked his head back with a start — barely in time to escape the roving eye of Breach who, from a nearby niche, sat leaning over Spy's neck taking in the view. Lean Bone lay still for a moment or two and then eased himself forward more cautiously. He took a long look, stretching his neck as much as he dared in the direction of the cave, but its opening was hidden by the trees and a jutting angle of stone that would also rob Breach of the view. Lean Bone rolled back, thoughtful and uncertain.

Already disturbed by Breach's threatened ambush of Sirgal, and further distressed to see him now cutting off Lean Bone's path, Steven leaned forward and moaned, "Now he will never get to the cave, unless he knows another way down!"

Again Steven and his anxieties were left to themselves, because the all-seeing screen had suddenly drawn attention to Falling Star not far away. Shielded in the deep forest from the prying eyes on the cliff, she was nevertheless hobbling slowly towards them, the faithful Trish at her heels. On reaching a spot where a sprinkle of sunlight tumbled down through the leaves, she stopped to hang for a moment on her crutches, panting for breath. Hot and weary, she raised her eyes to gauge the progress of a fast-climbing sun whose mottled shadows shifted playfully about her upturned face. But unlike the dancing rays that fell upon it, the little face looked tired, verging on despair, a window on the thought of Walking Owl's sundial where, minute by minute, the pencil-like shadow was shrinking towards its style and the appointed hour faster, it seemed, than she was approaching her goal. Worn but determined, her eyes searched the trail for the encouragement of a familiar landmark. Then, drawing a deep breath that might have been a sob, she lowered her head to the task, and leaning forward, resumed her toilsome advance oblivious of the flight of a white-tail through the neighbouring thicket.

Now as her flagging strength diminished, Falling Star was stopping more frequently, and so it was that after a short distance she again paused for breath. This time when she looked ahead for encouragement she was rewarded beyond expectation, because through the trees she could make out the dull grayness of the cliff, and between swaying branches, could glimpse a darker patch that was the cave's entrance.

"I see it, Trish, the cave!"

With new-found energy, Falling Star lowered her head and leaned forward for the final effort, but at that moment a sound rumbled in Trish's throat and erupted in a low, warning growl. Falling Star hesitated, then turned to see what the matter could be. Trish, her ears erect, was twisting between the shafts and trying to look back over their trail. It was a moment before Falling Star's eye caught the moving figure behind them, and a moment more before she recognized Alabak.

Surprised by Alabak's sudden appearance at such a time and place, and at a loss to account for it, Falling Star stood quietly watching her approach, uneasy over her presence but not suspecting any real danger. Then, as the young witch swept down upon them like an angry bird of prey, Trish caught and fathomed her mood. She stood for only an instant looking back before baring her teeth and spinning around — or trying to spin around — to meet Alabak head on. Alas! The travois could not be turned in the narrow space between the trees, and finding herself stuck halfway, Trish squirmed to be free, and her squirm quickly became a struggle.

Seeing the dog caught at a disadvantage and being thus assured of the upper hand, Alabak's lips curled in a malicious smile. Drawing her knife as she closed the remaining distance, she went for the ill-taken animal in a flying leap.

No longer in any doubt about Alabak's intentions, but shocked and horrified, Falling Star half cried, half sobbed, "Trish!" and forgetting all else, started to the aid of her companion, but losing her imperfect balance, fell instead to her knees. Unable to do more, she threw a crutch more in despair than expectation, because it fell far short of doing any good.

Trish herself, infuriated as much by being caught so awkwardly as by the peril of Alabak's raised knife, was making a frenzied effort to be free. Wriggling, straining and snarling, she reared fearlessly to meet the attack. It was then that Falling Star's poorly tied bindings gave way, and with their abrupt release, Trish shot forward as if catapulted from a sling.

Caught off balance by the unexpected assault, Alabak was bowled over, and losing her knife in the confusion, suddenly found herself at the mercy of her victim. Scrambling to her feet with difficulty, for Trish as over her like a pack of wolves, she stumbled back the way she had come, the enraged Trish still snapping at her heels.

All but overwhelmed by those few breathless moments, Falling Star could only stare after the departing figure, bewildered by the suddenness of Alabak's appearance and Trish's dramatic stand. She remained thus on her knees, having scarcely stirred a muscle, while Trish, not to be lured from her post, ended the chase and returned to give her mistress an encouraging lick. The gesture was enough to restore the child's shaken nerve. Recovering her crutches, she lost no time hobbling over the remaining distance to the cave.

Once free of the dog and far from beaten, Alabak had turned back, ready to follow at a safe distance. As soon as the child and her dog had left the scene of the scruffle she hurried forward, where a hasty search of the trampled ground rewarded her with the lost knife. Again armed, she chased after the fleeing couple in time to see Falling Star disappear into the cave. Trish remained at the entrance, and sitting on her haunches, watched Alabak's movements.

Alabak approached closer, trying to peer past Trish into the cave, but a warning snarl kept her at a distance. "I know you are there!" she called out. She looked up at the sun impatiently and balanced the knife as if ready to throw it at Trish. "If you stay in there until I tell you to come out, I will spare the dog."

The offer was met with silence, because Falling Star would have gone straight to the chimney. Alabak waited a moment and again looked anxiously at the sun. "All right, if you want to keep your dog, just stay in there out of the way … or else!" Apparently satisfied that the child was frightened enough to obey her order, she turned and hurried off through the trees to the pool.

Steven breathed easier. Things had looked pretty black for awhile, but Good was beginning to win back the ground it had lost to Evil. Walking Owl was vindicated; Falling Star was safely in the cave; and Lean Bone had not only freed himself from Alabak's prison but, having sighted Breach first, had avoided falling again into enemy hands. He settled back and could not restrain an expression of relief. "Now, if Lean Bone knows another way down, the star could go anytime."

"Not if the little girl is to have her wish." The unsettling words came from Thalamus, putting Steven's short-lived cheer on hold. "Unless she lied to the dog," the wizard observed, "she will be wishing for the safety of her grandfather, since she believes him destined for the stake."

Thalamus was right. Steven had to agree. The children knew nothing of Chikchik's confession, and Falling Star's intentions would not have changed. Even when Lean Bone reached the cave, it would be only to hear his sister's account of Walking Owl's peril at the hands of the angry villagers, and he would naturally accept what had to be done. It would have been better if Lean Bone alone had reached the cave.

It came to Steven that things were not moving towards their proper end, and he found himself very much distressed. He had been drawn into the children's cause so gradually he had not realized how deep his emotional involvement had become, much as Breach had angered him. Yet, even with Breach's alarming entry into the affair, he had still cradled in his mind a dreamlike acceptance that everything was going to turn out all right under the Gardinelle's supervision. Suddenly things seemed to have taken on a course of their own, and he was beset with doubts. He turned from Thalamus to the Gardinelle. "Your Highness. It means that she would be wishing for nothing. That isn't the way it was to be."

"Who will ever say how things are to be, my dear Steven, until the very last wish has been granted?"

"I mean, she was to get her special wish," Steven faltered.

"Nor has it been denied, Steven, and has yet to be wished. A

250

wish must be wished before it can be granted, and what is programmed in our stars, MEGOS will reckon."

The Gardinelle's words could not be questioned. At the same time they were not all that reassuring. And now as he watched the scene, Steven's uneasiness over the outcome was given even greater cause, because instead of looking for another way down, Lean Bone had wriggled into a position where he commanded a safer and better view of Breach. His behaviour was most disturbing. He was resting on his elbows; his breath was deep and uneven; the uncertainty with which he had viewed Breach moments earlier had become a mixed expression of resolution and fear. Though his eyes were fixed on Breach, they were directed in a frozen stare fused with apprehension. While his teeth were tightly clenched, his lips quivered a voiceless whisper of agonizing thoughts. The knuckles on his left hand stood white from the firmness of his grip on the stave of his bow, and his free hand trembled as it made ready to string the deadly venata!

That Lean Bone had resolved upon a chilling venture was clear beyond any doubt.

"Great Heavens!" The exclamation came from the Captain of the Guard, for Garth, coming to join the group, had just entered. He had stopped short behind Steven, his attention drawn to the mounting scene. "Whatever is that boy up to?" he asked incredulously.

If Steven had chided Lean Bone over being distracted by the white-tail, he was more than ready now to concede the boy's courage. Hunched tensely over the edge of his stool, he reacted to the tone of Garth's question with pride and admiration for his fellow Cheechikois. "He wants to reach the cave, but Breach is in the way."

Garth's eye passed over the page boy with a sniff and settled on Keep.

"Breach is in the way on two accounts," Keep offered. "He is barring the boy's path to the cave, and he has a scheme going with the witch to ambush Sirgal."

251

"The boy is on our side," Thalamus added dryly.

"How fortunate," replied Garth with equal dryness. "If Breach is in the way we can have him out of there in a hurry."

"No, my dear Garth," the Gardinelle quickly objected. "There is no need to stir up an open conflict at this point. Sirgal was to have gone only in response to an alternate wish, but he will meet Breach as a matter of honour if need be."

"If need be, Your Highness?" Garth contemplated Lean Bone for a moment. "A bow and arrow in the hands of a boy against a cabolt lance in the hands of Breach would seem to spell need without an if."

"Lean Bone has a venata," Steven declared.

Garth snorted. "A venata or whatever, it had better be deadly, or he will face the consequences of engaging a deadly knight."

"It had better not be deadly, or he will face the consequences of breaking a deadly oath," Thalamus countered.

Steven had forgotten the oath, but needed no reminder that a Cheechikois broke his oath only on pain of death. He wondered whether it had slipped Lean Bone's mind in the excitement, or whether he would remember it in time. But no. Lean Bone was even now fitting the venata to his bowstring.

Garth nodded soberly. "I see. Either way the boy won't reach the cave." He scratched his nose. "I smell the hand of Fulgor himself. I doubt whether Breach for a moment planned to ambush Sirgal — he knows we would be onto him. I would say this whole act has been to draw Sirgal into a trap all right. I would say that Breach is only the bait and it is Fulgor's band who lie in ambush."

"That would stand," Thalamus agreed.

The Gardinelle studied the faces of her councillors in silence.

Garth shrugged. "A show of strength would be enough to get Breach out of there, Your Highness, if you would only say the word."

"If Fulgor is really behind it as you suggest, he would surely accept the challenge," the Gardinelle demurred. "You would provoke a pitched battle on the spot."

252

"So much the better. We now have something to surprise him with." Garth made a deferential bow, and stepping to the Dome's side, invited the Gardinelle to look below.

On the near edge of the stadium grounds, facing a solid stone wall that stood along the far side, a company of knights was drawn up on their mounts in lines abreast. On a command from their captain, the front rank levelled its lances, and leaping forward, skimmed over the ground in a breakneck charge towards the wall. Ere the flying knights had covered half the distance, their lance points flashed with life, streaking the way ahead with sizzling vapour trails that broke against the surface of the wall in a frenzy of little mushroom puffs. Under the onslaught, the barrier wavered, blurred and dissolved like gossamer before a searing torch. As the charging line swept on over the crumbled ruins, Garth rubbed his hands with delight. "The micropar lance, Your Highness. Something to raise an eyebrow and counter the awe of Fulgor's signs, yet, bearing in mind the preference of Your Highness, not excessive for exposure to a Quick's wishfulness."

"I would still question the wisdom of going near the Quicks with so much as that," the Gardinelle remonstrated.

"But to do nothing will encourage Fulgor to more of this," Garth warned, taking in Wamwiki with a sweep of his arm. "Today these children are denied their wish, tomorrow it will be Quicks everywhere — if fear is to be the guide of wisdom."

"But the children," Keep broke in. "What will become of them if we draw Fulgor into a battle about their heads?"

"I can guess what will become of the boy if we do not make a show of strength, and quickly," Garth insisted. "And as for the wish, if I am not mistaken, the boy has already decided he would rather go for a shot at Breach."

Garth's observation was undeniable, because Lean Bone was settling down, and drawing a tentative bead on Breach, gave every indication of carrying out his plan.

"At least the boy has courage," Garth concluded.

"There is truth in all you say, my dear Garth," the Gardinelle replied, "but courage is more than to ignore consequences. For our part we face a choice: If we reveal the micropar in a show of strength, we risk exciting the Quicks to a premature and pernicious wish for it; if we withhold the micropar, we may by default see the fear of evil go on to deny those who would dream a paradise and wish to make their dream come true."

A voice from the Dome's monitor interrupted the Gardinelle's words. "Your Highness, the star is on final countdown."

The Gardinelle paused to draw breath for her decision.

Steven's heart sank. His eyes swept from face to face seeking assurance or hope, and returned to stare anxiously into the cosmoscreen. Breach had ruined everything. A feeling of helplessness crept over him to heighten his resentment and indignation. Why should Breach inflict such injury on people who had nothing whatever to do with him? Why did he have to show up in Wamwiki of all places, and at this of all times? If only Sirgal could have stopped him at the orbiter ramp! If only.... In bitter frustration Steven's mind began to course through the 'if onlys', only to remind him of his own part, and to sharpen his feeling of guilt for having failed to tell Keep he had heard Kwah's call to Eks; for having failed to expose the very one who had helped Breach escape with the orbiter; and for having failed to grasp the simple fact that no one can be a mere spectator — that wherever it lurks and however remote it might seem, evil was everyone's business. If not challenged it was free to gather where it chose, like rain in a beaver pond, and when it could no longer be contained, would burst forth to sweep all before it, heeding nothing and sparing nothing — neither wish nor prayer — just as Breach's shameless and evil intervention was denying Falling Star so dear a benefit for the mere purpose of settling a peevish score with Sirgal. It had not been the flag that egged him on in the first place. He was simply evil!

Thus tumbling through his mind, Steven's thoughts agitated his usually mild temperament and raised a keen anger. Yet, what he could have nipped in the bud with little more than a word was now a deadly match — a match that pitted a boy no more than himself against the ruthless Breach, if not the might of the shadowy Fulgor himself. Driven the more by the bitterness of self-reproach for his own part, Steven could at that moment have let fly the venata himself. He would have given anything to turn the tables — to reach out and drag Breach from his niche — to flush out Fulgor and destroy all he stood for. He wished he were the Gardinelle's councillor. He would counsel her to follow at least her stated preference to Garth's megamicropar: sacrifice such trovium as was needed to counter Fulgor's evil, and save the greater part for those who dreamed of a paradise for the Quick Side. He looked at the Gardinelle in silent exhortation. Go for the micropar! Now was the time! It must be used!

The momentary silence had lasted an eternity, and the ominous ticking of a timepiece seemed to grow louder with each count. Thalamus cleared his throat and registered a last word. "I think it safe to say, My Lady, that the primitives of Wamwiki have neither the faculty nor the words to wish for a micropar."

The Gardinelle nodded as one who was already of such a mind, for she turned to Garth. "The Knight Courier Sirgal will bear the micropar lance, and you will have your company stand by should Fulgor be waiting in ambush."

Never had so few words fallen with so much relief on Steven's ears. They were like an instant wish. Kindled with urgency, his eyes darted to Garth.

The old warrior was already in motion. "If only the boy will hold off long enough," he muttered as he fled the room.

"You have until the star!" Thalamus called after him. Then to the room, "The boy is smart enough to see that if the witch can take her cue from Breach, so can he. That way he can have both a wish and a shot at Breach."

In the sanctuary, as if sensing an impending storm, the chatter of squirrels, the twitter of birds, and the familiar trill of the little green frogs had ceased. In their place a deathly stillness now reigned over all.

Arriving at the pool, Alabak paused behind the cover of trees. Despite being pressed for time, she peered through the branches, searching the cliff for her accomplice. A flash of sunlight on Breach's lance told her he was already in place. She hesitated only to brush a twig out of her hair and smooth her rumpled costume before stepping out beside the pool. Making her way to the spot where Sirgal had met with the children, she took up her position and made ready to watch Breach for the signal. Keeping one eye on Breach, she rehearsed her lines in a low murmur:

> *The wish is strong,*
> *The flesh is weak,*
> *Let Sirgal come,*
> *Of faith to speak.*

"And I hope the Sisters of the Five Dreams don't hear me wishing that!" she finished with a mutter.

From his post, Breach swept the sky with his eyes, and settling back to wait, lowered his lance in readiness.

Lean Bone looked on calmly now, and steeling himself for the final hour, felt the reassuring pressure of the lynx tooth against his chest. An almost inaudible whisper fell from his quivering lips: "Aunt Alabak will see that a Cheechikois is not afraid to die."

In the cave, Falling Star was staring up the chimney, not daring to blink. Then suddenly it was there! High above the opening, a star with a long scintillating tail moved slowly and serenely across Falling Star's little circle of sky. She closed her eyes, crossed her fingers, and hurriedly moved her lips.

Beside the pool, Alabak caught the flash of his lance as Breach's hand stirred to make its upward swing. Fingers crossed behind her back, but keeping one eye half open so as not to miss anything, she muttered the embarrassing wishwords.

Eyes fixed on Breach and clutching the amulet for comfort, Lean Bone, too, saw the hand move. The lynx tooth dropped free, his eyes snapped shut, and his lips formed the wishwords. Opening his eyes, he drew the bowstring full back.

Lean Bone's audacious move had brought Steven to the edge of his stool. Horrified, he closed his eyes, and his own lips moved fervently.

Zing! went the venata.

All was in the Big Computer.

22

Even before Lean Bone's head had fallen back into the cradle of his arm, there was a blinding flash of lightning accompanied by a crash of thunder. The earth around shook like jelly.

"Fulgor!" Thalamus honked.

In less than a trice, a tumbling billow of black cloud was carried in on the crest of a whirling maelstrom to engulf the sanctuary. Lashing out with unbridled fury, the howling winds drove all impediments before them, sweeping the trees clean of their leaves and twigs in a single breath and bending their naked skeletons to the quaking ground, there to tear them limb from limb. Lifting the tangled remnants, the gale spun them aloft in a frenzied swirl of rubble, like chaff from the thresher's chute. As if to purge the denuded ground of any trace of living things, vicious tongues of lightning snaked out in all directions, snapping at every nick and crevasse.

In the Dome, enunciators of every description in the system monitors erupted in a cacophony of conflicting signals, at once announcing levels of success surpassed and danger limits exceeded. Computer hooters and overload buzzers, alert sirens and cosmic beeps, bells and trumpets — all combined in a bedlam of information. Lights too — red and green, blue and amber — lights flashing achievements and concerns from every recess and receptacle of the Dome's array of panels, merged their special hues to cast an odd flickering glow over the Gardinelle and her astonished councillors.

Bewildered by the jangle of sound and unnerved by its uncontrolled urgency, Steven covered his ears, involuntarily shrinking back onto his stool.

Though she sat more stiffly erect, the Gardinelle herself seemed outwardly unmoved. Her attention was turned to the computer work station where the printer had sprung into action and was spouting a stream of paper in an excited clatter of its own. Then as abruptly as it had begun, the din ceased, rendering all in the Dome still and quiet. Outside, the tempest continued to rage soundlessly on all sides until, in response to a flicker of the Gardinelle's hand, the cosmoscreen shrank back into its monitor.

The lull was no more than momentary, because Keep had jumped to his feet. "The bells! The wishing bells rang for a Perfect!"

"And the trumpets!" exclaimed the Gardinelle, seemingly as much surprised as Keep. "The miracle trumpets!"

Miracle trumpets? Steven was now more than ever bewildered. If he had witnessed a miracle it was anything but the likes of a butterfly unfolding its wings.

"See what is recorded," the Gardinelle was saying.

"First things first," Thalamus honked. "There is a red alert, and there will be Fulgor to pay if we are caught unprepared."

Bearing out Thalamus at least, the wail of sirens persisted from the direction of the barracks and penetrated the walls of the Dome. Steven found the plaintive tone irresistible. He ran to look out, and there below in a burst of activity, the grooms were racing to ready chargers while eager young knights, leaping onto saddled mounts, were speeding to their units and hurriedly dressing ranks. In the distance, still other units of micropar lancers had joined a battle line of mobile launchers and starball transports. Even as Steven looked, they moved away, gathered speed, and streaked off into space. It was a spectacle to make anyone tingle with excitement, and the thrill of it drew what was very much a hurrah from Steven's lips. "There go the knights to show the flag!"

At the mention of knights, the Gardinelle's attention swung back to the cosmoscreen. In an instant the Dome was once more transported into Wamwiki's turbulence where the villagers, swarming after Alabak, were slowing their pace in an excited babble of voices. Ahead of them a churning black cloud had swept down over the ridge, and reaching into the flat with tentacles of lightning, a giant arm blacker than the rest was stirring up the forest and flinging it about helter-skelter. Awed by it, the villagers slowed and stopped in their tracks, pointing and trembling with fear.

"The devil's wind," Steven breathed, for so it was known amongst the ancient tribespeople. It was the source of many legends of disaster and courage, and Steven had listened to Gorse's accounts of them on many a stormy night. It would suddenly appear from nowhere, the devil's wind, dropping out of the sky to wreak its havoc. Not the buzzing rattles of the shamans, not the humility of the masked dancers, no invocation — nothing — could turn the avenging hand from any village that had displeased the spirit.

So it was that the rush of angry villagers came to a halt while they cowered around their leaders, not knowing which way the rampaging arm might reach out, and so not knowing which way to turn and flee.

And at the heart of the turmoil, his very being assailed by the nightmare of sound and fury about him, Lean Bone was clinging desperately to a tangle of roots which was all that remained of the lookout tree, while nearby, aloof from the torment, sat Breach, unmoved and unmoving. Lodged in the crest of the rascal's headpiece, the gently rustling yellow and black feathers of the venata was all that had changed. Behind his shoulders in the distance, gathering in the shredding vapour, a host of restless shadows hovered. Surging in the void about his feet, a murky cloud of scud and litter swallowed up darting fingers of lightning that threaded into its depths to claw at the hidden ground beneath, feeding yet more litter to the scouring winds. Then suddenly the cloud opened as by a master hand, and there in the devastation below, looking up expectantly, poised and ready on his rearing mount, was Sirgal.

With a cry on his lips, Breach sank his spurs into Spy's flanks, and Spy, uttering a chilling scream that could be heard above the storm, swept down upon the good Knight Courier. Answering Spy with an equally piercing cry, Welkin echoed a challenge and bore his master upwards to meet the evil foe while phantom shadows, milling in the turbulence, crowded about to hem the contest in.

Now, levelled across the gulf of boiling vapours from opposing lances, micropars and cabolts sliced the space with incandescent rays that met head-on to explode in blinding flashes, mingling the savour of stardust with the acrid fumes of brimstone. So the riders closed upon each other for combat, to wheel, rear, and spin about in a wild exchange of thrust and parry, adding to the shrieking elements a tattoo of clacking hooves, clashing arms, and the unearthly screeching of their mounts.

By now overtaxed and far too numb and dazed to heed the dueling horsemen, Lean Bone had reached the end of his resistance. Little by little his grasp weakened until at length, utterly exhausted and unable to endure longer, he closed his eyes. As the triumphant winds plucked him loose from his hold and spun him aloft, the swirling vapours suddenly gathered themselves in, and engulfing all in their impenetrable mass, rolled upward and over the brow of the cliff and away from the scene.

In furious pursuit, there swept out of the sky a legion of knights bearing the colours of Quotaris. With micropar lances spurting luminescent trails, they fell upon the retreating cloud like a swarm of angry bees, harrying its billows over the hills as they passed on out of sight.

With the cloud moving off in a direction away from them, and finding themselves bathed once more in the light of a bright and friendly sky, the awestruck villagers regained their deserted courage. Aroused by the spectacle of armed horsemen swooping down out of nowhere, and wondering what had befallen Alabak and the child, they regrouped and pressed forward again.

Under the clear blue sky an empty silence had settled over the sanctuary. Where minutes earlier the luxurious forest had concealed the children's secret rendezvous, a semicircle of trees now hedged an open field in the shadow of the cliff, clean and bare of anything save a glassy pool. Nor at the foot of the cliff was there any cave to be seen, but only a mound of stones and shattered rock where the entrance once had been.

In the Dome, Thalamus broke the stunned silence. "It scarcely looks like a happening for bells and trumpets at the moment, My Lady."

"Faith, my dear Thalamus," the Gardinelle murmured. "A happening is no more than what it gives life to, and what is a stone thrown into the water if not the beauty of the ripples that dance on in the sunlight?"

When it seemed that all life had well and truly departed the spot, there rose from the pool the trill of a little green frog. Far off in the sky above the cliff a tiny speck appeared, and as it grew in size, so the trill from the pool increased with more voices. Nearer still, the speck had grown to a great white horse bearing two riders, and in what was no more than a hop, skip and jump, Welkin touched the brow of the cliff and bounded to a halt by the pile of rubble at its base. There, ending at last the boy's perilous tumble through space, Sirgal lowered Lean Bone to the ground, then losing no time dismounting, the Knight Courier fell to work on the pile of stones.

Now too, the air was filled with the clamour of voices as the first braves broke through the forest and spilled into the clearing. Awed by the storm's handiwork, the leaders stood for some moments in astonishment before perceiving the frantic efforts of Sirgal, whereupon they ran forward to lend a hand. In no time the rocks were flying with such energy as to send any idlers scurrying out of the way for safety, and in little more time a large stone fell away, revealing the edge of what was left of the cave's passageway. Willing hands worked on to enlarge the hole, and to everyone's surprise a dusty creature suddenly filled the opening, and out scrambled Trish with a grateful bark. But grateful or not, she was grabbed by the forepaws and spilled unceremoniously down the stone pile while the workers, spurred on with hope, bent their backs with even more vigour. When at last the opening had been enlarged enough for passage, Sirgal himself wriggled through. As his feet disappeared after him, the workers crowded in closer to peer anxiously into the dark recess.

In the Dome, Steven looked on no less anxiously, and indeed had scarcely moved a muscle until, exhaling a deep sigh of relief, he saw Sirgal reappear at last with a pale and faint child in his arms. Amid cheers from the waiting villagers, Sirgal carried his burden to a shady nook and there applied himself to Falling Star's revival.

The Gardinelle, too, seemed relieved, and with the affair in hand, renewed her interest in explanations. "Now, my dear Keep, what does the Record say of the bells and all?"

Before the Gardinelle had finished speaking, Keep had seized the printout, and detaching its length, began to search what was there. "Ah," he said, "here is the start very much as we expected." He read aloud. "I wish only for them to break it, the children's spell the kind...." Keep hesitated and wrinkled his brow somewhat perplexed. "... strong flesh is a pneumatype pony of the Five Dreams?" He stopped and looked at Thalamus. "This is very much garbled. Your computers have chosen a bad time to go faulty."

Thalamus snatched the dangling sheets, fixing Keep with an offended glare. "The computers make no mistakes," he honked. He shifted his glare from Keep to the garbled lines. Keep cocked his head expectantly for an apology. Instead, "This, my good man," Thalamus honked, "is the input when everyone was wishing at once. To unravel it you must interrogate the sorting register." Hanging the printout around Keep's neck, he turned to the work station. With a sprinkle of fingers he composed an instruction, causing the printer to spout more paper which he tore free and laid over Keep's arm with an exaggerated flourish.

Accustomed to Thalamus and his ways, Keep accepted the implied reprimand and printout with equanimity, and turning to the Gardinelle, took up where he had left off. "I wish only for them to break it, the kind pneumatypes, the children's spell, so everyone can be friends and they won't hurt him, my grandfather, the braves." He looked up. "That was, of course, the little girl."

"A pity to have sacrificed her special wish unnecessarily," the Gardinelle sighed. "Yet how nice to have turned a Regular into a Proper that embraces the Second Complement of Being. Still, that would not be enough to ring the bells. What could the boy have wished?"

"It seems to be just as he practised the wishwords behind the hollow tree, Your Highness," Keep replied, then with a hasty second look, "Except he added something. Yes. And for myself a white pony I can ride like Sirgal to protect everything in the sanctuary for my sister." Keep smiled sympathetically. "His preferred penalty for breaking an oath, no doubt."

"That, too, would be a Proper, drawing on the Third Complement as it does — but still only a Proper, though engaging Breach to save the wish was a selfless commitment indeed. But, my dear Keep, neither the girl's nor the boy's wish can account for the bells, let alone the trumpets. What must the young witch have done?" the Gardinelle asked.

"Nothing more than repeating the alternative wishwords, Your Highness," Keep replied, and looking up added, "Thus committing a Proper." He smiled at the thought.

The Gardinelle nodded. "Yes, technically, a Proper for the witch. But there must be something more," she urged, extending her hand to receive the printout as if she would study it herself.

At that moment Thalamus, who had been stroking his chin deep in thought, raised his arms and exclaimed, "My Lady, I see what has happened." His thin smile was one of curious amusement. "WAND was programmed for the wish, and having received it in three forms simultaneously, each drawing upon one of the Complements, presumed to have registered a Perfect." Thalamus confirmed his conclusion with a nod. "A technical Perfect would, of course, ring the bells."

"Oh, how delightful!" The Gardinelle clapped her hands with pleasure. "And to think it was the witch herself who actually brought it about and against her most evil intention. What a clever way of turning evil into good — and with a Perfect wish, which merits a transcendental favour!"

Keep, too, was now beaming, and airing a not unacceptable voice, began putting the words to a familiar tune. He was immediately joined by the others including Thalamus, who for once gave way to an expression of pleasure, and honking along with the others, helped make the Dome ring to the strains of the *Maple Leaf Forever*.

> *They hold all things, the magic rings,*
> *The wished with unwished twinned and spun,*
> *Wherefrom the least endowment springs,*
> *Nor good nor bad, for all is one.*

> *They grant all things, they hold no bars,*
> *Their all a Paradise will bring,*
> *For it is written in the stars,*
> *That all is one — but faith is King.*

To Steven, the tune was certainly the *Maple Leaf Forever*, but those were not the words in Miss Adley's book of songs. However, the phrase 'all is one' fell on Steven's ears like light in the dark. All is one! That was it! The pictographs had led the old shaman in a circle simply by saying that all is one. That was the First Complement of Being! Steven experienced a momentary feeling of exultation, but only momentarily. That the riddle was linked to the Complements of Being was to be expected where the Gardinelle was concerned, but it gave no clue as to the balm or how it was prepared. Nevertheless, Steven gained an optimistic feeling of closing in.

As if nudged by Steven's ongoing thoughts, the Gardinelle, jubilant herself, was addressing Thalamus. "Surely, my dear Thalamus, this must put the Quicks of Wamwiki in a properly receptive mood. Now must surely be a favourable time to share with them the triunium."

"Just so, My Lady," Thalamus agreed.

"But what of the miracle trumpets?" a voice piped up.

In her delight over the Perfect wish, the Gardinelle had momentarily neglected the need for a separate explanation of the

264

trumpets. "To be sure, my dear Thalamus," she reacted, "how are the miracle trumpets to be accounted for?"

Once more bending his mind to the matter, the wizard joined Keep to pour over the printout in search of an explanation. "There is nothing more here than Keep has already given us," he confirmed. "The little girl, the witch, and the boy together making a Perfect, which explains the bells, and then the trumpets." Thalamus paused. "Ah! FIRST the bells, THEN the trumpets. NOT the bells AND the trumpets together! So, something must have accompanied the Perfect — something evidently not within the jurisdiction of WAND." Thalamus, head down in deep concentration, paced the room. Suddenly he paused, and slowly turned to face the Gardinelle. "My Lady. Someone prayed."

For the wizard it was a simple and unadorned statement of fact — neither accusing nor commending. Yet Steven could feel a flush mounting his neck. He shrank back to conceal it. The impropriety of having interfered by breathing a small prayer only now occurred to him, but it had really been an involuntary reflex and not lack of faith in the Gardinelle. Steven dared not look at Thalamus, for though he no longer feared the reformatory, he was feeling deeply embarrassed. But strangely enough, Thalamus had said there was nothing in the Record, so it was Steven's secret. And if his prayer had not reached WAND and if it was not known to Thalamus and the Gardinelle, he was back to the unanswered question: How was the sorting done?

Intruding on Steven's reflections, Thalamus was asserting the facts. "Yes, My Lady, a Devout prayer coming on top of a Perfect wish through a coincidence of three Propers, is a happening of exactly one in a million. Fulgor's trap was surely cogged by a miracle!"

For Steven the revelation brought more than unexpected relief. Thalamus was saying that far from interfering, he had actually assisted in a miracle and had performed a worthy service to all, including Sirgal. It filled him with elation, lifting the feeling of guilt from his former sins of omission, and removed any cause for embarrassment if he were to confess to having prayed. And in owning up, he would at the same time be given an opportunity to find out about the sorting. He gathered himself for the effort.

Too late! Steven's resolve was interrupted by a commotion among the villagers. They were looking up, pointing excitedly to something overhead. Their voices rose in a hubbub that grew in volume until to Steven it seemed to be coming not out of the cosmoscreen but right through the very shell of the Dome. He cast his ears about, trying to orient the true source in his mind, and still unable to do so, finally looked outside. What he saw made him press his face hard against the transparency for the fullest view. To his disbelieving eyes he was soaring, or at least the chateau was soaring, high in the air — high in the air over Wamwiki! There below was the cliff, and reaching out from it was the desolation left by the devil's wind. The loud babble outside was coming from the chateau's own occupants who were leaning from the towers and crowding onto the roof, shouting and waving like homecomers on a cruise ship. For the chateau had indeed become a ship — a giant spaceship. Steven had not realized it before, but now the unusual shape of the Dome explained itself, and he could well imagine how it appeared to those below: the great main hall with its spiked dome nosing out ahead of the rakish conical roofs of the towers, and the four towers themselves, attached to the hall's flanks like mammoth pencil stubs, housing in their foundations the powerful trovium thrusters.

Steven's head automatically spun around to see how the Gardinelle was about to manage this new turn of events, but to his consternation she was no longer there. Nor was Keep or anyone else. The place was deserted, but forming a sea of upturned faces in the cosmoscreen, the villagers were looking and pointing directly at him, or so it seemed.

With more going on outside than filled the cosmoscreen, Steven scampered for a better view, afraid of missing something. At that moment he would have preferred to be watching from below, because the chateau must have been something to behold as it descended in a lazy spiral, the flags and pennants of Quotaris fluttering from its spires. Then as it settled gently to the ground at the edge of the clearing, the curious villagers pressed forward in a

266

wide semicircle. In their midst stood Sirgal with the reins of Welkin's bridle draped over his shoulder. From the charger's back, Falling Star was waving to the villagers about her; and Lean Bone, holding Sirgal's lance, flirted its pennant saucily.

As the tribespeople crowded expectantly before the chateau, the portal slowly swung open, and when it stood wide, a frolicking white pony, eager to be out, clicked his heels and bounded down the ramp. He paused just long enough to scent the air, and then with a captivating toss of his head, made straight for Lean Bone, his mane wildly atumble.

Lean Bone's eyes opened like saucers, and he turned to search Sirgal's face questioningly. The unspoken answer would have been clear to any boy. Without a moment's hesitation, Lean Bone sprang down from Welkin and ran out to meet his prize. As the pony bore down upon him, he opened his arms wide to embrace its shaggy neck on the run, at the same time swinging himself up and onto its back. And away they went like the wind, pennant flying as if in victorious contempt of Fulgor and his defeated band, the freedom to dream and to wish without fear preserved.

Steven watched with pride as the young Cheechikois flaunted the Gardinelle's flag for a complete circuit of the pool before coming to a breathless halt beside Welkin. "If I were the Gardinelle," he mused aloud, "I would untilt the maple leaf so it would be seen in its fullest!" Welkin merely nudged the pony with a sniff as if to say, "I thought you were left at home."

During this time a guard of Knights Courier eased their high-stepping mounts down the ramp to take up positions on either side. Following behind, the councillors in their ermine-trimmed robes of velvet moved onto the ramp, and making a lane for the heralds, lined the sides. It was the flourish of trumpets announcing the Gardinelle that finally brought Steven to his senses. The Gardinelle! He was neglecting his duty. He turned and ran to the stairs, and thence half sliding, half stumbling, circled downwards at breakneck speed.

23

By the time Steven had reached the ramp, the landau had moved off to the centre of the clearing, and there from its vantage — Falling Star at her side with Keep still trailing the printout — the Gardinelle was addressing the villagers. The villagers themselves were listening with rapt attention as the Gardinelle spoke of the Three Complements of Being and how, when given their place in wishes for the betterment of lots, they would lead to a world as satisfying as the happy hunting ground. Unable to make his way closer without creating a disturbance, Steven was forced to play the part of onlooker and to content himself with a quiet study of his ancestors while the Gardinelle made her point. "And so," she announced, "through the sharing of this great experience of selfless devotion between the children Falling Star and Lean Bone and their grandfather, your wise teacher Walking Owl, the tribespeople of Wamwiki have earned a special place in the march towards the greatest of all wishes."

While she spoke, the Gardinelle beckoned among the attendants, and it was Sylvester who stepped forward with a potted seedling, its curiously twisted stems already promising a stately triunium. Taking the little plant and holding it for all to see, the Gardinelle concluded, "So it is that we have brought to your keeping the wishing tree itself. Symbolic in the grace of its form, it reminds us that just as its three stems unite to bear an autumn crown of unparalleled splendour, so too as they are embraced, the Three Complements of Being will crown your efforts with the greatest of all wishes: a world fraternal and at peace. Let it now be your guide."

As the Gardinelle gave the pot to the delighted Falling Star, the villagers shrieked their wholehearted approval, which lasted some moments before quieting so that Falling Star could be heard. "Just look how perfect it is already, the little tree!" she cried. "I only wish it could grow right here in the sanctuary where they could share it together, the tribes and the forest creatures, the wishing tree."

Falling Star's wish was no problem. "We have all come for the planting ceremony," the Gardinelle replied, and as she spoke, the chateau's boisterous residents poured down the ramp in a stream to mingle with the tribespeople. At the same time, Sylvester offered his hand to Falling Star and helped her alight from the landau. It was then that Steven could see she was no longer a cripple, but moved with the elegance of a dancer.

Sirgal, in turn, saw to the Gardinelle, and now with the royal party at their heels and everyone crowding along, Falling Star and Sylvester led the way to a planting spot by the pool. There Thalamus produced a silver trowel, and handing it to Falling Star, bade her set the plant in the ground. When she had done as in-structed, Thalamus stepped to the edge of the pool and drew from his pocket a dainty silken handkerchief which he dipped into the water with an elaborate sweep of his hand. Returning to the plant, he held the delicate shred aloft, and sliding his fingers gently down its length, produced a shower of water. But the water failed to stop with the removal of his hand, and continued in such a stream it would have washed away the pot and all had Thalamus not rushed back to the pool, where he held the hand-kerchief while it released yet the better part of a tubful. The per-formance so caught the villagers by surprise that it was some moments before they burst into applause and laughter. But they were to see much more.

Thalamus removed his cape, and first waving it in the air, passed it over the little plant. As he drew the cape slowly up and away, the plant sprouted in pursuit, growing taller and taller until in a matter of seconds it was a beautiful sapling fully the height of the wizard. But not stopping there, it continued to grow while Thalamus, leaping back in mock astonishment at the tree's behaviour, stood and watched it develop into a stately old triunium, its trunk branching into three gnarled limbs that curled upwards to reunite and rise as one into the unequalled majesty of a maple's shimmering crown.

With the tree having reached its growth, the Gardinelle raised her hands for attention. "It is for the young people that the message of this creation holds the greater promise," she declared, "and to express that message to the young citizens of Wamwiki, Sylvester has come to speak for his classmates." Nodding to Sylvester with an approving smile that included the folded paper in his hand, the Gardinelle drew back a step, so yielding the stage to the young man.

Sylvester had already polished his spectacles, and taking his cue, struck a masterly pose with arm akimbo, the written word dangling unfolded between his fingers.

> *The old wishing tree holds a guide to embrace,*
> *Its stems forming pathways, each one of a grace:*
> *The oneness of all things that breathe or but lie,*
> *Declared in the stardust that sprinkles the sky,*
> *Wherefrom and through nations fraternal on earth,*
> *Each keep of a spirit enjoys equal worth,*
> *And third comes the strength from one's faith undenied,*
> *The complice of wishing, an arm at your side.*
> *Who draws on a wish giving life to all three,*
> *Can move the world closer to what it should be,*
> *Who strives for a paradise, here finds the key,*
> *Which bides in the form of the old wishing tree.*

The finish of his lines was greeted by such a show of appreciation that Sylvester was encouraged to a second bow, though it was the Vroomers flying overhead who may well have deserved most of the credit. When a fresh wave of shouts rose from many throats at the rear, the boy was contemplating yet a third bow when he perceived, as did everyone, the litter bearers with Walking Owl and the parents emerging single file into the clearing.

A way was quickly opened to let the newcomers through, and as the litters moved forward to be placed in the shade of the tree, the gaiety of the villagers gave way to an unhappy moan. "Alas, Alabak is said to have escaped with the spirit Breach on the back of his charger. The secret of her potion has been lost! The children are doomed — and so, too, will be peace between the Maliskaps and the Montakins."

But now, even as Maliskap reserves broke out of the forest armed for revenge, and as if the whole affair were no more than a stage setting for his act, Thalamus stepped to the fore. Seeing the wizard thus waiting, a silence descended over the scene. With all eyes upon him, Thalamus slowly removed his cape, and then suddenly whipping it over his head in a crackling arc, stood back looking up into the tree. Before their very eyes, the villagers saw first one leaf and then another and another turning colour, until in a breathtaking flood of changing hues, the shimmering foliage passed from green through yellow and orange to bright crimson. And when all were of a richness the leaves began to fall, fluttering gently down onto the deathly-still litters until they were covered in a thick blanket. Then in the stillness a rustling could be heard. The leaves stirred, and awakening from their stupor, the girls sat up to find themselves bathing in a mound of autumn leaves. Thereupon they leaped up with shouts of delight, and gathering handfuls of the tree's foliage, began showering each other in play. Uttering their own cries of joy which were echoed by their neighbours, the happy parents themselves fell upon the children come to life, smothering them with endearments and voicing gratitude to the visiting spirits, while once again strains of the *Maple Leaf Forever* rose from the orchestra.

Being as always of a mind to expose the lesson in any happening, the Gardinelle was ready to set this occasion in appropriate words. "Now," she cried, "may your tree come to flourish throughout the land, casting its message as it casts its leaf, like a balm over the tribes and their differences, that all who seek to make a paradise of the Quick Side may wish upon its leaf as on a star, for the stars and the leaf are one."

Short and to the point though the Gardinelle's words were, they were for Steven more than a declaration and more than speech. They were a whole story. They were the legend of the miraculous balm. He stood with his mind turning. The leaf is the balm; the balm is something — not something to heal a wound, but something to heal discord. The balm was the Gardinelle's preceptual guide to the greatest of all wishes! Caught by the simplicity of what had once seemed such a riddle and now seemed so apparent, Steven was almost stunned — so much so that for the moment he had no thought of the need to sort a prayer from a wish, whether it were the greatest of all or the least.

But short and to the point as the Gardinelle's words may have been, they were as much as the children could silently endure. Now with Falling Star and Sylvester leading, they joined hands to dance around the tree, kicking up the leaves in their path and filling the air with song. While the Choral Society, too, lent its voice to the rhymes, Thalamus, bringing his magic to bear on the matter, saw the tree clothed in a fresh mantle of leaves, and even wrought its seasonal changes to suit the words:

> *We greet with glee the wishing tree,*
> *Whose starry leaves auspicious,*
> *Should lead the wise to realize,*
> *The greatest of all wishes!*

> *Its boughs are bare in winter's care,*
> *When Season's Wishes go*
> *With Christmas cheer in carols clear,*
> *And sleighbells in the snow.*
> *When rosy buds the branches stud,*
> *In springtime's sunny rays,*
> *We wish, and wish, and wish again*
> *For summer holidays.*

> *We greet with glee the wishing tree,*
> *Whose starry leaves auspicious,*

272

Should lead the wise to realize,
The greatest of all wishes!

When leaves are green in satin sheen,
'Midst summer's flowery wealth,
'Tis time to fly the flag on high,
And wish the nation's health.
When yellowed leaves and golden sheaves,
Foretell the teacher's rule,
Though wishes reign, 'tis all in vain,
And we must back to school.

We greet with glee the wishing tree,
Whose starry leaves auspicious,
Should lead the wise to realize,
The greatest of all wishes!

When orange sheen of Halloween,
Bedecks the branches gay,
The Quicks get kicks with dirty tricks
In wishes gone astray.
Though leaves of red to freedom wed,
Are gone with autumn passed,
Its three stems bide a wishing guide,
That will forever last.

We greet with glee the wishing tree,
Whose starry leaves auspicious,
Should lead the wise to realize,
The greatest of all wishes!

When the jolly roundelay had run its course and the children, their energy spent, had little breath left for screams, the Chief sprang up. "Now will we honour this gift from the spirits, and now will our braves bury the hatchet forever to take up the pipe of peace in the path of Walking Owl. While our tomtoms spread the words of the spirits from the great waters to the great mountains and from the burning sun to the frozen snows, let the tribespeople come forward and pledge themselves to the greatest of all wishes, for the leaf and the stars are one." Whereupon he put his hand to his mouth, and throwing back his head, gave vent to a resounding whoop that echoed back from the cliff. Resting his hands on Walking Owl's shoulders, the Chief urged the old shaman ahead of him in a tribal dance around the tree. The tribespeople fell in behind, and in no time the braves and womenfolk were chanting and prancing to the stimulating beat of the tomtoms, Montakins and Maliskaps together.

Now too, the citizens of Quotaris joined in, and taking up the beat, the gnomes and giants, little people, ladies, knights and all, tripped their favourite steps beside the villagers, while above them the Vroomers were flitting over the treetop with the ecstasy of birds in spring. Not to be outdone in the home of his ancestors, Steven tied his handkerchief in a band around his head, and screaming his enjoyment, chased after the somersaulting Sima until he lost a shoe. With no more ado, he kicked off its partner and his tasseled stockings, and continued to swing along barefoot. Even the gardener and the matron were clicking their heels, and while the Choral Society chanted "money, money", Keep, with computer printouts swirling about him, took Muster by the waist with his free arm and skipped with her like a schoolboy let out. So it was that all abandoned themselves to the carnival mood, and while among the happy faces Muster's bore a smile as much of triumph as of delight, there were none to match the gratified smile of Sawni, who in his elfin way had been helping out at the lemonade bowl.

In the midst of it all, Steven experienced a special flush of joy, for he unexpectedly found himself behind a familiar ponytail that was tossing and swaying to the rhythm of the tomtoms. As he watched its fascinating motion, the head turned, and Marcie was smiling at him. "Hello Steven," she called, "you dance well."

Their hands joined and they tripped along together. "Wasn't it fabulous the way all this happened?" Marcie panted lightly.

Steven thought back over their first meeting when she had giggled over his somewhat gauche reply to her question, and resolved to make a better impression. "I was the one who prayed, you know," he said, trying not to show too proud, though the words had slipped out unintentionally in his anxiety to gain credit in her eyes. Now he suddenly found himself looking directly into her eyes, for she had stopped to turn and stare at him.

"You were the one?" she asked, her mouth agape.

Steven nodded modestly.

Marcie's eyes twinkled in an expression of scandalized amusement. "You prayed — during a wish?" She put her hand to her mouth, her shoulders bobbled, and she quickly looked right and left either to see if they were overheard or to find her confidante to share the pearl.

Steven could not quite read in Marcie's reaction whether his act was to be considered daring or foolish. He decided to go for daring. "I was lucky WAND didn't give me away," he confided, feigning relief over his escape from the near complication.

"WAND give you away?" Marcie giggled. "WAND doesn't sort prayers."

Abashed that he had made an unclever remark again, Steven shrank a little, and his embarrassment showed. In the momentary pause, Marcie began to drift away from him, for they were being jostled along by the crowd which was no longer circling the tree but was flowing towards the chateau.

"You didn't know?" Marcie searched Steven's face in surprise. "You get that in Third Year, in Petitions Two." Her giggle burst into its infectious tinkle. "Prayers and wishes are sorted by EGOS!"

"EGOS?" Steven stopped in his tracks. "But EGOS is me!" he exclaimed.

Marcie was now being swept away in the surge of bodies.

"Marcie!" Steven shouted, "Wait!" He tried to squirm forward to catch her, but she was swallowed up in a swirl of villagers. Steven pushed and wriggled, trying to make his way through them, but to no avail. Keen to see their visitors off, the villagers were stopping to ring the chateau's portal in a solid wall that would not give. "Let me through. I'm with the Gardinelle," he cried. He tried to slip through between two tall braves, but they were as immovable as stone. It was like repeating his chase after Breach all over again. In desperation he jumped up and down on the spot to see over the heads in front, calling out "Marcie! Thalamus! Keep!" Momentarily gaining sufficient height to see beyond, he caught a fleeting glimpse of Falling Star, who stood with the Gardinelle on a parapet in the last rays of a setting sun, waving good-bye to the crowd. At the same time, a low hum sounded from the depths of the chateau, and as it grew to a roar, the chateau rose slowly into the air, its residents waving to the cheering villagers from every niche, while Steven, flagging with his jacket and crying out frantically, went unnoticed and unheard. Then, as the chateau circled aloft, and as if to punctuate its departure, Welkin rose from the cliff to carry Sirgal in pursuit, followed by Lean Bone on his pony, bow and quiver over his shoulder, the pennant of Quotaris rippling from the tip of its staff.

Exhausted, disheveled and dismayed, Steven felt his heart sink, and as the chateau moved away, his arms fell limply to his side, the matron's velvet jacket, now soiled and torn, falling to the ground at his dusty feet. His lost hopes grasping at straws, Steven told himself they would soon miss him and would come back. Others besides himself must have been left behind in the hurried departure. He looked about for any who were sharing his predicament but saw only a few straggling villagers melting into the forest. Of the milling throng no one remained — save Walking Owl. He was kneeling among the roots of the triunium, intent on a tiny object that lay embedded in the trampled ground. In the dimness of the tree's shadow, the object glistened with a ghostly luminescence. Picking it out of the earth, the old shaman drew with it the tangled thongs of Lean Bone's amulet, and stopping, remained motionless, bent over it in quiet contemplation.

Seeing Walking Owl thus, Steven was the more conscious of his own abandonment. Even the tree was left standing alone and apart in the empty clearing. Its crown of crimson leaves — stars of the Cheechikois — shimmering with radiant beauty in the last rays of the dying sun, was draped with a festooning printout. The folds of the printout formed a gently swaying stairway which descended from the paradise of colour bearing its message.

276

Steven looked at it for some moments before the truth dawned on him. The stepped figure on the shaman's robe was a computer printout! It was all very clear. The words again tripped through his mind. The leaf is the balm ... the balm is ... the printout — the message.

The shaman's riddle was now resolved in every detail.

24

The rumble of the trovium motors had subsided with the diminished size of the chateau, but well after it had shrunk to a speck and disappeared from view, Steven's ears throbbed with the departing sound. The Gardinelle — the Elder Woman of Lots — had come and gone, leaving behind the tree and its leaf. Now they belonged to the Cheechikois. Now they would become history on the shaman's robe. Now too, the tree was casting its softening evening shadow over Steven's feet, but its deserted beauty was casting a more profound gloom over his spirits. That it had yielded the riddle of the miraculous balm and the key to realizing the greatest of all wishes, was cold comfort. All the elation he might have enjoyed was lost in the distress of this unexpected turn of events — in the carelessness, or irony, of the Elder Woman of Lots who with one hand had led him to find the truth, and with the other had cut him adrift in a long lost world. The total peril of his bizarre plight grew more apparent to him with the deepening solitude. He was a deserted boy standing beside a deserted tree — a tree that was supposed to symbolize the very precept of concern for one's fellow — the Gardinelle's sole concern — in effect, her flag! There could be as much comfort in a haircut, Steven began to tell himself as his despair became edged with a bitterness which all but dulled his awareness of a faintly intruding sound. He dressed himself with a start and listened intently. Yes! The distant sound of powerful motors could be heard. His heart leapt with relief. They had already missed him.

The Gardinelle was returning!

Soon the muffled roar had grown to a throbbing beat. It seemed to hang in the air and slowly, stubbornly, penetrated his outer consciousness until at last having drawn him into partial wakefulness, was retreating again into the distance.

Listening to the dwindling sound, Steven experienced a new and more dread feeling of being forsaken. Overcome by a rising horror at the thought of being truly and finally abandoned in such a way, he broke into a cold sweat, and calling out in panic for Keep and Thalamus, roused himself into outright wakefulness, their names hanging on his lips. The cozy sheepskin slipped from his shoulders, and he blinked about the room in sleepy confusion, his mind still floundering in the freshness of his waking sensations.

As he gradually recaptured the detail of his night's lodging, Steven sank back with a sigh of relief at finding himself thus comfortably safe. His relief turned to satisfaction, and approached exultation as he lay thinking what a surprise it would be to Gorse and Aunt Becky when he told them about the robe and all — Aunt Becky could be teased — he would tell her first that the star of the Cheechikois was a leaf all right, then watch the look on her face when he explained how the balm was a preceptual message, and the leaf just the messenger — it was strange, though, that with all the maple trees around, no one had ever heard tell of a triunium — what could have happened to it? Did its seed produce only ordinary maples — like apple seeds don't grow true? — but what about the leaf? It would still be the guide to the greatest of all wishes — Miss Adley would buy that. It was strange that, quite on her own, Miss Adley came up with the idea of her Maple Leaf flag granting wishes, like for freedom and refuge — where would she get it? — Remspruk? — but she didn't say about a balm — although anyone can see that as the flag took over the country, the tribal differences were forgotten, and the tribes began working together as they should — of course they were supposed to do it themselves but didn't — so it would have to be a coincidence — but maybe not — maybe when the tribes could no longer read the pictographs, the Gardinelle thought she might as well let the newcomers take the maple leaf, so Remspruk sent the idea enzyme — still, if the tribes could no longer read in the faded pictographs that they should lead the world to the greatest of all wishes, could the Chief be blamed? — and anyway, can you really give people a flag? — like, the Gardinelle herself said that flags and people are the source and the reflection of each other, so a flag is something that has to come out of the people themselves — maybe the Gardinelle realized her mistake and waited to try again when the newcomers were ready for a flag — but notice she didn't bring it to them like to the Cheechikois — just let Remspruk do it quietly — same as with Miss Adley? — unless Miss Adley found her idea in a book — or could she have learned from the old shaman, too? The shaman!!!

In the stillness, the fading sound of the distant motor filled the room like the murmur of the old man whose voice seemed to have no more than paused. Yet, turning his head in the dim light, Steven found the rocking chair resting empty and motionless. He was alone in the cabin, deserted of both the vision and the prompting voice of its author. Author? Steven's witness!

Steven sat upright, catching his breath with a sobering question: When did he really fall asleep? When did the shaman leave? Was it before, was it during, or was it after his account of the pictographs? In short, did the solution to the riddle come out of the shaman's mouth, or had Steven conjured it up in a fanciful dream?

Steven questioned his surroundings with a more critical eye, searching for justification for the vivid experience of his dream. Of the seductive embers, only cold gray ashes remained in the pit, concealing in their flaky powder the misty pathways that entwined reality and dream. Covering the wall, the gathered mementos of tribal days seemed less mysterious and intimidating than when they were bathed in the shadowy flicker of firelight. Now, in their quiet immobility, they heightened the stillness of the room as with the stillness of the past, while the massive fireplace shared them an aura of durability and permanence.

Allowing his gaze to mount the narrow alcove, Steven encountered the sightless masks. Hanging with their thoughts preserved in wooden silence, they did nothing to reaffirm the keen reality of his experience, and in a desperate effort to stem its escape, he swung about to face the pictographs in a half defiant, half conspiratorial appeal. To his further dismay, he was met with stony indifference, because where the ceremonial robe ought to have been hanging, the wall was bare.

It was only with his head bent back that Steven became aware of a string around his neck, and looking down over his chin, found the dangling lynx tooth. To his surprise, it was not hanging by a shoelace but by a fine leather thong. Puzzled, Steven looked first at the empty rocking chair for an explanation, and then turned to stare at the door pensively, as if expecting the old shaman to enter and confess. On the point of kicking away the sheepskin, he stiffened and remained listening. The throbbing beat was on the rise again. It seemed in no hurry to arrive or to pass by, but growing clearer, assumed the recognizable character of a helicopter. Its persistence was no longer to be denied. Steven snatched up his jeans, and without stopping to draw them on, ran to the door.

Leaping out into the morning light, Steven slid to a halt in astonishment, totally unprepared for the sight that confronted him, because the scene was one of utter devastation. In a broad swath stretching away on both sides of the cabin, the forest lay stripped, broken down, uprooted and shattered. Whole trees and remnants of trees — trees large and small — were levelled and strewn along the swath as if a tidal wave had swept down the valley. Even the big tree, with the inviting crotch he had almost taken refuge in, was no more. Its gnarled remains, broken, twisted, splintered and charred, were scattered in disorder almost to his feet. Fulgor himself could not have laid greater waste. Steven could only swallow and stare in amazement, while his hand stole absently over the lynx tooth. "Creepers!"

The noise of the helicopter, by now loudly dinning in his ears, drew Steven out of his shocked contemplation of the spectacle. He looked up to see the aircraft slowly coming into view low over the shoulder of the valley. Still in a state of bewildered wakefulness, he could be no more surprised by the appearance of a helicopter than by an orbiter or a soaring chateau. It was as though he had either not been dreaming or had not really awakened, but that his adventure was continuing.

The machine slowed to a stop and hovered as if making up its mind. Its olive drab fuselage bore the words SEARCH AND RESCUE, and above them the red and white Maple Leaf decal showed in sharp contrast before the pilot altered course and headed directly towards the spot where Steven stood agape. The Air Force! None had ever come so close before, and in the closing range it looked disconcertingly austere if not threatening. Not knowing what to make of it, Steven could only watch as the machine moved into position scarcely a stone's throw away. There it pivoted slowly and smoothly like a curbed beast, its throbbing power held in check by a skilful master. Electrified by its very proximity and buffeted by the turbulence from its pulsing vanes, Steven tingled with an apprehensive excitement. He became aware of faces peering at him through the transparencies. His amazed stare was being met with smiles! Relieved by such friendliness amidst the overpowering noise and the chaos of his surroundings, Steven waved. Then, incredibly, the machine settled to the ground, and its confusing din immediately subsided.

Before the swishing vanes had spun to a reluctant halt, the door slid aside allowing an officer to jump free. "I hope you are Steven Rainmaker," he called out, approaching Steven at a regulation lope.

Steven's nod was positive if somewhat tentative.

"Good." The officer passed a solicitous eye over Steven. Only then realizing he was still holding his jeans, Steven made an effort to jump into them, almost toppling in his embarrassed haste. The officer caught and steadied him with a firm hand. "You were reported missing after the tornado, Steven," he informed the boy, allowing his own incredulous gaze to sweep the area. "We have been hoping for a sign of you since dawn."

By now Steven had fully rejoined the real world in mind as well as in body, though it still took him a moment to fully digest what the officer was saying — not that he had never been the object of a search before, not at least if you counted his family.

282

But that he should be the object of a search by the Air Force seemed on first thought unbelievable, on second thought flattering, and finally (Steven swallowed with a tremor of emotion) somewhat touching. Touching because these were of the dauntless hands that guided the scrambling jets over the reservation by day and night. How often he had lain there, eyes closed, picturing the hurtling meteorite as it receded into the night, disdaining the whole of creation in its shroud of noise, its cloistered crew insulated from all intrusion in a metallic shell guarded by electronic robots watchful and wary of any approach; strange beings separated even from each other in their alien garb, too intent on the babble of synthetic voices, too absorbed in the ghostly glimmer of their instrument panels to be mindful of the faceless millions below, let alone to distinguish them as persons. And suddenly they were asking after Steven Rainmaker, being not only aware, but caring that a single one of the many millions was missing — and interrupting their precipitous sorties to search him out by name. Steven wondered what Thalamus would say to that, when in Quotaris by comparison, the miracle trumpets paid tribute to the accounting of one in only one million. The Maple Leaf was not to be underrated!

The officer turned his head from the devastation and lowered his gaze back to Steven as the boy zipped up his jeans. "Yes," he said with a rueful smile that both regretted Steven's close call and congratulated his escape, "we were almost ready to give you up."

The turn of phrase gave Steven a start, and with the sensation of being abandoned still fresh in his mind, sent a prickly chill down his spine. The words awakened the spectre of being huddled in the middle of an endless waste beneath a tattered shirt that beckoned limply for help from the end of a stick, while just beyond the horizon, word is being passed among a weary crew, "Our fuel is running low — we will have to give him up."

The fleeting vision ran through Steven's mind in less time than it took to draw a startled breath. It sent his eyes darting over the officer's face in an involuntary expression of encouragement, which was quite unnecessary because he was looking into the blue-gray depths of eyes that reflected the devotion to duty of a

Knight Courier. And the officer was smiling reassuringly, "Still, you look okay. Are you all right?" The question and its tone might have fallen from the lips of Sirgal himself. Perhaps it was that, and perhaps it was the sunlight catching the Maple Leaf on the waiting helicopter that sent an echo of the Gardinelle's voice ringing across the ravaged valley. "Nor can a knight bear greater trust than the flag and its message, for they who ride ahead with the flag, colour it, and all who follow behind are coloured by it."

Steven's head had already started to move in a mechanical nod of assurance before he fully realized that, surrounded by the destruction along the valley, his escape unscathed was lucky if not a miracle. Thinking of the old shaman's strange absence, Steven looked about uncertainly, terminating his nod in a confused hunch of his shoulders. "I don't know what happened to the shaman," he faltered. At the same time his wandering eye caught something in the wreckage of the big tree. It was coloured and out of place, and it filled Steven with a dread premonition of what it could be. Turning towards it, he half ran, half stumbled to the spot and fell on his knees. Looking down, he reached out with a tremulous hand — and touched the protruding edge of the shaman's clothing.

Just as quickly, the officer was at Steven's side, signalling to the helicopter crew for help. So it was that in very little time the heavy pieces of tree had been lifted away, exposing the body of the old man. He lay face down, clothed in the ceremonial robe, the crumpled headdress beside him. Still and cold, his hands were stretched above his head as if thrown out to protect a little circle of bones. Seeing him there very nearly as he himself had lain in the darkness staring at the ghostly glow of the lynx tooth, Steven shuddered. Then as a final length of seared bough was raised and cast aside, there separated from it a single leaf — all that remained of the tree's once profuse foliage — bright and crimson — a beautiful maple leaf.

Steven watched the leaf flutter down into the circle to settle upon the divining bones as if to say, "Amen."

"Look!" exclaimed one of the crew, "Just like autumn. Would you have believed lightning could do that?"

"Yes." Steven did not utter the word aloud, but it was on the point of his tongue, because he knew now that it had been no ordinary storm and no ordinary lightning. He looked at the shattered stump and mutilated boughs that lay about him, trying to piece them together in his mind. Their gnarled and twisted fragments could have been those of the picturesque old tree that had stood in the chateau's courtyard and later in the ravaged sanctuary beneath the cliff. Beneath the cliff? His eyes scanned the valley's rising shoulder, imagining the erosion of time, and dropped back to the leaf, unconscious of the old shaman being wrapped in a sheet and carried to the helicopter. His experience could not have been all a dream, he told himself, because no dream could have been so real. Anyway, suppose you did dream things that were true, and when you awakened they were really going on. How could you prove that your part was just a dream? Like the Gardinelle said about happenings — they are neither more nor less than what of them lives on. So dreams that come true must be happenings — like the tree. And if the tree could be real, so could the rest — and he was looking at the star of the Cheechikois — miraculous balm to heal differences and lead the way to a world fraternal and at peace — the greatest of all wishes!

From the helicopter the soulful wail of an actuator lamented the boarding of the grisly new passenger, and sharing its mood, the officer took Steven gently by the shoulders and turned him to the waiting machine. "We sometimes have to accept these things, Steven," he said.

But Steven slipped free, and returning to the little circle of bones, removed the lynx tooth from his neck. He stooped and pressed it into the ground amongst the roots as he had found it. Slowly, thoughtfully, he took up the leaf in exchange, and with a parting look at the spot, rose and allowed himself to be ushered away.

Aboard and seated, Steven watched the blades overhead begin to turn slowly, each one briefly cutting the sun's rays in its passing, and accelerating under the urging of the powerful motor, they sent such a swirling billow out over the old tree's remnants as to remind him of his arrival in the chateau's garden. The visions tripped anew through his mind in a fast-forward procession to the sanctuary. He could see the triunium maple in all its splendour, the radiant crimson of its luxuriant crown enveloped in a halo of gold from the setting sun. "Now," cried the Gardinelle, "may your tree come to flourish throughout the land, casting its message as it casts its leaf, like a balm over the tribes and their differences, that all who seek to make a paradise of the Quick Side may wish upon its leaf as on a star, for the stars and the leaf are one." Again everyone was dancing around the tree, and once more Steven found himself hand in hand with Marcie, her ponytail bouncing a rhythmic cadence to the wild beat of tomtoms.

The beat of tomtoms suddenly moderated, and Steven was looking down at the ravaged valley, for the helicopter had risen above the rim of the valley and began to cruise off in a wide arc. The swath of wasted forest took on a less awesome appearance as it fell away, and finally it seemed no more than a scar which stretched along the hillside. The broadening world below drew Steven's attention; he had never before been given such a view of the reservation and its surroundings. He thrilled at the strangeness of familiar landmarks from his elevated station, and watched the now squat trees slide past like Trovian satellites under the orbiter.

All too soon he was over the schoolhouse where the machine hovered for an instant, preparing to make its descent towards the open playground. While it hung there, the cabin turned slowly like a weathercock, and as it did so the highway below unravelled to Steven's view like a ribbon being pulled free from amongst the steel trellises and girders of the arching bridge, thence to snake out across the countryside. Then as if coming to the end of its travel, Steven's window ceased turning. So too, the scene below arrested its motion as if caught with the click of a camera. For a few moments Steven's eyes gobbled in what to him was a sensational view of the land of his ancestors, inhabited without change from time immemorial, but which in no time at all, by comparison, had been completely transformed by the hand of the newcomers. Yet the river as ever, holding within its broad expanse the line of division fixed by the newcomers, and still enjoying the fullness of its springtime flow, dominated the landscape. Even from the air, it bespoke the mighty spirit the tribes had long revered — now a pathway for the never-ending flow of commerce that served the industries and homes of half a continent. From the air, too, its accomplishments were more evident than from the rail of the bridge, where, in the yearly line of onlookers, Steven watched the springtime waters scour their shores as they had done since the beginning of time. Now he could see them carrying their winnings off towards the sea, to return nothing of them, and leaving nothing in their place. Nothing, that is, but the formidable channel they had cut to divide the ancient tribal lands and impede the fraternity, if not the unity, of the tribespeople. And even as it had stealthily eroded the territory and silently undermined the fraternity of the tribes, so too, the river had tempted the newcomers with opposing banks on which to distinguish and cultivate their differences.

"Can you read?"

The words popped into Steven's head as if the old shaman had murmured them into his ear. His head turned in a reflex towards the silent sheet on the cabin floor, and back to the living pictograph below. What more was to be read? He had answers to all the questions — except what happened to the Chief's fine resolution.

But if it were to be read, the view below held the story of a happening that was marked by an enormous X: a sprawling cross formed by the timeless river flowing eastward to the sea, and the ribbon of asphalt threading its way to the bridge. And from the air it could be seen that if the river had long halved the land in carving out its scheme, the highway had come to quarter it. If the river had bestowed its favours and disfavours equally upon its either bank, the highway, bounding the reservation in its retreat from the bridge and its guardian flag, traced a line of contrast — a line of contrast between the formality of the ordered townsites and affairs of the newcomers, and the informality of the tribespeople's spreading community.

It was that, descending into the valley, the quiltwork of farms on the one side grew more prosperous as it approached the river, the newcomers more populous, and their works more imposing until they reached a climax of progress at the water's edge. There overshadowing the village steeples and their crosses which now glinted under the caressing rays of the early sun, the nuclear power stations rose like alters at the feet of the great river, yielding their imposing height only to the Maple Leaf atop their domes.

Across the highway, as it, too, descended into the valley and its roots penetrated the moistening soil, the forest strove to recreate the majestic habitat of its vanishing denizens, while the tribespeople's invading forage patches and cottage plots grew more consuming of the providential storehouse, their demands terminating at the river's edge in a phalanx of piers which pointed over the water like fingers directing the cast of the fisherman's line and the set of his net. And on the elevated shore in the shadow of the forest, easily yielding in height to the heraldic leaf's pristine paradigm in the overhanging branches of a towering maple, stood the modest long house. Unlike the churches of the newcomers, however, the unsteepled long house bore no cross, but within the customs of traditional tribal culture, it held a symbolism that preserved the affirmation of old faiths — and the spirit of the river.

Thus, to the untutored reader, the highway drew a line of contrast between different life styles, if not to say conflicting paths, and though both sides featured the maple leaf in their own way, it fluttered over seemingly opposite goals. But Steven had learned something of truth and the reading of things. He knew if the Gardinelle were to speak at this moment, she would say that just as a vehicle is transport and not a direction, so a destination is a direction but not a path — which is to say that destinations were not to be read in the lifestyles but in the steeples and the long house — not in the paths but in the affirmations of faith which, whether of the old or the new, were in fact the affirmations of a shared reverence and a common goal.

So it could be said that the contrast was not of conflicting paths or destinations, but of differing accommodations — differing accommodations to the rules of an exacting adversary.

But what had Thalamus said of rules? Thalamus had said that in any contest the rules were the game. The newcomers had long come to recognize that such was indeed the case. That being so, they had studied the rules, even tracing their origin into the depths of the very stars themselves, thereby opening new vistas of points to be won and wishes to be gained. Having long enough endured the vicissitudes of fortune, and wishing to balance the good and bad of it on their own, they now sought to distil primordial good and evil in the likes of their nuclear domes. Having thus surmounted the fear of evil, and preserving their right to wish, they were learning the meaning of unity (if not the means to a paradise on earth), and on the way they had already put the rules to use transforming the countryside and building their bridge from whose dizzy height they could mock the mighty river. Despite the great obstacle it once had posed, they had linked the divided lands with their bridge. Despite the guardian flags on its either approach, the lines of traffic flowed steadily across its span. Despite their differences and the estrangement of continental distances, there was far more communication across the bridge and into the far reaches of the highway than across its narrow width.

Thus, the bridge was to be read not so much as a conquest of the river, but as a conquest of the division and segregation of peoples; not a defeat for the spirit of the river, but a victory for a greater spirit — the spirit of fellowship. Thus put, and however they had come to take up the leaf and its message, the newcomers were in truth carrying out the Chief's resolution for him. So it must be read that the purpose of the leaf had not been lost to the tribespeople after all. Rather, the Chief's resolution had fallen from the phantom express and had been recovered by a committed ally.

Yes, Steven told himself, dropping his eyes to the silent sheet; yes, he could read, and far better than when he had stumbled into the old shaman's cabin but a few hours earlier, dripping and breathless. Now too, he had something to write for Miss Adley — a commitment — and in his own words! The voice of the old shaman and his robe would not be stilled, but would be carried across the hills again with renewed life, and this time in words that would not fade, and in the hand of friendship, which knows no border. Yes, whether it came by miracle or by magic, and whether this great legacy is to be called the Star of the Cheechikois or the Maple Leaf, it travels a path already rich in wishes on the way to the greatest wish of all. Indeed, he had more than that for Miss Adley. He had something to harmonize in the schoolhouse rafters with her favourite admonition to wish for the moon and strive with faith. It was to say that everything, however great, must start with a wish, but no wish, however small, can be realized without the faith of commitment. So it is that commitment can be the difference between a Perfect and a wibble, and wibbles don't count in any amount. So said the Gardinelle.

The guardian flag sank from view behind the treetops as the helicopter descended into the schoolyard, where a waiting crowd of concerned villagers craned their necks for hopeful news. Catching sight of Steven's smiling face in the port, their arms rose in a wave of relief, and their cheers could be heard above the roar of the machine. And there in the centre of the group, standing with Stella beside her in the little gray convertible (very like the Gardinelle in her landau among the Wamwiki tribespeople), Miss Adley was waving more vigorously than the others. Perhaps it was because she read in Steven's smile the promise of an essay that would bring inspiration to his classmates and credit to the school; perhaps, too, she could hear the voice of spirits and orchestral strings, for as the machine settled to the ground, the sound of its relieved motor and whistling vanes, rejoicing over the lessened demands on their labour, seemingly intoned *O Canada.*

Perhaps that was so, but more likely it was because in returning Miss Adley's wave, Steven was still holding the miraculous balm — crimson herald of an autumn splendour soon to come — annual pageant of blazing colour which would envelop the land in a fellowship of nature. And as the dazzling leaf embraced the highway without distinction of sides, so the heraldic Maple Leaf, offering the hand of fellowship without distinction of diversity, would be seen everywhere as the New World message: not as a symbol of lordship over a people, but of guarding their human values; not as a symbol of exclusion, but of refuge and hospitality; not as a symbol either of division or of temporizing with evil, but of a commitment to truth; not as a symbol of conquest, but a symbol of the greater fellowship — and guide to the greatest of all wishes.

FINIS

The Author

Albert Henry (Harry) Hall, P. Eng. was born and educated in Edmonton, graduating from the University of Alberta with the degree of B.Sc. in Engineering Physics with high distinction. Awarded a postgraduate fellowship from the National Research Council, he subsequently received an M.Sc. in Aeronautical Engineering from the California Institute of Technology.

Mr. Hall chose a career with the National Research Council in Ottawa, and was head of the Structures and Materials Laboratory, National Aeronautical Establishment, prior to retiring in 1979. In addition to his work with N.R.C., Mr. Hall served for many years as a Canadian representative on panels of the Advisory Group for Aeronautical Research and Development (NATO), and the Commonwealth Advisory Aeronautical Research Committee. A fellow of the Canadian Aeronautics and Space Institute he served for a time as an associate editor of the Institute's journal, and farther afield, assisted in the work of the Operational Research Committee of the Canadian Association of Chiefs of Police, in which organization he holds honorary membership.

In earlier days, Mr. Hall was an avid canoeist in Alberta's hinterland. Later interests included, tree farming, beekeeping, keyboard music — and writing. He lives in Ottawa with his wife.